FAMILY SECRETS AT HEDGEHOG HOLLOW

HEDGEHOG HOLLOW BOOK 3

JESSICA REDLAND

Boldwood

First published in Great Britain in 2021 by Boldwood Books Ltd.

Copyright © Jessica Redland, 2021

Cover Design by Debbie Clement Design

Cover Photography: Shutterstock

A CIP catalogue record for this book is available from the British Library.

Paperback ISBN 978-1-83889-098-8

Large Print ISBN 978-1-80162-716-0

Hardback ISBN 978-1-80162-715-3

Ebook ISBN 978-1-83889-100-8

Kindle ISBN 978-1-83889-099-5

Audio CD ISBN 978-1-83889-226-5

MP3 CD ISBN 978-1-80162-712-2

Digital audio download ISBN 978-1-83889-097-1

Boldwood Books Ltd
23 Bowerdean Street
London SW6 3TN
www.boldwoodbooks.com

To Gary, taken too soon, RIP with love xx

RECURRING CHARACTERS FROM NEW ARRIVALS AT HEDGEHOG HOLLOW

Samantha Wishaw, aka Sam or Sammie
Former district nurse and tutor at Reddfield TEC. Owner and full-time manager of Hedgehog Hollow

Jonathan Wishaw
Samantha's dad
Veterinary surgeon at Alderson & Son Veterinary Practice

Debs Wishaw
Samantha's estranged mum
Identical twin to Chloe's mum, Louise

Chloe Turner
Samantha's cousin, who married Samantha's ex, James

James Turner
Samantha's ex-boyfriend, now married to her cousin, Chloe

Samuel Turner

Chloe and James's baby

Louise Olsen
Samantha's auntie/Chloe's mum
Identical twin to Samantha's mum, Debs

Simon Olsen
Samantha's uncle/Chloe's dad

Josh Alderson
Samantha's fiancé
Practice owner and veterinary surgeon at Alderson & Son Veterinary Practice

Paul Alderson
Josh's dad and former business partner

Beth Giddings
Paul's girlfriend/Josh's ex-girlfriend

Archie Alderson
Paul and Beth's young son

Lottie Alderson
Paul and Beth's newborn daughter

Connie Harbuckle
Josh's mum
Non-identical twin to Lauren
In a new relationship with Alex Williams

Lauren Harbuckle

Josh's auntie
Non-identical twin to Connie
Samantha's former boss at Reddfield TEC

Thomas Mickleby
Elderly widower befriended by Samantha
Left Hedgehog Hollow to Samantha in his will on the proviso she ran it as a hedgehog rescue centre

Gwendoline Mickleby
Thomas's wife, whose dream it was to run the hedgehog rescue centre

Rich Cooper
Ambulance paramedic. Good friend of Samantha/partner of Dave

Dave Williams
Builder. Good friend of Samantha/partner of Rich

Alex Williams
Dave's uncle
In a new relationship with Connie

Hannah Spiers
District nurse, on maternity leave
Samantha's best friend

Toby Spiers
Hannah's husband/James's best friend

Amelia Spiers
Hannah and Toby's baby/Samantha's goddaughter

Lewis
Josh's best friend from school

Danny
Lewis's younger brother

Fizz
Trainee veterinary nurse
Volunteer at Hedgehog Hollow

Terry
Has brought in several rescue hedgehogs/hoglets and has
befriended Samantha

THE STORY SO FAR...

For Samantha Wishaw, the owner of Hedgehog Hollow Rescue Centre, and her boyfriend Josh Alderson, May kicked off with a busy weekend of activities to celebrate the official opening. The events went swimmingly but Sunday finished on a low when Josh's ex-girlfriend Beth – pregnant with her second child by his estranged father Paul – showed up at the farm, demanding to speak to him. Josh had refused to have anything to do with Paul or Beth after their relationship came to light and he wasn't about to change his mind. He had no intention of building a relationship with his half-brother, Archie, either.

Beth returned to Hedgehog Hollow a week later but collapsed, meaning Josh had to make contact with his dad for the first time in eighteen months. Their reunion was far from pleasant. It was a challenge for Josh to have his dad thrust back into his life when he'd sworn he wanted nothing to do with him ever again, especially after the impact the news of the affair had had on his mum, Connie. She'd been devastated by the affair and had unintentionally over-dosed on paracetamol. Josh had found her and, although she made a full recovery, he could not forgive his dad for what might have happened.

Connie, now re-training as a counsellor, was in a really positive place. She absolutely was not looking for love but that changed when Alex came back into her life. They'd briefly met five years previously but nothing had happened, and they were both grateful for a second chance.

Samantha asked Josh to officially move in. While her friends Rich and Dave helped him move his belongings across, she visited her cousin Chloe in Whitsborough Bay. Chloe seemed uninterested in the news about Josh moving in. She only became animated when Samantha admitted that she was struggling to balance her many responsibilities. With word spreading and more hedgehogs arriving, Samantha was concerned she'd taken too much on, trying to run the rescue centre alongside a full-time job.

While Samantha was at Chloe's, her mum paid an unplanned visit and their encounter was as unpleasant as usual, resulting in Samantha leaving early and driving a wedge between her and Chloe yet again.

The barn was defaced by graffiti in the early hours of the following morning and the arrival of a first litter of abandoned hoglets added more pressure to an exhausted Samantha. Josh mooted the idea of her resigning from her job to work full-time at the rescue centre, where her heart lay. Now living with her, his salary could cover the food and bills, but she didn't want to let anyone down by leaving her tutoring role after less than a year.

But after fainting at work, Samantha admitted that things had to change and accepted Josh's financial support and her boss Lauren's blessing to resign from her job with immediate effect.

Beth asked Josh to meet her. Knowing she'd never leave them in peace if he didn't, Josh reluctantly agreed. She revealed that Paul had been diagnosed with Hodgkin lymphoma – a form of blood

cancer. The first round of chemotherapy hadn't been the anticipated success and he was about to embark on a second round while
looking for a stem cell transplant donor.

Josh and Samantha visited his dad but a neighbour told them
that the family had been taken away in an ambulance. Fearing the
worst for Paul, they raced to the hospital to discover that Beth was
the one in danger. It had been raining heavily and she'd slipped
and fallen down the wet communal stairs. Baby Lottie had to be
delivered early while Beth fought for her own life.

Both proved to be fighters but the family were going to need a
lot of support, so Samantha suggested to Josh that Beth and Paul
move into the farmhouse. The time Josh spent at the hospital
supporting his dad had massively improved their relationship, so
they accepted the offer to move in after Beth and Lottie were
discharged.

Samantha took a pregnancy test to rule that out as the cause
of her fainting and was surprised to feel relieved by the negative
result. She'd always wanted children – or believed she had – so
she invited her best friend, Hannah, to the farm to discuss it. It
came out that she was terrified of having children in case she
turned out to be like her own mother, who had treated Samantha
so cruelly all her life. Hannah encouraged her to open up to Josh
about her fears, even though Samantha was afraid that telling
him she didn't want children could mean the end of their relationship.

Josh was understanding and, although he'd have ideally liked
children, Samantha was more important to him. He didn't want her
to make such a major life decision based on a belief that her mum's
personality had changed after Samantha was born so he invited her
dad, Jonathan, to the farm to discuss it. Jonathan revealed that Debs
(Samantha's mum) had changed as a result of a trauma some years
before Samantha was born. After walking home alone, drunk, she

was raped and left with long-term emotional wounds, for which she refused support.

Samantha secured a new friend and committed volunteer – trainee veterinary nurse, Fizz – when she brought in some rescue hoglets. While Fizz was helping feed them, the barn came under attack again. Samantha was assaulted when a box of eggs was hurled at her, splitting her cheek open. The Grimes cousins – Brynn and Cody – were already behind bars and it turned out that Cody's younger brother, Connor, and a friend of his had picked up the mantle. They were both on parole so were sent back to continue their sentences and the police assured Samantha and Josh that the extended family had been spoken to about the serious consequences of anyone else getting involved.

Paul's family moved into the farm and, a few days later, Josh, Paul and Beth addressed what had happened and why. The past couldn't be changed and the hurt caused wasn't going to be forgotten anytime soon but a fresh start was needed for everyone, so Josh drew a line in the sand and agreed to move on.

Samantha started to accept she wasn't like her mum and that children might be a possibility. Josh didn't want her to feel pushed into it so he decided the timing was right to show her he loved her unconditionally. On the night they released the last of the original rescue hedgehogs, he proposed and she accepted.

1

I sat on Thomas's bench with a mug of tea in one hand, the other hand stroking Misty-Blue's warm belly as she lay sprawled across my lap.

'Listen to that,' I said to her, cocking my head to one side. 'Isn't it so peaceful?' The only sounds were the chirp of birds, the buzz of insects and Misty-Blue's gentle purrs.

'No babies crying for once,' I added, not that I really minded. Archie and Lottie were adorable. Their parents, Paul and Beth, were also great house guests. They couldn't have done more to help with the cooking and cleaning despite Beth still recovering from a near-fatal fall down the stairs at her flat and Paul, Josh's dad, having Hodgkin lymphoma – a type of blood cancer.

Closing my eyes, I tilted my head back towards the sun. It was a bright, warm Sunday in the middle of June, so Paul and Beth had taken advantage of the gorgeous weather and driven Archie and Lottie to the coast. Josh – owner of Alderson & Son Veterinary Practice – had been called out to a goat emergency an hour ago so I was on my own at Hedgehog Hollow, enjoying a rare and precious moment of tranquillity.

After a few minutes, I opened my eyes and sipped contentedly on my tea. My heart fluttered as the diamonds on my engagement ring sparkled in the sun. We hadn't made any plans for when we'd marry yet. It didn't feel right to set the date until Paul had been through the next round of chemotherapy later this month and we were, of course, still hoping a stem cell donor would be found.

Everyone had been thrilled at the announcement of our engagement. We'd invited our closest family for afternoon tea last Sunday so we could share the news. After that I'd called my best friend Hannah, who excitedly squealed down the phone.

I tried my cousin Chloe next but she didn't answer. Loyalty towards her after years of close friendship meant it didn't feel right for her mum – my Auntie Louise – to hear first so I held off phoning her, trying Chloe repeatedly over the next few days but without success. On Thursday, fed up that messages to get in touch urgently had seemingly been ignored, I phoned Auntie Louise, who was also delighted. Then I texted Chloe:

✉ To Chloe

Josh asked me to marry him! I'm so excited. I've been trying to get hold of you all week as I ideally didn't want to tell you my big news by text but you haven't responded to my messages and I'm worried. I hope you're okay. HOT TIP! There's a woman on a farm in Huggleswick who is always here for you. You know where she is if you ever need her xxx

So far, she hadn't responded and I was determined not to let it dampen my excitement. If Chloe had decided to have an epic strop, I wasn't going to bend over backwards this time. I'd waved the white flag plenty of times and now it was her move.

I'd also sent a quick text to Mum:

✉ To Mum
I hope all's well with you. Just letting you
know that Josh asked me to marry him and I said
yes. Not planning to set a date yet. Sam x

She hadn't responded but I hadn't expected her to, although I had hoped she might, even if it was just one word: 'congratulations'. I wasn't going to let her dampen my excitement, either.

I swallowed my last mouthful of tea. 'Right, Misty-Blue, it's back to the hoglets for me.' She leapt off the bench and bounded towards the meadow to chase butterflies and I headed for the kitchen.

As I rinsed my mug and plate in the sink, I gazed out of the window and spotted a car driving at speed along the farm track. Hedgehog emergency? I dried my hands and rushed to the farmyard to help, then stopped dead, my heart thumping. *Hang on! That's Chloe's car!*

She screeched to a halt with a spray of gravel beside me, yanked on the handbrake and leapt out. 'Did you mean your "HOT TIP"?' she cried.

'What?'

'In your last text. You said you were always here for me. Is that true?'

'Of course. What...?'

She removed her sunglasses, revealing red, swollen eyes. 'Good, because Samuel and I need to stay here. I've left James.'

I stared at her, mouth agape. Surely not. She and James were devoted to each other. Gathering myself, I held out my arms and moved towards her but she backed up against the car, clearly not wanting a hug.

'What happened?' I asked, thrusting my hands into my jeans pockets.

Her jaw tightened. 'I don't want to talk about it.'

I wasn't going to push it. That tone clearly announced: 'no-go-zone'.

She pushed a strand of straggly hair behind her ear and I couldn't help but notice how dishevelled she looked, in a creased T-shirt and leggings, with her long, blonde hair pulled back into a messy ponytail. She was make-up free and her cheeks were blotchy. It was such a contrast to what I was used to: a woman who normally wouldn't leave the house without her hair styled and wearing full make-up.

'So can I stay?' she demanded.

'Yes. Of course you can. Slight problem, though. We don't have a spare bed.'

She frowned. 'How come? Did your dad move in after all?'

'No.'

'Then I can have his room.'

I shook my head. 'Josh's dad and his family are living with us at the moment. They have what was going to be Dad's room and—'

She planted her hands on her hips. 'What? Why? You told me Josh hates his dad and wants nothing to do with him and his little slapper.'

I winced at the insult and bit down the urge to point out that it was like the pot calling the kettle black, considering Chloe had slept with James while we were still together. 'I know, but a lot's changed recently.'

'Would have been nice to have been kept in the loop.'

Well, perhaps if you'd returned my calls, you might have been. But there was no point in retaliating.

'Seems I'm always the last to know things,' she added in a softer voice, her eyes glistening before she put her sunglasses back on.

I wasn't sure whether that last statement was a dig at me or whether it was linked to the reason she'd left James so I decided to try again. 'What's he done?' I asked, gently.

She shoved her shades up onto her forehead and glared at me. 'What part of "I don't want to talk about it" don't you understand?'

'Okay. Sorry. I won't ask again.' I put my hands up in a surrender sign. Clearly Chloe was distressed and I needed to focus on that. I had meant it when I'd said I'd be here for her. I wanted to help if I could. I glanced towards the farmhouse – a three-storey ivy-clad stone building – trying to think of the best solution.

'I can offer you one of the two rooms on the top floor and—'

'The attic?' She screwed up her nose in apparent disgust.

'It's a proper storey and the rooms are huge. They're clean and freshly painted but there's no furniture in them yet. We've got an airbed and some bedding but that's the best I can do for now. Like it or lump it.' I could hear the sharp edge to my voice, but what did she expect? Turning up unannounced and expecting five-star luxury accommodation to be ready at the click of her fingers then insulting my beautiful home was not the best start. Especially when she'd been ignoring my calls and had been hostile when we last saw each other.

She sighed. 'Okay. It'll have to do. I'll take whichever one's en-suite.' She obviously spotted my grimace. 'Oh, my God! Tell me there is at least a bathroom up there.'

As tears pooled in her eyes, I felt guilty. Something pretty horrendous had to have happened if she'd left James, and me being defensive about my home was not helpful. I softened my voice. 'Sorry. I wanted to live in the house for a while before I decided how to use the space.' *And I wasn't expecting three adults and three babies to move in with me before I could do that!*

'Shall we start by getting Samuel and your stuff inside?' I asked, keen to break the uncomfortable silence. I opened the back door on her car and reeled back at the overpowering stench.

'Oh, yeah. I had to stop to feed him on the way and he puked afterwards. I think he might have had an explosion at the other end too. Babies are so adorable.' There was humour in her tone but the high pitch of her voice and the awkward shuffling on the spot suggested it was no laughing matter and she was close to hysteria.

Taking a deep breath, I poked my head back into the car. There was no 'might' about it. There'd *definitely* been a double-ended incident. Samuel was asleep, his face smeared, his clothes drenched. The back seat was going to need several sponge-downs followed by a damn good airing; a task I could not see Chloe willingly taking on. I already knew she'd turn on the tears and I'd feel sorry for her and offer to do it. It was how it had always been with us and I hated that I knew it yet would still let her manipulate me.

My poor little namesake could not be comfortable. In Chloe's situation, I'd like to think I'd have found somewhere to pull over again and do my best to clean him up with some baby wipes, change his nappy and dress him in fresh clothes. But I wasn't in her situation. I didn't even know what her situation was.

'We'll need to get him bathed and changed,' I said, lifting out the baby carrier and passing it to Chloe, who curled up her lip and held it out away from her body. 'I'll grab the things we need for Samuel now and we can get the rest later.'

'I need to get showered and changed too.'

I winced at her whiney tone and counted to three in my head before I could answer, knowing I'd have snapped otherwise. 'You can but we need to sort him out first. Look at him.'

'But I...' And then the tears started and I knew it would be me sorting Samuel out. And that, very likely, this would become a recurring theme for however long she stayed.

2

CHLOE

Earlier that morning

'Waaahhhh!' Each high-pitched cry made my head thump and sent a shudder down my spine. I squinted at my phone. 9.07 a.m. on a Sunday morning and just over two hours since his last feed. Urgh.

'I'll go.' James rolled over to a sitting position, pulling the duvet with him. A blast of cool air chilled my now exposed arm and leg, bringing me out in goose bumps.

'And what good's that going to do? Can your body produce milk?'

'No, but...'

I tutted as I flung back what he'd left me of the duvet. 'And don't even think about suggesting bottle-feeding him again. He's not even four months old yet.'

'Wouldn't dare.' The words were muttered under his breath but I gave him a hard glare so he knew I'd heard and I wasn't impressed.

'For God's sake, Samuel. Where's the fire?' I shouted as I stormed across the landing to the nursery.

I whipped off my PJs top, grabbed him out of his cot and

plonked down on the nursing chair. Within seconds he was sucking greedily on my sore nipple. Clenching my jaw, I focused on the view out of the window, not that there was much to look at. Samuel's nursery was at the rear of our new-build house and, from where I was seated, I could only see the back of the house behind us. Not exactly the most awe-inspiring vista to take my mind off the agony.

'Maybe you should ask your midwife about the pain.' I hadn't heard James approach.

'I've told you before, I don't like the woman. She's a patronising cow.'

'Then ask for a different midwife. Or ask Sam for help.'

I glared at him. 'Sam? You're joking, right? The Lady of the Manor hasn't got time for me these days. Barely notices my existence. Especially now that she's got the amazing Josh, super-vet.' I steeled myself for some comment about sarcasm being ugly but none came.

'Didn't you say she phoned the other weekend?'

'A fortnight ago? Oh, yeah, and a great conversation that was. Barely lasted five minutes.' I hadn't told James that I was the one who'd hung up. Even I could see that it didn't paint me in a good light, although who could blame me? All she'd done was witter on about the weather and ask about Samuel. What about me? Didn't I matter anymore?

I hadn't told James that Sam had been trying to get in touch with me all week either. I'd come so close to answering each call but couldn't face the awkward, stilted conversation, as though we were strangers. And then she texted me telling me she was engaged. Texted! Who does that? Biggest news ever and she lets me know by text. That certainly put me in my place – right at the bottom of her priority list. Thanks a lot, Samantha Wishaw.

James ran his fingers through his dark blond hair and gave me a gentle, understanding smile. I looked into his piercing blue eyes and I swear my heart skipped a beat. From the moment I first saw him, I was lost to that man. He somehow always seemed to manage to calm me down; something he'd had to do a hell of a lot recently. I smiled back, hoping it conveyed an apology for being so snappy. Again.

'Don't worry about Sam,' he said, his voice full of reassurance. 'You'll probably hear from her a lot more often now that she's working with the hedgehogs full-time.'

I stared at him, my eyes wide with disbelief and that brief feeling of calm disappeared. Working with the hedgehogs full-time? Since when? When she'd visited last month, she'd admitted she was finding it a struggle running the rescue centre while teaching full-time, but she'd also said resigning from her job wasn't an option. So what had changed?

'I thought you weren't in touch with her,' I snapped.

'I'm not.'

'Then how do you know more about her life than I do?'

'Because Toby told me when we met up.'

'And why were the two of you talking about Sam? Desperate to hear all about your ex-girlfriend?'

James sighed and shook his head slowly. 'I can't talk to you when you're like this.' He turned to leave.

'Like what?'

'Angry. Jealous.'

'Oh, so there's something to be jealous about, is there?'

With another sigh, he left the room.

I held my breath as he thundered down the stairs and, moments later, slammed the front door. I closed my eyes as I shakily exhaled.

'That went well,' I told Samuel. 'Another delightful day in the wonderful life of Chloe Turner.'

* * *

Samuel and I were downstairs when I heard a car outside about ninety minutes later. I carried him over to the window and peeked through the blinds. James was back, and about time too. I'd been worried sick. I sat down on the sofa with Samuel on my knee and listened for the front door opening.

'Where the hell have you been?' I shouted the moment he closed the door. 'Would it have killed you to text me?'

James appeared in the lounge doorway looking sheepish. He held a stunning bouquet of flowers in one hand and a paper bag in the other. 'I drove to the beach, went for a walk, and then I got you these.' He thrust the flowers towards me but I didn't take them.

'What's in the bag?'

'I thought you might like some croissants for breakfast.'

I knew the right thing to do was to thank him. The flowers were beautiful and fresh croissants were my favourites, but I'd worked myself into such a state while he'd been gone – terrified that he'd finally seen sense and left me – that I couldn't seem to do the right thing. All I could do was shout.

'So you've been to the supermarket and you never thought to do the weekly shop? Nice one, James. Really helpful.'

His expression was one of clear dismay. 'I thought you'd done an online order.'

'I began one but Samuel started crying and I never finished it.'

'Why didn't you say? I could have done it.'

I winced at the all-too-familiar tilt of his head and expression of pity in his eyes. That right there? *That* was the reason why. I couldn't bear to admit that I'd failed at yet another thing and get that sympathetic look which only made me feel even more inadequate. I was sick of everyone else having to come to my rescue. Why couldn't I get a grip on anything? And not just with Samuel. Our wedding would have been a disaster if Sam hadn't taken control of most of the plans.

'I need a shower.' I thrust Samuel towards him.

'Should I put the oven on to heat up the croissants?'

I couldn't be bothered to answer. It wasn't exactly important. Like everything about my life.

* * *

I desperately needed to relax. My whole body felt rigid and my teeth ached from the constant grinding. Yet even the powerful massaging flow from the shower couldn't work its magic and untense me. I seemed to constantly ache these days. I kept replaying this morning's spats with James. Two so far. We'd be in double figures before bedtime.

I knew that an extreme lack of sleep made me crabby and James got the brunt of that but, honestly, it wasn't all my fault. He had to accept some blame because he never thought things through. The situation just now was a prime example. If he'd told me he was planning to go to the supermarket, I could have asked him to do a full shop but, no, he'd stormed out of the house in his pathetic little man-strop and... I shook my head. I could hardly blame him for storming out of the house, either. I'd caused that. And he probably hadn't been planning to go shopping at all but had thought some flowers and croissants might cheer me up after a bad start to the day. So now I felt even more of a bitch for having a go at him as usual when he'd been trying to do a nice thing.

Switching off the shower, I squeezed the excess water from my hair before rubbing it with a towel. With a fluffy bath sheet wrapped round me, I slumped down onto the toilet seat, head in hands, as the tears flowed. Was this it? Was this my new reality? No sleep, no sex, permanently tired and achy and sod all time to do anything?

I couldn't decide whether weekdays or weekends were the

worst. During the week, I was doing well if I managed to brush my teeth before lunchtime. Days passed me by in a blur of tears, dirty nappies and feeding but at least there were no arguments... until James arrived home from work. And then all we seemed to do was argue.

Why was it all so damn difficult? Or was it only me who found that? Other new mums seemed to manage. Little Miss Perfect at the end of the road definitely did. She'd had her second baby a month after Samuel was born and I spotted her every day without fail, pushing the double buggy past our front window, a huge smile on her perfectly made-up smug face. She wasn't wearing smelly, creased PJs and looking like she'd been dragged through a hedge backwards. And she had two kids under the age of one to cope with! Unless that was her secret. She'd sussed it out with her daughter so the son was a breeze. Although I couldn't help feeling it was me messing it up. Like I always did.

* * *

James didn't need to say a word. The look he gave me when I stepped into the lounge said it all. Raised eyebrows. Parted lips. I obviously disgusted him. I looked down at my crinkled T-shirt and grey sweatpants, such a world away from how he was used to me dressing pre-Samuel.

I glared at James. 'They're clean.'

'I didn't say anything.'

His soft voice, tinged with the usual Chloe-can't-cope sympathy and that tilted head wound me up again. 'You didn't have to. They're comfortable, okay? And it's not like we're going anywhere.'

James winced. 'But we are.'

'Where?'

'My mum's surprise sixtieth.'

My stomach did a backflip before I realised he was winding me up. Badly timed but I couldn't face another argument on an empty stomach. I grabbed a croissant off the plate on the lamp table and took a bite.

'You're hilarious,' I mumbled, my mouth full of warm pastry. 'That's *next* Sunday.'

'It's *this* Sunday.'

'No, it's the fourteenth.'

'And today *is* the fourteenth.'

It couldn't be. His phone was resting on the arm of the sofa. I jabbed at the screen with a greasy finger and frowned at the date it showed. *Mid-June already? Really?* My mind raced as I looked towards Samuel lying on his back on his playmat, kicking his legs, his right hand gripping a Peter Rabbit comforter. Could I refuse to go? Say I was tired? Feeling ill? It's not like I'd even be lying. I genuinely felt like crap.

James stood up, put his arm round my shoulder and kissed the top of my head, making my heart race. 'It won't be a late one. I promise. You know how much my mum loves her Sunday evening TV.'

His tone was gentle but persuasive and I knew there was no way I could back out. It wasn't fair on him or his mum. My parents lived a short walk away but Nancy lived in York, an hour away. She was nervous behind the wheel and found driving to the local shops an ordeal, so driving to Whitsborough Bay was out of the question. Trains made her anxious, too. She was paranoid about missing her stop, even though Whitsborough Bay, being on the coast, was the end of the line, so impossible to miss. Yet it was a ready-made excuse so we always had to traipse through to York instead. That meant she didn't get to see her grandson nearly as much as she'd have liked because no way was I willing to make that trip every weekend and I certainly wasn't going to drive through on my own so she could coo over Samuel and barely notice my existence.

I looked up into James's pleading expression and my resolve crumbled. I could do it for him. I'd do anything for that man. And it was his mum's birthday so it was only fair that we were the ones to do the travelling today.

'What time do we need to leave?' I asked, trying my hardest to keep my tone light when a two-hour round-trip for a two-hour meal was my idea of hell right now. All I really wanted to do was lie on the sofa and, instead, I'd have to face a permanent replay of the same intrusive conversation from James's relatives: *How's Samuel? How often does he wake up? Are you feeding him yourself? How soon before you give him a brother or sister?* And it would be as though I didn't exist. As though I was merely a vessel for baby-production. They'd all want to hold him, too, and I hated that. I needed him close to me.

James squeezed my shoulder. 'Ideally we need to be out the house in an hour but we could push it by another fifteen minutes if that works better for you and Samuel. I know you're tired but hopefully Samuel will sleep in the car and you can have a nap too.'

'Fingers crossed.'

He gently pushed a strand of wet hair behind my ear then brushed his thumb over my cheekbone, gazing at me with such love that my heart started to race. Was he going to kiss me? We hadn't kissed properly since we brought Samuel home from hospital. That evening we'd laid on our bed with our new baby between us, all bundled up in a soft knitted blanket, fast asleep. James thanked me for giving him a beautiful son and kissed me with such tenderness that my insides felt like liquid. That was almost four months ago. Since then it had been quick pecks, brief hugs and lengthy arguments.

Samuel sneezed and the moment broke. Reality returned.

'I'll be ready in half an hour,' I muttered, dropping the croissant back on the plate, my appetite gone.

How had I not registered that it was Nancy's birthday today? Thank God James had sorted out the card and gift because, if it had been left to me, that could have been awkward.

Upstairs, I paused by Samuel's nursery. I'd planned to order him something special to wear. Messed that up, too. Maybe he already had something. It had been a tough pregnancy and, stuck at home under strict orders to rest and avoid stress, I'd been hideously bored. So I shopped online. Quite a lot. I might have got a tad carried away. We'd been given clothes as gifts too and I seemed to remember someone – no idea who – had bought him a cute trouser, shirt and cardigan combo. That would be perfect.

I opened the wardrobe door and a pile of freshly washed but unfolded clothes tumbled out. Crap. I'd forgotten about shoving them in there ready to sort out later. I stared in dismay at the pile on the floor and then at what remained in the wardrobe. Why hadn't I had the foresight to organise anything before Samuel came along? Why was everything all jumbled up, still in gift bags or delivery packages? The wardrobe had two rails full of pale blue plastic hangers and they'd never been used.

Shuddering at the enormity of the task, I shook my head, left the nursery and closed the door. The outfit he was wearing would have to do. If only I could get away with my PJs.

'I'll go and do the shopping while you're getting sorted,' James called up the stairs. 'Samuel's in his bouncer. Do you want me to bring him up?'

'I'll come down and get him.'

'Okay. See you soon.'

I peeked out of the front window and watched him reverse off the drive and exit our street, undecided on how I felt about his supermarket run. There'd be food in the house tomorrow – a good thing – but did he have to be such a martyr? It made me feel even more guilty that I'd failed to accomplish something as simple as the online shop. And him going out also meant that I needed to look after Samuel again. So much for giving me some time to get ready in peace.

Sighing, I went downstairs. Samuel was in his bouncer in the middle of the lounge floor. I bent down to pick it up and frowned. Was that James's phone on the rug? He must have put it down while he strapped Samuel in and had forgotten to retrieve it.

I lifted up the phone and stared at it. Should I...? I'd never checked his phone before, although it had crossed my mind shortly before Samuel was born when I'd suspected James might be having an affair. How wrong could I have been? He'd actually been having treatment for testicular cancer – thankfully now in remission – but hadn't wanted to tell me about his diagnosis while I was meant to be avoiding stress. Typical James, putting me first.

'Promise me you won't tell Daddy,' I said to Samuel. 'If I get his pin code wrong on the first attempt, it's a sign that I'm not meant to check.' I tapped in his birthday. Wrong.

'Three attempts. But that's it. I'll probably be locked out after that anyway.'

My heart raced as our wedding date unlocked the screen. I stared at the phone then put it back down on the floor. I couldn't do it. It wasn't right. But, then again, if he'd been stupid enough to leave it lying around, he was inviting a spot of snooping. I picked it up again.

'Where first, Samuel? Texts, you say? Toby's top of the list. Let's see your daddy slagging me off and asking about Samantha.'

I scanned through the recent conversations with his best friend. Boring. All the texts were about football, golf, a sci-fi series they were both into and confirmation of times and places to meet up.

Conversations with his mum were dull, too, the subjects

including the weather, gossip about her neighbours, and her bunion troubles. There were loads of texts to her sister – his Aunt Beatrice – but they were all about the surprise party and our birthday gift of a weekend away for the pair of them. No mention of me.

I scrolled down his text list further, past texts from me, his boss and his mobile phone provider. Nothing.

'Emails?' I asked Samuel.

James's inbox appeared to be full of marketing emails. Then I stopped scrolling, heart thumping, as one name jumped out at me.

'Oh, my God!'

I clicked into the email. My cheeks flushed and I started shaking as I worked my way back through a series of three messages.

'No, no, no, no! Oh, James! Why? And why her?'

The phone slipped from my hand and onto the rug. I swallowed down the panic rising in my throat. This was going to wreck everything.

3

I felt like a packhorse as I led the way across the gravel farmyard and along the wide path in front of the house, Chloe traipsing behind me with her handbag hooked over one shoulder, holding Samuel out to the side. Somehow I'd ended up with Samuel's changing bag and a large sports bag strapped across either shoulder, a backpack on my back and two large binbags in each hand.

Stuffing everything into binbags strongly signalled leaving in a hurry and it was killing me not knowing what had happened. Not because I was intrigued by any potential gossip – absolutely not my thing – but because I was worried. My cousin was prone to the dramatics but packing up and leaving in a rush seemed extreme, even for her.

I pushed open the front door and paused on the step as a thought struck me. 'James does know you've left him?'

She looked down and kicked at some gravel on the path. 'I thought you said we needed to get Samuel bathed and changed.'

'We do, but—'

'So stop asking me complicated questions.' She pushed past me into the large hall and placed Samuel's carrier down.

Inwardly sighing, I closed the door behind us. Shafts of light filtered through the glass panels round the door, illuminating the green, cream and blue patterned Victorian tiles.

I usually felt lifted the moment I stepped inside, welcomed back into my beautiful home but, right now, I felt uneasy as I dropped the binbags onto the tiles, removed the other bags and rolled my burning shoulders.

Chloe glanced towards the staircase. 'Where can I get showered and changed?'

'What about Samuel?'

Her lip quivered and tears sparkled in her eyes. 'I was hoping you could do it. He'll need feeding afterwards and, if I don't get showered now, I won't get a chance. I'm covered in sick. Please, Sammie.'

So we were back to using Sammie, were we? After the rift, she'd ditched the affectionate shortened name that she, Dad and Josh called me and it had become more formal. But now that she needed something from me...

I could have pointed out that Samuel had been rear-facing and there was no way Chloe could be covered in sick unless she'd tried to clean him up – which she hadn't – but what would that achieve? The important thing here was this little baby and I wasn't going to let him fester in soggy, smelly clothes any longer.

'I'll need the main bathroom so you can use the en-suite in my bedroom. It's the last door at the front of the house.'

'Towels?'

'In the storage cupboard in the main bathroom. Second door at the back of the house.'

Chloe grabbed the sports bag from me and ran up the stairs, no doubt desperate to get away before I changed my mind.

I gazed down at Samuel and my heart went out to him. 'Hang

on a bit longer, little one. As soon as I've found some clothes, I'll have you sorted out.'

Crouching down, I untied one of the binbags. It looked as though Chloe had swept the entire contents of Samuel's wardrobe and drawers into it as everything was in a jumbled-up mess and there were even clothes still in gift bags and online delivery packages. I found a T-shirt for his age but couldn't find any trousers that would fit. I untied the next bag but with no success. Sick of rummaging, I grabbed a baby blue sleepsuit.

'Sorry, sweetheart. This will have to do for now. Your stuff needs some serious sorting.'

* * *

Samuel remained asleep while I peeled his clothes off in the family bathroom and flung them straight into a binbag with the soiled nappy. The vomit would have washed out but I wasn't convinced about the other incident. Best to just dispose of the lot.

As soon as I lowered him into Lottie's Pooh Bear baby bath within the large claw-foot bath, his eyes opened and he emitted the most ear-piercing scream. Not that I could blame him. I cursed Chloe under my breath for abandoning me and then cursed myself for letting her. The state Samuel was in, this was definitely a two-person job, especially as the water needed refreshing after I'd initially sponged off the worst of the mess. Goodness knows how I'd have managed if I hadn't got used to handling slippery babies through helping bathe Lottie and Archie over the past couple of weeks.

'It's all right,' I said in what I hoped sounded like soothing tones, despite me feeling far from relaxed at that point. 'Not long and then we'll get you in some fresh clothes and your mummy can feed you.'

He continued to screech. I'd thought Archie and Lottie were loud but, even when their cries were combined, Samuel eclipsed them. Poor Chloe and James. Their ears were probably ringing.

Samuel's cries reduced to whimpers by the time I'd dried him off and secured his fresh nappy. I was fastening the final few poppers on his sleepsuit when the doorbell rang.

'Chloe?' I called, poking my head out of the bathroom. The shower in the en-suite was still going so I grabbed a fresh towel and swathed Samuel in it to keep him warm before making my way downstairs.

An auburn-haired woman of about my age stood on the doorstep. 'Is this where I bring poorly hedgehogs?' she asked before smiling at Samuel, who'd nuzzled into my shoulder.

'Yes. I'm Samantha. Hi.'

'Hi. This hedgehog has been curled up in my front garden for a few hours. My next-door neighbour says they shouldn't be out in daylight. Is that right?'

'Mainly. Mums can be out foraging for food or materials for a nest during the day but they'd normally be moving quickly and with purpose. If there's one stationary or slow-moving during the day, it's very likely something's wrong.'

She opened up the handles on a bag for life. 'Sorry. I didn't have anything else to put it in.'

I peered into the bag. A large hedgehog with mainly dark spines was curled up in the middle.

'Do you know what's wrong with it?' the woman asked.

'I couldn't tell you without picking it up and...' I indicated Samuel.

'I adore babies so I don't mind holding him. I'd love to know that the hedgehog's okay before I go.'

She gently placed the bag down and I passed over Samuel. As I pulled on the pair of thick gloves I kept by the door, I smiled at her cooing over him.

'Flystrike,' I announced after I'd given the hedgehog a quick check. 'You see these white bits?' I pointed to a couple of patches of what looked like small grains of rice between the spines. 'These are fly eggs which, if left, would hatch into maggots, which would then burrow into the hedgehog's skin and can cause some serious damage.'

'Urgh! That's disgusting.'

'It's really common and it's easily treated when the hedgehog is brought in quickly before the eggs hatch.' I turned the hog over and it allowed me to unfurl it briefly before curling back into a ball. It was enough time to check the gender. It was a male, which meant I didn't need to worry about a nest of abandoned hoglets somewhere. 'Would you like him releasing back into your garden?'

She screwed up her face. 'I'd like to say yes, but I work away a lot. You'd struggle to catch me at home. Can he be released here instead?'

'That's fine. Thanks for bringing him in. Do you want your bag back?'

She laughed lightly. 'Fly eggs? Maggots? I might pass on that.'

'Probably a good idea.'

She handed Samuel over then left.

'Well, young Samuel, our new arrival needs treatment quickly, so Mummy is going to have to take care of you whether she's ready or not.'

Leaving the hedgehog in its bag by the door, I took the stairs two at a time, calling Chloe's name. She didn't respond but the shower had stopped. I knocked on my bedroom door then went straight in to find her standing in front of my cheval mirror wrapped in a towel with a towel turban on her head, prodding the skin round her eyes and frowning.

'I'll need to leave Samuel with you,' I said.

She spun round, looking surprised to see me there. 'I'm not dressed.'

'Then get dressed. I've got a hedgehog emergency.'

'What am I supposed to do with Samuel?'

'Whatever you normally do while you get dressed.' I didn't have time for a discussion.

I glanced round the room in despair. What a mess! There were a couple of soggy towels dumped on the stripped floorboards and she'd emptied the contents of her sports bag all over the bed. Trying not to sigh, I shoved everything aside, grabbed our pillows, positioned them in a square in the middle of the bed and placed Samuel in between. 'See you later.'

Chloe's protests followed me down the stairs and, as I closed the front door, it struck me that I'd rather listen to Samuel's cries than Chloe when she was in full whinge mode.

* * *

'Don't worry, little one,' I said as I took the hedgehog over to the barn. 'I'll soon get rid of those nasty fly eggs and you'll feel so much better.'

Gently placing the bag on the floor, I disinfected the treatment table, covered it in blue paper towel, grabbed a new chart and the scales, then weighed the hedgehog.

'You're a good weight,' I told him, scribbling it down on his chart. 'Would you like a name?' We'd started with hedgehog-related names like Spikette, Sonic and Mrs Tiggy Winkle but quickly exhausted ideas and moved onto famous characters from books or movies. Although we'd barely scratched the surface on that category, I fancied a change. 'How about classic authors? Thomas's favourite book was *Great Expectations* so you can be Dickens. It suits you.'

I set about cleaning up Dickens. Although there were several patches of flystrike, the cuts beneath them weren't deep. It looked as though he'd squeezed under some barbed wire or something similar and it had scraped him in several places. Eggs typically hatched within twelve hours of being laid so the woman's quick reaction in bringing Dickens in had made a massive difference. Time was so important, which was why I'd had to put my foot down with Chloe.

By the time I'd cleaned Dickens up, given him a shot of antibiotics and settled him into a crate with food and water, some of the hoglets had started squeaking so it was feeding time once more, which was quite a task. We'd had triplets brought in during the week, bringing our hoglets total up to seventeen, although I only had fourteen to hand-feed as three were with their mum, Trinity. Four more adults had joined us but we'd released a couple of healed patients so, including Dickens, we now had twenty-four adults.

As I plugged in the heat pads and prepared the formula, my thoughts returned to Chloe and James. What could possibly have gone wrong for Chloe to pack up her stuff and turn up unannounced at the farm? It had to be bad, otherwise she'd have moved in with her mum instead, so she clearly wanted to be somewhere less obvious and put some distance between her and James.

I was convinced James knew nothing about her leaving. She'd evaded my direct question and why else would everything be hastily shoved into binbags? He had to be worried sick, assuming he'd discovered she was gone. I doubted Chloe had left him a note. Running out was far more her style. Could James have rung me on the off chance she'd turned up? Could Auntie Louise have? My phone had been charging on the kitchen worktop when I'd seen the car approaching and I'd rushed out without picking it up. It was still there now.

Tomorrow would signify exactly two years since Chloe and James did the dirty on me. Much as I hated what they'd done, I couldn't deny that they were perfectly suited. James's calm, considered, mature approach to life seemed to balance out Chloe's impulsive, reckless and often juvenile outlook. He definitely brought out the best in her. Or at least he had before they'd married. I had little experience of them as a married couple, having been pushed out of Chloe's life at their wedding. What if that amazing first year together had been down to the excitement of a new relationship and a wedding on the horizon? What if the reality of married life then straight into expecting their first child had been too mundane for Chloe? And, with James's diagnosis with testicular cancer, they'd had a lot to deal with. Had it been too much? I hoped not, because it would be very sad for them and for Samuel if it was over already.

If Chloe wanted to stay here and wanted my help, I just hoped she'd fill me in. James was bound to track her down to Hedgehog Hollow – assuming he wanted to find her – and the last thing I wanted or needed was to be stuck in the middle of a war between my ex-boyfriend and my semi-hostile cousin.

4

CHLOE

I'd heard Samuel screeching while I was in the shower. Even an extractor fan and a torrent of water hadn't been able to drown out the worst sound in the world. Looking at him sound asleep on Sam and Josh's bed right now with his hands curled into little fists by his ears, his soft blond hair like a cap of fluff, it was hard to reconcile that it was the same baby. Shame it wouldn't last. He'd be awake and demanding food soon. I shuddered at the thought of that ordeal.

I removed the towel turban from my head and shook out my hair. Washing it twice in one week was a novelty. Twice in one day was unnecessary and indulgent but how else was I going to get a moment to think, especially after the journey from hell? I'd been stressed enough trying to gather everything together before James arrived home without having to stop to feed Samuel and then him decorating the car soon after. I should have stopped and tried to clean him up. I knew that now but, at the time, all I could think about was getting some distance between me and Whitsborough Bay. Fast.

I pulled on a pair of black leggings and rummaged for a T-shirt among the pile of my clothes on Sam's bed. I lifted one up and opened it out and tears pricked my eyes as I stared at the 'World's Best Mummy' slogan emblazoned across it. James's eyes had shone with excitement when he presented me with it and a matching 'World's Best Baby' sleepsuit for Samuel a fortnight after he was born. I'd laughed, said it was adorable, and worn it proudly the following day. But that was the last day of James's paternity leave. That was the last day as a happy family of three. I hadn't felt anything remotely resembling happy again after that and everything had started to fall apart without him. World's best mummy? What a joke. World's biggest failure, more like. I hadn't been able to bring myself to wear it again and I certainly couldn't wear it now.

Another rummage and I found a creased but clean plain pink T-shirt and pulled that on instead. I gazed round the room. It was beautifully decorated in a pale duck-egg blue on three walls and a darker shade behind the bedhead. Two large windows either side of the bed looked straight out over fields. The farmyard and the barn where Sam ran her hedgehog rescue centre were to the left but I'd need to be by the window to actually see them.

Feeling weary but not wanting to sit on the bed for fear of prematurely disturbing Samuel, I lowered myself to the floor and dragged my handbag towards me. My heart thumped as I reached inside for my phone. Seventeen missed calls from a mixture of James, Mum and Dad. Five voicemails. A stack of text messages. A tear trickled down my cheek as I numbly dropped my phone back into the bag. Not now.

I rested my head against the foot of the wooden bed and looked up at the canvas of a wildflower meadow on the wall opposite me. The colours were vibrant yet soothing at the same time. Gazing at it, I could imagine the flowers swaying in a gentle breeze, hear the bees buzzing, feel the... my eyelids started to droop.

'Waaahhhh!'

And now I was wide awake. Again. I pulled myself up and, moments later, Samuel was latched on while I shut my eyes tightly, trying to block out the pain.

5

After a full round of hoglet feeds, I returned to the farmhouse in search of Chloe. I could hear Samuel's cries as I approached. It was just past four and I felt a twinge of guilt for abandoning her for a couple of hours. Hopefully she'd understand that I had a business to run and couldn't drop everything just because she'd turned up out of the blue demanding accommodation. It had only been fortunate timing on her part that I'd been between feeds when she arrived so had been able to bathe and change Samuel for her.

In the lounge, I found her pacing the floor, hair dishevelled, cheeks red, attempting to soothe Samuel by bouncing him in her arms. Except it looked more like the poor lad was on the receiving end of an electric shock, being jolted up and down.

'Where the hell have you been?' she demanded over his cries, her eyes flashing with anger.

My twinge of guilt fled the building. 'Hedgehog emergency and hoglet feeding. Cup of tea?' My refusal to get sucked into an argument was either going to inflame her further or calm her. I prayed for the latter.

'That would be nice,' she said, her voice softening.

'Coming right up.' I strained my ears for a 'thank you' as I stepped into the hall. None came. A thank you from Chloe was a rare and precious gift.

* * *

In the kitchen, I checked my phone. There were missed calls and texts from James and Auntie Louise as expected. I clicked into the first voicemail, left at 11.37 a.m.

'Sam, it's James. I'm sorry to bother you but I don't suppose you've heard from Chloe. Let me know. Cheers.'

He sounded quite cheery in that message but the second one left fifteen minutes later told a different story: 'Hi, Sam. Sorry. It's me again. Chloe's gone and she's taken Samuel but I don't know where they are. I got back from the shops to find their stuff gone. No note. No warning. She's not answering her phone and I'm getting really worried now. Can you call me, even if you haven't heard anything?'

I ran my hand through my hair and sighed. So I'd been right and she hadn't let him know. That wasn't fair. I'd always thought of James as the ideal person to have around in a crisis because he seemed to be able to keep a cool head no matter what, but who could keep a cool head when their wife and son had just vanished?

There was one more message from him left at 12.18 p.m. This time he sounded weary: 'Me again. I'm on my way to York. It's my mum's sixtieth and there's a surprise meal planned. I'm the one picking her up and I'm so late but I can't not go. I'll have my phone on. Please, please get in touch if you hear anything. She might even turn up at yours. She's not at her mum's and I can't think where else she'd go. If she is with you, don't panic. I'm not going to turn up tonight and try to drag her back. I don't know why she left but she obviously needs some time away from me and I'm going to respect that for now. I just need to know they're both safe.'

There was a voicemail from Auntie Louise, too: 'Hi, Sam. I know James has already left a message. Chloe's not here or at your mum's. We have to assume she's with you. Where else would she be? I don't know what's gone on between them to make her leave and, right now, I don't really care. The important thing is that Chloe and my grandson are okay. Please can you let me know either way? Thanks, sweetheart.'

I put my phone down with a sigh. I'd make a fresh brew and try to convince Chloe to at least call Auntie Louise, even if she didn't want to speak to James. If she refused, I'd call them both myself. It wasn't fair to let them stew, no matter what James had done... or what Chloe thought he'd done. She did have form, after all, for letting her imagination run away with her.

When I returned to the lounge with the drinks, Chloe had her back to me and was still trying to soothe a screaming Samuel. In the mirror on the other side of the room, I could see her wiping her wet cheeks before she turned round.

'He's trying out for the baby Olympics. I think it's a safe gold in the loudest cry competition, don't you?' Her voice cracked and tears glistened in her eyes even though she had a smile plastered across her face.

I'd talk about making contact with Auntie Louise and James once Samuel was placated. 'Why don't you sit down and have your tea while I give him cuddles?'

She didn't need any convincing. I'd no sooner put the mugs down on the coffee table than he was thrust into my hands. He paused, looking at me with big blue eyes, then started to howl again.

'What's the matter, sweetheart?' I adjusted my hold and the

smell hit me. I turned to Chloe. 'He's filled his nappy again. That's why he's crying.'

'But you just bathed and changed him.'

'I know, but you've fed him since then. Given what happened in the car, he's probably got a dodgy tummy.'

With a sigh, Chloe put her mug down and made to get up.

'It's okay. I'll change him. You drink your tea.'

She picked up her mug again but she didn't look at me. Or thank me.

* * *

'All clean and happy now,' I said to Chloe as I returned to the lounge ten minutes later.

Samuel's cries had eased as soon as I had him cleaned up and in a fresh nappy but I'd wanted him to be fully settled before I came back downstairs, allowing Chloe some time to gather herself together. It didn't take a genius to see that she was struggling with Samuel and possibly had been for quite some time.

'I honestly couldn't smell anything.' Chloe looked at me, her ice-blue eyes all big and innocent. 'You have to believe me.'

'You've probably grown immune to it.' There was no way she could have missed it but I didn't want to make her feel any worse than she clearly already did.

When Chloe made no move to take Samuel from me, I sat down on the other end of the corner sofa from her with him on my knee. 'I'm listening.'

'I don't want to talk about it.'

'And I'm not buying that. What happened with James?'

'None of your business,' she snapped.

'You made it my business by seeking refuge here. Come on,

Chloe, you know you're going to have to open up eventually so you might as well just get it over with.'

She scowled at me. 'So you can gloat and tell me it's karma for me stealing your boyfriend?'

'You really think I'd do that?'

'Yes!'

I raised my eyebrows at her.

Her shoulders slumped. 'I don't know. Maybe. Okay, no then. But you'd probably be thinking it.' The whine was back.

'It was two years ago, Chloe. So much has changed for us all since then. I've got Josh now and he's my forever. James never was. He was always meant to be with you.'

'Yeah, well, things change.'

'What things? What happened?'

She fixed her eyes on mine and I thought for a moment that she was going to let me in. Then she shook her head. 'Nothing. It doesn't matter.'

'I need to go back to the barn shortly. If you're not going to tell me why you've run out on James, that's your choice, but there's one thing I insist you do. You *have* to let James and your mum know you're safe. I've got missed calls and texts from them both, and I bet you have too.'

The colour rushing to her cheeks confirmed that.

'It's not just about you,' I added. 'There's a baby caught up in all of this and his dad has a right to know where he is. He's left me three voicemails and he sounds frantic.'

'I don't want to speak to him.'

'Then don't speak to him but at least send him a text.'

She stared at me, defiance in her eyes, then she sighed. 'Okay. You win. I'll text him.'

I was about to retaliate and say it wasn't about winning but I decided against it. Turning this into an argument wouldn't accomplish anything. She'd agreed to make contact and that was the important thing for now.

'Will you speak to your mum, too?' I stood up and waited for an answer but she stared at her nails instead. 'I'll get the rest of your stuff out of your car.'

'Samuel's baby bouncer is in the front passenger footwell. Can you bring me that first?'

'Okay.' I handed over Samuel and left the room.

My phone beeped with a text from Josh before I reached the farmyard:

✉ From Josh
Goat saved & sorted. Home in about 20 mins.
Missing you xx

I'd better warn him what he was about to walk into:

✉ To Josh
We've had 3 new arrivals. Dickens has flystrike,
Chloe has an attitude problem and Samuel's cries
measure on the Richter Scale. Chloe says she's
left James but won't tell me why. It's been an
interesting afternoon! Really sorry xx

I added the shocked and confused emojis then sent it. Josh wouldn't be happy. Chloe hadn't exactly endeared herself to him, although she didn't endear herself to many people, tending to be cold and guarded around strangers.

✉ From Josh
Please don't be sorry. Definitely not your
fault. My mum always taught me that, if I don't

have anything nice to say, I should keep quiet.
So this is me keeping quiet ;-) xx

✉ To Josh
I know how you feel. Hopefully it will turn into
a classic Chloe drama and she'll be back with
James tomorrow xx

I was lifting the last of the binbags out of the boot when Josh pulled into the farmyard.

'Anyone in need of a hug?' he asked out of the window.

I dumped the bags on the gravel. 'Me, please. A big one.'

'Why's she parked in the middle of the farmyard?'

'She kind of dumped it there. I'll move it shortly.'

Josh parked then ran over to me and pulled me into a tight hug. I felt quite tearful as I clung onto him.

'How is she?'

'Snappy. Stressed.'

'And you don't know what happened?'

I stepped out of the hug and shook my head.

'Do you think something big has actually happened or do you think Chloe's just been a bit more melodramatic than usual and is too embarrassed to admit that?'

'The thought did cross my mind.' Part of me hoped that would be the case. All I wanted now was for Chloe and James to be happy and, if this was simply a bit of over-reacting on Chloe's part for something mundane like James failing to put the toilet seat down or take the bins out, then it should be easily resolved. But I couldn't shake the feeling that it was way more serious, otherwise she'd have gone to her mum's.

'Where's she going to sleep?'

'Top floor, on the airbed you bought for the barn. She can use the bedding we got for Dad's room and... oh, no! What was she thinking? There's nowhere for Samuel to sleep. I've emptied the car and there was no travel cot or Moses basket or anything like that. The car seat's covered in sick, not that he could settle in that for the night even if it wasn't.'

'Mum can probably borrow that cot from her next-door neighbour again. I'll ring her now.'

Connie had looked after Archie while Beth was in hospital and her neighbour, who had a young son, had come to the rescue with a travel cot and bedding.

I parked Chloe's car properly while Josh was on the phone with his request.

'She'll call me back when she's spoken to Sian,' he said. 'Load me up.'

Josh insisted on carrying the remaining bags so his hands were full when his phone rang as we were walking towards the farmhouse. I fished it out of his pocket.

'I've got the cot and some bedding,' Connie said after we'd exchanged greetings. 'Alex and I are heading to the coast for a walk along the beach this evening. We can drop everything off around six, if that suits.'

'That would be perfect. Thank you so much. See you both later.'

'At least that's one thing sorted,' I said when I disconnected the call. I glanced back towards the farm track. 'I keep expecting to see James, Uncle Simon or Auntie Louise racing down the track.'

'Do they know she's here?'

'I've no idea. I told her she has to let them know she's safe and she promised she would, but what Chloe promises and what Chloe actually does can sometimes be poles apart.'

6

Through the lounge window, I watched a jeep approaching on the farm track. Super-Josh. As he parked up, then hugged Sam, I felt a stab of jealousy. It was a long time since James had held me like that.

'We don't like him, do we?' I muttered to Samuel, tearing my gaze away from the window and focusing on him wriggling in his bouncer. 'He moved in and proposed pretty damn quick. Who does that?'

Plonking myself down on the grey corner sofa, my eyes scanned round the large room. Like the master bedroom, it was decorated beautifully with a soft grey, blue and warm cream palette. A log burner set in a brick alcove had a large driftwood mantlepiece above it and a basket of logs on the hearth. My cousin definitely had a good eye when it came to home furnishings.

'Someone who wants to bag themselves an enormous farm. That's who. Well played, Josh.'

I heard their voices a few minutes later as they passed the window, then the front door opened.

'That's the rest of your bags,' Sam announced, stepping into the lounge and tying her long dark hair into a ponytail. 'Josh has gone back to the barn for the airbed. Might as well get that blown up and ready for you.' Her eyes widened and she pressed her fingers to her mouth. 'I've just had another thought. There's no curtains or blinds on the top floor. It'll be dark by about ten tonight but sunrise is before five.'

'Great. So what you're saying is I've got zero chance of any sleep in the attic.'

'I didn't say that. I just said it'll get light early.'

'The combination of three screaming babies, an airbed, early dawn and a trek downstairs to the toilet aren't exactly conducive to a good night's sleep, are they?'

'I can't do anything about crying babies but you can sleep on the sofa instead if you prefer or you can have the airbed in here. There's a downstairs toilet and it'll be...' She paused and frowned. 'Actually, scrub that. It'll have to be upstairs.'

'Why? Because I'll be in everyone's way down here?'

'No. It's because you won't want to sleep down here. Thomas—'

I jumped up, goose bumps prickling my skin. 'Oh, my God! He died in this room, didn't he? Where?' Sam knew stuff like that completely creeped me out and had done for years, thanks to an incident in the summer between school and college.

Sam wasn't fazed by death, although I suppose it went with the territory, being a trained nurse. She'd found Gramps in his home the morning after he died and had stayed there alone with him until my parents and hers arrived. I could never have done that. I'd never been able to return to Meadowcroft knowing he'd died there.

'There are no ghosts here,' Sam said, her voice gentle. 'But, if there were, they'd be friendly ones.'

Ghosts weren't the issue. I wasn't convinced they even existed. It was death that gave me the jitters. 'We'll manage upstairs.' I smacked my palm against my head and my stomach plummeted to the floor as my stupidity hit me. 'Samuel! I haven't got a cot. I haven't even got any bedding for him.' I could feel panic welling inside of me. How could I have been so stupid?

Sam placed her hand on my arm. 'I noticed. It's all in hand. Josh's mum has borrowed a travel cot and some bedding from her neighbour. She'll drop it off later.'

Josh returned, a folded-up airbed tucked under one arm and carrying an electric pump. 'Hi, Chloe.'

'Josh.' It came out as a bit of a snarl. It was his fault. If he'd smiled or injected any enthusiasm into his greeting, I might have believed I was welcome but he hadn't, so I wasn't going to gush over him.

There was a moment's awkward silence then he turned to Sam. 'Where do you want these?'

'I'll take them upstairs and sort out the bedding.'

And leave me to make small talk with Super-Josh? No way. I stood up. 'I'll help you. You can watch Samuel, can't you, Josh?'

I bundled Sam out of the room and up the stairs before he had a chance to object.

* * *

My eyes burned with tiredness as I lay on the airbed in one of the attic rooms a few hours later, staring at the pale crescent moon through the round window on the side of the farmhouse.

The airbed was more comfortable than I'd expected, although getting up off it was a trial. Just as well there was nobody around to see me take an undignified roll onto the floor, hauling myself up from there, arse in the air.

Sam had loaned me a bedside light from her room and Josh had carried up a wooden chair from the kitchen so I could sit some-where and feed Samuel after we'd realised there was no safe way for me to lower myself onto the airbed with a baby in my arms. It wasn't the ideal set-up, although nothing about the current situation was ideal.

I glanced towards Samuel asleep a few feet away in the borrowed cot. How stupid did I feel for not even thinking about sleeping arrangements for him? To be fair, I couldn't have taken his cot apart and we had nothing at home that I could use as an alternative, but I could have at least grabbed some bedding. What an idiot! I hadn't been thinking clearly, though. I'd just wanted to get out of there.

Josh's mum, Connie, had insisted on putting the travel cot up for me. I'd met her briefly at the Family Fun Day at the start of May and it was rare that I warmed to someone immediately, but there was something very warm and natural about her. I got the impression that she didn't make immediate judgements about people and that was also rare. People make snap assumptions about me all the time and I hate it. Her boyfriend, Alex, seemed friendly too. Cute couple.

I wasn't so convinced about Josh's dad, Paul, and his girlfriend, Beth. They arrived back from a trip to the beach just after I'd made my bed. Well, after Sam had made the bed while I watched. To be fair to Paul, he'd looked drained and had taken off to bed after dinner but that Beth was certainly a piece of work. She'd smiled and acted as though she was delighted to meet me – *any friend of Sam's is a friend of mine* – but I saw through her. How long had she known Sam? A month? She was all: *Sam's so amazing, Sam's so lovely, Sam's a sugar-coated angel sprinkled in fairy dust and sent from heaven.* Okay, maybe I'd made the last one up but she was definitely over the top with how grateful she was to Sam and how pally they supposedly were, tripping over herself to share pointless boring anecdotes: *Do you remember when we did the washing up together, Sam, and I got some bubbles in my hair? Ooh, it was soooo funny.*

Sam was *my* best friend, not hers. Or she had been until I slept with her boyfriend, threw her out of our wedding, turned Mum against her, accused her of having an affair with James... I bit my lip as the offences kept stacking up. And that was only over the past couple of years. Better not dwell on the preceding years. It was a wonder she still put up with me after everything I'd done to her. But that was why I'd run to her because, no matter how much I pushed, she was always there for me. The only true friend I'd ever had.

Samuel gave a small cry and I propped myself up on my elbows, waiting for all hell to let loose, but silence fell instead. Settling back on my pillows, heart rate regulating once more, my thoughts turned to James. I pictured him arriving back from the supermarket, panicking as soon as he clocked that my car wasn't on the drive. He'd probably have worried that something had happened to Samuel and I'd had to rush him to hospital. As soon as he'd gone upstairs, he'd have seen the open wardrobes and drawers, contents decimated, and he'd have known. There'd been no need for a note. It was obvious what had happened. Not so obvious why.

Would he see his phone in the middle of the lounge floor and guess that I'd been snooping? And, if he did, would he work out what I'd found? I hated the thought of him being worried about us but escape had felt like the only option at the time. With the car packed and Samuel secured in his car seat I'd snuck back inside, unlocked James's phone again and hastily taken photos. I wasn't sure why. Fear he'd delete them and tell me I'd imagined things? I hadn't imagined anything. I'd seen her name and I had the photos to prove it.

7

'I'm off to work,' Paul said, poking his head into the kitchen the following morning and smiling warmly at me. 'Beth's gone back to sleep. Are you okay to bring Archie down later?'

I put my spoon down in my cereal and smiled at him. 'That's fine. Have a good day.' Archie was a little too heavy for Beth to carry downstairs and she certainly couldn't carry him and Lottie together.

Josh appeared a few minutes later and poured himself a bowl of cereal.

'You've just missed your dad.'

He sat down opposite me and added milk. 'How did you think he looked?'

'Drained, although he did his best to hide it as usual.' Since moving in, Paul seemed bright and cheerful most of the time but he didn't fool either of us. We could tell he was shattered and one glance at him in an unguarded moment revealed the fear and worry of what would happen if the treatment failed again. He didn't like to talk about it much but I'd picked up enough from snatched conversations to know that he was more worried about the impact of a terminal diagnosis on Beth and their young family than he was for himself. What a burden to bear.

Josh sighed. 'At least he's only got three more days. Although he wouldn't have had to work at all this week if he'd taken the job with me.'

I shook my head. 'It wouldn't have made any difference. You know what your dad's like. He'd have insisted on working his notice.' Last week, Josh had offered Paul the vacant position of veterinary nurse at his practice. Paul had been genuinely touched and I suspected he viewed Josh's offer as another step in the healing process in their relationship, knowing what a big thing it would be for Josh to have his dad working alongside him after everything that had happened. He'd talked it over with Beth and had decided that the timing wasn't right, pre-treatment, but he'd see how he felt afterwards and reconsider Josh's offer when he felt ready to return to work.

I watched as Josh half-heartedly chased his cereal round the bowl but made no effort to scoop any of it up. 'You're worried about him, aren't you?'

He pushed his bowl aside. 'I can't help it. What if the treatment doesn't work? What if we don't find a donor? What if...?' His eyes raised to the ceiling in the direction of the nursery. 'They're babies. They wouldn't even remember him.'

As his voice cracked, I rushed round the table and hugged him close. 'I know it's hard but try not to think like that. Fizz should have the testing dates confirmed from the colleges and university this week. We'll hopefully get a good take-up and, the more we test, the more likely we are to find a match.'

I sat down beside him, took his hands in mine and looked into his eyes. 'But if there's no match and the chemo doesn't work, we'll find a way through it together. And Beth and the kids will never be alone. We're their family now.' I blinked back my own tears, desperately hoping it wouldn't come to that. 'Stay strong, yeah?'

Josh took a deep breath, nodded, and smiled weakly. 'Have I told you lately how amazing you are and how much I love you?'

'Yes, but it never grows tired.'

He cupped my face in his hands and gave me a soft kiss, making my heart race. We'd been through so much already and there were still plenty of hurdles ahead but we were so strong together, we could face anything. I just hoped we wouldn't have to face the worst.

* * *

I sat forward on Thomas's bench later that morning, my hands clasped round a mug of tea, thinking about Paul and the battle he was about to face with his second round of chemotherapy. My heart felt so heavy for him, facing an uncertain future. He had three more days at work and then he was going to spend five precious days with his family before treatment resumed.

Sighing, I sat back and looked up. Ribbons of white clouds stretched across the pale blue sky and, as a light breeze blew a tendril of hair across my face, my thoughts turned to Gramps.

'Happy birthday, Gramps,' I whispered, raising my mug towards the sky. 'I miss you.'

I closed my eyes, breathing in the tranquillity, then opened them again a few minutes later on hearing the crunch of gravel.

'It's a bit cooler this morning and I spotted this in the kitchen.' Beth held up my favourite cardigan. 'I thought you might like it.'

'Thank you.' There was a definite chill in the air so I put my mug down and gratefully pulled the cardigan on. 'Are you joining me?'

'Only if that's okay. I can go back inside if you want some alone time.'

'I was about to check on you anyway.' I smiled at her as I shuffled along the bench.

'They're asleep but probably not for much longer.' She sat down, placing the baby monitor beside her. 'It's so peaceful out here. You looked deep in thought just now.'

'I was. I was just thinking about my Gramps. If he'd still been with us, he'd have been seventy-seven today.'

'You were close?'

'Really close. And to my Nanna. They were amazing grandparents. It's been two years since Gramps left us and seven for Nanna but I still miss them both.' My voice cracked and I swallowed down the lump in my throat.

'I've often wondered what it would be like to have grandparents.' Beth sighed. 'I never knew who my dad was so that ruled out knowing my paternal grandparents. My mum's dad died when I was a baby and she had a massive fall-out with her mum when I was about six or seven. I've no idea why. Mum would never talk about it. All I'm left with are some vague memories and a couple of crumpled photos.'

From her wistful smile, I guessed that she was picturing her grandma. 'What was she like?'

'She was this lovely round lady with rosy cheeks and wispy blonde hair. Always baking, always smiling, always singing. But, after the fall-out, Mum moved us to Hull for a fresh start and, as far as I know, she never let Grandma know where we were.'

'Aw, Beth. That's so sad. So you never saw her again? You don't even know if she's still alive?'

'I haven't a clue. Sometimes I imagine she's devoted years to trying to find us and that one day we'll have this emotional reunion. But then I ask myself how hard could it have been to track us down?

Lincoln to Hull is about an hour and a quarter. Not exactly the other side of the world. So it somehow hurts a little less to think that she's dead rather than that she didn't try to find her only grandchild.'

'I'm so sorry.'

She shrugged dismissively but I could see the sparkle of tears in her eyes. 'I feel bad for Archie and Lottie. With Paul's parents gone, they won't know what it's like to have grandparents either.'

'What about your mum?'

'She's never shown any interest in meeting her grandkids, although I shouldn't be surprised at that when she barely remembers she has a daughter. She lives on Corfu and runs a yoga retreat, of all things. If you'd ever met her, you'd know how hilarious that is because she's the most stressed-out, highly-strung woman you could ever meet. I've only seen her three times in the last twelve years.'

My mind raced with the maths. Beth was twenty-six now, which had to mean...

'She abandoned me when I was fourteen,' she said, as though reading my thoughts. 'Went Greek island-hopping with some bloke she'd barely known for five minutes. She fell out of love with him within a couple of months but fell in love with Corfu.'

'What did you do when she left?'

'Stayed with our elderly next-door neighbour until it became obvious it wasn't only for a week like Mum had promised her. Mrs Jennings had a few health problems and a teenager in the house wasn't ideal so...' She sighed and shrugged. 'After that, the concept of home was a fluid thing. Friends, boyfriends, a couple of hostels and the occasional shop doorway.'

I gasped, shocked at what I was hearing. Even though it was years ago, the pain was still obvious in her voice. 'Oh, Beth! That's awful.'

'It wasn't great but I only slept rough a handful of times and the one thing it taught me was that I might have had my problems but there were people a hell of a lot worse off than me. Besides, I always knew it would be temporary until I got my qualifications and a job. Luckily, when I started college, I made a new friend whose parents had a granny flat above their garage so I lived there until Paul bought the flat in Wilbersgate.'

'I had no idea you'd had such a tough time.'

She picked up the baby monitor and gazed down at her hands as she twiddled with it. 'I never told Josh about it. He knew Mum had buggered off to Corfu and we were barely in touch but he never knew the rest.' She looked up at me and frowned. 'Paul rang Mum when I was in hospital. He told her I might not make it and she should get a flight quickly. She said she couldn't afford the airfare. I might have been dying and my own mother couldn't jump on a plane to see me. Of course, Paul offered to pay for her ticket and do you know what she said then?'

I shrugged, although I could well imagine the response. It sounded like Beth's mum had a lot in common with mine. Mum hadn't bothered to visit me while I was in a coma following the arson attack on the barn and she hadn't even had the excuse of living in another country.

'She said she couldn't afford the time either but if he wanted to transfer her the money he would have sent for the airfare, she'd be very grateful.'

'That's harsh.' No wonder she sounded so bitter. How appalling!

'That's my mum for you.' A cry sounded through the monitor and Beth stood up. 'That's Archie awake. I'll leave you in peace. Thanks for listening.'

'If you want to talk some more, let me know. I... erm... I have a difficult relationship with my mum, too. I know how hurtful it can be.'

She gave me a sympathetic look. 'Thank you. I might just take you up on that.'

When she'd gone, I sat back against the bench and pulled my cardigan a little tighter round me. That had been unexpected. Poor Beth.

I'd thought a lot about what might happen when she and Paul moved into Hedgehog Hollow, but making a new friend hadn't been something I'd anticipated. Yet every conversation I had with her, I warmed to her even more. I'd never get my head around what either of them put Josh and Connie through but I felt like I was beginning to understand Beth as a person. Josh had called her a manipulative liar and he'd been right. That's who she had been. It wasn't who she was now. Even Josh had commented on how much she'd changed. It was probably down to a combination of getting older, motherhood, Paul's cancer diagnosis and her own brush with death. I liked the woman she'd become and was in awe of the strength she demonstrated.

From the looks that Chloe had been shooting us both across the kitchen table last night, my cousin didn't like our blooming friendship. No surprise there. Chloe didn't like to share. She'd always struggled with my friendship with Hannah and I suspected it was going to be the same with Beth. We had enough to contend with right now without adding petty jealousy into the mix.

My mug was empty and it was getting colder, which signalled time to retreat indoors and see if Chloe was up. Josh had spent the night in the barn on hoglet-feeding duty while I stayed in the house in case Chloe needed me. The walls and floors were thick but they'd done nothing to stifle Samuel's cries. He'd awoken demanding a feed every couple of hours, which was far too often. At his age, I'd have expected Chloe to be feeding every three to four hours. If this was her normal, it could explain her erratic behaviour and mood swings.

Hannah had phoned me a couple of weeks ago, concerned at what James had shared after a night out with Toby. He'd spoken about them arguing and about Chloe being tearful and spending all day in her PJs. If Samuel was demanding two-hourly feeds, was it any wonder?

* * *

I tapped lightly on Chloe's bedroom door. Getting no response, I gently nudged it open. She was seated on the chair nursing Samuel with what could only be described as a look of sheer agony on her face. She was biting her lip; her eyes were scrunched up and tears were flowing.

She must have sensed my presence as she snapped open her eyes and swiped at her wet cheeks. 'How long have you been there?' she demanded.

'I brought you a cup of tea.' I held up the mug. 'How long has breastfeeding been painful?'

'Who says it's painful?'

Ignoring her question, I took a couple of steps closer and knelt beside her. 'Have you asked your midwife for help?'

'I don't like her. She's patronising. Keeps saying I'm doing things wrong. How can there be a *wrong* way to breastfeed a baby?'

I hesitated, trying to find the right words that wouldn't make her jump down my throat. 'Sometimes the baby doesn't latch on properly so they end up feeding for a long time but not actually getting much milk. It's nobody's fault. It's just one of those things. The problem is the baby ends up hungry so demands feeds twice as often and poor mum's left in pain.'

'Yes, well, we're fine. I know what I'm doing. Was there something else you wanted?'

'No.'

'Then a little privacy would be nice.'

'But you look like you're suffering.'

'Has moving into your manor house somehow taken away your ability to listen? I said we're fine.'

Wincing at her rudeness and the volume of her voice, I turned and left. I wanted to help but she clearly didn't want me to, and I wasn't going to stick around to be yelled at and insulted in my own home. I'd had plenty of that from my mum growing up. And what was that reference to 'manor house'? That certainly smacked of jealousy and, if she'd ever bothered to find out anything about my friendship with Thomas, she'd have known that I'd far rather be living in a tiny one-bed flat and still have Thomas in my life than be in his home without him.

8

CHLOE

I stared at the closed door, cursing under my breath. Why had I just done that? Why was it so hard to admit that I needed help? Because I absolutely did. This level of pain could *not* be right. I refused to believe that so many women chose to breastfeed if it was. Who'd willingly continually subject themselves to this?

With the ordeal finally over, I pulled my clothes back into place and wiped my damp cheeks again. It wasn't just the feeding that hurt. Between feeds, my skin felt like it was on fire. I'd barely slept last night for the pain.

'I might have to ask Sam if she can help me, like your daddy suggested,' I told Samuel as I placed him back in the cot. 'I'll get you dressed first. If I can find any clothes that fit.'

I emptied the contents of each binbag into a pile on the wooden floor, then immediately regretted it. Rummaging through one binbag had been bad enough but now I'd created a clothes mountain that looked impossible to conquer.

'Would anyone notice if you didn't change clothes?' I asked after the first six items I picked up were either too big or too small. I chewed on my lip. Sam would notice. And that Beth probably would too. I bet her kids didn't wear the same thing two days in a row. I bet all their clothes were organised and ironed to perfection.

* * *

Silence greeted me downstairs when I'd finally found a cute T-shirt and dungarees in a gift bag and wrestled Samuel into them before stuffing the rest of his clothes back into the binbags.

'Hello?' I called. 'Sammie?'

Standing in the wide hallway with Samuel in my arms, I felt quite lost. What was I doing here? And, for that matter, what was I doing with my life?

I shuffled into the lounge and lowered myself onto the sofa. How had it gone so wrong? On paper, I had everything I'd ever dreamed of: gorgeous husband, comfortable new home, no financial worries and a family. Yet, lately, I'd never felt more miserable. Except once. No need to go there.

A shiver ran down my spine and I leapt to my feet. I couldn't stay in that room on my own knowing Thomas had died there. I didn't know any of the details – Sam and I weren't in each other's lives back then – and I wouldn't have wanted to know even if I had been. But all I could think about now that I knew Thomas had died in the room was Maud Pickles. And thinking about Maud Pickles meant thinking about everything that happened afterwards. I shuddered. Not now.

I needed to find Sam. Presumably she'd be in the barn. I didn't have the energy to traipse back upstairs for a coat or cardigan for Samuel but there was a basket of what looked to be fresh laundry on the floor with a hand-knitted pink blanket folded up on the top, presumably belonging to Lottie. That would keep Samuel warm and his wellbeing was the main thing. I was still in my PJs but I didn't care. We were in the middle of nowhere, so who was going to see me? There was a wooden shoe rack near the door holding a pair of hedgehog-print wellies. Sam's feet were a size bigger than mine but they'd do. A large waterproof jacket – presumably Josh's – hung from a set of driftwood coat hooks and I pulled it on.

It was chilly outside, with quite a breeze, and I was sure I could feel drops of rain. I wrapped the coat round Samuel to protect him further.

As I approached the barn, I glanced across the farmyard and my heart skipped a beat. My car! Someone had broken into it. The boot and all four doors were wide open. I raced towards it, drawing up short when I spotted a couple of buckets and a plastic caddy containing cleaning products. Oh, my God! Sam had cleaned the car for me. I'd completely forgotten about it but she obviously hadn't. She wouldn't make a fuss about doing it either, probably just casually dropping into conversation later that it was all sorted and I could... I shook my head. All sorted so I could go home. She wanted rid of me. And who could blame her? She'd probably been kept awake half the night by Samuel and then I'd yelled at her when she'd tried to help me.

My shoulders sank. I couldn't go home. I needed to get my head clear about the emails I'd seen on James's phone and what it meant for us. I'd have to look at those photos I'd taken and decide on my next steps, but I wasn't ready to do that yet. It could be several days before I could face that, so I needed Sam onside. She'd be perfectly justified in sending me packing after the way I'd behaved so far so I needed to make it up to her, starting with an apology for earlier and a huge 'thank you' for cleaning up Samuel's mess.

As I approached the barn, I heard laughter and stopped dead. Was there someone with her or was she on the phone? The only cars in the farmyard were Sam's, mine and Beth's so she couldn't have visitors as it wasn't somewhere you'd visit on foot.

I hovered by the door with my hand outstretched but couldn't bring myself to open it. I definitely wasn't in the mood for strangers.

Stepping back, I glanced down the side of the barn. There was an open window near where Sam treated the hedgehogs. I took a few steps closer then hesitated, hearing Nanna's voice in my ear: *Eavesdroppers never hear good of themselves.* But I wasn't specifically planning to eavesdrop. I just wanted to work out who was with Sam before I went inside to thank her.

Sam's voice drifted through the window: '...never came to see me in hospital either, so I know how hurtful that is. It was always difficult between us but, like you, I thought that deep down she felt some love for me and would see my brush with death as an opportunity to start over.'

I frowned. Sam never talked to anyone outside our family about her relationship with her mum, yet there was no mistaking that was who she was talking about.

'I can't believe we have something so awful in common. I'm so sorry.'

Beth? Sam was confiding in Beth? What the hell was the world coming to? The woman who'd broken Sam's fiancé's heart had somehow waltzed into her life, moved into her home, and they were discussing their deepest tragedies. Even worse, they had bad relationships with their mums in common. Beth was clearly desperate to take Sammie away from me. Why couldn't things be left alone? Why did someone always have to come along and take what was mine?

9

SAMANTHA

At lunchtime, I locked up the barn. I'd expected Chloe to join me at some point, bored and in need of company, so was surprised that she hadn't put in an appearance. She'd either plonked herself in front of the TV or gone back to bed in a sulk. Even though it was her who'd shouted at me, it would somehow be my fault. Chloe could be funny like that, never quite able to accept responsibility for the part she'd played.

I glanced over towards her car. What a mug I was for cleaning it for her, but it couldn't be left any longer. It should have been dealt with yesterday, but I'd been busy organising dinner for everyone and it had slipped my mind afterwards. Josh would have told me it was Chloe's problem and it was up to her to sort it but I kept picturing her face contorted in pain as she'd fed Samuel this morning. She wouldn't accept my help with him and she wouldn't talk to me about James so cleaning her car was one small kindness I could show her. I just hoped she appreciated it, because it had been pretty grim.

Passing the lounge window, I could see Beth on the rug playing with Archie so presumably Lottie was asleep in her cot upstairs. I'd had a lovely chat with Beth in the barn this morning. She'd turned up with the babies in their buggy then produced a packet of biscuits and some photos of her grandma, saying that our conversation on Thomas's bench earlier had triggered some more memories. I put the kettle on and, over drinks and biscuits, told her all about Nanna and Gramps. Before I knew it, I was opening up about Mum. Beth was so easy to talk to and it was refreshing to chat to someone who so clearly understood how it felt. While I was a district nurse, I'd had patients who had toxic relationships with one or both parents but I'd never met anyone outside my work who did. Josh understood the hurt after his dad's affair with Beth, but he hadn't experienced the persistent cruelty.

In the lounge, I smiled at Archie, who was determinedly trying to force a wooden rectangle into a circular hole on his shape sorter.

'Have you seen Chloe at all?' I asked Beth.

'No, but I could hear Samuel crying upstairs when we got back from the barn so I'm assuming she's in her room.'

'I'd better check on her and see if she wants any lunch.'

Upstairs, I gently tapped on Chloe's door. No answer. I pushed it open. Samuel was asleep in the travel cot and Chloe was curled up on the airbed.

'Are you awake?' I whispered.

Silence.

'Chloe?'

I waited for a few moments then turned and left. I hoped she was catching up on some sleep but I couldn't shake the feeling that she'd been wide awake and was ignoring me.

* * *

Beth and I had lunch together at the table in the middle of the kitchen, with Archie next to her in his highchair. There was a separate dining room downstairs but it was currently being used for storage while Josh and I decided what to do with it.

The table was one of the few pieces of Thomas's furniture I'd hung onto. It was sturdy oak, beautifully crafted and I knew how much it had meant to him as Gwendoline had been a passionate baker and he'd had it especially made for her. As part of the farmhouse refurbishment, my good friend Dave had sanded and waxed it and it now looked as good as new, flanked by a new set of solid chairs.

I pushed my empty plate aside and stood up. 'I'd best get back to the barn and finish getting ready for the invasion on Wednesday.'

'Are you looking forward to it?' Beth asked as she scraped the last of Archie's food onto a spoon and handed it to him.

'I'm really excited about it, although I'd be lying if I said I wasn't a tiny bit nervous. I'm used to a class of teenagers but a class of primary school children may be a little more challenging to organise.'

Shortly after we opened, I'd received a generous delivery of cat and dog food courtesy of nearby Bentonbray Primary School. The children were studying British wildlife and had wanted to direct the profits from their Easter fair to the rescue centre to help us recover after the arson attack. The head teacher mooted the idea of a visit by the children and I'd been happy to oblige. It was a small village school with only 120 pupils, so we'd arranged four half-day visits for thirty children at a time. My new friend and volunteer, Fizz, had offered to help and having two groups of fifteen swapping between two activities was a less challenging prospect.

'I'll sort the dishes,' Beth said when I picked up the plates. 'You get on with your planning.'

'Thank you. If Chloe comes down, can you tell her there's a sandwich in the fridge for her and that I'd love to see her in the barn if she fancies some company?'

'Will do.' Beth wiped Archie's face. 'Is she okay?'

I shrugged. 'She won't talk to me but my gut reaction is no, she's far from okay.'

That thought was hounding me as I wandered across to the barn and, try as I might, I couldn't concentrate on preparing the worksheets for the children. I'd plugged my earphones in to listen to some music but I barely registered any of the songs, my mind filled with worries about Chloe.

After half an hour of re-doing my work, I closed my laptop, picked up my phone and stopped the music. I was going to have to call Auntie Louise to let her know that Chloe and Samuel were safe and with me, in case Chloe hadn't got in touch yesterday. With my earphones still in, I called her on FaceTime.

'Sam! Thank goodness!' she cried, answering my request after only one ring. 'Are they with you?' Her eyes were wide and her usually rosy cheeks pale.

'Yes. They turned up yesterday afternoon.'

'That's one less thing to worry about, then.' The relief in her voice and on her face was obvious.

'Didn't Chloe let you know? She promised she would.'

She shook her head. 'She texted me to say she was safe and staying with a friend and she insisted it wasn't you, but who else could it be? Chloe doesn't have any other close friends.'

Although true, it saddened me to hear the words spoken aloud. 'I half-expected you or Uncle Simon to turn up yesterday.'

'We wanted to but she'd gone to such pains to say she wasn't at Hedgehog Hollow that we felt we needed to give her space. Do you have any idea what's happened? Poor James is in such a state.'

'I can imagine. I honestly don't know what's gone on. She won't talk to me and I'm worried about her. She looks exhausted, I can tell she's struggling to feed Samuel even though she won't admit it and—'

'She's struggling to feed him? In what way?'

'I think she's in pain. And he's feeding too often so I don't think he's getting enough milk.'

She frowned. 'I wasn't aware of that. She never said anything.' Her tone was soft and I knew she'd be thinking she'd somehow let her daughter down.

'I think she's scared of asking for help.'

'Why?'

'Because that would be another admittance of failure. You and I know that's not the case but you know how Chloe's mind works.' My cousin was confident and self-assured if she was in her comfort zone – which was doing anything connected to arts and crafts, drama or sport – but she hated trying new things. She'd declare herself a failure or useless before she even gave whatever it was a chance.

Auntie Louise sighed. 'I have no idea where that comes from and it's so ridiculous.'

'I agree. What about James? Has he given any clue as to why she left?'

'He doesn't know. He says they had an argument that morning but it wasn't about anything major – just the usual niggles.'

'Are they arguing a lot at the moment?'

'If they are, she hasn't told me about it. She's always seemed upbeat when I've seen her.'

'I hate to say it, but she's far from upbeat at the moment. I think she's struggling with motherhood. I don't think it's what she expected.'

Auntie Louise's eyes widened. 'You can't mean that. Chloe adores children. She works with kids every day.'

'But she doesn't work with babies. Her job wouldn't have helped prepare her.' Chloe was currently on maternity leave from her role as a pre-school assistant where the youngest children were age three. 'She had a tough pregnancy and now—'

The barn door burst open, stopping me mid-sentence. Chloe, dressed in her pyjamas and my hedgehog wellies, stormed towards me. 'How dare you talk about me like that? Who's on the phone?'

My stomach did a backflip.

'I said who's on the phone?'

I'd never heard her shout so loud. It was just as well Samuel wasn't with her – presumably asleep in the house – or she'd have scared him.

'Your mum.' I unplugged the earphones and thrust the phone towards her so she could see I wasn't lying.

'Hello, sweetheart,' Auntie Louise said. 'Don't get mad with Samantha. We're both worried about you.'

'I'm fine,' she snapped.

'You don't look it and you don't sound it.'

'Well, I am, and I resent the accusation that I can't cope with Samuel.'

I gasped. 'That's not what I said.'

Chloe glared at me. 'You said I couldn't cope with motherhood. Same thing.'

'I said I thought you were struggling. Different thing.'

'*Same* thing.'

I wasn't going to get embroiled in an argument. She'd obviously somehow heard my side of the conversation and, to be fair to her, I could understand why she'd taken that as an inability to cope even though I hadn't meant it like that.

'I just think you might need some help.'

'Because I can't cope. You're not making it any better, Samantha.' She pronounced every syllable of my name, clearly expressing her disgust.

'Sweetheart, Samantha's only worried about you.'

Chloe turned her gaze to my phone. 'And you agree with her?'

'I don't know. But you did run out on your husband.'

'Cheers, Mum. Thank you both for the vote of confidence. Why does everyone think I'm such a failure at absolutely everything?'

'Nobody thinks that.'

'Yes they do. You, James, Samantha. Everyone!' She slammed my phone down on the treatment table and ran towards the door.

'Chloe!' I grabbed my phone and winced at the cracks across the screen. Auntie Louise had her hand clapped across her mouth.

'Sorry,' I said. 'I'll go after her and call you back.'

'No need. She clearly needs help so I'm coming over. I'll be with you as soon as I can.'

'Okay. Probably a good idea. I'll try to speak to her but I think you might have more luck when you get here.'

I hung up and hastened after Chloe but, as I stepped outside, an elderly couple walked towards me, the man holding a plastic washing up bowl. A new arrival and the timing could not be worse. I glanced towards the farmhouse to see Chloe disappear inside. I'd have to catch her later as the hedgehog had to be my priority. At least it would give her a chance to cool off.

'Are you the hedgehog lady?' the woman called.

I grabbed the thick gloves I kept by the door and walked towards them. 'Yes, hi. I'm Samantha. You've got a patient?'

She smiled. 'We've got six.'

I reached them and peered into the bowl. A large adult with a damaged back leg lay on its side on a towel with five hoglets huddled close to it. There was fresh blood on the adult so it was clearly a recent incident, which was good news as that meant limited opportunity for infection.

'Can I ask where you found them?'

'By the side of the road into Little Tilbury,' the man said. 'The big one was on its side like it is now, so Mary went back to our daughter's for some gardening gloves and the bowl while I kept it safe from passing traffic.'

'When I came back, Stan had found the babies in the hedgerow.'

'That was lucky. Thanks for acting so quickly.'

The couple explained that they were in the area visiting their daughter, but she had an enclosed walled garden which was unsuitable for a hedgehog release. We agreed I'd release them on the farm when the time came.

I hesitated by the barn door as they pulled away, looking towards the farmhouse. Ideally I'd check on Chloe but it would have to wait. I needed to get the hoglets warm, relieve their mum's pain then get her to Josh's veterinary practice for an X-ray.

'We'll call you Beatrix after Beatrix Potter,' I told her as I cleaned her wound.

She had three boys and two girls warming on heat pads and I decided to name them after characters in Beatrix Potter books: Peter, Benjamin, Jeremy, Jemima and Flopsy.

I rang Josh and told him about our new arrivals, then gave him a brief overview of the situation with Chloe.

'Sounds like she definitely needs help,' he agreed. 'Why don't you bring the hoglets with you too? You can get back to Chloe and be there for your Auntie Louise arriving and I can bring them all home with me tonight.'

'That would be a brilliant help. Thank you.'

10

I was shaking with rage as I stormed out of the barn and over to the farmhouse, ignoring Sam's calls. How dare they discuss me like that? How dare they pass comment on my ability to be a good mum to Samuel? What did they know about it?

But by the time I was halfway up the stairs, anger gave way to embarrassment. Had I really shouted at them both? Nanna had been right about the perils of ear wigging and I'd now experienced that twice in the same day. Served me right.

A little later, I lay on my back on the airbed, staring at the vaulted ceiling, cursing myself for letting everything spiral so badly out of control. When we first met, my feelings for James had been so deep and so intense that I'd allowed myself to believe we could overcome anything the future threw our way. In my typical impulsive approach to life, I hadn't paused to think about what the past might hurl at us.

Samuel lay beside me, fast asleep, his hand curled round my

little finger. I turned onto my side and looked down at him, my heart bursting with love.

'It's just you and me now,' I whispered, a tear escaping and trailing down my cheek and neck. 'I'm sorry I failed you. I really thought your daddy and I would last but I don't think there's any chance now. I should have known this would happen eventually. I should have warned you.'

When I was little, I'd constantly hear the same thing from relatives or friends of Mum's. They'd gaze at me admiringly, then turn to Mum and say, 'She's so beautiful, Louise. She's going to be such a heartbreaker when she's older.'

They were wrong. It was me who always ended up heartbroken. Being 'beautiful' was more of a curse than a blessing, particularly when I was a teenager. Girls eyed me with suspicion and envy and boys leched after me. I struggled to hold down female friendships, confronted with accusations of flirting with their boyfriend or trying to outshine them if ever we met up outside of school, free of the constraints of uniforms and sensible shoes. It wasn't my fault I wasn't spotty, rarely had a bad hair day and knew how to dress for my figure. What did they expect me to do? Wear overalls, a hat and oversized shades so nobody would notice me? So I steered clear of girls and spent more time with the boys who I thought were my friends. Big mistake.

I was fourteen when the rumours started. Bloody Mark Daniels, the lying git. All we'd done was kiss and it had been a crap slobbery one at that. After that, barely a week went by without a fresh allegation about who I'd had sex with or some daring place where the deed had occurred. It was pointless protesting because everyone preferred to believe the lies and the more direct action – thumping Mark Daniels – landed me in trouble at school. My protests somehow gave gravitas to the assumptions they'd already made about me: dumb blonde who shags her way through life because all she has is her looks. I moved from one boy to the next, each time thinking this might be the one who was different, each time getting my heart broken.

When I was sixteen, I met Travis Enderby-Bowes. He was eighteen and worked behind the bar at Kellerby Cliffs Holiday Park. A man instead of a boy. I believed him when he told me he loved me and we'd be together forever. If only...

A knock on the door interrupted my thoughts. I wiped at my damp cheeks. 'Go away, Sam!'

'It's Beth.'

I sighed. 'What do you want?'

The door opened and she poked her head round it. 'Sorry for disturbing you. I just wanted to check you'd got the text from Sam to say she's had to rush a hedgehog to surgery.'

'My phone's on silent.'

She glanced at Samuel and nodded. 'Can I get you anything?'

'No.'

'Okay. Well, you know where I am if you need anything.' She gave me a big smile then closed the door.

Who did she think she was? The owner of the house? My landlady? I should have demanded champagne and strawberries. That would have wiped the stupid grin off her face.

'Fake,' I muttered under my breath. I hated people like Beth. Pretending to be my friend when all she wanted to do was take what was mine. I'd fallen for that once before but never again. I'd learned my lesson the hard way.

11

SAMANTHA

As I drove back along the farm track later that afternoon after dropping Beatrix and her hoglets off at Josh's practice, my stomach did somersaults. I hadn't had time on my side to go into the house and risk a confrontation with Chloe so I'd texted her and Beth to say where I was going. I'd checked my phone at the practice and Beth had replied to wish me luck but Chloe hadn't responded.

When I drove over the brow of the hill, Chloe's car in the farmyard came into view and I relaxed a little. I was worried she'd have done another runner which wouldn't have resolved anything.

The rest of the hoglets needed feeding so I had to do that before I could seek out Chloe. By the time I'd finished, it was late afternoon. While I was locking up the barn, Auntie Louise pulled into the farmyard.

'Sorry I couldn't get here sooner,' she said, rushing over to give me a hug. 'I had to finish some things off.'

'Is she okay?' she asked when she stepped back. 'Have you spoken to her?'

'I couldn't. I'm so sorry. A hedgehog and five hoglets arrived and I needed to get them to Josh urgently as the mum needed an X-ray.'

The words spilled out at a higher pitch and speed than normal. 'Then the hoglets needed feeding and I had antibiotics to give to some of our other—'

Auntie Louise pulled me into another hug. 'It's okay. Breathe.'

I held her tightly, trying to quell the rising panic. Since Josh's family moved in, I'd been able to successfully balance my time between the hedgehogs and helping Beth. Even though Beth was stronger and more independent with each passing day, she still needed some assistance, especially with lifting. I really could have done without the added responsibility of Chloe and Samuel, especially with all the accompanying drama.

'Listen to me,' Auntie Louise said, taking both my hands in hers and fixing her eyes on mine. 'You have a job to do here and nobody's expecting you to drop everything because Chloe's upset.'

I suspected Chloe did but I wasn't going to say that. 'It was my fault she got upset earlier. I *was* talking about her, after all.'

'To me! To her mum! It's not like you were gossiping about her to some random stranger.' Auntie Louise linked my arm and we set off on a slow walk towards the farmhouse. 'I'm sorry you've been dragged into this.'

'I want to be here for her but it's not easy when she won't let me in and keeps yelling at me.'

'We'll get to the bottom of it and I'm sure it's nothing that can't be sorted. This thing between her and James is probably a misunderstanding and an over-reaction on Chloe's part. A few days apart will give her a fresh perspective on that.'

I hoped she was right because I was already feeling anxious after only one day and didn't relish much more of this. After returning to work too soon following the arson attack and collapsing at work as a result of the stress, I was meant to be taking things easy, and life with Chloe was usually far from easy.

12

CHLOE

Standing by the back window in the attic room, I rocked Samuel in my arms. I'd never been into nature like Sam, but even I could see that Hedgehog Hollow was set in spectacular surroundings. Fields in varying shades of green, gold and brown stretched for miles, interrupted occasionally by a line of trees or a copse. Horses, cows and sheep grazed in some of the fields and a red tractor drove up and down another. The scene was reminiscent of crayon pictures I'd created as a child. Such a contrast to the boring view at home of nothing but other houses.

I'm not sure how much time had passed since Beth's appearance. My phone was still on silent, upside down, in the far corner of the room. Because Samuel had awoken and demanded another painful feed, I suspected a couple of hours had drifted by. Was Sam back yet? I toyed with moving to the front window to check but it would require effort and I simply couldn't be bothered.

'Sammie's very lucky living here, isn't she?' I asked Samuel. 'Could you imagine growing up on a farm? All that space to run round in.'

Another knock on the door interrupted us. With a sigh, I flung it open, assuming it would be Beth pestering me again. 'What do you want?'

'If that's the way you've been speaking to Samantha since you got here, I'm amazed she hasn't sent you packing.'

'Mum?' I genuinely hadn't expected that.

'How's my gorgeous grandson?' She reached for Samuel and showered his cheeks with kisses. When she stopped, she looked at me with a solemn expression. 'And what about you? How are you?'

I wanted to be able to give her a confident – possibly sarcastic – response, especially as her first priority had been to hug Samuel but, as soon as I opened my mouth to speak, my voice caught in my throat and the tears started.

She put an arm round me and pulled me to her chest. 'It'll be all right. We'll soon get things sorted and back to normal.'

'They can't be,' I wailed.

'*Everything* can be sorted.' She stepped back. 'Why don't you get yourself showered and changed and I'll look after Samuel? Come downstairs when you're ready and we'll have a chat.'

I had no energy to argue. A shower could be good. But if she thought I was going to tell her what was going on, she'd had a wasted trip. I wasn't ready to go there yet because, once we started down that route, there'd be no going back.

It was amazing the difference a shower and fresh clothes could make. I felt so much more human as I made my way downstairs but, the moment I opened the lounge door, the sense of calm I'd felt was swept aside by a wave of rage. Samuel was in his bouncer and Mum, Sam and Beth were all kneeling on the floor, rummaging through the binbags of his clothes. One of them must have been up to the attic to retrieve them while I was in the shower. Sneaky little sods.

'What the hell are you doing?' I demanded.

Sam looked up warily. 'We thought you might like a hand sorting them into size.'

'Did you, now? And it never occurred to you to ask me if it was okay to do that?' I hadn't meant to shout but I was fuming. How dare they?

'Chloe! What's got into you?' Mum looked shocked.

'Oh, sorry, have I stepped out of the shower into a parallel universe where it's acceptable for strangers to rummage through your belongings?' I fixed my gaze on Beth, whose cheeks coloured before she stood up and muttered something about checking on her kids and scuttled out of the room.

'That wasn't very nice,' Sam said as soon as the door closed.

'It was downright rude,' Mum added sharply. 'And I did not bring you up to behave like that.'

'But she was—'

'Stop talking and sit down. Now.'

It was my turn to be shocked as I swiftly lowered myself onto the sofa. Mum hadn't used that strict tone on me since I was at college and we barely spoke for a year except in anger.

Sam placed the outfit she'd been folding into a plastic crate and sat on the rug, cross-legged, facing me. Mum sat on the other end of the sofa and raised her eyebrows expectantly. I could feel the disapproval emanating from both of them.

'Why are you both staring at me like that?'

'We're waiting for you to tell us what's going on.' Mum's tone had softened but it was obvious she was still mad with me, which wasn't fair.

'How would you like it if I invited a stranger to rummage through your belongings?'

'Beth was doing you a favour but that's an aside. This isn't about her. Talk to us, sweetheart. What's going on? What's happened with James?'

I wanted to tell them. I wanted to share the burden but where could I start? It was too big, too complicated, too scary. And how could I give 'it's too big, scary and complicated' as the reason for my silence without being bombarded with questions? So I merely shrugged.

Mum shook her head. 'That's not an answer. Why did you take off without even leaving a note? James is beside himself, you know. He was in tears last night.'

'Why are you telling me this? Are you trying to make me feel guilty?' *Because there's no need. I already feel guilty. And not just for yesterday.*

'No, but I'd have thought you'd have shown more concern for the man you married. Why did you leave?'

I don't know what made me say it. Stalling for time, perhaps? 'Why don't you ask him?'

'I have and he doesn't know.'

'He would say that.' Again, a stupid thing to say but I needed to deflect her questions.

Mum lightly placed her hand on my forearm. 'Is it because you had a row on Sunday morning?'

I rolled my eyes at her. 'What do you take me for? If a petty row was enough to make me walk out, we'd never have even made it up the aisle.'

'Was it because you didn't want to go to his mum's party? I know you find Nancy frustrating but it was her sixtieth.'

My jaw tightened.

'You could have at least put in an appearance out of courtesy, even if you weren't feeling up to it.'

It was barely audible but I was sure I heard Sam gasp, and one look at her wide-eyed expression confirmed it.

Mum was on a roll. 'You put him in a really tricky position, you know. He couldn't not go so he had to make up an excuse for you. Nancy was really disappointed that she didn't get to see Samuel on her birthday.'

Sam's head was bowed, a clear sign of her discomfort. Was this like déjà vu for her? Was this how it felt to be my cousin, having your mum always thinking the worst of you? I knew my parents adored James and had welcomed him into the family like the son they'd never had but I never thought they'd take sides, especially when they didn't know the full story.

'Why did you bother coming over today, Mum?' I demanded.

'Because I was worried about you.'

'So worried that the first thing you did was give Samuel cuddles. Then you sent me for a shower. Then you accused me of leaving my husband because I didn't want to celebrate his mum's big birthday. Great to know what you think of me and whose side you're on.'

'I'm not taking sides.'

Standing up, I shook my head at her. 'Could have fooled me.' I turned to Sam. 'Do you want me to leave?'

She looked startled. 'Erm... no. You're welcome to stay as long as you need to.' She almost sounded like she meant it but the words were there and that was enough for me for now.

'Good. Then you can help me carry my son's clothes back upstairs so I can sort them out for myself.' I started gathering them up and squashing them into the plastic crates. 'I am capable of some things, you know.'

'I'm sorry about the clothes.' Sam started to fill another crate. 'It was just that I couldn't find anything to fit him yesterday and I thought it might be easier for you to have it all organised.'

'I'd have done it myself if I'd had anywhere to put them.' I bit my lip. Harsh. I could hardly expect Sam to suddenly conjure up a chest of drawers and a wardrobe.

'So that's it?' Mum said. 'You're going to disappear upstairs without talking to me?'

'Looks like it.'

'Chloe! Don't be so silly.'

'I'm silly, am I? As well as shallow and selfish and—'

'I didn't say any of those things.'

I stopped scooping the clothes and looked up at her. 'You might not have said those exact words but the meaning came across loud and clear.'

'I'm sorry. It's not what I meant. Please talk to me.'

'No! Look, I don't want to fall out with you again, Mum, but did it not occur to you that there's a reason why I came here instead of staying with you and Dad?'

'I assumed it was to get some distance from James.'

'It was. But it was also to get some distance from his biggest fan. You! I knew that, if I stuck around, all you'd do is go on about how wonderful you think he is, how bad I am for running out on him, and you'd keep trying to push us back together. What did you do just now? Exactly what I predicted.' I unstrapped Samuel from his bouncer as I continued. 'I don't want to talk about what happened with James. I know I'll have to at some point but I'm not ready yet and I need everyone to understand and respect that.'

I hoisted Samuel onto my shoulder. 'For the record, I did *not* leave James because of any arguments, although you might as well know that we've argued pretty much constantly since his paternity leave ended. I do *not* find Nancy frustrating. What I find frustrating is that she would love to see more of Samuel but makes a fuss about travelling so, instead, we have to organise two adults and a baby and travel to her. Not quite so easy. As for her birthday, I got my dates muddled and thought it was next weekend. Even though I wasn't prepared, I would have gone and smiled and been happy for her because she's family and, whatever you think of me, I'm not so petty that I would have deliberately kept her grandson from her because of my diary screw-up. But none of those things caused me to run. Right now, I am *not* ready or willing to talk about what did. Have I made myself clear?'

'Yes,' they both muttered.

Sam placed a lid on one of the crates and looked up at me. 'You're welcome to stay but I have a condition. You say you're not ready to talk about what happened and you don't appreciate being asked so I'm going to do as you've requested and not ask you again. However, you *cannot* throw that back in my face later, suggesting I wasn't interested because that's absolutely not the case. I won't be asking but I'll be here for you if and when you're ready to talk. Do we have an understanding?'

I looked at Sam's earnest expression. She'd never have stood up to me like that before and I couldn't help admiring the way she'd changed since moving to the farm. There was a self-assurance I hadn't previously seen, yet the kindness I'd always associate with my cousin was still there. 'We have an understanding.'

Turning to Mum, I gave her a half-smile. 'I'm sorry you've had a wasted journey and I appreciate your concern, but do you understand why I'm annoyed with you?'

She nodded. 'You got it wrong, though. Your dad and I *do* love James but do you know why? Because we've seen how good he is for you. Since he came into your life, you've been so happy. You've been more relaxed than we've ever seen you. You've stopped putting yourself down and stopped talking about being a failure. You've been you. Because of that, I want you to work things out with James because the two of you are great together. However, if he's done something that makes a reconciliation impossible, then it would never be a question of your dad and I picking sides. We have always and will always stand by you, no matter what.'

My throat felt tight and my eyes burned and I could tell from the shake in her voice that she was on an emotional precipice too as she stood up and gathered Samuel and me in her embrace. I let her hold us but I didn't hug her back. I was still too pissed off with her for that.

When we stepped apart, her eyes glistened. 'I'll say goodbye for now but – and don't get mad with me for saying this – there's more to this than you and James. You've got Samuel to think about too. James has a right to see his son and Samuel should get to see his dad. If you don't want to talk to me, please talk to Samantha and do it sooner rather than later. For Samuel's sake but also for your own. Promise me?'

I stiffened. She was doing it again. 'Oh, my God! You can't help yourself, can you? You think I don't know that?'

'I don't know, Chloe. I don't know what's going on with you right now. I don't understand any of it.'

I grabbed Samuel's bouncer and stormed towards the door, shaking my head in disgust. 'Nobody's asking you to understand it. It's nothing to do with you.'

'Of course it is!'

'It isn't. This is between James and me.' I yanked the door open.

'But it isn't, is it? Because James has no idea why you've left.'

I gave her a hard stare. 'So we're back to Team James again. Thanks for all the support.'

Slamming the door behind me, I stomped up the stairs with Samuel but I hadn't even made it up the first flight before my shoulders slumped and the anger abated. I shouldn't have shouted at Mum like that but she'd pushed all the wrong buttons. I already felt crap about everything and she'd managed to make me feel a million times worse.

I hesitated on the landing, cuddling Samuel's soft cheek against mine. The right thing to do was to go downstairs and apologise, but when had I ever done the right thing?

Taking a deep breath, I continued up to the top floor. The confrontation had been bad enough but, the mood I was in, going back down would only make it worse. Mum would keep pushing for an explanation and I couldn't give her one. Not yet. I would need to get her back onside, though. When I did feel strong enough to tell her and Sam what was going on, I'd need them both so very much because the truth was going to rock all of our worlds.

13

SAMANTHA

I slowly folded a couple of Samuel's T-shirts, head down, as I listened to Chloe stomping up the stairs. That was hideous. I had no idea what to say so I looked up at Auntie Louise and gave her a sympathetic shrug.

She sighed. 'She's not going to come down again, is she?'

'I doubt it. How about a cup of tea? Give her time to calm down then you can maybe go up to her?'

She stood up, shaking her head. 'I think she'll need longer than that. I'd better go. I can't seem to say anything right.' Tears glistened in her eyes and there was clear defeat in her voice and on her face. 'It was like her first year at college all over again.'

'Chloe's a bit emotional at the moment. I'm sure she'll be in touch with an apology in the morning, if not tonight.' I wasn't sure at all but I didn't want to make my auntie cry.

'I won't hold my breath,' she said, her expression grim. 'What a disaster. I shouldn't have come. Thanks for looking after them for us.'

I stood up. 'Happy to help. I'll walk you to the car.'

'What do you think's going on?' Auntie Louise asked.

'I'll tell you in a moment.' Closing the front door behind us, I glanced up at the house to make sure there were no windows open, then threaded my arm through Auntie Louise's as we set off towards the farmyard. The sky had turned dark grey with the threat of heavy rain any moment.

'When she turned up yesterday, I'll admit that I thought it was a classic Chloe over-reaction to something fairly minor but now I think something significant has happened and it's so big she needs to get her head round it herself before she can share.'

'Like what? The only thing that springs to mind is that she's discovered James is having an affair but I honestly don't think he'd do that to her.'

'Neither do I, especially after the misunderstanding just before Samuel was born.'

'Then what else could it be?'

We'd reached the car and I let go of her arm. 'I genuinely have no idea and I think it's probably best not to speculate. I know it won't be easy but try not to worry. I'll look after her.'

She hugged me tightly. 'I know you will. I just feel so useless.'

'Stay in touch so she knows you care but don't rush her. That's all you can do for now. She'll be ready to talk eventually and, when she is, I have a feeling she's going to need you.'

Auntie Louise got in her car and wound down the window. 'Thanks again for looking after them, sweetheart. See you soon.'

'Give my love to Uncle Simon. And say "hi" to Mum from me. Actually, don't bother. She won't be interested.'

'I haven't given up hope for you two.'

'I have. Less painful that way.'

I waved her off then returned to the farmhouse, quickening my steps as I felt the first few spots of rain. Auntie Louise was right: that had been a disaster. What could possibly have happened between Chloe and James?

* * *

Back inside, I bundled the rest of the clothes into the crates, carried them upstairs and knocked on Chloe's door.

'Has Mum gone?' she asked after calling me in. She was seated cross-legged on the airbed with Samuel in his bouncer on the floor next to her.

'Yes. She feels really bad.' I moved the crates into the room.

'You could see why I was pissed off with her, couldn't you? She morphed into your mum for a moment.'

'She's aware of that. Welcome to my world. It's not a nice place to be, is it?'

'It was enlightening. I've heard Auntie Debs speaking to you like that so many times and it never really had an impact on me until I was on the receiving end of something similar just now. I couldn't bear five minutes of that. How did you cope?'

'I think the answer to that is that I didn't. Not really. But I learned not to react, or at least not in front of her. I'd often hide in my room in tears, licking my wounds.'

'I never appreciated quite how crap it feels.' She patted the bed beside her – an invitation that I could stay and talk, although clearly a discussion about James was off the agenda.

'Don't let it come between you,' I said, lowering myself onto the airbed. 'They might be twins but our mums are very different. Never forget that.'

'I suppose so. So, do you want to help me sort out these clothes?'

I really wanted to check on Beth, and the hoglets would need feeding shortly too, but this was Chloe's way of asking for help and she might not do it again if I abandoned her.

'I'd love to. I'll need to go over to the barn in half an hour, although I'm guessing Samuel will need feeding around then anyway so you'll want some peace.'

As I sat beside her, sorting the clothes into size, Chloe chattered about how she hadn't had a chance to organise anything yet so Samuel had been wearing the same few outfits on rotation. She shook her head in despair at how many unworn outfits were now too small. Although she kept her tone light and there was plenty of laughter and rolling of her eyes, I couldn't help noticing her choice of words. Failure. Useless. Disaster. Hopeless. Did she really think that about herself? Although she'd made similar comments over the years, it had usually been in a self-deprecating manner. More typically I thought of her as a strong and confident woman who knew what she wanted and went for it, often to the detriment of others: what Chloe wants, Chloe gets. Could that have been an act? Had the confidence been her attempt to cover up how she really felt about herself?

When Samuel started crying, it signalled my chance to leave Chloe and get on with things. The hoglets would be squeaking for food but I couldn't leave the house without checking that Beth wasn't upset by Chloe's behaviour. I found her in her bedroom watching *Peppa Pig* with Archie.

I leaned against the doorframe. 'I'm so sorry about earlier. Are you okay?'

'I'm fine. I get why she was annoyed. I shouldn't have touched her stuff without permission.' She paused and frowned. 'I know it's none of my business but is Chloe okay? I heard shouting.'

'I don't think she is but she won't talk about it so there's not a lot I can do to help right now. Whatever's going on with her, though, there's no excuse for being rude or unkind. Let me know if she's off with you any time I'm not around.'

'I don't want to cause any trouble.'

'You wouldn't be. If she wants to stay here, she needs to play nicely.'

* * *

While I attended to the hoglets a little later, I heard a car and peeked out of the barn window to see Paul arrive back from work and dash for the house with a newspaper over his head to keep off the now heavy rain. Ten minutes later, Josh returned and came straight to the barn with a carry case.

'Wow! That rain's torrential,' he said, shaking off his arms by the entrance. 'One bandaged up hedgehog and five happy hoglets checking in to the rescue centre.' He placed the case on the table and kissed me, instantly making me feel so much calmer.

'Are they all okay?'

'Beatrix had a clean break in one place so that should heal nicely. The hoglets all seem in good health.' He pulled a chair out and studied my face. 'You look tired.'

'I am. It all kicked off when Auntie Louise got here.' I explained what had happened while I settled Beatrix and her hoglets in the crate I'd prepared for them.

'And you really have no idea what this could be all about?' he asked when I'd finished.

'I've been racking my brain and I've come up with nothing.'

'Do you think James will turn up?'

'I think it's inevitable at some point. I'm surprised he hasn't already.'

'If it kicked off with your Auntie Louise, imagine what it'll be like if James appears.'

I shuddered at the thought. 'It won't be pretty.'

Josh bit his lip and wrinkled his nose. 'You know I'm not Chloe's number one fan, especially after the way she's treated you, but I do understand the bond you have so I get why you want to help her. But does she have any idea what's going on with you at the moment? Unless you've been having cosy catch-ups since she rocked up – which I don't get the impression you have been – I'm pretty certain she doesn't know that you fainted at work.'

'She doesn't.'

'I thought not. So she's clueless as to what you're dealing with.' He started counting on his fingers. 'It's hoglets season meaning feeds round the clock, you have the normal day job here, you have a series of school visits starting on Wednesday, you're helping Beth with Archie and Lottie, my dad's about to start chemo and you and Fizz are organising stem cell testing programmes to help with that. For someone in full health, that would be more than enough to deal with but, in the past two months, you've been hospitalised, assaulted and you've collapsed. And now you have another two house guests accompanied by a whole pile of drama.' He took my hand in his. 'I'm worried about you, Sammie. This is more stress instead of less. Way more.'

Concern was written all over his face and it warmed my heart to feel so loved. 'I promise I'm okay. I'll admit that I *am* tired but that's not down to Chloe. I would have been anyway.'

'I think you should tell Chloe you've been ill.'

'How would I say that without sounding like I'm accusing her of causing me extra stress?'

'You're great with words. You'll find a way.'

I appreciated the vote of confidence but I knew how Chloe's mind worked. Our conversations were short and perfunctory at the moment and I suspected that wasn't going to change while she was working through things in her head. There was no way to just slip into casual conversation that I'd left my teaching job because I fainted from being under too much stress. It would be obvious it was a warning to her not to push me over the edge which would either lead to another outburst or she'd retreat completely and I'd never find out what was going on. I couldn't do that to her, especially when her self-esteem was clearly rock-bottom.

'I'll think about it.' I squeezed Josh's hand. 'And I know the signs. If I feel it's getting too much, I'll say something.'

He slipped off his chair and drew me into a hug. 'Make sure you do.'

I wished I could stay right here, forever comforted and protected. The barn was one of my happy places, surrounded by my gorgeous patients, with a soundtrack of snuffles, scratches and squeaks. There were no tantrums, no crying babies and no secrets here. But it was time to go back to the farmhouse which, right now, was rife with all three.

14

I lay on the airbed listening to the rain hammering against the windows, turned to my side, turned to my other side, rolled off and looked out the front window, then the side, then the back. Back to the airbed. Lying. Sitting. Curled up. No matter what I did, I couldn't settle and relax and I knew exactly why. James. Any minute now, he could turn up and demand to see me. Up until Mum's appearance, I hadn't even considered it but now it seemed inevitable. Tonight? Tomorrow? I felt sick.

Rolling off the airbed again, I grabbed my phone and clicked on the photos I'd taken of James's emails but my stomach lurched and I couldn't bring myself to read them. I tossed my phone back into my bag and lay face down with my head in the pillow, the fabric and feathers muffling my panicked squeal. I was going to have to face up to things. But not yet.

As soon as I tried to focus on something different, all I could picture was Mum's hurt expression earlier. It seemed naïve now but I honestly hadn't expected her to track me down and turn up like that. Why, at a time when I was going to need her more than ever, had I pushed her away? Aside from the year from hell when I was at college, we'd always been close, which made what happened earlier even harder to stomach. I'd pretty much thrown her out... and it wasn't even my house! What was wrong with me? All I seemed to do at the moment was yell at people and stomp about. Even worse, they were all people I loved and needed. It was like I had this self-destruct button on relationships that I kept pressing every time things were going well.

I'd have to text Mum later and apologise for being so stroppy and hope she accepted tiredness as an excuse. We needed to be friends again because, when it all came out – which it would – I needed her to be on my side. I needed her to understand.

I released another cry into the pillow and pounded my fists on it. How was I supposed to get Mum to understand when I didn't understand it myself?

* * *

Sam poked her head round the bedroom door a little later. 'You don't have to hide up here.'

'I thought it was safer to be where other people aren't.'

She gave me a weak smile. 'Paul and Josh are making a chilli. It'll be ready in about twenty minutes. Will you come down and join us?'

I was ravenous but I couldn't face another evening of Beth sidling up to Sam like a lovesick teenager. Josh and his dad would have heard all about this afternoon and they'd all hate me for it. I'd feel it emanating from them. Nope. Definitely couldn't deal with that tonight.

'Can you bring me some up instead?' I gave her my best puppy dog eyes. 'I'd rather be on my own tonight.'

'Okay. I'll bring you a tray up before we...' She stopped and shook her head. 'Actually, no. Sorry, Chloe. If you don't want to join us to eat, that's your choice and I'm not going to beg you, but I'm not bringing your food up. I'm about to help Beth bath Archie and Lottie because she's still recovering from her operation and isn't meant to be doing any heavy lifting. Then I'll be sitting down to eat. If you want your food hot, you either join us or you collect your own meal. I'll see you later.'

'That's me told,' I muttered when she closed the door, but something about the tone of her voice stopped me feeling angry. She sounded weary, although was it any wonder if that Beth had her running round after her kids? Sounded like she'd really made herself at home and had poor Sam at her beck and call, cheeky cow.

I toyed with skipping dinner but my empty stomach protested loudly. No point. Twenty minutes she'd said. I'd better check the time and set myself an alarm in case I dozed off. Which meant looking at my phone. Which meant seeing all the texts and missed calls.

I ignored the ones from James but Mum had sent me a long message on WhatsApp:

✉ From Mum
I'm back home and so sorry about what I said earlier. Can we put it down to nervous gabbling because I was worried about you? You are and always will be my proudest achievement and the most important person in my life. I'm here for you whenever you're ready to talk but I won't push you. All I ask is that you please stay in touch, even if it's just to tell me what you're wearing, whether the sun is shining, what you're watching on TV, what you're eating, whether Samuel smiled etc. Missing you. Please give that

```
little boy a big kiss from me. Cuddles for you
both xxxxxx
```

I couldn't be mad with her. I knew she hadn't meant it. Re-reading it, I winced at her third sentence. When the truth came out, I could pretty much guarantee I would no longer be her proudest achievement.

```
⊠ To Mum
Consider it forgotten. I'm wearing the same as
earlier, the sun has nearly gone to bed and it's
bucketing down outside, there's no TV in my
room, it's chili for tea and Samuel is asleep.
I'll give him his kisses and cuddle when he
wakes up. I appreciate mine xxx
```

I lay back down, hands clasped across my stomach, waiting for the alarm to sound, focusing my mind on the meal I was about to eat because food was a safe subject and I could not let my thoughts drift elsewhere. No way. Too dangerous.

15

SAMANTHA

My T-shirt was soaked from carrying Archie from the bathroom to the nursery but I didn't have the time or energy to dry it or change. He'd taken his first few tentative steps over the weekend and now the little tyke was extremely squirmy. He'd splashed like crazy when I lifted him out of the bath and it was impossible to keep a towel wrapped round him for longer than three seconds.

'Five-minute warning for food,' Paul said, appearing beside me as I lay Archie down on the changing station. 'Do you want me to relieve you?'

'If you don't mind...' I thanked him and left him to get Archie dressed for bed while Beth sorted Lottie.

Down in the kitchen, Josh was stirring the chilli bubbling on the Aga. It smelled delicious and was the perfect comfort food after a tough day.

'All clean?' He turned towards me and laughed. 'Was there any water left in the bath or are you wearing it all?'

I rolled my eyes at him. 'I swear your brother uses me for target practice.' I removed a tray from the dresser and added one of the place settings to it for Chloe.

Josh tutted. 'I take it she's not gracing us with her presence tonight.'

'She'd rather eat in her room.' I added a small bottle of fresh orange juice from the fridge. 'But I told her nobody will be taking it up for her. She has to come down and collect it.'

'Good. As long as she knows this isn't a hotel. We all muck in.' He raised his eyebrows and pointed his wooden spoon at the pan of chilli.

'I know. I'll talk to her tomorrow about helping out.'

There was no reason for her not to help. If Beth could manage when she had two babies to look after while recovering from a major operation, Chloe could manage with one baby and no health issues. She'd likely kick up a fuss because she hated cooking and avoided it wherever possible. If she wanted to take responsibility for loading and emptying the dishwasher instead, that was fine. Or she could make lunches. Even Chloe could manage sandwiches. The important thing was that she contributed in some way.

A sudden lashing of rain at the kitchen window made me jump. Either the wind had strengthened or it had changed direction. 'I can't believe how heavy it is.'

Josh glanced towards the window. 'I had the wipers on full coming home and they barely cut through the water. There were loads of floods across the roads already. I bet there'll be a few roads impassable by morning.'

I stepped closer to the window and shuddered. It was shortly after 8 p.m. but already as dark as winter. 'I hope you don't get called out in this.' Even though he had a 4x4, meaning water and mud weren't too much of a challenge, the reduced visibility through the windscreen was a worry.

'Me too, but I'll take it steady if I am. Food's ready if you want to shout upstairs. We should probably invest in one of those giant gongs to call everyone to the feast.' He winked at me and I smiled.

As I called up, I wondered whether Chloe would appear or if she'd stay in her room sulking because I'd refused to wait on her. If she didn't come down, it would take a lot of willpower not to warm her dinner in the microwave and deliver it to her after we'd eaten, but I was going to have to stay strong. If I weakened, she'd continue to walk all over me. I'd let her do that so often in the past.

We were about halfway through our meal – still no sign of Chloe – when a loud rap on the door knocker made me drop my fork with a clatter, flicking rice across the table.

'You're jumpy tonight,' Josh observed.

He was right. That was the second time I'd over-reacted to a loud noise. It had to be the weather putting me on edge. 'I'll get it.' I pushed my chair back from the table. 'Probably a hedgehog emergency.'

But it wasn't. It was James, pale-faced, his hair plastered to his head, his suit dripping wet.

'Oh, my gosh, James! What are you doing coming out in this?'

'I have to see her.' Only five words but every one of them emphasised his pain.

It was a bad idea that he was here – although not entirely unex-pected – and I would have kept him on the doorstep and explained why but there was no way I could leave him outside in such horrific weather. I grabbed his arm and pulled him into the hall.

'I don't think she's going to want to see you.'

'What did I do wrong?'

His eyes beseeched mine and I wished I could offer him some-thing. 'I don't know. She won't say.'

'If I knew what I'd done wrong, I could try to put it right.' He ran his hands across his beard and through his dark blond hair, spat-tering droplets of rain on the wall and the floor tiles.

He looked so lost that all I wanted to do was wrap my arms round him and reassure him. If anyone needed a hug right now, it was James. But I didn't dare. Josh would understand if he saw us but Chloe wouldn't. She'd probably accuse me, yet again, of trying to steal her husband from her like she did at their wedding. I couldn't face opening up all that once more.

'Stay here. Let me grab you a towel.'

Josh looked up expectantly as I returned to the kitchen. I grimaced. 'It's James.'

His eyes widened. 'In this weather?'

I pulled a couple of hand towels out of a drawer and shrugged apologetically.

Josh stood up. 'I'll put the kettle on. What does he usually have?'

'White coffee, no sugar. I'll take him into the lounge then go up and tell Chloe.'

Back in the hall, James had removed his suit jacket and tie and hung them on one of the coat hooks. His jacket clearly hadn't given him much protection from the rain as his pale blue shirt was sticking to his skin. 'Go into the lounge,' I said, tossing him the towels. 'I'll ask Josh to get you a dry T-shirt.'

'Thank you.'

I returned to the lounge moments later to find him perched on the edge of an armchair rubbing a towel over his hair. He'd lost weight since I'd last seen him about six weeks ago at the press launch of Hedgehog Hollow. He looked gaunt, his eyes were bloodshot and dark rims below them suggested fatigue. I hoped it was down to the situation with Chloe and that the cancer hadn't returned.

When Chloe and James got together, it hurt to be around him but I never felt uncomfortable in his presence; we'd been good friends, after all. Although I'd have preferred that he hadn't fallen for my cousin, it wasn't like him being with someone else had been a bolt out of the blue. He'd been honest that I wasn't his forever and I'd always known I'd lose him sooner or later when he found someone with whom he had the chemistry he felt was missing between us.

Josh wasn't James's biggest fan but that was because of James cheating on me with Chloe rather than a dislike of the man himself. He didn't fear I still had feelings for James and he didn't interpret me talking to or laughing with him as flirting. So why did Chloe? Would me being engaged to Josh make her any less insecure, because insecurity was surely what it was? And why was Chloe insecure in the first place? She was the one with the looks. She was the one who James had chosen. How could I possibly be a threat to what they had?

'Thanks for that.' James placed the towels on the floor and sat forward with his hands between his legs. 'How is she?'

'Hard to say. Have you spoken to her mum?'

'She rang me when I was on the train home. I drove straight here from the station.'

That would explain the suit. 'Didn't Auntie Louise tell you not to come?'

'She did, but I had to do something. If I could just talk to her...'

The lounge door opened and Josh stepped in holding a couple of mugs, a T-shirt draped over his arm. 'You picked a grim evening for a visit to the farm,' he said jovially, handing James a mug and the T-shirt. 'How were the roads?'

'Flooded. I had to do a couple of detours.'

'I'm not surprised.'

Josh handed me a hedgehog mug and, with his back to James, mouthed, 'Do you want me to stay?'

I answered him with the slightest shake of my head.

'Shout if you need anything,' he said, before leaving the room.

I averted my eyes while James changed into the T-shirt, praying Chloe didn't pick that moment to appear.

'What happened, James?' I asked when he settled back onto the chair with his coffee. 'Auntie Louise says you don't know but you must have some idea. She wouldn't have taken off like that – especially with Samuel – without a reason.'

He shrugged. 'That's the thing. *Nothing* happened or at least nothing that would lead to this.' He ran through the events of the morning and, although it didn't sound pleasant, nothing he told me should have triggered Chloe's reaction.

'It makes no sense,' I said. 'There has to be a reason for her walking out.'

'I was awake all night going over it all and I can only come up with one thing.'

'What?' I sat forward, my pulse quickening.

'She doesn't love me anymore.'

'No, James. That's not it. Of course she still loves you.'

'Does she, though? I'm not so sure.'

'You two are brilliant together.'

'I used to think so but now I...' He broke off and shook his head.

'Go on,' I urged.

'I wonder if her being with me is just some silly one-upmanship that got taken too far.'

'One-upmanship? Over whom?'

He fixed his eyes on me. 'You.'

My stomach did somersaults. 'What? Why would you think that?'

'Isn't there some sort of weird competition between the two of you?'

'No! Of course not! Although...' Something Chloe had said in the hospital after Samuel was born popped into my head. She'd admitted she sometimes intentionally set out to hurt me because I seemed to have it easy: 'You found school easy and walked out with straight As, you have a great career, you have loads of friends and you're never bothered about how you look or what people think of you. I've found everything a struggle so I took from you whenever I could. I wanted to be you.'

We didn't get a chance to discuss it any further and it had gone out of my mind until now. There was no way Chloe would have gone after James just to hurt me. Was there?

'Although what?' James prompted.

'Nothing. I can't believe... She wouldn't...' I shook my head vigorously, slopping my tea over my hands. I barely noticed the pain of the scald as I kept replaying that evening. I'd specifically questioned her as to whether one of the ways she'd tried to hurt me was by going after James when she didn't love him and she'd promised me it wasn't and that she loved him with all her heart.

'Sam?'

'It's nothing. She did say something about the one-upmanship thing when Samuel was born but it's not some weird competition. I've certainly never tried to upstage her or compete against her. Anyway, she told me at the time how much she loved you and I honestly don't think that's changed. I reckon you're both struggling with a new baby in your lives and you probably need to talk to each other more – proper talking instead of arguing – so that you can find a way through it as a partnership instead of enemies.'

'We argue constantly,' he admitted, head down. 'I can't seem to say or do anything right and... That sounds like I'm blaming it all on Chloe. It's probably my fault.'

'It's more likely you're equally to blame.' I put my tea down on the floor. 'Let me tell Chloe you're here. I'll do what I can but I can't force her to see you.'

'I appreciate you trying. I'm 99 per cent certain she won't see me but there's that small percentage of hope. If I hadn't come over, I'd only get it thrown back in my face, accused of not caring although driving over is potentially about me not respecting her need for space. Go figure!'

He was definitely stuck between a rock and a hard place. 'I'll do my best.'

＊ ＊ ＊

Chloe was kneeling on the floor changing Samuel's nappy when I stepped into her bedroom.

She twisted round to face me and blew a strand of hair out of her red face. 'Don't have a go at me for not coming down for my food. I was going to but Samuel needed feeding.' She turned back to continue what she was doing.

'That's not why I'm here. James turned up.'

She stopped rigid but didn't turn round. 'And you told him to get lost.'

'That's not my decision to make. He's downstairs.'

She whipped her head round, eyes wide. 'You let him in?'

'Have you seen the weather? He was drenched.'

'But you let him in?'

I winced at the volume and tried hard not to shout back but there was no mistaking the harsh edge to my voice. 'Yes. Because it's bucketing it down out there and James is in remission from cancer. No way was I about to leave him to drown on my doorstep.'

Her expression softened. 'Is he okay?'

'He was soaked through but Josh loaned him a T-shirt so he's warm and dry now. He wants to see you.'

She clapped her hand to her mouth and shook her head. 'I can't see him. You can't make me.'

'No, I can't, but I think you should talk to him.'

'No! I'm not ready.' She sounded afraid.

I crouched down beside her, my voice gentle. 'Why? What's happened?'

'You promised you wouldn't push me.'

'I'm not pushing. I'm just trying to understand why you won't speak to the man who you recently told me you love so much that it hurts. He's your husband, Chloe. He's your son's father. You can't just shut him out.'

'You make it sound simple. Nothing about this is simple.'

'Then explain it to me.'

'You won't understand. None of you will.'

'How do you know until you try us? We all love you. We're here for you no matter what. Surely you know that. Me especially. Think of all the crap you and I have been through since the wedding and how difficult things have been between us yet you chose to come to me and I've been happy to let you stay. Doesn't that speak volumes about our relationship that, no matter how bad things get, we're still here for each other? Let me in. You can tell me anything.'

Tears filled her eyes and I thought for a moment that I'd got through to her but she blinked rapidly, gulped and turned back to Samuel. She finished fastening the poppers on his sleepsuit then handed him to me.

'He can see Samuel but he can't see me. Sorry. I know you think I'm being unfair but I'm not ready to confess.'

'Confess? Confess what? Oh, Chloe. Is it you? Have you been seeing someone else?'

A tear slipped down her cheek. 'I almost wish that was it. That would be so much easier.'

Samuel gave a small cry and I cuddled him into my shoulder and stroked his back. 'Are you saying it's something you did rather than something James did?'

She bit her lip and nodded slowly. 'But I can't say any more. I won't.'

'Okay.' I sighed as I stood up. 'I'm not going to rush James with Samuel.'

'I know.' She stood up too and handed me a blanket and a soft toy from out of the cot.

'Which means you have time to change your mind about seeing him yourself.'

'That's not going to happen.'

'We'll be in the lounge if it does.'

I closed the door softly behind me, my heart breaking at the unmistakable sound of my cousin sobbing.

As I slowly carried Samuel downstairs, I felt like an amateur sleuth trying to piece it all together but none of it made sense. Chloe wasn't having an affair and I believed her. I believed James wasn't either. They'd argued about something and nothing, he'd gone out to get the shopping and she'd gone upstairs to get changed for his mum's birthday. At some point in the hour or so while he was out, something had happened to make her flee. But what could it be, especially when she'd just admitted that it was something she'd done and not James? My head hurt just thinking about it.

* * *

James was hunched up with his head in his hands when I pushed open the lounge door. He looked up at me expectantly and his eyes filled with tears as he clocked his son.

Instantly, he was on his feet, holding Samuel close, breathing him in, kissing his soft hair. I wanted him to enjoy the moment without me stating the obvious.

'Chloe?' he asked after he'd settled back in the chair with Samuel.

I shook my head. 'I'm sorry. I tried.'

He exhaled loudly. 'Thanks anyway. Can I have a moment alone with him?'

'Of course. I'll be in the kitchen. You take as long as you need.'

I closed the door behind me, a lump in my throat. This was so heartbreaking and so unfair. I only hoped Chloe could get her head together quickly and face up to whatever it was she'd done before it was too late.

* * *

After I finished my meal, I heated Chloe's up in the microwave and carried her tray upstairs. It wasn't right to make her forfeit her dinner just because James was here. We'd offered James something to eat but he'd declined. I'd offer again later.

'Has he gone?' Chloe asked when I opened her door.

'No, but I thought you might be hungry.'

She eyed the chilli appreciatively. 'I'm starving.'

'Do you want some company?'

'No.'

'I'll bring Samuel up later.'

'Okay.'

Silence.

I turned and reached for the door when I heard the two words which Chloe spoke so rarely. It was barely audible but there was definitely a 'thank you'.

16

CHLOE

Even though my stomach was churning with nerves, knowing that James was downstairs, I couldn't deny how hungry I was. Sam had no sooner closed the door than I pounced on the tray contents, eagerly glugging back some of the fresh orange juice then raking in the chilli. The meal was a welcome relief from the memories of the past tumbling round in my mind and getting steadily more vivid by the hour.

But eating couldn't last forever. When I'd scraped the bowl clean, there was nothing else to focus on. Samuel's clothes were organised and I'd even sorted through mine and arranged them into piles at one side of the room. I had my Kindle with me but a book wouldn't have held my concentration for long, not with my mind so active.

I lay back down on the duvet, my hands clasped across my full stomach, and stared yet again at the vast space above me. Sighing, I closed my eyes and tried to relax but I didn't know how. As a child, I'd found it hard to concentrate on one thing at a time. Hyperactive, they said. I wasn't. It was just that there always seemed to be so many exciting things to do and not enough hours in the day. I loved variety and wanted to have a go at everything.

At secondary school, I hated studying – tediously boring – but I wasn't daft. I was astute enough to know I needed to pass my exams and bright enough to do it with reasonable grades. Not like Sam. She aced every subject, although that was hardly surprising. If my mum had treated me like Auntie Debs treated Sam, I'd probably have hidden in my bedroom with my nose in a textbook too.

While academic subjects weren't my bag, there were three things that came naturally to me: drama, sports and arts and crafts. Drama was the only subject I passed with an A and I always landed the lead role at the local theatre school. I represented the school in netball, volleyball, athletics and tennis and attended several arty/crafty after-school clubs. Always on the go. Always active. Always doing something.

At college, I was the same but it wasn't because of my love for variety and excitement. It was because I was afraid that, if I slowed down, the truth would catch up with me. And now it looked as though it finally had.

I opened my eyes and turned onto my side, facing the front of the house. The rain battered against the pane and I shivered. Torrential rain always made me think of *him*. That dark hair, those full lips, the tenderness in his eyes and the softness of his touch when he told me he loved me. Travis Enderby-Bowes. The one who nearly destroyed me all those years ago.

The one who was about to destroy my life now.

17

Thirteen years ago

'Yes!' Scarlett waved her job sheet in the air on Monday morning. 'I've escaped again this week. Have you drawn the short straw, Chloe?'

I grabbed my sheet off the top of my cleaning cart, scanned down the numbers of the caravans I'd been allocated and grinned at her. 'Nope. Not this week. Which must mean—'

'No!' our colleague Lorna wailed, stamping her foot. 'Why do I always get Mouldy Pickles?'

'Because you were very bad in a previous life,' Scarlett quipped.

'As opposed to being very bad in this life, like you?'

'No fighting please, ladies.' I held one hand out towards each of them, like a referee in a boxing match. They both jostled me, fists raised, but it was all done in jest. They were the best of friends at work really.

Mouldy Pickles – or Maud Pickles to name her properly – owned a static caravan at Kellerby Cliffs Holiday Park, where we all worked. We mostly cleaned the holiday lets but the permanent residents could pay for a cleaning service too.

It was always with trepidation that we checked our randomly allocated job sheets at the start of the week to see who'd got the raw deal. Maud Pickles lived like a pig. How one elderly lady living alone in a small space could create so much mess remained a mystery. Her caravan reeked of mould – despite there being no physical evidence of any – and so did Maud.

A petite woman in her mid-eighties with long white hair and pale eyes, she was friendly enough, but that was part of the problem. She'd keep you chatting and that meant longer in 'the caravan of stench'. After only ten minutes in her van, the smell clung to our uniforms and we'd find ourselves itching for the rest of the day.

Mondays – linen change day – were the worst. You had to literally peel the sheets off the mattress. Seriously grim way to start the week.

'It's been three weeks in a row,' Lorna whined. 'Come on, girls, can one of you swap with me this week? Please.' She gazed at us both pleadingly.

Scarlett scraped her long, dark hair into a high ponytail and shook her head. 'How many times did you swap with me last year when I kept getting Mouldy Pickles? I told you it would come back and bite you on the arse this year.'

Lorna fixed her gaze on me and I knew what was coming.

'Pwetty pwease, Chloe.' She played with her auburn braids and widened her brown eyes. She was eighteen – same age as Scarlett – but her petite 5' 1" frame and spattering of freckles helped create the illusion of a small child when she put on her needy voice; the one she knew I struggled to resist.

'I'll wuv you forever,' she added.

'Argh! Oh, go on, then. But if I end up getting her three weeks in a row after this, you're taking her back for at least one of them.'

She stood on tiptoes and gave me a squelchy kiss on the cheek.

Laughing, I playfully pushed her away as Mr Bowes, the duty manager, purposefully strode into the room for our morning briefing.

Situated ten miles south of Whitsborough Bay, Kellerby Cliffs Holiday Park was one of the region's biggest employers of students each summer. With over a thousand static caravans, forty wooden lodges, a leisure centre, a small fun fair, shop, bars and restaurants, there was a massive range of jobs available from cleaners to bar staff to lifeguards. Those who worked hard were rewarded with an offer to return the following summer, so it was no wonder they received thousands of job applications each year.

Aged sixteen, I'd applied for a job in the kids' club. I'd always wanted to work in a pre-school and, with the long summer ahead of me before starting at college to study childcare, I hoped to get some practical paid experience. I'd been gutted when I received the phone call telling me I wasn't experienced enough but might I like a cleaning job instead? As if! I was about to tell them where to stick their job offer when it struck me that it could be my way in. What if I worked hard, got noticed and managed a transfer? So I had accepted and started five weeks ago in early July, although annoyingly it didn't look like there'd be any chance of a role change.

Scarlett was assigned as my buddy for my first week. Her purpose was to educate me in how to do the job but it was obvious from day one that Scarlett relished the opportunity to educate me in more than cleaning toilets and changing bedding.

'How old do you think Mr Bowes is?' she'd asked as soon as we stepped outside with our cleaning carts on my first day.

'Erm, not sure. Late thirties maybe?' At well over six foot with broad shoulders, a shock of dark hair and a youthful face, he definitely looked younger than my dad, who was forty-three at the time.

She laughed at me. 'Fifty-four. Can you believe that? He's seriously hot. Definitely a DILF.'

My jaw dropped.

'A dad I'd like to—'

'I know what it means! I just wasn't expecting you to say that.'

She curled her lip up. 'Oh, God, don't tell me you're easily offended because we're not going to be friends if you are. I get enough of that from my mate, Lorna. I haven't got room for two of you in my life.'

'No! Nothing like that. It's just that you're only eighteen and he's your boss and...' I paused as I clocked the mischievous expression on her face. 'Unless you've already...'

She winked at me. 'Lots of times.' Then she laughed and indicated we should head down the path with our carts. 'I'm winding you up. I absolutely would, given half the chance, but that man is completely devoted to his wife. Married for thirty years and still besotted. Sickening, really. I don't think humans are designed for monogamy. You won't catch me settling down with one man or woman for the rest of my life.'

'Woman?' I asked. 'You're bisexual?'

'I don't do labels. Too restricting. I love men but I'm attracted to women too. You've got to mix it up a bit. Women's bodies are far more attractive than men's. Don't you think?'

'I haven't really given it much thought.'

'You should. Don't know what you're missing till you try it. You've got a boyfriend, then?'

'Not at the moment.'

'Good. So I won't hear you prattling on about him all the time. I'll introduce you to Lorna when she's back in tomorrow. She's been with Seb since she was, like, five. They're getting married next year.' She pointed her finger down her throat and made gagging sounds. 'Right, you, better stop slacking and clean some vans.'

As she taught me my role that first week, she also taught me a hell of a lot more. Lorna called her a 'potty mouth' and frequently said I should tell her to 'stop talking filth' but I was fascinated. Contrary to the rumours from school, I hadn't lost my virginity. I'd had lots of boyfriends and always started each new relationship full of optimism that, this time, it would be different. This time, it would be about them getting to know me instead of being all about them trying to get in my knickers. It never was. So, broken hearted, I dumped them, only for them to further break my heart with all their lies. I wanted my first time to be special and, with Scarlett's unexpected lessons, I felt confident I'd know exactly what to do when the right man came along.

* * *

On the Monday morning of the job sheet swap with Lorna, I rolled my cleaning cart up the ramp onto the deck running down one side of Mouldy Pickles's van: Dolphin 23. I took a few deep breaths; last chance for some fresh air before I stepped into 'the caravan of stench'.

I knocked on the door. 'Hello, Ms Pickles. It's Chloe from cleaning.' I tried the handle but it was locked. 'Ms Pickles? It's Chloe. I'm here to clean.'

Nothing.

Stepping back, I glanced at the lounge windows at the front of the van and the bedroom ones at the back. The curtains on both were closed. She must be having a lie in.

I knocked again. 'Ms Pickles? I'm coming in to clean, so make sure you're decent.'

The familiar stench of mould, which usually clawed at me as soon as I opened the door, seemed worse than usual. I gagged and turned my head to inhale some fresh air.

'It's a warm day,' I called. 'I'm just going to prop the door open with my cart.'

I stepped into the gloom and flicked on a light. 'Ms Pickles? Are you home?'

The green anorak she always wore when she went out – even on a hot day – wasn't hanging in its usual place by the door and her grubby beige canvas shoes weren't there either. She must have gone out, although I wasn't sure why she hadn't opened the curtains first.

Dirty dishes were piled high in the sink and the remnants of what looked like an Indian takeaway festered in foil trays on the work surface. The bin was overflowing and there appeared to be debris everywhere, from newspapers to sweet wrappers to twigs. It was going to take way longer than usual to clean today.

I billowed out a binbag, dropped the food trays into it, added the contents of the kitchen and bathroom bins, threw in some of the lounge mess and tossed the full bag outside.

With a laundry bag and fresh bedding draped over one arm, I opened the door to the master bedroom and reeled back, gagging once more. I was going to have to open the windows before I could strip the bed. I pressed my hand over my mouth and nose, switched on the light and my heart leapt out of my chest when I spotted her.

'Ms Pickles?'

She was sitting on the floor in front of the wardrobe, wearing her green anorak and canvas shoes, staring at me.

'Are you okay?'

I took a step closer, my heart thumping.

'Maud?'

She was far too still. Her skin had a greyish tinge. And she was looking at me but not really looking.

I shuffled even closer and reached out a hand to gently nudge her, only just managing to stifle a scream when she slumped to one side. Deep down, I'd known it as soon as I saw her. She was beyond help. I'd seen enough hospital and crime dramas on TV to know that she was long gone.

'Oh, my God! Oh, my God! Oh, my God!' I rubbed at my forehead as I swallowed the lump in my throat. What to do? In my week with Scarlett, I'd learned a hell of a lot of things but none of them were what to do when you found one of the residents dead.

Phones were confiscated at the start of each shift to avoid us being distracted from our work, there were no phones in the caravans and Ms Pickles didn't own a mobile. I was going to have to hoof it up to the clubhouse and track down Mr Bowes.

I wheeled my cart inside and locked the door behind me. We'd always been told not to run round the site so I did the fastest walk I'd ever done in my life, smiling and greeting passing guests, all the while stifling the urge to scream. I'd seen a dead body! I'd touched a dead body! My skin was crawling.

A wild goose chase took me to the restaurant, the shop, the pool and the arcade. Why did nobody have a radio on them? All the while, panic was building. I kept picturing her face, grey and contorted. I could feel her cold skin on my fingers and desperately wanted to wash my hands.

I burst through the door to the empty bar and slammed straight into someone.

'Hey, where's the fire?' he cried.

'Sorry.' I realised from his branded shirt that he was bar staff. Dark hair. Maybe a few years older than me. 'Mr Bowes. I need Mr Bowes.'

'You've literally just missed him.'

'I can't have. I need... There's...' My heart was racing so fast and I was struggling to breathe by this point. My mouth was dry and I couldn't seem to form any more words.

He led me by the arm and pressed me down into a chair then crouched beside me.

'Are you okay? What's happened?'

'Urgent. She's... I can't...'

'Breathe,' he urged. 'Look into my eyes and follow my breathing. Slowly. Deep breaths. In. Out. That's good.'

Wide-eyed, I stared into the stranger's kind grey eyes. He had the longest eyelashes I'd ever seen on a male, and thick dark eyebrows, which made his gaze intense yet reassuring.

'You're doing well. Keep breathing, slower still.'

I finally managed to catch my breath, the urge to scream fading.

'You need Mr Bowes?' he asked.

I nodded. 'Urgent.'

'And it's definitely urgent?'

I nodded vigorously this time. 'Dead. She's dead.'

'One of our guests?'

'Maud Pickles. Dolphin 23.'

He gently squeezed my hand. 'Stay here. I won't be long.'

Adrenaline fading fast, I wasn't sure my legs would carry me anywhere so was more than happy to stay.

Moments later, the barman returned and crouched beside me again. 'Uncle... sorry... Mr Bowes will be here in two minutes. I'm Travis, by the way.'

'Chloe. Mr Bowes is your uncle?'

He wrinkled his nose. 'I'm not supposed to tell people that in case they think it's nepotism but I don't know why because that's *exactly* what it is.'

I had no idea what nepotism was but I didn't like to show my ignorance. I'd have to ask Sammie later if I could remember the word. She was clever and knew stuff like that.

'I told him that people would guess. We've got the same surname. Sort of. He's my dad's brother but my parents double-barrelled our name so I'm stuck with Travis Enderby-Bowes. I sound like some posh kid from Eton or Harrow.' He glanced round him and, even though there were no customers, he lowered his voice. 'Is she really dead? Maud?'

I shuddered as I pictured her again. 'She was icy cold and stiff and grey.'

'You poor thing.' He gave my hand another squeeze and my heart raced at his warm touch. 'Ah! Here he is.'

Mr Bowes stepped through the door with the confident air of a man completely in control. Head held high, shoulders back, he beckoned me with the slightest flick of his hand.

'Hope to see you around,' Travis said.

My stomach did a somersault as he gave me a cheeky wink. I hoped so too. Travis Enderby-Bowes was absolutely gorgeous.

* * *

Travis was outside when I exited my final caravan at the end of my shift that afternoon.

'Travis! What are you doing here?' I asked, surprised but delighted to see him.

'I was on my break and I fancied a walk.' He gave me broad smile. 'I might have planned to coincide it with your finish time.'

'Why was that?' I asked, looking at him shyly through lowered lashes; something Scarlett had taught me. Now that I wasn't in a panic, I could see that he was even more gorgeous than I'd thought earlier. He had thick dark hair, piled high on his head in an effortlessly messy style. Long sideburns, chiselled cheekbones and full lips gave him a sexy, brooding appearance.

'Two reasons. First, I wanted to make sure you were okay. Are you?'

'Still a bit upset, but getting there. Your uncle was lovely. He offered to pay for a taxi home and said I'd still get paid for my shift if I left, but I preferred to stay.'

'He's a decent bloke, is Uncle Chris. He won't stand for anyone slacking and he notices those who work hard. You'll have scored yourself serious bonus points today. You'll be on his radar now. If you want to change jobs, you'd just have to say the word and he'd make it happen.'

'Really? I'd love to work in the kids' club. I applied but I was told I didn't have enough experience. I'd even be happy to do a few hours volunteering after my cleaning shift.'

'Leave it with me.'

'And the second reason?' I asked.

'To ask whether you'd like to go out sometime.'

Would I ever?

* * *

A couple of days later, Mr Bowes called me into his office and said he understood I was interested in working in the kids' club. He'd arranged a one-week voluntary trial for me starting the following Monday after my cleaning shift each day and, if the feedback was good, I could leave my cleaning post and work there full-time for the rest of the summer.

Travis happened to be 'passing' Mr Bowes's office when I came out, grinning from ear to ear.

'Did you sort that out?' I asked him. 'Nepotism?' I'd remembered the word and asked Sammie what it meant.

'Why have relatives in high places if you can't benefit from it? Looks like I might need to take you out to celebrate your new job.'

'I haven't definitely got the job yet. I have a trial first.'

'Then that gives us an excuse for a second date. But how about organising that first one?'

Present day

I didn't usually close the lounge curtains at night – no need when there's nobody around to peer inside – but tonight's grim weather definitely warranted it.

'Are you okay?' James asked, his voice full of concern. 'You seem a bit twitchy.'

I felt it. I couldn't seem to sit still. Every time a gust of wind blew the rain more heavily against the window, I jumped.

'It's this weather. It puts me on edge.'

After I'd pulled the curtains closed at the other end of the room, I curled up on the sofa and picked up one of the cream fluffy cushions. Cuddling it to me might help settle my jitters.

'I wondered if it was because of me. All I seem to have done over the past year is cause you pain and hassle. I'm so sorry, Sam.'

Samuel, asleep in his arms, made a grizzling sound and he looked down at him and smiled, making my heart melt.

'It hurt at the time but I'd do it all again in a heartbeat because it made me leave Whitsborough Bay and led me here. Now I've got a beautiful home, the most rewarding job in the world and an amazing fiancé.'

He sat up straight, eyes wide. 'You're engaged?'

'Chloe didn't tell you?'

'No. Oh, my God, Sam! Congratulations. When did this happen? When's the big day?' His voice was full of enthusiasm and possibly a hint of relief that I'd moved on and was happy.

'It was last Saturday night out the back, overlooking the meadow. Nothing flashy but absolutely perfect.' I raised my hand to flash my ring. 'We haven't set a date yet.'

He gave me a wide smile, his eyes twinkling. 'I'm so pleased for you both. Josh seems like a decent bloke.'

'He is. He's the best. Thank you. But, as I say, it wouldn't have happened without you and Chloe getting together. So now we need to work out a way to keep you together. Assuming that's what you still want.'

His smile faded. 'Definitely. Chloe and this little one are my world but I feel so helpless. I honestly don't know why she left like that. Has she *really* not said anything to you?'

'She won't talk about it.'

'But that's madness. How can I put things right when I don't know what I've done wrong?'

'I think it's more complicated than that. I don't actually think the problem is something you've done.'

'Then why run out on me if it's not my fault?'

I shrugged. 'That's the bit I can't work out. From what I can gather, something happened on Sunday that, I don't know...' I searched for a suitable word, '... spooked Chloe in some way and put her in flight mode. But as to what that could have been, I have no idea.'

The sound of the front door opening made me jump. Moments later, Josh stepped into the lounge, shaking his wet hair.

'It's wild out there.'

'Are the hedgehogs okay?'

'They're all fine. Fed, watered, given medicine.' He sat down next to me. 'Your dad's here but he says you're not to attempt to go across in the rain. He'll catch up with you in the morning.'

Josh looked over towards James. 'I take it Chloe didn't come down.'

James shook his head. 'Unfortunately not.' He glanced towards the clock on the mantelpiece and frowned. 'I'd best be making tracks. Samuel will probably need a feed soon.'

'There's no way you can drive home in this,' Josh said. 'Crap visibility aside, the roads are flooded. You can't get back to Whitsborough Bay tonight.'

'But I can't stay here.'

'You can and you will.' I stood up. 'I'll speak to Chloe.'

* * *

There was no answer when I knocked on Chloe's bedroom door so I tentatively opened it. The bedside lamp I'd loaned her was switched on casting a soft glow from the corner of the room. Chloe was lying on the airbed, wrapped up in the duvet.

'Are you asleep?' I whispered.

'Just dozing.' She squinted at me. 'Has he gone?'

'He's staying tonight. You can hear the rain. It's not safe to drive and, even if it was, the roads are flooded so he can't get back.'

I steeled myself, ready for a tirade of objections, but none came.

'Where will he sleep?' She sounded resigned rather than annoyed.

'We're running low on options so it has to be the sofa. We don't even have any more bedding but we've got a couple of throws and plenty of cushions so he should be warm and comfortable.'

On the way up the stairs, I'd wondered whether Chloe might bend and suggest James share the airbed with her. It would be the logical solution and he was her husband, after all.

She pushed herself up on her elbows. 'I know what you're thinking but I can't. I'm sorry. It's right that he stays. I'd worry about him driving in this but I can't face him yet, Sammie. Please tell me you understand that.'

I knelt down beside the bed and sighed. 'I understand that you wouldn't want to share a bed with him when you're struggling to even see him but I don't understand what's going on with you. You made me promise not to keep pushing you but you do realise you're going to have to talk to him sooner rather than later, don't you?'

She slumped back on her pillows with a sigh. 'I know. I just need a bit more time. Tell him...' She fell silent for a moment and I prayed she was going to ask me to tell him she loved him. 'Forget it. Don't tell him anything.'

'Are you sure? Because he said to tell you he loves you.'

Chloe held my gaze, her eyes glistening, then she turned onto her side and closed her eyes.

I stayed there for a minute or so but she didn't move. Sighing once more, I stood up, gathered her empty pots onto the tray and opened the door. 'I'll bring Samuel up when he wakes for his feed.'

No response.

* * *

I might have loaded the dishwasher a bit too aggressively because the clattering caused Josh to rush into the kitchen.

'Are you okay? Has she had a go at you?'

'I'm fine. Sorry. Surprisingly, she didn't have a go but I think I might have preferred it if she had.' I put the tablet in the tray and set the dishwasher away then turned and pressed my back against it. 'Obviously I can't stand being shouted at but at least I know what's on her mind when she's having a rant. I don't recognise her like this. She's prone to sulking but, in the past, I've always known why. This is different. This isn't sulking. This is distant and angry and upset and I have no idea how to get through to her. I've never seen her like...' I paused and frowned. 'Actually, I have. Once. But we're talking years ago.'

'What happened?'

'It was when we were at college. I went to the sixth form and she went to the technical college. She absolutely loved it at first. She was studying childcare – exactly what she'd always wanted to do – had made new friends and was really happy. But then she split up with her boyfriend and fell out with one of her friends and she took it out on the rest of us. There was a right atmosphere over Christmas. She snapped at everyone, was really sulky and withdrawn and had a huge fall-out with Auntie Louise. It went on for well over a year because I remember her still being really funny the following Christmas. I tried to get her to talk to me but she wouldn't. I barely saw her that year. It was really hurtful, especially when I was leaving for university so wouldn't see her much then, but I gave up trying to spend time with her. I got sick of the rejection. She's as distant now as she was back then although, in many ways, it's worse now because she's living under our roof.'

Josh hugged me. 'She'll tell you eventually. And if she doesn't, she needn't think she's living here for a year or more till she sorts herself out.'

'Oh, gosh. Could you imagine?'

'I'm trying not to. I'll have nightmares if I do.'

19

I couldn't sleep, knowing James was downstairs. I kept expecting him to thrust open the bedroom door and demand to know what the hell was going on. I would have done if I'd been in his shoes. But that was where we differed. Like Sam, James was calm and patient. They both thought things through and considered other people whereas I was reckless and impulsive and never paused to think through the consequences. I tended to grab onto an idea and run with it.

Mum was right about James being good for me. He provided balance. He grounded me. He made me stop and think instead of doing something or making a decision I might regret or that might hurt someone else.

So often since our wedding day, I'd wished he'd been with me when Sam arrived at the reception, several hours late and covered in mud. He'd have handled the situation completely differently. I should be able to look back on my wedding as the best day of my life, filled with happy memories of love and laughter. Instead, my lasting memories were bitter and angry: shouting at my cousin, accusing her of trying to steal my husband, demanding she leave and being so wound up by the whole thing that James and I didn't even do our first dance.

Thanks to that ugly incident, the marriage was nearly over before it started. James and I had a huge bust-up at the airport and almost didn't board the plane for our honeymoon. I'd told Mum afterwards that I'd been the one having a go at James, livid that he'd checked on Sam on our wedding night and I'd caught them embracing. The reality was that I'd calmed down and realised that I'd over-reacted, but James was fuming with me for what he called my 'appalling behaviour'.

I'll never forget the look of disappointment on this face as we sat in departures, having barely spoken a word all the way to the airport.

'You've got to talk to me eventually,' I said.

'I still don't understand what happened at the wedding, Chloe. How could you turn on Sam like that?'

'What did you expect me to do? Congratulate her for still being in love with *my* husband?'

'No. I'd have expected you to show compassion for her. She pushed us together when she could see that you and I had what she and I didn't. Imagine how difficult it must have been for her to be around us, helping you plan the wedding, being your bridesmaid, all the while wishing it was her.'

I flashed my eyes at him. 'Have you heard yourself? She was jealous of me. She wanted what I had and she was determined to keep making a play for you.'

He shook his head. 'Have *you* heard *yourself*? Sam doesn't have a jealous bone in her body. She gave us her blessing to be together, she stepped back from the friendship with me and she never said or did anything to try to win me back. I was the one who went looking for her that night and I was the one who hugged her to say sorry for all the pain I'd caused. She didn't even want me to do that. She kept telling me to leave her alone and be with you.'

'How would you feel if one of my ex-boyfriends was still in love with me?' I snapped.

'It wouldn't bother me unless you were still in love with him. I'd never loved Sam as anything more than a friend and you knew that. All she's ever done is try to make you happy and you've repaid her by turning against her and turning your family against her too.'

'If Sam's that special, perhaps you should have married her instead of me.' I knew I sounded like a spoilt brat but I couldn't help it. Everything he said was right and I couldn't stand it when I was called out on my faults. It made me feel even more inadequate than I already felt.

James stood up and shook his head. 'I don't recognise you at the moment. Can the woman I fell in love with please come back? I'm not convinced I like this imposter.'

'James!' I cried as he walked away, shoulders hunched. 'Where are you going? We'll be boarding soon.'

A few long strides and he disappeared from sight. I sank down in my seat, trying to avoid the curious glances of the other holiday-makers. Was that it? Was our marriage over before it had even started?

My heart thumped as I waited for him to return, fear gripping me that he might have walked out for good. It thumped even faster when the call came for the first wave of passengers to board the plane. Then the second wave. Then all remaining passengers.

Departures emptied and I felt sick as our names were called out over the loud speaker. What the hell was I meant to do? Wait and hope he reappeared? Board the plane and go on our honeymoon alone?

Our names were called again. Final call. Home or honeymoon? Much as the thought of a honeymoon for one filled me with dread, returning home and admitting that I'd single-handedly destroyed my marriage was even scarier, especially as I was expecting a baby; news that we were planning to announce to our immediate families after the honeymoon.

Stomach churning, I picked up our hand luggage, passports and boarding cards and shuffled towards the departure gate.

'Chloe! Wait!'

My heart leapt at his voice. I spun round to see James running towards me but his expression was sombre. 'Come back for the car keys?' I asked bitterly, convinced from the dark look in his eyes that this was the end. I handed him his backpack and he took hold of it with a sigh.

'No. I've come back for you and our baby. I'm hoping a bit of sun, sand and sea will bring back the real Chloe Turner because she seems to have gone missing in action. Do you think there's any chance of us finding her?'

'We really need you to board now,' one of the flight crew said, clearly cringing at having to interrupt us.

I handed James his passport and boarding card and nodded. I couldn't speak. Not even to say sorry. If he'd said he'd just come back for me, I'd have thrown my arms round him and whispered 'sorry' a hundred times. But he'd said he'd come back for our baby and I couldn't shake the feeling that the tiny life growing inside me – only about eight weeks old – was the main reason he hadn't walked out of the airport and out of my life. If there'd been no baby, he might not have returned. I wasn't enough.

A couple of weak cries brought me back to the present and I glanced over to Samuel's cot. His cries intensified and I rolled off the airbed and began the ritual of pain.

As Samuel fed, I imagined James downstairs trying to get warm and comfortable on the sofa under a couple of throws and tried to block out the guilt. Had he heard Samuel just now? Was he thinking about me or was he only concerned about his son? The longing to feel his arms round me was so intense, I could almost feel his strength and smell his forest-pine scent.

After Travis, I never expected or even wanted to love again. I was scared of letting someone in and history repeating itself but I hated being alone. So I moved through a string of boyfriends who I knew were bad choices; a bit of fun but not a long-term prospect and definitely not men I'd fall for. When they proved themselves to be exactly what I'd expected – users, liars, cheats – I ditched them and moved onto the next.

And then I met James.

The ferocity of my feelings the instant I saw him at Gramps's birthday party was both astonishing and overwhelming – a gorgeous stranger in a sharp suit and shiny shoes – and I couldn't take my eyes off him. I genuinely had no idea who he was. Sam and James had been together for about eight or nine months at that point but I'd never actually met him because she always went across to York to see him rather than him coming to Whitsborough Bay. He wasn't on social media so I'd only seen a few photos Sam had taken and hadn't paid much attention to them. Perhaps if I had, things might have been different, but I assumed he was a guest from another party who'd wandered into the wrong room.

He'd noticed me too and I felt drawn towards him. I excused myself from Gramps's neighbour, flicked my hair over my shoulder, and strode across the room, butterflies dancing in my stomach. It felt as though we were the only ones there as we moved ever closer, eyes locked. We joked later that it was like Cupid had fired an arrow straight into both of our hearts. Instant. Lasting.

'Hi,' he said as we reached each other, electricity crackling.

'Hi. I'm Chloe.'

'James.'

His name should have set off alarm bells but I barely registered it. All I could do was focus on his lips and imagine what they felt like pressed against mine. I'd never had such an intense reaction to anyone. Not even Travis.

I racked my brain for something intelligent or clever to say but all I could think about was how fit he was and I could hardly blurt that out. Think!

'Nice suit,' I said. 'It's good to see someone making an effort.'

'Thanks, but I have to confess that the suit is because I came straight from work although, if I hadn't, I'd have still made an effort. Seventy-five years is pretty special.'

So he was in the right place. Who was he? 'You know the birthday boy, then?'

'Yes. Sort of.'

He didn't give me any more detail and I didn't ask. I could hear my heart hammering despite the chatter and the music and wondered if he could hear it too.

I became aware of a couple of people beside us but couldn't seem to avert my gaze and neither could James.

'Sammie's boyfriend,' Gramps declared loudly. 'So pleased you could make it.'

And at that moment we both snapped out of it. This was Sammie's boyfriend? Shit! Close call. Off limits. No-go zone. Step away from the completely unavailable man.

Yet I couldn't do it. A voice in my head kept telling me that they didn't love each other. They were just having a bit of fun until the real thing came along. Sammie had told me that. So he wasn't completely unavailable after all. He was fair game.

I turned to see Sammie next to Gramps and my stomach clenched with nerves. She asked James about his day at work and I probably should have made my excuses and left them to it but, instead, I found myself questioning what he did and actually gushing with excitement when he told me he was a marketing director. I might even have touched his arm, desperate for some physical contact.

Suddenly we were alone again. Sammie and Gramps had gone and it was just the two of us. I'm surprised our hair didn't stand on end with the volume of electricity crackling between us. I couldn't stay there and make feeble small talk and I couldn't walk away either. I needed to make sure I wasn't imagining it.

'You feel it too, don't you?'

James gulped as he nodded.

'What do you think it means?'

'I don't know. It's never happened to me before.'

I glanced round the room. We needed to talk and the function room was too loud, too busy and too full of people I knew.

'Follow me. There's somewhere quiet we can go.' My fingers lightly touched his and I gasped at the shockwave throughout my body.

A colleague of mine had held her wedding reception at Sanderslea House Hotel the previous summer and I'd stayed overnight. There were turrets on each corner and, allocated a top floor room, I'd gone exploring, hoping to climb up one, only to discover they were bedrooms. I mentioned to another of my colleagues, Sandy, that I hadn't seen turret rooms on the hotel's website or I'd have booked one. She asked me if I could keep a secret. Could I ever? Keeping secrets was something I excelled at. Sandy's sister used to work at the hotel and had told her they weren't really bedrooms and the numbers on the doors were an illusion. There wasn't enough space in the turrets for a king size bed so they weren't viable as rooms but they could be hired out for small meetings. They were meant to be locked but the card reader on the back left one didn't work.

So Sandy and I went to explore and her sister was absolutely right. The door opened to reveal a winding staircase up to a turret room with 360-degree views.

'Wow! It would be amazing to sleep up here,' I said, turning in a circle at the top.

The only pieces of furniture in the room were a velvet chaise the colour of black cherries, a pair of matching chairs and a coffee table.

'It would be amazing to have sex up here,' Sandy responded with a giggle.

And, even though I'd planned to whisk him away to talk, that was all I could think of as I led James by the hand up the spiral staircase on the night of Gramps's birthday party.

At the top of the stairs, we took a moment to take in the views. It was getting dark and a mixture of streetlights and illuminated houses near and distant appeared magical like fairy lights.

'That's amazing,' James whispered.

We faced each other, eyes wide and, next moment, our lips met. I gasped as he ran his fingers through my hair.

As suddenly as it started, it stopped.

'I can't.' James stepped back, shaking his head. 'Sam. We can't do this to her.'

'I'd agree if you loved each other but I thought it wasn't serious between you.'

'It isn't.'

'I thought you were only together until one of you met someone else.'

'We are.'

I pointed to my chest. 'Someone else. Right here. You admitted downstairs that you felt it too and, even if you hadn't, that kiss told me.' I stepped a little closer and traced my index finger lightly across his lips.

'She's your cousin.' His hand stroking my cheek weakened his protest. 'I don't want to cause problems between you.'

'I can handle Sammie. She'll understand.'

If I'd known back then that Sammie really loved James, would I have done anything differently? Probably not. I'd have focused on her feelings being unreciprocated and convinced myself she'd get over him eventually. I hadn't known, though. I hadn't cared. All I wanted was James.

From the moment I set eyes on him, I was lost to that man. After more than a decade of avoiding anything real, I finally felt ready to let someone back in and James was that person.

Every day I loved him a little bit more. Even over the past few months, when all we seemed to do was argue, he still held my heart tightly. All I wanted him to do was hold me and kiss me and tell me that, no matter what happened, he'd love me forever. No matter how crabby I got, how much I pushed him away, how cruel I could be when I lashed out, I needed to know his love was enduring and he'd never leave my side.

Until we got married, I believed I was his world but, since becoming husband and wife, I wasn't convinced he loved me as deeply as I loved him and it terrified me. I couldn't stop picturing his disappointment at the airport, the way he said he'd come back for our baby, and how there'd been no intimacy since the night we brought Samuel home from the hospital. It felt like I'd played my part and given him a son and now he could let me go.

When Samuel finished feeding and I'd changed his nappy and settled him back in his cot, I stood by the closed door. I touched it with my fingertips then rested my head against it, as though that could connect me more closely with my husband downstairs. I had to fight back the urge to race down two flights and throw my arms round him.

'I'm sorry, James,' I whispered. 'I love you more than you can ever imagine but it's how it's got to be.'

It hurt so much to be apart but I had to keep him at a distance. It would be easier for him when the truth came out. He likely already hated me for leaving him and that would build the longer I stayed away but that was how it had to be. That way, the truth wouldn't hurt him quite so much.

The thought of telling him made me feel sick. That look of disappointment he'd given me at the airport would be nothing compared to the look he'd give me when he heard what I'd done. There was no way he'd forgive me. I hadn't ever forgiven myself, so how could I expect him to?

20

SAMANTHA

I could smell smoke. The barn! The hedgehogs! Surely it couldn't be happening again. The Grimes boys had been caught and were behind bars.

The smell permeated my nostrils, making me cough. Heart racing, I tried to fling back the duvet but I couldn't seem to move. Something was pinning me down.

I opened my mouth to call out to Josh but no sound came.

A man laughed and a cat yowled. Misty-Blue! I needed to find her. *I'm coming.*

I was outside. Smoke hung in the air and my eyes watered. I could hear the crackle of flames, someone running through long grass, glass smashing. Orange flames danced in the dark sky and I felt weak with fear.

'Get her!' a man's voice yelled, deep and sinister.

I tried to run but my feet were rooted to the spot. Something hurtled towards me and hit me on the cheek, cracking the bone, and I screamed.

A bright light made me squint and I screamed again as someone grabbed me. 'It's okay, Sammie. I'm right here.'

'Josh?'

'You're safe,' he said. 'It was just a bad dream.'

'The hedgehogs!' I thrust back the duvet and ran to the window but there were no flames coming from the barn. It was still raining, although not nearly as heavily. I pushed the window open and inhaled. No smoke either. I put my hand to my cheek. Nothing.

Closing the window, I turned back to Josh, frowning. 'It seemed so real.'

He scrambled across the bed and joined me by the window. 'Look. You can see the light's on so your dad must be up feeding the hoglets. Everything's fine. Come here.'

I gratefully relaxed into his embrace, wrapping my arms round his waist, feeling safe.

'You're trembling.'

I couldn't seem to stop. 'It was awful. The barn was on fire and I couldn't move. They were after Misty-Blue. I could hear someone running through the long grass behind the barn, like last time, then they threw something at me again.'

'You're safe and so are the hedgehogs and Misty-Blue.'

I turned to look towards the barn.

'Would it help if I went and checked?' Josh asked gently.

'It's the early hours and it's still raining. I can't ask you to do that.'

He squeezed me and kissed my forehead. 'I'll be back soon.'

My nightie was drenched with sweat so I pulled on a fresh one then dived under the covers, shivering. 'Just a nightmare,' I muttered. 'But frighteningly real.'

It had been like re-living a blended version of the arson attack by cousins Bryn and Cody Grimes on the original barn and the evening of the assault on the re-built barn when Cody's younger brother and his accomplice smashed the upstairs windows, chased Misty-Blue and hurled a box of eggs at me, splitting my cheek open.

I ran a couple of shaky fingers across my cheek and shuddered once more, snuggling further down under the duvet, heart racing.

When Josh returned roughly ten minutes later, my heart rate had finally steadied, the trembling had ceased, and I'd warmed up.

'Everything's fine in the barn. There've been no disturbances, no graffiti, and Misty-Blue's curled up on a cushion in the boot room.'

Relief flowed through me. 'Thanks for checking. I know I was being silly.'

Josh climbed back into bed and cuddled me to him. 'You wouldn't have settled if I hadn't and I wouldn't have settled knowing you were worried. Are you okay now?'

'I think so.'

He kissed me then switched the light off and we settled back down under the duvet.

But now that I was awake, my mind was active once more, worrying about the situation with Chloe and James. We weren't hormonally imbalanced teenagers anymore. She couldn't just push James away for a year like she'd pushed me away when she was at college. She was married with a baby. She was going to have to talk to him.

After nine months together, I'd like to think I knew James pretty well. He was a patient, tolerant man but even the most patient of people had their breaking point. Would driving through a storm and sleeping on a sofa under a couple of throws while being ignored by his wife be James's? He'd be perfectly justified if it was.

21

CHLOE

I was placing Samuel back in his cot shortly after 4 a.m. when I could have sworn I heard a woman's scream. I pulled Samuel's covers over him and my heart thudded as I listened but all was silent. Damn lack of sleep wreaking havoc with my imagination.

Shortly after, I heard the sound of the front door closing – definitely not my imagination – and peered out of the window. The rain had eased from torrential to a steady patter. Could that be James leaving? My stomach did a backflip as I watched someone hurrying along the path towards the farmyard. Definitely male. Hunched in the rain, I couldn't tell if it was James or Josh.

If it was James, it seemed ridiculously early to be leaving. Although, if he had to detour to avoid the floods, maybe it wasn't that early. He'd need to get home, changed, and out again for the first train to work. I doubted he'd have managed much – if any – sleep and that was my fault. All of this was my fault.

The security light illuminated the farmyard and the figure disappeared into the barn. It had to be Josh. I glanced towards the cars and James's was still there. I was surprised to feel relief flowing through me. Weird. I'd wanted James to leave yet I was glad he hadn't. How did that work?

I was still by the window when Josh returned to the house. I heard the front door shut and, moments later, a door closed on the floor below. Then silence.

The urge to go down to James was back with a vengeance. Was there any way I could see him without having to explain what had happened? I paced up and down the room, working on a speech.

I'm really sorry I ran out on you and for all the pain I caused. I know this might not make any sense to you right now but I can't explain why I had to leave so please don't ask me to. I promise I will explain eventually. I want you to know that it's not because we've been arguing although I'll admit that the last few months have been tough. I haven't met anyone else and I don't want to and I'm not ill so please don't start speculating about anything like that. The problem is me and I need some time to get my head around a few things before I can tell you what's going on. I know I've tested your patience a lot since we've been married and it's a lot to ask you to be patient again but please try to be. I do love you and I always will but you might not love me when you know what...

I sighed and kicked at the airbed. Too vague. Too cryptic. Too bloody inadequate. Try again.

I'm really sorry. I know none of this makes sense right now but I promise it will eventually. It's nothing you've done. It's me.

I ran my fingers through my hair in despair. If I said that, he'd think he was being dumped. The classic, 'It's not you, it's me,' line.

I'm really sorry. I know none of this makes sense right now but I promise it will eventually. Please be patient and I will explain it all. I do love you and I always will.

The front door closed again and I rushed to the window. Was that Josh going back to the barn? I squinted through the rain but, as the security lights illuminated the yard once more, I could see that it was James heading for his car. My heart raced as I pressed my hands against the glass. No! He was leaving. He'd be halfway down the track before I made it down the stairs.

I glanced at my phone. Unless I rang him. I picked it up and hovered over his name then tossed it onto the bed. Perhaps it was better this way. I hadn't even worked out what to say and it was unrealistic to expect him to stand there and say, 'Okay, you take your time, I'll be right here waiting.' He had every right to question me and it would turn ugly. I didn't want our marriage to be over. I didn't want to lose him. But, by running out with our son and refusing to see him, might I have already damaged an already fragile relationship too deeply? Could I actually have hammered that last nail into the coffin before the truth even came out? Or would the truth be the final nail?

I was the one who'd walked out on him but I could pretty much guarantee he'd be the one to walk out on our marriage when he knew it all.

22

✉ From James
Thanks for last night. I left early when the
rain eased. There didn't seem any point in
staying any longer when Chloe wouldn't speak to
me. At least I got to see Samuel. The roads were
still flooded but I made it back safely. Sorry
you're caught in the middle of this mess. Wish I
knew what had caused it. Look after them for
me x

I'd still been awake when I heard the front door closing and had gone to the window to check it was James leaving rather than Chloe doing a moonlight flit. I'd texted him to ask him to let me know he got home safely so it was a relief to hear from him.

'Poor bloke,' Josh said after I read out James's text while he dressed for work. 'Chloe should have spoken to him last night. That was rude of her.'

'I know. All I can do is keep encouraging her but I can't make her do anything. Chloe has always done whatever she wants.' I pulled on a hoodie. 'Right, that's me sorted. I'll go across to relieve Dad.'

* * *

Dad was washing his hands when I entered the barn. 'Perfect timing,' he said. 'I've just finished feeding them all. They're getting really lively now.'

'Aren't they? They'll be ready to make their own way in the world before we know it.'

Dad dried his hands then joined me at the treatment table. 'How are you? Did you manage to get back to sleep after your bad dream?'

I shook my head. 'I tried but my mind was too active.'

'Thinking about Chloe and James?'

'I just don't understand what could have happened. She won't talk to him or me. She won't even talk to Auntie Louise.'

'I'd offer to have a word but it was always your mum who was close to Chloe; not me.'

'Thanks, Dad. We're just going to have to hang on in there and hope she finally opens up. I'm trying so hard not to pick sides here but I can't help leaning towards Team James and I feel so mean for that when Chloe's in such a state.'

'Don't feel bad about it. You've taken her in and you've already gone over and above by cleaning her car and acting as a go-between. You've shown you care and you've shown empathy. That's all you can do right now. She'll talk to you when she's ready. Unless...' Dad frowned. 'This may be a bit out there but do you think she'd speak to your mum? Remember when she was at college and she was all snappy with everyone and fell out with your Auntie Louise? Your mum seemed to be the only one Chloe would speak to back then.'

I remembered it well. They'd always been close, which had been upsetting when Mum was so distant towards me but that year had felt even worse seeing them all cosied up together and completely shutting me out.

'It's worth a try.'

'I'll give her a ring at lunchtime.' Dad stood up and gave me a hug. 'I'd better head home. Good luck with the school visit tomorrow. You and Fizz will be amazing and you'll have the next generation of volunteers lined up by the time you're done.'

'That would be so lovely. If it goes well, I'll probably get in touch with a few more schools and offer something similar.'

'Sounds good. I'll see you later.'

As soon as Dad left, I opened up my laptop and searched for a list of local primary schools. Not being from the area, I had no idea how many there were. With hedgehogs now officially classified as 'vulnerable to extinction', engaging with the local community was one of my top priorities and schools were such a great way to do that. My hope was that we could inspire the children to want to save the hedgehog and their enthusiasm would inspire the parents to make their gardens hedgehog-friendly and perhaps drive a little more slowly when out at night. Small changes could make such a difference to the dwindling population.

I bookmarked the schools link then clicked on my to-do list. There was nothing else needed in preparation for the school visits but I was feeling in a productive mood. First on my list was finding someone to maintain the rescue centre's accounts. My system so far was an ever-growing pile of receipts and invoices in a box file; far from ideal. Before I left my tutoring role at Reddfield TEC, my boss Lauren – who was also Josh's auntie – had suggested that I might be able to find a volunteer from the accountancy course to keep on top of Hedgehog Hollow's accounts. The accountancy tutor, Adam, had loved the idea of having a live set of accounts for one of his students to work on so I emailed him with some details about the rescue centre and the small time commitment I anticipated. Hopefully there'd be some interest and someone could start soon.

I also emailed the animal care tutor, Vanessa, to offer some work experience opportunities. The students undertook a two-week placement as part of their course. I had a feeling I'd already missed the boat this year but I could offer some hours around lessons or even on an evening if that would work for them.

A reply came back from Vanessa within half an hour:

To: Hedgehog Hollow Rescue Centre
From: Vanessa Coulson, Animal Care Tutor, Reddfield TEC
Subject: RE: Work Experience Opportunity at Hedgehog Hollow
Hi Samantha,
Great to hear from you and your email couldn't be better timed. As you suspected, our students have already done their work placements but one of them fell through last minute so the student missed out.
Next week, they start a two-week research project. I'd organised a placement for that student to do alongside his project but I've just picked up a voicemail to say it has also fallen through. The student will be devastated but you've just thrown a lifeline. Would it be too soon for you to offer a two-week placement starting on Monday? I'd need to sort some paperwork and do a risk assessment but I can give you lots of help and guidance. Would this be at all possible? Can you come back to me before morning break and, if it's a yes, I'll run it by the student?
Thank you!

Next week? It was a bit sooner than I'd be thinking, but why not? There'd be another couple of school visits with which he could help and it would be good for him to see how a rescue centre can work with the community. If he wanted to use hedgehogs for his research project, I had plenty of ideas and lots of guidance I could give.

To: Vanessa Coulson, Animal Care Tutor, Reddfield TEC
From: Hedgehog Hollow Rescue Centre
Subject: RE: Work Experience Opportunity at Hedgehog Hollow
Hi Vanessa
So sorry to hear about both placements falling through. Next week for a fortnight would be fine as long as you can definitely help with the paperwork and run through what's needed. I have a couple of school visits this week and a few family commitments so would struggle to squeeze in much preparation time otherwise.
If the student is interested, I'm happy to drive up to the TEC this afternoon or Friday to meet you both.
I look forward to hearing from you.

Vanessa replied, reassuring me about the paperwork and support. She'd be in touch again when she'd spoken to the student.

By 10 a.m. I'd crossed loads off my to-do list, fed the hoglets and administered medication to the hedgehogs who required it. I needed to get back to the farmhouse to see if Beth wanted any help with Archie and Lottie. I felt bad that they were effectively trapped upstairs until I could carry Archie down. Beth insisted it wasn't an issue but I always aimed to get back to the barn by mid-morning to help her. I was therefore surprised to see her in the lounge with Archie and Lottie when I passed the window.

'Morning! I was just coming to help you,' I said, poking my head round the lounge door.

'We were up and organised before Paul left for work so he carried Archie down.'

Lottie was asleep but Archie was busy navigating his way round the room, holding onto furniture to balance himself.

I smiled at him. 'A few more days and I reckon he'll be walking without the furniture.'

'I think you're right.'

'I haven't had any breakfast yet so I'm going to grab a bowl of cereal. Do you want one or have you already eaten?'

'I haven't had a chance yet. Cereal would be great, thanks.'

A few minutes later, we sat down on the sofa together with our breakfast while Archie continued to navigate round the room.

'Did James see Chloe last night?' Beth asked.

'Unfortunately not, but he got to spend some time with Samuel which was good. He texted earlier to say he'd made it back to Whitsborough Bay after a bit of a detour.'

'Paul had a couple of detours on his way to work too. That was a hell of a storm last night. The torrential rain took me right back to my fall. I kept thinking how much worse it could have been and how I could have lost Lottie. I was really unsettled all night.'

'I'm not surprised. I was unsettled too. I had a nightmare about the barn being on fire again.'

'Did you scream? Paul said I'd imagined it.'

I grimaced. 'I was hoping nobody heard. It was awful. It felt so real. Poor Josh went out in the rain so he could reassure me that Dad and the hedgehogs weren't in danger.'

When we'd finished eating, I stood up and took Beth's empty bowl. 'I'd better check on Chloe. I'll see you shortly.'

I made a mug of tea and took it upstairs. There was no answer when I knocked on Chloe's bedroom door so I pushed it open. She was seated on the kitchen chair feeding Samuel and, once more, that look of sheer agony contorted her face.

Her gaze met mine and my heart broke for her as tears steadily tracked down her cheeks and she whispered, 'Help me. Please.'

23

CHLOE

I hadn't planned to ask Sam for help but the pain was so intense that the words tumbled out. Something was definitely wrong and I was starting to worry about Samuel's health. Sam had said something yesterday about babies not latching on properly and not getting enough milk. Could I be depriving him? I couldn't bear the thought of doing anything that might put him at risk.

Sam rushed over and placed her hand on my arm. 'I'm not an expert but Hannah is.'

I shook my head vigorously. No way. Too close to home.

'Chloe! You're in pain and she'll be able to help. She's breast-feeding Amelia and she's an NCT volunteer.'

'She'll think I'm a failure. She'll tell Toby and he'll tell James and he'll take Samuel away.' I could see from Sam's frown that my comment made no sense to her. It would when she knew.

'You're not a failure,' she said gently. 'Most new mums need help. I'll phone Hannah and ask her if she can come over but I'll ask her not to say anything to Toby.'

She placed my drink on the floor and left the room. I wiped my cheeks once more with the palm of my hand and sniffed. I wasn't thrilled about Hannah coming round but if it meant easing the pain and doing the right thing for Samuel, I was going to have to accept it. I'd have to trust her not to say anything to Toby as it would definitely get back to James and I didn't want him to know how bad it had become, especially if Sam was right and Samuel wasn't getting enough milk. James would think I was a crap mum. And he'd be right.

Sam reappeared as I was pulling my PJs top back into place. 'Hannah's coming over at half eleven and she's promised not to say anything to Toby. I thought you might like to get washed and dressed while I change Samuel.'

Without waiting for a response, she took Samuel from me, grabbed the outfit I'd laid out on the bed and his changing bag, then paused by the door. 'There's loads of options for breakfast in the kitchen so feel free to raid the cupboards and fridge then come over to the barn to get Samuel when you're ready.'

'Do I have any choice?' I muttered when she'd gone, feeling a bit miffed that she was treating me like a child, telling me what to do.

I jumped when the door opened again. 'Sorry. I've just realised it probably sounds like I'm rushing you but time's really tight for me. I'll need to feed the hoglets again shortly and I've got loads on.'

She closed the door and my stomach sank. Had she heard me and felt the need to offer an explanation? She hadn't sounded defensive and surely she'd have been snappy if she had heard. I certainly would. I sighed. That was where my cousin and I differed.

Moments later, laughter filtered up to me from the room below – Beth's kids' temporary nursery – and I felt riled again. 'Got no time for me but you can pause for a laugh with your new best friend, Beth. Nice to know where your priorities lie.'

An enormous yawn made my jaw click uncomfortably. I rubbed at it, frowning. Was it possible to feel any more shattered than I did right now? An airbed in the middle of an empty room had never looked more appealing. Could I...? Samuel was being looked after. I wasn't needed. Just ten more minutes. I lay down, curled into a foetus position and closed my eyes.

* * *

'Enjoy your sleep?'

I flicked my eyes open to see Sam standing over me, arms crossed, jaw tight.

'What time is it?' I asked, rubbing my eyes.

'Twelve.'

'What?' I sat upright. 'Why didn't you wake me earlier?'

'Because I assumed that you could be trusted not to go back to bed and because I've been over in the barn working and looking after your son.'

'Where is he?'

'Downstairs with Hannah, ready for a feed. Can I trust you to sort yourself out and come *straight* down?'

I flinched at her tone. It was what she called her 'super-stern nurse voice' which I knew she used to use on patients who weren't taking their meds or following dietary guidance. She'd never used it on me before and I felt well and truly chastised. How old did she think I was? Five?

'I'll be down after my shower,' I retorted. I knew I was pushing it but where did she get off ordering me about?

'You don't have time. Samuel needs feeding and Hannah's here to help you. So it's toilet, teeth then downstairs, please. I'll see you shortly.'

The moment she left, I grabbed a pillow and tossed it towards the door with a frustrated cry. If I wanted a shower, I'd have a shower and she couldn't stop me. I grabbed some fresh clothes, stomped down the stairs to the bathroom and yanked open the shower screen door, but I heard Samuel's cries and my resolve crumbled. My son needed me. Sighing, I closed the screen and filled the sink with water instead.

* * *

Loud voices and laughter drifted up to me as I emerged from the bathroom. It sounded like there was a party going on in the lounge. My steps slowed on the stairs as I tried to tune into the conversation, listening out for my name. From what I could pick up, they were talking about Beth's eldest, Archie, taking his first steps over the weekend. The way they were gushing about it, you'd think the kid had just run a marathon. At least it meant they weren't talking about me.

My stomach tightened listening to Beth's voice. She'd better not be hanging around. It was bad enough having to rope Hannah in to help but, with James being best friends with her husband, at least I actually knew her. Beth was a stranger. I wasn't even convinced I wanted Sam to stick around. I couldn't bear the thought of having an audience judging my incompetence.

When I stepped into the lounge, Sam and Hannah were on the floor with three babies of assorted sizes spread out on a playmat. Beth stood just in front of me, cuddling a fourth one. She smiled at me but I didn't feel like smiling back.

'Your son is absolutely gorgeous,' she gushed. 'I couldn't resist a cuddle.' She passed the baby towards me and I realised with a jolt that it was Samuel she was holding; not one of her own.

I took him from her and he immediately released a wail. Typical. Weren't babies meant to love their mothers unconditionally?

Beth leaned over and stroked his cheek. 'Don't worry, Samuel. Mummy will feed you in a moment.'

I stepped back, shocked at her over-familiarity, but she didn't react. Neither did Samuel and I felt quite smug that the crying continued. She may act all gooey and charming but at least she wasn't a baby-whisperer.

'I'll leave you in peace,' Beth said. 'Sam, are you still okay to help me with the buggy?'

Sam scrambled to her feet. 'Definitely.' She picked up the smallest baby and handed her to Beth then picked up the largest and turned to me. 'Beth's taking Lottie and Archie for a walk. I'll help Beth then it's up to you what you want. I can stay here with you or I can go with Beth if you'd rather have some privacy.'

I *didn't* want an audience but I *didn't* want her being all cosy with Beth either. 'If you could come back to help, that would be great.' I flashed her my sweetest most grateful smile but it was lost because both Beth and Sam were too busy fussing over Beth's kids.

Standing in the middle of the lounge with a screaming Samuel rigid in my arms, I felt completely useless.

'I'll be back shortly,' Sam said and they both left.

'Why don't you pass me Samuel while you get yourself comfortable?' Hannah suggested when the door closed.

As I plumped cushions, she asked me questions about the regularity and length of Samuel's feeds, how it felt and what adjustments I'd made, if any, to try to ease the pain. I was hesitant at first but she was extremely encouraging and it was clear that the more detail I gave her the more likely she'd be able to help and put an end to this agony.

* * *

Sitting sideways on the bench outside, I pulled my knees up to my chest, wrapped my arms round them and dipped my head, battling the desire to cry yet again.

At least I had a diagnosis now. Breast engorgement and mastitis,

Hannah reckoned. Being a district nurse and a breastfeeding counsellor, I had no reason to doubt her verdict. The former explained why Samuel needed feeding so often as it was caused when more milk was produced than the baby was taking and, as Hannah showed me, he never latched on properly like Sam had suspected so struggled to take what he needed. The latter – caused by a blocked duct – explained the recent burning sensation. It also explained some of the fatigue and the general achy feeling.

I needed a course of antibiotics as I'd let it go on too long without treatment and an infection would have developed. I'd panicked when she said that, unable to face driving back to Whitsborough Bay to see my doctor. She couldn't prescribe anything herself with being on maternity leave but was able to pull in a favour and secure me an emergency appointment with one of her colleagues on her district nursing team.

'I thought you might like a cup of tea.'

I looked up at Sam, standing in front of the bench, holding out a mug with a hedgehog on it.

Nodding, I adjusted position and took it from her.

'There's some lunch inside too when you're ready.'

I nodded once more.

'Hannah's secured you an appointment with one of her colleagues at 3.45. You'll need to leave by about ten past three. I'll give you some directions.'

'You're not coming with me?' I'd assumed she would take me and the idea of going on my own filled me with dread.

'I can't. I'm sorry. I've got an appointment at Reddfield TEC.'

'What for? I thought you didn't work there anymore.'

'I don't, but a student on the animal care course is starting work experience with me from Monday so I'm meeting him.'

I raised my eyebrows at her. 'You're offering work experience already?'

She shrugged. 'An opportunity came up.'

'Sam! That's far too soon. You've only been doing this for five minutes.'

Her eyes widened. 'Thanks for the vote of confidence.'

She sounded hurt and I didn't mean to upset her. It just seemed a lot of responsibility to take on when she'd only just got the place up and running. We occasionally offered work experience placements at the pre-school where I worked but my manager hated doing it because of the amount of preparation and paperwork involved.

'I only meant that it's a big commitment, especially when you're still learning yourself.'

'So?'

'So surely it's difficult to teach someone else when you haven't got all the answers yourself?'

'Keep digging that hole, Chloe.'

Why did I keep saying the wrong thing? No wonder Sam looked offended. It sounded like I was criticising her knowledge when I was really more concerned about the amount of work I knew these things involved. I'd try one more time.

'I'm just thinking about you. Haven't you got enough on your plate at the moment with Josh's family invading and demanding so much of your time?'

Sam planted her hands on her hips and raised her eyebrows. 'Josh's family have not "invaded". They're invited guests and are very welcome here.'

My stomach lurched at that and I got the full meaning: I was *not* an invited guest and therefore *not* welcome. I was about to retort but Sam was on a roll, a hard edge and impatience in her voice that I wasn't used to.

'They don't demand any of my time either. Beth only needs help with lifting and Paul has never asked me for anything. And, by the way, they both do their fair share of the cooking and cleaning, which certain people don't, so you're going to need to do something around the house if you want to stay.'

An image of me all alone in a Cumbrian holiday park lodge attempting to make a meal flashed into my mind and I shuddered. 'I'm not cooking. You can't make me.'

She stared at me for a moment, eyes narrowed, then she sighed and softened her voice. 'I was going to suggest you take charge of loading and unloading the dishwasher or making sandwiches at lunchtime. You can't exactly call that cooking.'

I scowled at her. Her request wasn't unreasonable and I could just about cope with making sandwiches but, me being me, I had to make a snide remark. 'I suppose you'll expect me to make sandwiches for Beth too. And to load her plates into the dishwasher.'

'Oh, my gosh, Chloe!' She pressed her fingers against her temples, looking shocked. 'What is it with you and Beth? Why are you so hostile towards her?'

'I don't trust her.'

'With what?'

I lowered my eyes. I couldn't explain that it wasn't just Beth – it was any female – without opening the door to my past. I offered a feeble shrug instead. 'I'm thinking about you. She's Josh's ex. Aren't you worried about having her in the house knowing they have a history?'

'No. Because it's exactly that: history. There's nothing between them anymore just like there's nothing between James and me.'

Although she said it softly, that was definitely a dig. 'I just don't get why you're so pally after what she did to him.'

Sam sat down beside me. 'She's done nothing to me personally so I take her as I find her. She's a good person who lost her way and made some mistakes but she's making up for them now. Besides, life's too short to hold a grudge.' She stared at me pointedly. 'Otherwise you wouldn't be here and we wouldn't be having this conversation, would we?'

'That's not fair.'

'And you're not being fair to Beth. I really like her and I'm sure you would too if you gave her half a chance.'

My stomach churned. So she'd done it; Beth had taken Sam away from me. Why did it keep happening? Evidently Beth was welcome because she hadn't personally hurt Sam but I wasn't because I had. 'If you want me to leave, why don't you just come out and say so?'

'What? How did you interpret that from what I just said?'

'It's obvious. Josh's family are welcome because they're "invited guests", but your own flesh and blood dared to show up without an invitation and it's been a massive inconvenience. You were lying when you said you'd always be here for me.'

I expected her to apologise and convince me I was forever welcome – typical Sam reaction – but she shocked me by jumping up and pacing in front of the bench waving her hands in the air, her voice raised. 'This is doing my head in. I can't keep having the same non-conversations with you. Do you never listen? Do you never notice things?'

'I *do* listen.'

'Really? You've listened to everything I've said since you got here?'

'Yes!'

'Then how am I not here for you? I've let you stay; I've provided meals and I've looked after Samuel. I cleaned him up when you arrived and I cleaned up the mess in your car, both of which you never even bothered to thank me for.'

My stomach lurched. I'd been on my way to the barn to thank her for cleaning my car yesterday when I'd overheard her talking to Beth so I'd returned to the farmhouse and it had gone out of my head. I was about to thank her now but she was still pacing and ranting.

'I've begged you to let me in but you wanted me to stop asking so I respected that on the proviso you didn't throw it back in my face later. You've sulked, you've shouted and you've stomped about. You've had a go at Beth and your mum, you've barely spoken to Josh and now you've insulted my knowledge and my business decisions. You're not making things very easy.'

'I'd better pack my things, then.'

'You're still not listening! I'm *not* asking you to leave. I'm asking you to stop taking out whatever it is that's upsetting you on everyone else and to start pulling your weight but do you know what the one thing is that I really, really desperately want you to do?'

I shrugged.

She stopped pacing and sat down beside me once more. 'Talk to James. He deserves to know what's going on. And if you need help working through that conversation, talk to me or your mum or even my mum but just bloody well do something.'

I winced. Sam hated swearing. If the high pitch and volume of her voice hadn't already conveyed her anger, the use of the word 'bloody' certainly did.

'Hiding out here is not the solution. It's not fair on James and it's not fair on Samuel. You say you love James and you claim that it's nothing he's done. That would suggest to me that the last thing you want is for your marriage to be over. But don't you see that every day that passes where you ignore whatever it is that caused you to leave James is making the situation worse?'

I pondered on her words. 'What if the thing you claim I'm ignoring is likely to end my marriage anyway?'

'Then I say you take that risk because, if you don't face up to it and you keep cutting James out of your life like this, you may not have a marriage to save anyway.'

She was right. I knew she was right and the thought terrified me. I loved James so much and I couldn't bear the thought of a future without him but all I could picture was his disappointed face at the airport and his words: 'I don't recognise you at the moment. Can the woman I fell in love with please come back? I'm not convinced I like this imposter.'

What haunted me was whether the Chloe he fell in love with really existed or whether it was her who was actually the imposter. I'd spent so much of my life acting that I wasn't sure what was real anymore. Was the real me the person who was angry and bitter and pushed away the people I loved? And was the real me the person who'd done that terrible, unforgivable thing nearly twelve years ago?

I was terrified that it was. I stared at the meadow, feeling a scream welling up inside me. I didn't trust myself to speak. Memories whirled round my head, begging to be let loose. Sam was right about me hiding out but she probably meant from James. I was definitely hiding, but it was from the past.

I couldn't look at Sam. I knew she was waiting for me to say something but I couldn't form the words. Not yet. If I ignored her, hopefully she'd leave before I yelled or screamed or collapsed to the ground in a sobbing mess.

24

I waited for Chloe to open up but she wouldn't even look at me. She just sat on Thomas's bench, staring at the meadow.

'I'm here now,' I prompted, my voice soft once more. I was furious with myself for shouting, even more furious for swearing and I have no idea where the pacing came from. I was never impatient with people, no matter how much they tested me, yet I couldn't seem to help myself around Chloe at the moment.

Stony silence.

'You can't keep whatever it is bottled up forever and you know you can't stay here forever, which is not me asking you to leave. This is me concerned about you, your son and your marriage.'

She turned her head away from me so I couldn't even see her profile.

'Suit yourself,' I said eventually, standing up. 'I'll text you the details for your appointment.'

I paused but she remained facing the other way. If her shoulders had been slumped, I'd have thought she might be crying, but her head was held defiantly high, as though she was mad with me. That was hardly fair. Yes, I'd got impatient and I'd even sworn but surely she could see that I had every right to be mad with her for insulting my work experience plans and for waltzing into our lives and expecting everyone to rally round her without giving anything in return.

Despite saying she was welcome to stay moments ago – and meaning it – her defiance right now made me seethe. I'd changed my mind. I wanted her to go. I could feel the words on my tongue. *This isn't working. I think you'd better leave before one of us says something we regret and we fall out for good.*

But she was still my cousin and we had been close for most of our lives. The chasm between us kept growing now but it wasn't impassable. Yet. I wasn't the one who could build the bridge, though. That had to be Chloe.

'I'll be in the barn if you need me.'

No response. With a sigh, I walked away, muttering under my breath.

* * *

Inside the barn, I had to pace up and down several times to work out my anger and tension before I texted Chloe with the name of the surgery and some basic directions.

Once I'd sent the text, I took a deep breath, closed my eyes, and reminded myself that I was in my happy place with my hedgehogs. I focused on the tranquillity, the occasional scratch or squeak from the crates, and the song of the birds outside.

Another couple of male hedgehogs arrived that afternoon. Chaucer had a bad case of flystrike and Orwell appeared to be severely dehydrated so treating them gave me a welcome focus away from Chloe.

I'd settled Orwell into his new home after giving him some

rehydration fluids and was about to start on Chaucer when a text arrived from Chloe:

✉ From Chloe
I need to get some things after my appointment
so I'll be out for a few hours. I wouldn't want
to put you to any more trouble so don't include
me in your dinner plans. I'll eat while I'm out

I shook my head. Why did she always have to take things the wrong way? Her text reeked of stroppiness. I'd have to hope that she'd reflect on our exchange while she was out and see that her behaviour was unreasonable because, if things didn't change, I might have to ask her to leave. Or Josh would as this situation wasn't doing any of us any good. I'd promised to look after myself but I could feel my stress levels soaring.

* * *

It was strange being back at Reddfield TEC for my meeting with Vanessa and Zayn, the work experience student, that afternoon. Only five weeks had passed since I'd fainted at work, leading to my premature departure to work full-time in the rescue centre, yet so much had happened during that time that working at the TEC seemed like a lifetime ago.

I'd only just sat down when I spotted them approaching along the corridor. Zayn had that swagger his generation seemed to have mastered. Wearing branded sportswear, his ebony hair was short at the back with a crown of corkscrew coils that bounced as he moved.

Vanessa shook hands with me then introduced Zayn. His expression was serious and I hoped he hadn't been forced into this. The last thing I needed was a sullen teenager.

'It's great to meet you, Zayn,' I said, enthusiastically. 'So how do you feel about spending a couple of weeks rescuing hedgehogs?'

Suddenly he beamed at me and his dark eyes sparkled. 'Are you for real? Hedgehogs? They're wicked.'

'Zayn was telling me earlier about the hedgehog who visits their garden.'

'We call him Winston. We've got this sick house for him...'

As he raved about Winston and his love for all hedgehogs, I pushed aside Chloe's earlier negativity. This was going to work.

* * *

It was a little after 6.30 p.m. when, from the kitchen window, I spotted Chloe's car on the farm track. Paul was in the lounge with Archie and Lottie, and Josh was upstairs getting changed after work while Beth and I prepared a cheesy pasta bake and salad.

I dashed into the hall as soon as I heard the door open a few minutes later, determined to catch Chloe and smooth things over. She had Samuel strapped to her front in a grey baby carrier. It had to be a new purchase as she hadn't had one of those when she moved in. She had paper carrier bags in each hand: one from the chemist and one from the supermarket.

'How did the appointment go?'

'Fine.' She walked towards the stairs without even looking at me.

'Is that all you're going to say about it?' I fought hard not to sound irritated.

'You already know Hannah's diagnosis. They said the same at the surgery and I've got some tablets to take.' She continued up the stairs.

'We're making pasta bake for dinner.'

'Well done, you. I hope you enjoy it.'

I winced at the unnecessary sarcasm.

Beth was emptying the large pan of pasta into a colander over the sink when I returned to the kitchen. She turned round to look at me, obvious sympathy etched across her face.

I plonked myself down at the table, grabbed a block of cheese and slammed it against the grater. 'I know what you're thinking. I shouldn't let her speak to me like that.'

'Actually, I wasn't thinking that. I was wondering what could have hurt your cousin so deeply that she keeps lashing out.' She put the pasta down and leaned back against the sink. 'When my mum abandoned me, I used to be like Chloe. I told you I stayed with our next-door neighbour, Mrs Jennings, until it was obvious Mum wasn't going to return, but that wasn't the full reason I left. She was a lovely woman but even she couldn't cope with my mood swings. I was so angry. I'd stomp about, slamming doors and shouting and it was too much for her. She wasn't in the best of health but my behaviour was making her worse. She cried the day she asked me to leave but it was absolutely the right thing to do for her and for me. That was my rock-bottom moment but I needed to hit that low before I could get my act together. I realised I couldn't control my mum's behaviour, but I could control mine. I could choose whether or not to let her selfishness ruin my life.'

'You think I should ask Chloe to leave?'

'No. I think that, in her case, it might make things worse. But keep being patient with her no matter how much she pushes you. I think your cousin's in a lot of pain and every time she snaps at you and pushes you away, she's really testing you. She needs to know that no matter how bad things get, you'll stay in her life. If you can keep putting up with her attitude, she might finally believe you when you say you're there for her.'

'You really think that could be it?'

She picked up the pasta and tipped it into a pan of cheese sauce on the Aga. 'I don't know Chloe. I know very little about your family history and I've barely spent any time in her company but I do know what it's like to be lost and alone. I'd tell Mrs Jennings that I didn't want to talk about it but I did. I just needed to know that someone cared enough to stick with me once they knew the truth about how angry I was and how, at the time, I wished my mum was dead.'

Could she be right about Chloe testing me? It was certainly possible. I couldn't face another confrontation tonight so it would have to wait until tomorrow, probably after the school visit. Unless she decided to leave before then.

'Thanks, Beth,' I said as I wrapped up the cheese. 'I'll keep trying.'

* * *

I sat bolt upright in bed, gasping for breath, a sheen of sweat covering my body. Another nightmare. The Grimes cousins had broken into the barn, taken our bald rescue hog, Gollum, and were pelting him and Misty-Blue with eggs. I tried to get to them but it was like my feet were encased in cement.

My heart thudded and I was trembling again but this time there was no Josh to comfort me. He'd taken the nightshift with the hoglets so that I could be fresh for my school visit this afternoon.

I shivered as I picked up my phone to check the time: 4.28 a.m. I had ninety more minutes until the alarm sounded. Retreating back under the duvet in the darkness, I closed my eyes and inhaled slowly and deeply, waiting for my heart to stop racing.

Once again, the nightmare had been terrifying and very real. The Grimes boys were all behind bars yet they were still affecting my life. It was so unfair.

Fifteen minutes later, my mind wouldn't rest. I kept running through the altercation with Chloe yesterday and what Beth had said. I was even more worried about Chloe now. What could possibly have happened that was so bad it could mean the end of her marriage?

By 5 a.m. I had to accept that sleep was off the agenda so I got up, showered, and wandered over to the barn wearing one of my hedgehog dresses. Fizz told me she'd be wearing a T-shirt with a cartoon hedgehog on it so I wanted to go for maximum cuteness effect too.

Josh was asleep on the sofa bed but he stirred as I crept down the barn. 'You're early.'

'I had another nightmare.'

He peeled back the duvet and I kicked off my wellies and eagerly clambered in, grateful for his strong arms round me and the warmth of his body.

'The fire again?'

'No. They were pelting Gollum and Misty-Blue with eggs. I tried to get back to sleep but I kept thinking about Chloe.'

'I don't understand why she doesn't just tell you what's going on. Surely the whole point of coming here was that she wanted your help.'

'I know. It's frustrating but Beth said something insightful about Chloe's situation last night and I think she could be onto something. I'm just going to have to dig deep into my patience banks for this one and keep telling her I'm here when she's ready.'

'You're a far better person than me. My patience reserves would have run dry by Sunday night.'

I snuggled in closer. 'That's because you don't know the lovely side of Chloe.'

'There's a lovely side?'

I gave him a playful nudge. 'There is. I promise.'

'Then why don't you tell me about it?'

Several examples came to mind and I thought for a moment about the best. 'When I left home for university, Chloe insisted on coming to Liverpool with us because she was so sad about me leaving. She'd had that weird blip at college but we'd got really close again over the spring and summer. When Dad and Chloe left me in my room and I started unpacking, I came across a box I didn't recognise. It was full of gifts from Chloe...'

I smiled as I pictured the special home-made contents of the box. She'd bought some seaside-themed material and made some bunting, a couple of cushions and a material noticeboard out of it. I still have them in my office. She'd drawn a caricature of us both onto a mug and she'd decorated a silver photo frame. She must have spent hours working on everything and all the items brought me so much comfort while I settled into an unfamiliar place and found new friends.

As I spoke, more and more memories surfaced of the moments over the years where Chloe had been kind and thoughtful. They were only occasional but they were pretty special when they happened.

But the thing I'd loved the most about my cousin was how she'd built me up each time Mum knocked me down. From what she'd said when Auntie Louise visited, she hadn't realised quite how painful Mum's putdowns felt, yet she'd behaved as though she had, hugging me, making me laugh. She'd helped me stay positive and strong and I would be forever grateful for that.

Now it was my turn to help her stay positive and strong.

CHLOE

I opened my eyes, squinting in the sunlight streaming through the curtainless windows. I reached for my phone on the floor next to the airbed. 9.17 a.m. How was it that late? I'd put Samuel down after his last feed shortly before half five and I'd been so exhausted last night that I'd dropped straight off after it.

In a panic, I sat upright, wondering if someone had taken him but he was on his back in the travel cot, his arms above his head, his head turned towards me, and I could see the steady rise and fall of his chest beneath the covers.

I lay back down, rolling my eyes. Who would have taken him? Why was I thinking crazy thoughts like that?

I'd forgotten how refreshing four hours of unbroken sleep felt. Why the hell hadn't I accepted help earlier?

I could feel that the meds had already kicked in. I wasn't aching so much and, although the burning sensation was still there, it wasn't as severe. If I could feel this much better already, I might actually feel alive again by the weekend. It would be amazing not to be so fuzzy-headed all the time.

Pushing back the duvet, I crept to the front window, not wanting to disturb Samuel. To the left, I could see Sam in the farmyard holding a cardboard box under one arm and speaking to someone through the window of a black 4x4. Could it be a hedgehog arriving or a delivery?

I sat back on the bed, chewing on my lip. I'd been at the farm for three nights so far and I'd just realised I hadn't asked Sam a single question about herself. I hadn't asked how many hedgehogs the rescue centre had or how she'd ended up being able to run it full-time when she'd previously told me she couldn't afford to leave her teaching job. I knew Josh, Uncle Jonathan and Sam took it in turns to sleep in the barn but I'd never thought to ask why. Did hedgehogs need round-the-clock care? I hadn't asked if she'd set a wedding date. I clapped my hand across my mouth. I hadn't even congratulated her or asked to see the ring. What the hell was wrong with me? Had I really been that focused on me and my problems that the only interactions I'd had with my cousin – the best friend I'd ever had – had been about me? I'd insulted her, shouted at her, placed demands on her. She'd pushed back a couple of times like letting James in, telling me to fetch my own dinner, asking me to pull my weight round the house and to be nice to Beth, but none of those things had been unreasonable. I'd been the unreasonable one. God knows why she hadn't sent me packing, especially after yesterday's incident.

Samuel murmured and I sighed. He was probably the reason. Although how many chances had she given me over the years before he came along? Maybe letting me stay wasn't just about him.

* * *

By mid-morning, Samuel was fed and changed, I'd had some breakfast, and I'd even managed a shower with him strapped into his bouncer in the bathroom. It was such an obvious thing to do that I wasn't sure why I hadn't tried it before. He was safe and occupied and I could see and hear him through the shower screen. I didn't need to worry about him.

I dressed in the bathroom then carried him back to the top floor in his bouncer. My phone was flashing with a text.

✉ From Auntie Debs
Hope you're okay. Everyone's worried about you, including me. I think we need to talk. I'm free tomorrow afternoon but I'd rather not come to the farm. Can you meet me at April's Tea Parlour in Great Tilbury at 3pm? xx

My stomach lurched even though I'd been expecting Auntie Debs to get in touch. She was right. We *did* need to talk. Mum would have told her exactly how I'd reacted when she'd visited and she might even have spoken to James. She'd have probably guessed there was a connection to the past but she wouldn't be able to work it out.

I shuddered, my stomach in knots, but I couldn't keep putting this off. Auntie Debs was the starting point.

✉ To Auntie Debs
Samuel and I will see you there xx

I lifted Samuel up and cuddled him to me, breathing in his delicious baby scent. 'It's getting closer,' I whispered. 'The truth will be out soon.'

Thirteen years ago

The day after Mr Bowes offered me the work experience opportunity in the kids' club at Kellerby Cliffs Holiday Park, Travis
Enderby-Bowes took me on our first date. He told me he'd pick me
up at three when my cleaning shift finished and would drop me
home after we'd eaten as he was working in the bar from 8 p.m.

'Nearly five hours together on a first date?' Scarlett curled up
her lip as we steered our carts back up to the storeroom. 'Rather
you than me.'

'Is that bad?' I asked, feeling suddenly nervous. 'Should I have
said no?'

'No, but five hours is, like, forever! You barely know the guy.
What if you run out of things to say after thirty minutes?' She gave a
dirty laugh. 'Although talking's overrated. There are far better ways
you could spend your time. Still don't need five hours, though.'

Lorna shoved her in the ribs. 'Seriously, Scarlett, does everything have to be about sex with you?'

'Yep.'

'Then you're missing out. Ignore her, Chloe. What's he got planned?'

'He won't tell me but he asked if I could swim, although he didn't ask me to bring a swimming costume or towel.'

'Ooh, maybe he's taking you skinny-dipping,' Scarlett gushed.

Lorna tutted. 'Will you just stop it?'

The pair of them were complete opposites. Lorna was sweet, quiet, studious and devoted to her fiancé. Scarlett was loud, brash and, as she liked to joke, 'available to all'. The bickering and the banter at work were clearly affectionate but I hadn't been surprised to discover that, despite both living in nearby Fellingthorpe, they didn't spend time together outside of work. Their outlooks and opinions were far too different.

Lorna put her arm round my shoulder. 'I'm sure it will be amazing, whatever he's got planned, and I look forward to hearing all about it tomorrow.'

'And I look forward to hearing all the juicy details. Hope you've shaved and waxed.'

'Scarlett!'

And so it continued until they both left on the minibus leaving me all alone, perched on a low wall at the holiday park entrance, my palms sweating and my pulse racing.

Moments later, a sleek silver Audi TT convertible pulled up beside me. When Travis said he had a car, I'd imagined something old and rusting. He surprised me even more by jumping out of the car, rushing round to the passenger side and opening the door for me. He looked effortlessly gorgeous in black jeans and a plain white T-shirt with the sleeves rolled up, revealing tanned, muscular arms. Yummy.

'I've been looking forward to this all day,' he said, beaming at me.

'Me too.' And I had. It was all I'd been able to think about while

I cleaned, which was a welcome change from picturing Maud Pickles's glassy eyes.

I glanced shyly at him as he pulled away, marvelling at how confident and composed he was behind the wheel considering he was only eighteen.

'Is it your car?' I asked.

'Yes.'

'It's very nice.'

'Thank you. Eighteenth birthday present from my grandparents.'

I tried not to but I think a little squeak came out. Not being old enough to drive yet, my car knowledge was virtually non-existent but even I knew that I was travelling in an expensive car.

'That's a very generous eighteenth birthday present.'

He gave me a sideways glance and smiled. 'I might as well put it straight out there. My grandparents own the holiday park plus two others.'

'Oh, my God! Really?'

'They set six up from scratch along the Yorkshire Coast and made their money selling the three further south. My dad's the duty manager at the Whitsborough Bay one, my Auntie Helena runs the Whitby one and, as you know, my Uncle Chris runs Kellerby Cliffs. Nanna and Granddad are retiring at the end of next season, at which point their kids will each get their own holiday park.'

'Will you stay in the family business?'

He shrugged. 'Simple question. Complicated answer. I want to but I don't know if I can. I've done various jobs at the parks since I was thirteen and have been at Kellerby Cliffs for the past two years. I love it and, if I was happy to get to middle management and stay there, I could have a job here long-term. Problem is, I've got ambitions. I want Uncle Chris's job eventually and I can't have it. He's got three kids and they all want to work here when they're old enough.

Uncle Chris has always been transparent that they'd be on a fast track to the top jobs and the only way I'd get a top position is if they decide they want different careers. It's the same at Whitby with Auntie Helena's three kids.'

'Why can't you work at your dad's park?'

He screwed up his nose. 'Long story. I'll tell you later if you like but, for now, we've reached our destination.'

Travis steered the car onto a gravel track between a stone wall. A slate sign had the words 'Kellerby Cliffs Grange' engraved onto it.

'Where are we?' I asked.

'My grandparents' house.'

'Oh. Okay.' I wanted to ask why. Taking me to meet his grandparents on our first date seemed a little strange but what did I know? My exes hadn't exactly been in the same league as Travis. Past dates were typically a trip to the cinema or ten pin bowling and a quick fumble in their bedroom, the park or a bus shelter.

Kellerby Cliffs Grange was seriously impressive. Built from light stone and flanked by a triple garage and what looked to be offices or workshops, it was enormous.

Travis pulled the car to a stop outside one of the garages. 'All the land you can see belongs to them too but this is nothing. Wait till you see out the back.'

He opened the car door for me and took my hand as he led me through a gate to the side of the house. I wondered if there might be a pool – especially after he'd asked me about swimming – but what stretched out ahead of me was far more unexpected and way better.

'Is that a private beach?' I asked, eyes wide.

'Cool, eh? Have you ever done stand-up paddleboarding?'

'No.'

'Then now's your chance.'

I recalled Scarlett's earlier comments about skinny-dipping and blushed. 'I haven't got a swimming cossie.'

'We've got loads in the beach hut. Come on. Race you.'

He sped off towards the sea, laughing, and I pelted after him. The perfectly manicured lawn gave way to longer grass dotted with wildflowers before descending onto the sand. Following Travis's lead, I kicked off my trainers.

There was a pale blue beach hut – which had to be at least six times the size of the ones in North Bay back home in Whitsborough Bay – with a large wooden veranda. Next to it was a smaller matching hut, which Travis told me contained deckchairs, paddleboards, bodyboards etc.

He unlocked the beach hut and propped open the two glass doors on hooks. I peeked inside and gasped. There was a bed in it!

'There's a chest of drawers over there full of swimming costumes and bikinis. They're all brand new. Nanna has this obsession with keeping a stock in case we have unexpected visitors. There are towels on the shelves and there's a couple of changing rooms at the back.'

He pointed towards two spaces with white saloon doors on them next to a kitchenette. 'I'll get the boards out while you change.'

I opened the top drawer and gasped. It was full of bikinis and tankinis in a range of sizes and colours. The next drawer down contained an array of full costumes. I hesitated for a moment, cursing Scarlett's words ringing in my ears, debating whether a bikini would send signals that I was up for the type of afternoon she'd have been up for, especially when there was a bed right behind me. But I did normally wear a bikini to the beach. I decided to go for the middle ground and grabbed what I thought was a raspberry pink tankini but, when I lifted it out of the drawer, it was a two-tone swimsuit with a red asymmetric bottom and a one-shouldered pink top. When I pulled it on, it tantalisingly revealing my toned stomach and the curve of my waist and hips. Very hot.

Travis obviously thought so too as he was all fingers and thumbs as he tried to select a short wetsuit for me to wear, muttering about how the North Sea was too cold for hot bodies like mine; clearly not what he meant to say.

I loved sports but hadn't tried watersports before, despite living on the coast. After half an hour on the board, paddling along the cliffs towards Fellingthorpe Brigg – a rocky outcrop stretching some distance into the sea off Fellingthorpe beach and only accessible at low tide – I wondered why. My natural core body strength meant I had a good sense of balance and, although I did topple off my board a few times until I got used to it, it wasn't a struggle to clamber back on.

'You're a natural.' Travis was clearly impressed. 'It took me ages to get the hang of staying on.'

I had found myself a new love: paddleboarding. Physically it was hard work but there was something surprisingly relaxing too about gliding over the water, seeing fish darting beneath us. A couple of seals bobbing about in the water near the Brigg made me squeal with delight.

We chatted as we paddled about everything from families to school to music we liked. He asked lots of questions and was so easy to talk to; something I'd never had with any of my exes. They'd either wanted to only talk about stuff they were interested in or they wanted to make out, so it was refreshing to have a proper adult conversation with someone who seemed genuinely interested in me. He also made me laugh and I loved that I did the same for him without even trying to be funny. We just clicked and I couldn't help thinking that paddleboarding might not be my only new love that day.

When we got back to the private beach after about ninety minutes on the water, we stripped off our wetsuits. Travis handed me a bottle of water from the fridge in the beach hut then suggested we have a swim.

'The water's still cold but, on a hot day like today, it's bearable.'

'Last one in's a rotten egg!' I have no idea what made me say something so juvenile or to squeal like a little girl as I sprinted towards the sea but it seemed to amuse Travis. He raced after me, catching up with me as I hit waist height, grabbing me round the waist and pulling me into the water on top of him. When we emerged, laughing, he kept his arm round my waist, his face suddenly serious.

'I realised earlier that paddleboarding was a daft idea.'

'Really? Why? I loved it.'

'It was great but it meant I couldn't do this.' He pressed his lips to mine and I snaked my arms round his neck as I responded to his salty kiss. Butterflies soared and swooped in my stomach and my heart raced as our kiss deepened.

* * *

The garden at Kellerby Cliffs Grange held more surprises, with an enormous patio area that was home to a summerhouse, firepit, woodburning oven and the biggest collection of outdoor furniture I'd ever seen. Travis had sent me for a shower in the main house and when I returned he was placing a pizza in the oven on the end of a long wooden paddle. He told me to help myself to a drink from the summerhouse where I found a fridge filled with a mix of soft drinks and alcohol. I grabbed a pineapple juice and gave it a shake as I stepped back into the sun.

'This place is amazing,' I said to Travis. 'I bet you spend loads of time here.'

'More than I do at my parents' house.' He wrinkled his nose. 'I lived here for a while.'

'Is that because of your dad?'

He indicated that we should sit down on the corner sofa and Travis took a swig of his Coke.

'My dad doesn't like me. I have an older sister, Genevieve. She's twenty-one and he doesn't like her much either. I think he liked the idea of having children but not the reality and he had no time for us when we were little. The holiday parks were his life and, of course, peak season is the school holidays so we never went on a family holiday with him. It was always just Mum, Gen and me. It was drummed into us from an early age that work always came first.'

'That must have been tough.'

'I think we accepted that's how it was as kids but, as we got older, we realised it wasn't how it should be. Dad also drilled it into us that the business would be ours one day and that we'd start working there as soon as we turned thirteen, whether we liked it or not. Gen's birthday fell on a Saturday and he scheduled in her first cleaning shift on her birthday. She hated working for Dad. Said he was constantly sniffing around, making it clear that he expected more of her because she was the boss's daughter and the holiday park was in her blood. She lasted two months before telling him where she'd like to shove her cleaning cart – right in front of everyone – and walking out. They've barely spoken since then.'

'And she's twenty-one now?'

Travis nodded. 'Seven long years.'

'I'm not sure I like the sound of your dad.'

He got up and checked on the oven. 'Pizza's ready.'

The conversation paused while he sliced it up and pointed to a bag of tortillas for me to tip into a bowl. We ate a couple of slices of pizza each in silence, except for appreciative sounds for how delicious the food was, then he continued his story.

'The thing about my dad is he's exceptional at his job. He's done some impressive things for the business, and the staff and guests all love him. If you're not family, he's a pretty decent boss to have.'

'But he treats you like crap if you're family? And that's why you can't work for him.'

'Nailed it. I was curious at first, wondering what could be so amazing that he cast his wife and kids aside so I happily but sceptically took up my post when I turned thirteen, and I was soon hooked. Dad was tough on me but I could see why the other staff rated him. I learned a lot about management by watching him. I asked lots of questions and even came up with some ideas that he liked and, for a couple of years, we actually had a pretty good relationship.'

'So what happened?'

'I er...' He visibly squirmed and rubbed his fingers through his hair. 'I got suspended from school for smoking dope.'

'Oh, my God, Travis! You did not!'

'Stupid thing was it was only the once but my mates buggered off and I was the one caught holding the spliff. Dad was livid. Sacked me from my job.'

'Your own dad sacked you?'

'Told me he wouldn't tolerate drug addicts at work. Can you believe that? A few drags on a spliff for the one and only time and I'm a drug addict.'

'What happened next?'

'Mum and Dad were arguing all the time because she thought he'd over-reacted so I moved in here for a bit, which was no hardship. Granddad had a word and the school retracted the suspension so I returned after a couple of days but that made no difference to Dad.'

'Your Granddad must be pretty persuasive. Which school was it?'

He grimaced. 'Whitsborough West.'

My eyes widened. Whitsborough West was a private school a few miles outside Whitsborough Bay and very posh and exclusive.

'Yeah, I know what you're thinking. Posh kid. It was because of my grandparents. They insisted on paying for all eight grandchildren to go through private education and that's why the suspension got retracted. Granddad threatened to withdraw the five of us who were there at the time and never send the three yet to start. Suddenly my offence wasn't quite so serious in the school's eyes but it was in Dad's. He only started speaking to me again when I aced my GCSEs. Apparently I wasn't a "waster junkie" after all. He even offered me my job back but I'd already started working for Uncle Chris and preferred to stay put.'

'Didn't your dad mind you working for your uncle?'

'He went ballistic but Uncle Chris didn't care. They couldn't be more different and never got on. So it's crunch time for me. Middle management with Uncle Chris, change career, or brave it with Dad.'

'Big decision.'

He nodded. 'Which is why I'm taking a year out to decide. I'll stay at Kellerby Cliffs until the season finishes at Christmas but I'm planning to see the New Year in overseas and spend the year travelling while I make up my mind.'

My heart sank at the thought of him leaving, which I knew was silly when we'd just met. We'd only spent a few hours together but there was something special about Travis Enderby-Bowes.

'Enough about me,' he said. 'Tell me more about you. What made you want to work with pre-school kids?'

While we ate, I talked about my fondness for art and crafts and how I'd loved teaching the younger ones at my after-school clubs. I'd considered primary school teaching at one point but creative play and early development interested me more.

When we'd finished eating, I asked him more about his travel plans. As he spoke about all the countries he hoped to visit, I drifted off into a little fantasy about travelling the world alongside him, spending our days in the most amazing places. Maybe I could convince him to put his plans on hold until I left college and we could do it together. Or I could put college on hold. And, as he kissed me again, I imagined how those nights might be.

* * *

As he drove me back to Whitsborough Bay a little later, Travis kept apologising for having to go into work that night.

'I knew you were going to be special,' he said. 'I'm kicking myself for not doing a shift swap. I'll be thinking about you all evening now.'

'Does that mean you want to see me again?'

'Definitely. Would you like to see me?'

'Definitely.'

Seeing him grinning, my stomach did a somersault. He was pretty damn special too. Completely different from any of the boys at school. Ambitious, driven, exciting. And, my God, could he kiss!

I lay in my bed that night, a huge smile on my face as I relived every detail of our afternoon and evening together. I brushed my fingers across my lips as I imagined him kissing me again, and a whole lot more.

* * *

'Did you shag him?' Scarlett asked the moment I arrived at the holiday park the following morning.

'No! It was only our first date.'

'What's that got to do with anything?'

Lorna rolled her eyes and tutted. 'Did it go well, Chloe?'

I grinned at her. 'It was the best. We went paddleboarding

which I loved and then we had a swim and a kiss which I also loved. And he wants to see me again.'

'Aww.' Lorna smiled at me. 'That sounds lovely.'

'Sounds dull as shit.' Scarlett made a gagging sound. 'You two are no fun with your cutesy virgin relationships.'

'Why does it bug you so much that Seb and I want to wait until we're married?' Lorna demanded.

'Because it's so twee.' Scarlett turned to me. 'Don't tell me you're going to wait till you're dragged down the aisle too.'

'Probably not, but I want my first time to be with someone special.'

'Oh, please!' Scarlett made another gagging sound.

Lorna must have spotted something in my expression as she exclaimed, 'And Travis might be that person.'

Suddenly Scarlett was interested, bombarding me with questions. What did he look like? How did he kiss? Had we done more than that? Had he had many girlfriends?

'You're going to have to introduce me to him,' she said as we pushed our carts towards the caravans after the briefing.

'Why do you need to meet him?' Lorna asked, an unexpected sharpness to her tone.

'To see if he's good enough for our little Chloe, of course!'

'That's Chloe's decision. Not yours.'

Scarlett stuck two fingers up at her. 'Maybe I'll nip up to the bar mid-shift and check him out for myself. See you both later.'

Scarlett took the left fork towards her allocated vans and Lorna and I continued in uncomfortable silence until the next fork where we needed to part company.

'Be careful around Scarlett,' she said, all mysteriously.

'What do you mean?'

Lorna's brow knitted and she glanced furtively around her then stepped a little closer. 'You've heard how she talks. She likes to shock. She's a complicated person. Don't let her talk you into anything you don't feel comfortable with.'

'Don't worry. I won't go all the way with Travis unless I'm sure about him.'

'It's not you I'm worried about. You seem to have your head together. It's Scarlett's influence that bothers me. She can be pretty persuasive when she wants to be.' She patted me on the arm. 'Just be careful. Please. I'll see you later.'

I said goodbye and we parted ways. I wasn't sure what Lorna meant about Scarlett. Was she jealous of my friendship with her and trying to warn me off? She didn't seem the jealous sort, though, and their friendship was only a work-based one. So what else could it be?

If I'd asked a few more questions or if I'd been a little less naïve, things could have been so different. Travis and I might have travelled the world together. We might have married and raised a family.

So many what ifs and maybes. That summer was full of them. If it hadn't been for swapping my job sheet with Lorna and Maud Pickles dying, I'd probably never have met Travis Enderby-Bowes because the cleaners and bar staff at the holiday camp didn't tend to cross paths.

How many times over the years had I wondered how different life could have been and how different *I* might have been if I hadn't been the one who found Maud? One thing I took away from it was never to do anyone a favour. Unless there was something in it for me, I wasn't interested in helping out. Why should I? That one moment of kindness had massive repercussions and, even now, I still couldn't bear to think about them.

SAMANTHA

Present day

I picked up a crate and gloves and made my way across to the black 4x4 parked in the middle of the farmyard. Nobody exited the car but the driver's window was wound down. A man in a dark suit, possibly in his early fifties, was in the driver's seat and a woman of a similar age dressed in a black dress was beside him, crying.

'We've got six baby hedgehogs for you,' the man said, his voice flat. 'They're in a box behind me.'

I put the crate down, opened the back door, lifted the box out of the footwell and peered inside. Six hoglets were nestled among several folds of kitchen towel.

'Where did you find them?' I asked, closing the car door.

'We were driving out of the village on our way to a funeral when we spotted a family of hedgehogs by the side of the road,' the man said. 'It looked as though they might cross at any minute so we stopped.'

'And then that idiot zoomed past on his killing machine,' the woman cried.

The man sighed. 'We were about to get out of the car to alert any other approaching vehicles when someone whizzed past on his motorbike.'

'He killed their mum.' The woman broke down sobbing.

The man nodded to confirm it and my heart broke for them. Imagine being on the way to a funeral – an emotional moment anyway – and witnessing that.

He took a deep breath. 'A neighbour doing some gardening saw it and she got the box and said we should bring the little ones to you as they wouldn't survive without their mum.'

'She's right. They're too young to fend for themselves. I'm sorry you had to see that.'

'Thank you. We have to go. Do you need anything else from us?'

I didn't want to delay them further by having a conversation about where to release the hoglets. 'No, that's fine. Thank you so much for bringing them in.'

I clutched the cardboard box to my side and waved them off, a sadness in my heart. What a waste of life. The hoglets were a good size but, even if they were healthy, it didn't necessarily mean they'd survive. The trauma of seeing their mum wiped out like that could still kill them. I needed to get them inside and on heat pads to warm them up. It was a good job I'd prepared everything for the school visits well in advance because six hoglets to treat was going to take up quite some time.

Back in the barn, I plugged in the heat pads then set to work weighing and checking the hoglets. There were four females and two males so, sticking with the literary classics, I chose the Brontë family for my theme. We already had a hoglet called Charlotte, named after Josh's grandma, so I went for Anne, Emily and Brontë for the girls plus Cathy from *Wuthering Heights*. I christened the boys Branwell – the brother in the Brontë family – and Heathcliff.

Five of the hoglets were a good weight but Cathy was quite a bit lighter so I'd need to keep an eye on her. There were no signs of infestation on any of them, although Brontë had a fresh scratch on her stomach so my priority needed to be Cathy and Brontë.

The arrival of the hoglets meant I didn't have time to go over to the farmhouse to check on Chloe and Samuel. In some ways, that was a blessing. I wanted to go into the first school visit feeling happy and excited instead of feeling upset after yet another confrontation with my cousin, and she needed some space to gather her thoughts.

Beth had texted me to say that they were organised before Paul left for work again so he'd been able to carry Archie downstairs and I needn't worry about going back over and helping them.

* * *

The first group of thirty children from Bentonbray Primary School were expected at 1.30 p.m. and Fizz was due an hour before to run through the final plans. I headed over to the farmhouse at noon to grab a sandwich before she arrived.

As I passed the lounge window, I noticed Beth on the sofa with Lottie on her knee and Archie tucked in beside her, watching *Tele-tubbies*. They looked so adorable all snuggled up together and I pictured a scene like that with Josh and our children. The idea of motherhood turning me into a carbon copy of my mum terrified me – irrational though I knew that was – but Connie was studying counselling and her supervisor had found me a counsellor who'd be able to help me. My first session was scheduled for a fortnight's time, after the school visits were done and dusted, and I was eager to get started.

I poked my head round the lounge door. 'Hi, everyone.'

Beth turned her head and smiled. 'Hi. Are you all set?'

'I think so. We had six hoglets arrive so that's kept me busy this morning. Luckily Josh and I laid out the tables and chairs last night. I've just popped back for a sandwich. Do you want one?'

'Chloe's making me one.'

My eyes widened. 'What? Are you serious?'

'She's in the kitchen right now. She asked if I'd like a sandwich and whether I thought you'd like one too. She even apologised for having a go at me the other day. I think she might have had her rock-bottom moment. Things should hopefully move forward from this point.'

'Let's hope they do. Do you need anything before I go back to the barn?'

'We're fine, thanks. Good luck. Not that you need it. You'll be brilliant.'

I gave her a grateful smile then closed the lounge door. Chloe making not just me but Beth a sandwich? That was certainly unexpected.

I stepped into the kitchen and, sure enough, Chloe was at the kitchen table chopping cucumber and tomatoes onto a board while Samuel, in his bouncer in the middle of the huge table, sucked on his Peter Rabbit comforter.

'Perfect timing,' she said looking up and smiling. 'Is ham salad okay?'

'Ham salad's great. Thank you.'

'You're welcome. Beth said you have a school visit this afternoon and someone called Fizz is helping you. Do you think she'll want a sandwich?'

'Erm... she might. She's coming straight from university so she might not get a chance to eat.'

'I'll do you a couple of buns each. Unless this Fizz is vegetarian.'

'No, she's not. This is really good of you.'

'Someone pointed out to me yesterday that I haven't been pulling my weight.'

'Chloe, I—'

'It's fine. You were right. I've emptied the dishwasher but I wasn't sure where some of the things lived so I've put them on the side. I thought the least I can do is make everyone some lunch.'

'It's really appreciated. How are you feeling today? Have the meds kicked in?'

'I'm feeling better than I've done in weeks. Samuel slept for four hours between his last two feeds and I actually got some sleep.'

Chloe raved about how amazingly helpful Hannah had been while I put the pots away in the right cupboards. She sounded so much more positive and I could see glimpses of the fun-loving woman she used to be as she talked.

She loaded a tray with mine and Fizz's lunch and pushed it towards me. 'Off you go. Good luck this afternoon.'

'Thank you.'

'I'm going out after lunch,' she called as I stepped into the hall. 'I'm meeting someone.'

I turned to face her, my interest piqued. 'James?' I tried not to sound too hopeful but I couldn't help it.

'No. I'm meeting your mum. She texted me. I thought you should know.'

'Where are you meeting her?'

'April's Tea Parlour.'

'Was that your suggestion or hers?' I knew I was punishing myself by asking but I'd only speculate and assume the worst if I didn't.

Chloe grimaced. 'It was hers. But don't go reading anything into that. She probably doesn't want to get under your feet.'

I could tell from the lack of eye contact that she was lying but I liked that she was trying to protect me. 'You don't need to sugar coat it. She doesn't want to risk bumping into me and that's fine. The last experience at your house wasn't exactly pleasant. We agreed on no relationship and she's simply upholding her part of the deal.'

'Please don't be upset.'

'I'm not upset. I've spent too much of my life being upset by what Mum does or doesn't do or say. I hope you have a good chat. Maybe she'll be able to help you. I'd better get over to the barn. I'll see you later.'

As I wandered over to the barn with the tray, I wondered whether Dad had spoken to Mum and asked her to have a word with Chloe or if she'd got in touch off her own back. I genuinely wasn't upset that she was seeing Chloe. If anything, I was pleased. Chloe and Mum had always had a strong relationship and Mum had acted as a go-between for Chloe and Auntie Louise during that difficult year at college. Maybe she'd get through to her. It was definitely worth a try. As for not meeting her at the farm, that *did* disappoint me. The other part of the deal we'd made was to be civil when our paths crossed. She'd been anything but civil when I saw her at Chloe's last month and she'd decided to completely avoid me this time. On a positive note, at least it meant I could relax this afternoon; or as much as I could with thirty children to take care of. If I'd known Mum was in my house or garden, I'd have been in a turmoil.

* * *

'That was a good sandwich.' Fizz licked her fingers. 'Please thank your cousin for me. So do you like the T-shirt?'

'It's amazing. Your friend's very talented.'

She'd told me over lunch that a friend of hers, Robbie, was an architect with a sideline in illustrations. He'd drawn what Fizz called a 'hedgicorn' – a hedgehog with a sparkling unicorn horn protruding from the midst of its colourful spines.

I loved how Fizz knew exactly who she was and didn't care what anyone else thought of her pink hair and her colourful dress sense. She was unashamedly proud of her passion for unicorns – the sparklier the better – and had a wardrobe full of unicorn-themed clothes. Her vibrant personality matched her clothes and five minutes in Fizz's company could cheer anyone up. Maybe I could introduce her to Chloe, although Chloe never warmed to my friends so maybe not.

'Robbie's done a few other designs and I've got some prices for bulk-printing if you ever wanted to consider some merch. Could be good for funds, especially if we do more school visits.'

I smiled at her. 'You're a never-ending supply of brilliant ideas.'

'I try my best. I'll email you the details tonight and you can look at them whenever you have a chance. No rush. So, talk me through the final plans for this afternoon.'

Fizz followed me upstairs where she was going to be based with half the group. It would be easier for me to stay on the ground floor in case any rescue hogs arrived.

'You'll be running the crafts we discussed up here.' I indicated her table, laid out with all the materials needed. We'd come up with a range of hedgehog-themed activities suitable for the various age groups.

Downstairs, I was running the more educational side of the visit, showing the children where the hedgehogs slept and discussing the reasons they might need to come to us, making sure it wasn't too graphic for the little ones. I also had a couple of hands-on activities, creating a comfortable hedgehog bed for inside and a hedgehog feeding station for outside (hoping they'd then feel inspired to create the latter if they had a garden at home) and a fun quiz involving them moving to a different wall depending on which of four answers they thought were correct.

'I think they're going to love it,' Fizz said as we made our way back downstairs for a drink before the minibus arrived. 'Let's hope they all learn something and can play their part in saving our little hedgehogs.'

A couple of minutes later, we sat down at the treatment table with mugs of tea.

'I've confirmed dates for stem cell testing at university and the TEC,' Fizz said. 'Just waiting to hear back from the sixth form.'

'That's brilliant news. Thank you so much for organising that.'

'Absolute pleasure. Obviously I'm hoping we can get a match for Josh's dad but I keep thinking of all those extra names on the donor register who could be a match for someone else.' She took a noisy slurp from her tea. 'Oh, and my brother says he'll take a test. He's also a leader for the local Young Farmers' Club so he's going to raise it at their meeting next week.'

'That's amazing. Thank you. What's your brother called?'

She rolled her eyes at me. 'Wait till you hear this. You know how I hate my real name – Felicity? That's nothing compared to what my brother got saddled with. He's called Barnaby. Even our parents admit they don't know what they were thinking. Everyone calls him Barney. Mildly better but still makes a twenty-eight-year-old sound like a pensioner.'

We'd finished our drinks and Fizz was washing the mugs at the sink when the minibus arrived. 'They're here!' she called.

I took a deep breath to quell a last-minute explosion of nerves and we both stepped outside to greet the teachers, supervising parents and children.

I dressed Samuel in a cute pair of navy dungarees with a yellow tractor on the bib, which I'd forgotten I had. Not wanting Auntie Debs to think I'd lost a grip on everything, I pulled on a pair of jeans and one of my favourite summery tops. I straightened my hair and applied some make-up while Samuel watched me wide-eyed from his bouncer, probably wondering who this stranger was in place of his normally dishevelled mummy.

'Are you ready to see your Great-Auntie Debs?' I lifted him out of his bouncer, wrapped him in a cardigan, then picked up my handbag and his changing bag.

There was a minibus parked in the farmyard alongside the barn and I could hear children laughing inside. I wondered what Sam had organised for them and whether she'd struggled with ideas. I'd have enjoyed helping her if I'd known about the visit. How bad was it that the first I knew was Beth telling me earlier? I couldn't blame Sam for that. It was my fault for shutting her out.

I strapped Samuel into the car then clambered into the driver's seat. A sweet peachy aroma hit me. I hadn't noticed it when I drove to my medical appointment yesterday. Sniffing the air and looking round, I spotted an air freshener attached to the air vent and another one hanging from the rearview mirror and tears rushed to my eyes. Sam must have put them in the car this morning. Only she would think to do something like that. I gasped. Oh, no! I *still* hadn't thanked her for cleaning it and she'd even mentioned it yesterday. How had I failed to do that twice? No wonder she was so clearly losing her patience with me.

* * *

I hadn't felt nervous about meeting Auntie Debs but, as soon as I drove past the village sign for Great Tilbury, nerves snaked through me and I shuddered.

I remembered April's Tea Parlour opening. I must have been about ten at the time. My grandparents lived in nearby Little Tilbury and they'd often taken Sam and me there for a lemonade and a cake when we visited. The last time I'd been to April's had been after Sam and I finished our GCSEs. Nanna was still with us and I hadn't yet met Travis. It had been such a good afternoon, full of laughter, as we celebrated freedom from school and spoke excitedly about the long summer ahead of us and starting college that September. Back then, I could never have predicted what was about to happen.

I spotted Auntie Debs's car parked alongside the village green and pulled up behind it.

'Time to face the past,' I told Samuel as I unbuckled him. 'Sam's right. I can't stay at Hedgehog Hollow forever and I don't want to keep you away from your daddy. I'm going to have to tell him what's going on.' I glanced towards the café. 'Unless Auntie Debs says not to.' I couldn't help hoping that would be the case.

I grabbed the bags and closed the car door. No. That really

wasn't an option. If I didn't tell James, someone else was going to. There was no doubt in my mind about that. I'd seen the emails.

* * *

April's Tea Parlour had been completely refurbished since my last visit. Death-by-pine-furniture and chintz patterns had been replaced with restful white furniture accented by pink, baby blue and mint green paint colours, accessories and crockery. The place looked much classier and bigger and I was so astounded by the change that it took me a moment to realise that someone had spoken to me.

I turned to a young blonde woman wearing a mint green apron over a white shirt. 'Sorry, miles away. It's been a long time since I've been in here. It looks so different.'

'It's gorgeous, isn't it?' she said, beaming. 'It's my mum's. I'm Daisy.'

I suddenly felt much older than my twenty-nine years. When I'd last been in, Daisy had been a five-year-old girl with curly blonde hair.

'It's really pretty.' I craned my neck to see into the next room. Most of the tables were occupied but I couldn't see Auntie Debs. Maybe she'd gone for a walk first. 'I'm meeting my auntie. It's Debbie Wishaw.'

'I'll take you to your table. Your auntie's here but I believe she's nipped to the bathroom.' She nodded towards Samuel. 'Do you need a high-chair or is he a bit small?'

'A bit small still but thanks.'

I dumped the bags on the floor, removed Samuel from his car seat, then sat down with my back to the room; less chance of anyone overhearing my side of the conversation that way. The table nearest to ours was unoccupied so we should be able to talk.

Auntie Debs emerged through a louvred door and smiled as she spotted me. I did a double-take every time I saw her these days. Mum and Auntie Debs are identical twins but I swear that, until recently, Auntie Debs looked at least a decade older, her forehead always bearing a deep frown, her heavy-framed glasses hiding eyes laden with sadness. She wore minimal make-up, kept her brown hair long and unkempt, and she only ever dressed in dark, drab colours. Now her hair was layered into shoulder-length waves with some chestnut highlights, she wore make-up, she'd ditched the glasses for contacts and her wardrobe burst with colour and floral patterns.

Over the years, I'd wondered whether her prematurely ageing appearance was my fault for involving her in my mess but the change since splitting up with Uncle Jonathan reassured me it wasn't. Or at least it wasn't *just* down to me. The change in physical appearance might make her look more like Mum's twin than her big sister but the transformation wasn't complete. Her eyes didn't sparkle like Mum's and the frown remained. She still had a burden to bear. Mine.

I stood up as she approached the table and eagerly accepted her hug, taking care not to squish Samuel.

'I thought you might stand me up,' she said when we broke apart. She took Samuel from me and kissed his cheek as we both sat down.

'I considered it.'

She nodded. 'I'm glad you came.'

'Does Mum know you're here?'

'Of course. You know I don't keep secrets from your mum.'

I raised my eyebrows at her.

'Except that one,' she added. 'She sends her love.'

'Did she tell you what happened on Monday?'

'Yes.'

'Was she upset?' I hoped she'd say no. I hadn't meant to upset Mum. I never meant to upset anyone, yet I always seemed to.

'I think she was more upset with herself than she was with you. She says you've been keeping in touch by text.'

I nodded. I never had anything to report but I sent her a text, as promised, morning and evening to let her know we were okay.

Auntie Debs frowned as she glanced round the café. 'It's busier than I expected. I'm not sure we'll be able to talk in here.'

That was fine by me. I was more than happy to delay.

Daisy appeared to take our order. I hadn't even glanced at the menu but Auntie Debs asked for a pot of tea and a cheese scone which sounded good to me so I ordered the same.

When Daisy left, Auntie Debs lifted Samuel up so she could get a good look at him. 'I'm sure he's grown since I last saw him.'

'He probably has.'

'And you've lost weight. Perhaps we should have ordered you something more substantial.'

'I'm fine. Just not had much appetite recently, for obvious reasons.'

An elderly couple were shown to the table closest to us. Auntie Debs scowled. 'Definitely can't talk,' she whispered.

Over tea and scones, we made small talk and reminisced about what April's used to look like. Samuel was a bit squirmy but swapping him between us seemed to settle him.

Daisy returned to clear our table and ask if we wanted anything else.

'Just the bill, thanks,' Auntie Debs said.

When she'd gone, Auntie Debs lowered her voice. 'The reason you left. It's got something to do with what happened back then, yes?'

My jaw tightened and my stomach moved into spin cycle. 'Yes. And I think it's about to catch up with me.'

'How?'

I glanced to my side, aware that the elderly couple were eating in silence so could potentially tune into everything we discussed. 'Not here.'

'Shall we go for a walk when we've paid?'

'Samuel's buggy's still at home.' There'd been no way I could have fit that in the car alongside everything else.

'There are benches round the village green. We can sit on one of those.'

* * *

We didn't make it as far as the benches. We'd only taken a dozen paces when Auntie Debs asked the question that had obviously been burning inside her: 'Does James know what happened?'

I stopped walking. 'No, but I think he's about to find out.' I shuddered. 'Just when I had everything I'd ever wanted; it's all going to disappear. I know I have to tell him myself. It's better he hears it from me but...' My shoulders slumped and I couldn't stop the tears. 'I don't want my marriage to be over.'

'You don't know that it will be.'

I swiped at my tears. 'You didn't see his face at the airport before our honeymoon. He was so angry and disappointed with me for how I'd been with Sam. He said he didn't recognise me and he walked away. It nearly ended then. What I did to Sam was nothing compared to what I did way back. He's not just going to walk out. He's going to run as fast as he can and who could blame him?' I stroked one of Samuel's tiny hands, my heart breaking as he curled it round my finger. 'And he might take Samuel away from me, although I probably deserve that.'

'It won't come to that.'

'It might.' And who could blame him? My actions all those years ago didn't exactly scream perfect mother material. 'How do I even begin to explain it to him?'

'I think the best thing is to try it on someone else first. And seeing as you've moved in with her, I'm thinking Samantha's the logical choice. Although I think you already know that and perhaps that's why you ran to her.'

I nodded. Not consciously, perhaps, but she was right. 'Will you come with me?'

'No, Chloe. I can't do that. Samantha and I... I'll support you in any way I can. I'll be there when you tell your mum if you want. I'll even be there when you tell James but me being there when you tell Samantha adds an unnecessary complication.'

'Please. I need you with me and...' I took a deep breath. 'The thing is, I haven't been completely honest with you. There are things you don't know.'

'What sort of things?'

I looked round. The village wasn't busy but there were people about. 'Someone might hear.'

She stared at me, frowning. I could imagine her head spinning with possibilities as to what I'd kept from her. Then she sighed. 'I guess we'd better get up to the farm, then.'

'You mean it? You'll come with me?'

'I'll come with you. But only because I'm worried about what it is that I don't know.'

She was right to worry.

29

Thirteen years ago

It was difficult finding time to see Travis around our shifts – especially during our first full week together when my hours were stretched to fit in my cleaning shifts and volunteering at the kids' club – but we somehow managed it.

It helped that he had a caravan on site. There was a section of the holiday park which housed some older caravans providing staff accommodation for anyone who worked late shifts and, as the owner's grandson, Travis had exclusive use of one. He gave me a spare key and, if he was on an 8 p.m. finish, I'd let myself in at the end of my working day and watch TV until his shift was over.

Every moment we spent together, I fell a little deeper in love with him and, although neither of us had said it aloud, I was sure he felt the same. Finding Maud Pickles dead had been traumatic but it had led me to Travis; the best thing to ever happen to me. Nanna used to always say 'everything happens for a reason' and now I understood why.

Scarlett had nipped up to the bar to check out Travis the day after our first date, like she'd said she would, and had gushed at the end of the shift about how hot he was. I noticed Lorna giving her dirty looks but Scarlett just turned her back on her and continued to rave about Travis.

After that, she wanted to know every little detail about our time together, but it didn't go unnoticed that she never asked in front of Lorna. There was tension between them and I wondered whether Lorna had said something to Scarlett after her mysterious warning to me and they'd had a bust-up about it.

On the Wednesday morning, six days after I started seeing Travis, Scarlett and I pushed our carts down to the caravans. It was A Level results day and Lorna had booked the day off so she and Seb could celebrate. Scarlett wasn't bothered about her results. She already knew she'd flunked a couple of her exams and was planning to take a year out and do re-sits. Mr Bowes had said she could continue working there full-time although, from what she'd told me, her parents were loaded and she worked out of boredom rather than financial need.

'I presume Travis has had other girlfriends?' she asked me.

'Quite a few.'

'And he's not all pure and innocent like you and Lorna?'

'He's not a virgin if that's what you're asking.'

She smiled mischievously. 'And you're not *completely* pure and innocent, are you? You may not have done the deed but you've done other stuff.'

'Yes but, as I've told you before, I'm not giving you all the graphic details. I don't like talking about stuff like that.'

'From what you've said, Travis will have aced his A levels. I'm thinking he might appreciate a congratulations blowjob.'

'Scarlett!'

'Oh, don't be such a prude. You've done it before. Although maybe not the Scarlett way...'

Cheeks blazing, I was torn between sticking my fingers in my ears or asking her to elaborate. But when she started rummaging on her cleaning cart for demonstration aids, I couldn't take it anymore and sped off with my cart, mortified, her laughter following me down the path.

Problem was, it was all that I could think about all morning while I cleaned. Travis was working from 2 p.m. but he'd told me he'd meet me in the caravan on my lunch break so he could tell me his results.

Three As and a B were seriously impressive and, from Travis's response, so was my choice of celebration. I might not have had tuition in 'the Scarlett way' but I felt sure she'd have been proud of me.

A week later, it was my turn to get my GCSE results, although they weren't anywhere near as impressive as Travis's – other than my A in drama. I'd also started working full-time in the kids' club after a successful trial so we had two things to celebrate.

Travis swapped shifts so he could have the evening free and, with his grandparents away, he suggested we go down to their private beach for a barbeque. He lit a fire and, after we'd eaten burgers cooked on disposable barbeques, we toasted marshmallows over the flames while the sun went down. He'd strung some twinkly fairy lights across the front of the beach hut which, along with the glow from the fire and solar lights round the edge of the cove, gave the beach such a magical romantic feel.

It was hard to believe we'd only been together for a fortnight. It felt as though he'd been in my life for years – a best friend who I could talk to about anything and who understood me.

Darkness fell and we snuggled together, gazing at the stars, listening to the gentle lap of the waves against the shore.

Travis took my hand in his and lightly kissed it, then he looked up at me with such tenderness in his eyes. 'I've never said this to anyone before but I love you, Chloe. I know it hasn't been long but, as I said on our first date, I knew you were going to be special.'

'I love you, too. And I've never said that to anyone either because I've never felt it before.'

His lips met mine with a kiss burning with passion. When he took me by the hand, led me into the beach hut and onto the bed, my heart raced. This was it. My first time in love, my first time having someone love me, and my very first time. I knew there was no expectation but I wanted him as much as he wanted me. The moment felt right and, embarrassing as it had been to listen to tales of Scarlett's sexual exploits, her lessons had gone in.

Travis and I were inseparable after that night. I met his grandparents, his mum and his sister, Genevieve, who was home from university for the summer, and they all warmly welcomed me to the family.

Mum and Dad said they liked him but I appreciated it was difficult to form a proper opinion from a few snatched minutes when he dropped me home, as he always needed to get back to work. I didn't mind, though. There'd be plenty of time for them to get to know him in the future.

As August gave way to September, everything felt perfect in my world. I loved my job at the kids' club, I was head over heels in love with my gorgeous boyfriend and, although I'd not met his scary-sounding dad, the introductions to both sides of the family had gone well.

I was dreading starting college because it meant our routine would be different but Travis promised me nothing would change between us. We wouldn't be able to see each other during the day but I could base myself in his caravan on evenings and weekends and do my coursework so I could see him during his breaks and after his shift finished. I even stayed over a few times and he rose early to drop me off at college in the morning. Mum and Dad weren't too keen on that but it would have been hypocritical if they'd kicked up a fuss as they'd got together when they were fifteen.

Despite my reservations, I settled in at college. I loved my course and made some new friends. It was amazing how the wary attitudes I was used to from females changed when they knew I had a serious boyfriend and was no threat to any relationship they might be in.

Sammie turned seventeen in mid-October and we went out for a family meal, which finally gave me the opportunity to properly introduce Travis to my family. I could see they all instantly warmed to him. Just as well because he was going to be around long-term.

My love for Travis grew deeper and, as we moved towards the October half-term, he talked about deferring his travel plans. His Uncle Chris's children were quite a bit younger than Travis so there was no immediate rush for him to leave Kellerby Cliffs Holiday Park to make way for them.

'I was thinking that I could work here for another two years,' he said as we cuddled up in bed in the caravan on the Friday night after college finished for the half-term holiday. 'I'm sure Uncle Chris would let me take on more responsibilities to get some good experience. Then we could travel together after you've finished college. What do you think?'

My heart raced. 'You'd really wait for me? You were so excited about going travelling.'

'I know, but I'd miss you too much to properly enjoy it. Two more years would give us more time to plan and more time to save. Will you be my travel-buddy?'

'Oh, my God, Travis! I'd love to.' I threw myself at him and kissed him passionately. I'd been hoping he'd say something like that. It felt like the ultimate confirmation of how much he loved me, willing to put his plans on hold just for me.

And so it was decided. I'd finish college, working at the kids' club at the holiday park during the holidays – something Mr Bowes had already agreed to – then Travis and I would travel the world together.

Mum and Dad, Auntie Debs and Sammie all urged caution. We were young. He was my first serious boyfriend. It might not last. What did they know? We were deeply in love and perfect for each other so there was absolutely no reason why the relationship would end.

I genuinely believe we would have lasted. We would have travelled the world. We would have married and had kids. We would have been happy.

If it hadn't been for Scarlett and her 'great idea'.

Twelve and a half years ago

Mr Bowes welcomed me back to my job in Kellerby Kids' Club for October half-term. On the first Saturday, I reported for duty and was stunned to see Scarlett wearing the bright yellow polo shirt worn by the kids' club staff.

'Surprise!' she cried, rushing up to hug me.

'What are you doing here? I thought you couldn't stand kids.'

'Ssh!' She pulled me to one side. 'I wanted to spend time with you. It's been lonely here since you bogged off to college and Lorna sodded off to uni with Saint Seb. So when I heard someone had dropped out last minute, I told Mr Bowes I adored children and would be happy to step in. It was easier for him to find cleaning cover for a week than someone reliable to work here so I did a two-day trial last week and here I am to brighten up your half-term.' She planted her hands on her hips and glowered at me. 'Can't you pretend you're pleased to see me?'

I smiled at her. 'Sorry. I am. You just really surprised me but it's a good surprise. It'll be fun.' And I was confident it would be, as long as she kept the X-rated conversations away from innocent ears. She really didn't strike me as kids' club material.

I hadn't seen Scarlett since starting college but we'd stayed in touch by text and social media. I was Facebook friends with Lorna but we never phoned or texted and I suspected we wouldn't stay in touch long-term. She'd definitely pulled away from me after I lost my virginity. She'd pulled away from Scarlett, too. I got why. There'd been so much I wanted to learn and Scarlett had the answers and Lorna didn't.

'Can we have lunch together?' Scarlett asked.

'I'm meeting Travis.'

'And I'm meeting Greg.'

'Who's Greg?'

'One of the lifeguards. He started here just after you left and he's mmm mmm mmm. Had to bag him before anyone else got their grubby mitts on him.'

'He's your boyfriend?'

'Be off with you! My boyfriend? I'm not you or bloody Lorna-Closed-Legs devoted to one man only. But he is a regular feature. Although he's far from regular. Large. Maybe even extra-large.'

I laughed. Those sort of discussions didn't embarrass me anymore. 'Well, I'm very pleased for you and your extra-large lifeguard.'

'So can all four of us be all disgustingly couply and have lunch together?'

'I suppose so. But not every day. I hardly get any time with Travis as it is.'

But it did become a regular thing when Travis's shifts allowed and, actually, it was fun. Travis and Greg got on immediately and it felt very grown up having a couples lunch, even though Scarlett was adamant she and Greg weren't exclusive and 'couple' was a label she never wanted.

Scarlett seemed really pally with Travis, which surprised me.

She laughed loudly when I mentioned it. 'You're not jealous, are you?'

'No. It's just that I didn't realise you knew each other so well.' I'd managed to introduce them during the summer but it had been brief.

'We didn't but I got transferred to the clubhouse cleaning team in late September and, on the back of that, I picked up some bar shifts. I thought I'd told you that. Maybe I didn't. Anyway, he's a good laugh and, oh, my God, is he hot?' She fanned her face with her hand. 'If he wasn't already taken...'

I laughed as I playfully nudged her. 'Well, he is, so keep your mitts off.'

'We could always share.'

'Erm, I don't think so. You've got Greg. He's hot too, so you can stick with him.'

Mum and Dad agreed to let me stay with Travis for the week as long as I rang home every night after work – which I dutifully did – so I didn't mind sharing our precious time together over lunch too much because I got him all to myself every night.

On the Saturday night at the end of half-term, Scarlett turned nineteen and the plan was to join her and Greg for a pub crawl in Fellingthorpe. It was a few days into November but really mild so Travis suggested we take some drinks down to his grandparents' beach instead. I had no objections. The cove was a special place and I loved spending time there.

I drank too much. We all did. Inevitably Scarlett steered the conversation round to sex. It started off pretty innocent – first kiss, first touch, first time – and moved onto best, worst and most embarrassing experiences. I had the least experience but I could still join in the conversation and it was hilarious listening to some of the anecdotes from Greg and Scarlett.

The more we drank, the more outrageous the stories seemed to get.

'Have any of you ever been attracted to anyone of the same sex?' Scarlett asked.

'Scarlett fancies women, too.' Greg grinned. 'She keeps promising me a threesome but hasn't delivered so far.'

She seductively pressed her fingers to his lips. 'I just need to find the right woman,' she purred. 'You can't rush these things.' She looked at me and Travis. 'Any attraction to the same sex?'

'Not me,' Travis said.

I shook my head.

'You'd love it,' she said, winking at me. 'What about you, Gregster? Fancy getting it on with another man?'

'That would be a no.'

Scarlett tutted. 'You three have no idea what you're missing and you...' she prodded Greg in the chest, '... have disappointed me. I thought you were up for anything.'

'I'm still up for a threesome. But with two women and *not* a woman and a man.'

Scarlett necked back the rest of her drink. 'Fantasies, then,' she announced. 'What's your ultimate sexual fantasy?'

'A threesome!' Greg cried, making us all laugh.

'I'm beginning to think the man might fancy a threesome,' Travis said. 'Put him out of his misery, Scarlett.'

'What about you, Chloe?' Scarlett asked. 'What's your fantasy? Does it involve me?'

It hadn't. I swear it hadn't but the moment she said it, I could picture Scarlett and me together. It didn't take much imagination as she'd stripped off in front of me in the changing rooms at work on plenty of occasions.

'Oh, my God! It does!' She squealed with laughter.

'It doesn't.'

'Liar! You're picturing you and me together right now.'

I glanced up at Travis but he was laughing along.

'So what if I am? It's only because you keep going on about it,' I protested.

'You could always kiss,' Greg suggested. 'I'm sure that would satisfy a few fantasies right here and now.'

I glanced at Travis again but he was still laughing. 'You won't hear any objections from me.'

And that's how it happened. That was the moment that changed my life forever. Because it didn't stop with kissing Scarlett on the beach. When she declared she had a 'great idea' – swapping partners – it genuinely *did* seem like a great idea at the time. Doesn't everything when your decisions are blurred by drink? If I'd had my wits about me, I might have remembered Lorna's warning. I might have thought about Scarlett's continual questions about Travis and her repeated declaration of how hot he was. But I didn't and that one decision had repercussions. Massive ones.

31

SAMANTHA

Present day

The school children had been with us for about forty minutes and it was going well. They were well-behaved, asked lots of questions and responded well to instructions including whispering to avoid frightening the hedgehogs, although we'd had a sticky moment. I'd forgotten how fascinated young children were by toileting. When I explained that I had to help the smallest hoglets go to the toilet by 'tickling their tummies' – a more child-friendly explanation for stimulating the bowels – there was an explosion of laughter.

We'd arranged for a biscuit and juice break before the two groups swapped over, which gave Fizz and me the opportunity to prepare for round two.

As I wiped down the treatment table there was a sudden loud bang. The light in the barn dimmed as, heart thumping, I spun round to face the window. Raw eggs were dripping down the glass.

'Fizz!' I cried, rushing towards the window.

'What's up?' she asked, breathlessly, as she appeared by my side.

'Can you put the hoglets in a crate under the table?'

'Which hoglets?'

What a weird question. 'The ones we're feeding.'

'We're not feeding any. Are you okay, Sam? What are you looking at?' Her voice was full of concern.

'The eggs.'

Fizz squinted in the direction of the window then linked her arm through mine.

'We'll be back in two minutes,' she called cheerfully towards the back of the barn. 'Just need to check on something.'

We stepped out of the barn and Fizz closed the door. I blinked in the bright sunlight, feeling completely disorientated.

Fizz stood in front of me, frowning. 'Are you okay, Sam? What just happened?'

I rubbed my temples. This was so weird. It had been dark in the barn, yet it was daylight now. I ran down the side of the barn towards the window. No eggs. Clean.

Fizz ran after me.

'I heard a bang,' I told her, reaching out and touching the glass to make sure my eyes weren't deceiving me.

'It was me. I dropped a ream of paper on the floor.'

I crouched down and rested my back against the barn as I looked up at Fizz. "It seemed so real, like I was re-living that night. I thought it was Connor Grimes and his mate again.'

'They're behind bars.' She crouched down in front of me, her brow furrowed. 'Do you want me to call Josh?'

'No. I'll be fine. I'm just a bit jumpy at the minute. Best go back inside before the teachers think they've been abandoned.'

'Are you sure?'

I stood up and took a deep breath. 'Early night for me, I think. Thanks, Fizz.'

As we entered the barn, the children didn't pay much attention but the teachers and parents looked towards us expectantly.

'Sorry for dashing out!' I called, striding across the barn towards them. 'We thought there was a hedgehog emergency coming but it was a false alarm.' I smiled brightly although I didn't feel very bright, butterflies waltzing in my stomach. 'Three minutes and then we'll get started again.'

Returning to the treatment table, I rested my hands on it and gulped, fighting back the tears. What just happened? The barn had gone dark. I'd seen the eggs on the window. I'd even been able to smell the formula we fed to the hoglets. The nightmares were bad enough without re-living the attacks during the day. Terrifying.

* * *

I turned to Fizz as we waved the minibus off. 'Is it just me or was that ninety minutes more exhausting than a normal full day?' My half-time incident certainly hadn't helped. There'd been no further occurrences but I'd felt on edge and it was tiring trying to look and sound bright and cheerful when I felt far from it.

She smiled. 'Not just you. I'm pooped. And we have it all to do again tomorrow.'

I held my face in my hands in mock-horror. 'And twice next week.'

'Argh! Don't remind me.'

We moved back into the barn to feed the hoglets, which needed to be the priority before clearing everything away.

'How are you feeling?' Fizz asked when we'd each settled with a hoglet in our hands.

'A bit unnerved but I'm sure it's nothing a good night's sleep won't sort out.'

Fizz's phone buzzed with a text while we were between litters of hoglets.

'It's my brother, Barney,' she said, picking it up. 'He's asking me for six tests. That's awesome.'

'Brilliant news. You said your brother runs your grandparents' farm?'

'Yeah. It's been passed down through the generations and it's all Barney's ever wanted to do.'

'You weren't interested?'

'It wasn't for me. I've got no interest in the behind-the-scenes stuff and it wouldn't have been fair to have a share but expect Barney to manage all that. It's how it should be with him in sole charge. I just wish he could meet someone who shares his passions.'

'He's single, then?'

She sighed. 'He keeps choosing women who couldn't be more wrong for him. They see the big house and the land and they imagine he's loaded so they'll live this romantic lifestyle. The reality is that he works bloody long hours in all weathers, the air smells of shit and anyone in Barney's life is going to have to grab some wellies and an overall and muck in. I don't know how many times I've told him to go for someone from a farming background but he's always drawn to flashy women with long, blonde hair in tight dresses and high heels. Couldn't be more incompatible as a farmer's wife. You don't know anyone suitable, do you?'

I pondered for a moment then shook my head. 'He'd probably fall for my cousin Chloe if he met her because she's exactly what you've described as his ideal woman, but she's ha...' I stopped. I'd been about to say 'happily married' but it was far from that at the moment. 'She's married with a new baby. I don't really know many women in the area yet, but I'll let you know if I have a brainwave.'

'Please do. I'm going to sound like our mum here but I worry about him all alone in that huge house. He's got the dogs but it would be lovely if he could have someone special.'

'And what about you?' I asked, spotting the perfect lead-in opportunity. 'Anyone special in your life?'

'Not at the moment. My ex-girlfriend, Nadine, dumped me shortly after I turned twenty-five. She used to love my quirky style but she suddenly decided that hitting a quarter of a century meant it was time to start dressing sensibly. She bought me all these "grown-up" clothes for my birthday and made an appointment for me to get my hair – which was purple at the time – dyed brown. I was so shocked that I went along with it but, the moment I sat in the salon chair, I came to my senses. I wasn't going to let anyone dictate my style so I walked out of the salon with bright red hair and Nadine walked out of my life.'

'Aw, Fizz. That's awful. But it sounds like you're better off without her.'

'I am, although I didn't think that at first. I was devastated. Then I had my little lottery win and guess who suddenly wanted me back? She turned up at the cat shelter where I worked with a huge bouquet of flowers and a list of ideas of how we could spend the money. I do literally mean she'd prepared a list and printed it out. Who does that? It was then that I realised what a lucky escape I'd had.'

'Good for you. You can't change who you are just to please someone else, otherwise you're going to end up miserable.'

'Exactly! That's why I worry so much about Barney. He keeps hoping these women will change for him. It's not going to work. Someone who loves fancy clothes, fine dining and expensive holidays is unlikely to transition into being a farmer's wife. I'd love for someone to prove me wrong, though.'

I swapped over to my next hoglet. 'By the way, I've got a work experience student from the TEC starting on Monday for two weeks, so we'll have another pair of hands at next week's school visits. His name's Zayn Hockley.'

'I know Zayn. He goes to Young Farmers. Nice lad and, once he's comfortable around someone, he never shuts up, so consider yourself warned.'

'Thanks for the tip.'

I took it as a compliment that he'd been so chatty yesterday. He obviously felt comfortable around me, which boded well for a fortnight together.

Vanessa had arranged to visit on Friday morning to go through the paperwork and she'd repeatedly assured me I wouldn't have too much additional work to do, but Chloe's negative reaction kept weighing on me. I wasn't concerned about Zayn but was I trying to do too much too soon? Was this afternoon's incident proof of that?

'Zayn will have such an awesome time here,' Fizz said, as though sensing my concerns. 'You're such a brilliant teacher and you know so much.'

I smiled at her gratefully. I could do this. And if I did it really well, Zayn might even want to stay on as a volunteer. Fizz was right and Chloe was wrong. It was going to be great and this afternoon's incident was simply down to fatigue. I hoped.

32

I was washing up the mugs shortly after Fizz left, ready to go over to the farmhouse for some rest when, through the barn window, I spotted Chloe's car pulling into the farmyard. Another car followed hers and my stomach lurched. Mum! What was she doing here? Possibilities swam through my mind. She might have talked Chloe into going back to James and had come to help her move her stuff. Chloe might have convinced her to say 'hello' to me. Or perhaps Chloe had decided it was confession time and Mum had come to offer her moral support.

They parked side by side and got out. Chloe lifted Samuel out in his car seat and she and Mum spoke for a few moments before both glancing towards the barn. I swiftly stepped back from the window. A bit more discussion, then they strode purposefully in my direction.

I dashed round to the treatment table and opened my laptop in an effort to look like I was in the middle of something rather than spying on them.

The door opened and Chloe stepped inside. 'Hi Sam. Erm... I've got your mum with me. Have you got a bit of time?'

'Yeah, sure, come in.' I hoped I didn't sound too flustered. 'Do you want a drink?'

My stomach did a somersault at the sight of Mum. She looked so different – so beautiful – in a pair of pale blue cropped trousers and a chiffon white tunic top covered in blue flowers.

Mum shook her head.

'No, thanks,' Chloe said. 'We had a huge pot of tea this afternoon.'

'Okay. Well, come down, grab a seat.' I indicated the sofa bed.

'Samantha,' Mum said in a low voice as she passed, barely glancing at me.

'Hi, Mum. How've you been?'

'Fine, but we're not here to talk about me. Chloe has something to tell you and she insisted on having me with her.'

That was me told. I should have known that the idea of her coming to see me was a ridiculous notion. But was this confession time at last?

They both sat down and Chloe placed Samuel's car seat beside her. He was sound asleep. I carried a chair across from the treatment table and looked at Chloe expectantly. Her brow was furrowed and she chewed on her lip, clearly nervous, before drawing a deep breath.

'You remember my boyfriend, Travis?'

'Yes.' How could I forget him? They'd been besotted with each other and the whole family had liked him, so it had been a shock when Chloe announced it was over after about three months and an even bigger shock when she told us why. I wouldn't have had him pinned as a cheater, although what did I know? At that point, I'd never had a serious relationship.

'You remember why we split up?'

'Because he cheated on you with a friend from work. Scarlett, was it?'

'Good memory.' Chloe glanced at Mum, who nodded encouragingly. 'It wasn't quite how I told it. He did have sex with Scarlett but it wasn't really cheating because I knew about it and said it was okay.'

'You gave your boyfriend your approval to sleep with one of your friends?' I tried not to look or sound too astonished but this was unexpected information.

'Yes, and I had permission to be with her boyfriend in return.'

Mum looked down at the floor, her jaw tight, clearly uncomfortable with this.

'So what are we talking here? A one-off partner swap? A wild party?' I couldn't bring myself to say the term that had popped into my head.

'A stupid drunken discussion about fantasies that progressed into reality for a week or so.'

I didn't know what to say. Chloe had worked through a string of boyfriends over the years but Travis had been her first serious relationship. Going from losing her virginity to partner swapping seemed like a huge step after only a short time together. I was also struggling with what this had to do with her leaving James, but it must have some relevance or why share it?

'You were happy with this arrangement?' I asked, trying to keep any sort of judgement out of my voice. Not that I had any right to judge. People in love could make crazy choices. I'd been there myself, pretending I didn't love James and making out I was more than happy to continue seeing him until he found someone else with whom he found the missing chemistry.

'It seemed like a good idea at the time and it was meant to be a one-off. A bit of fun. But it didn't stay as the one time...'

Tears glistened in Chloe's eyes and I could feel the hurt and betrayal even now.

'Go on,' I encouraged. 'What happened next?'

I could never in a million years have predicted what she was about to tell me.

33

Twelve and a half years ago

Scarlett laughed at me when I said I wasn't comfortable continuing with our little arrangement. It was the Thursday evening twelve days after the 'great idea' and I'd been waiting at the table in Travis's caravan for him to finish his 8 p.m. shift but, as usual, Scarlett had turned up. She kept doing that. I hadn't minded the first couple of times but now it was really pissing me off. With schools back, staffing levels for the kids' club were at a minimum but she'd picked up extra work behind the bar. Her shifts often coincided with Travis's so there was no need for her to encroach on what precious time I had alone with him.

'Oh, my God, Chloe!' Scarlett dramatically tossed her long hair over her shoulder. 'Why are you making such an issue out of it? It's just a bit of fun. It means nothing.'

'Maybe not to you but Travis and I love each other and this doesn't feel right. It's like cheating.'

'How's it cheating when you both know about it?'

Her hard stare unnerved me and, even though I wanted to offer her a confident objection, I felt way out of my depth and lowered my eyes to the table. 'I'm sorry, but I want it to stop.' I'd only actually slept with Greg that one crazy night but suspected she'd laugh at me again if I shared that.

She tapped her long red nails on the table and tutted. 'I should have known you'd try to ruin things.'

I looked up and flinched at her narrowed eyes. 'I'm not! I just want things to go back to how they were before.'

She threw her head back and released a pantomime-villain-style cackle. 'Good luck with that! Don't you see? Things can *never* go back to how they were before.' Her voice softened and she gave me a sickly-sweet smile. 'Aw, it's adorable how naïve and innocent you are. You might look like you're eighteen but you're like a little twelve-year-old inside.'

My stomach lurched as she reached across the table and brushed a strand of my hair behind my ear.

'And so beautiful.' She sighed. 'Tell you what. Why don't we ditch Greg and you, me and Travis get it on instead?'

There was something about the teasing way she said it that wound me up and I couldn't help thinking that it was all about her wanting Travis.

I straightened my shoulders and held her gaze. 'Not gonna happen.'

'Why not? I bet Travis would love it.'

'Well, I wouldn't.'

'How do you know until you give it a try? You enjoyed our kiss.'

'I've tried enough new things recently. I just want it to go back to Travis and me from now on.'

'Travis doesn't know anything about this, does he?' she asked, raising a perfectly manicured eyebrow at me, a smug grin on her face.

'I'm going to talk to him about it tonight.'

She cackled again as she stood up and grabbed her bag. 'Good luck with that, too. You're going to need it.'

'Meaning?'

'Meaning I know that Travis enjoys our time together too much to want to let me go and I *definitely* won't be letting him go without a fight. If you want to play big girl games, you have to live with the consequences.' She gave me a sickening smirk then opened the caravan door. 'See you later. Or not. Whatever. But I *will* be seeing Travis again and you can't stop me.'

I twisted round on the sofa so I could see out of the window. My heart thumped as I watched Scarlett sashay along the well-lit pathway, her hips swaying. Had that been a threat?

My breath caught as Travis approached her. They stopped, exchanged a few words, then she snaked her arms round his neck and kissed him. I expected him to push her away, knowing I was waiting for him, but he responded, running his hands over her backside and pulling her closer. I'd never experienced the green-eyed monster before but seeing them together like that enraged me. It was bad enough thinking about what they might have been doing behind closed doors.

I raised my hand to knock furiously on the window but stopped myself. I wanted Scarlett to leave before I confronted Travis and me making a scene would give her the perfect excuse to return and ruin things. If they weren't already ruined.

They pulled apart eventually and Travis headed towards the caravan. Scarlett turned and blew a kiss towards me then did a deep bow with flourished arms like a lead performer at the end of a show. Watching her, I realised exactly how naïve I'd been. This had all been a game to her. Lorna had known it and she'd tried to warn me. Whether Scarlett's plan all along had been about snaring Travis or simply about messing with the two of us, I didn't know, but we'd played right into her hands.

'What's going on with you and Scarlett?' I demanded as soon as Travis closed the caravan door behind him.

'You know exactly what's going on. Same as what's going on between you and Greg.'

'That's crap! I don't spend every day hanging around Greg. I don't kiss Greg when I see him like you just kissed Scarlett.' I lowered my voice. 'It's gone too far. It needs to go back to just the two of us or...' I tailed off. I hadn't intended to make any threats.

'Or what?'

'Nothing,' I muttered.

'It's obviously not nothing or you wouldn't have said it. So out with it. What will happen if I keep seeing Scarlett?'

'I don't think we can be together.'

He leaned against the kitchen units, arms folded. 'So you're giving me an ultimatum because you're jealous of her?'

I ground my teeth. 'It's nothing to do with being jealous. It's about me and you. We love each other and we were happy together until Scarlett disrupted things. If you love someone, you should only want to be with them. Unless you don't really love me and you'd rather be with her.' The idea that I might have just spoken the truth made me feel sick. I could feel my cheeks burning as I nervously waited for Travis to speak and I cursed the tears that started to run down my cheeks.

His face softened as he perched on the edge of the seat opposite me, but he made no attempt to touch me. 'I don't get why you're crying. You agreed to this. I thought you were having fun with Greg.'

'Not really. Not after that first night.'

He frowned. 'So I'm not allowed to have any more fun with Scarlett because Greg's crap in bed.'

'I didn't say that.' I'd met up with Greg a couple of times but, sober, I couldn't convince myself it was a good idea. I'd hoped that, if I let him have his fun for a couple more weeks, Travis would have come to the same conclusion but clearly not.

I moved round the table to stand next to him. 'Can't we go back to how things were before?' I pleaded, running my hands down his chest towards his belt. 'We don't need Scarlett and Greg. We're great together and you know it.'

I tried to channel Scarlett's sexy sultriness, but it felt more like desperation as I undid the buckle on his work trousers. 'Why don't we put it down to a drunken mistake and move on without them?' My voice sounded more like a whine than a purr.

He didn't answer and I felt every shred of my dignity running towards the door. Was I really having to work this hard to convince the love of my life not to continue sleeping with my friend? How could that be right?

Scarlett's words echoed in my mind: 'I *definitely* won't be letting him go without a fight.' Well, neither would I. I couldn't channel Scarlett – too close for comfort – but I *could* play a part. I was good at acting. I'd be – I plucked a name out of nowhere – Chantel Delacroix, lady of the night, mistress of the bedroom.

I pressed my lips against his, biting his bottom lip. 'You're going to stop seeing Scarlett because there's nothing she can do for you that I can't.' Acting a part was a good idea. I felt stronger and more in control as I ran my hands down his chest again and unzipped his flies. 'With her, it's lust. With me, it's love.'

His breath came short and fast as I kissed him passionately and maybe I'd have managed to convince him if I'd shut up and let my hands and body do the talking. But Chantel Delacroix was gobby and always got what she wanted. 'And you'll stop seeing that bitch at work, too. She needs to be out of both of our lives completely.' The minute the words spilled out, the sharp intake of breath told me I'd gone too far.

'What?' Travis shoved me back, eyes wide, mouth open. 'She has shifts with me. I can't avoid her.'

Although the shove hadn't been rough, it had been completely out of character. In fact, everything about his behaviour tonight seemed different. Where was the Travis I'd fallen in love with? Was this Scarlett's influence?

'You could if she wasn't working here anymore,' I suggested, my character gone, the whine back in my voice.

'You're suggesting I sack her?'

'It would solve the problem. You once said why have relatives in high places if you can't benefit from it?' The latter was a feeble attempt at a joke. Completely ill-advised. But I did mean it and it would definitely solve the problem. It wasn't as though Scarlett would struggle financially. Her parents would bail her out.

'We'll forget you just said that,' Travis snapped, his eyes flashing with anger. 'In fact, let's forget about the whole thing. Why should I stop seeing Scarlett just because you order me to?'

'I didn't order you. I asked you.'

'Yeah, right.' He stood up, zipped up his trousers and fastened his belt. 'I'll drive you home.'

'You're kicking me out?' The tears started again.

'I think we need some time apart.'

He marched to the caravan door and thrust it open. A cold draft blew in a few leaves and I shivered as I pulled on my coat and scarf.

I struggled to keep pace with him on the way to the staff car park. What did 'time apart' mean? An evening? Or forever? It couldn't be over!

Silence prevailed all the way to Whitsborough Bay. Travis tightly gripped the steering wheel, staring straight ahead, mouth set, brow furrowed.

I tried to reason with him but he turned up the radio to drown me out. I didn't dare turn it down. I had no idea what to do. This was my first proper relationship and also my first meaningful argument. Was I meant to put it right now or would one of us say sorry tomorrow?

This was all bloody Scarlett's fault. I stared out of the window, replaying every conversation we'd ever had about Travis and, the more I thought about it, the more convinced I was that it had been about getting her claws into him and Lorna had known it.

He turned the radio down as he pulled into my street. Outside my house, he remained seated instead of opening the car door for me.

'I'm sorry,' I whispered. I wanted to ask him if he still loved me but I was too afraid to hear the answer. I opened the door but made no move to get out.

'You're letting the cold in.' He didn't look at me and, once more, I got that sense of not knowing him. His voice was as chilled as the air outside.

'Sorry.' I hastily pulled the door to as I unclipped my seatbelt. 'Are we okay?'

'What do *you* think?'

'I don't know. That's why I'm asking.'

He didn't answer although I suppose the silence was an answer in itself. I got out, closed the door, and gulped as he floored the accelerator and screeched down the street.

I couldn't face going inside and being bombarded with questions as to why I was home so early, especially when I had no answers. But I knew someone who might. I took my phone out of my bag and texted Lorna as I strode down the street:

✉ To Lorna
Hi. Hope uni is going well. I need to ask you something. You told me to watch out for Scarlett. What did you think she'd do?

I wasn't sure if she'd reply. We hadn't spoken since our last shift together in September – our only interaction since then being a few 'likes' on Facebook – but I hadn't even reached the end of the street when my phone started ringing.

'What's she done?'

'Persuaded Travis and me to swap partners with her and Greg, this lifeguard she's being seeing.'

The sharp intake of breath was unmistakable and I could picture Lorna's shocked face. Saying it aloud, I could see that things had progressed at an alarming rate.

'It was a huge mistake and I said I wanted it to end—'

'But she's not willing to let Travis go.' The blunt declaration suggested that Lorna had predicted this in the summer.

'Something like that.'

She sighed and her voice softened. 'Oh, Chloe. I tried to warn you.'

'Did she always plan to break us up?'

There was a pause and another sigh. 'Probably.'

'Why?'

'As I said to you before, she's a complicated person. I like the 'work' Scarlett. She works hard and she's great fun in small doses but there's a reason we never met up outside of work. She's not friend material. She only looks after number one and she uses people. Which you've just experienced first-hand.'

I'd reached a bench at the end of the street and slumped down onto it. 'I feel so stupid.'

I could hear someone calling her name in the background.

'Sorry. I'm off to the cinema with friends so I've got to go. Don't blame yourself. She's clever and I'm afraid you never stood a chance against her. What Scarlett wants, Scarlett gets.'

'Like my boyfriend.'

'Sorry.'

'Thanks for trying to warn me. I should have listened.'

Her name was called again. 'Take care,' she said gently. 'Bye.'

She disconnected the call and I tipped my head back and looked up at the stars. What Scarlett wants, Scarlett gets. She'd pretended it was me she was interested in but, all along, she'd wanted Travis and she'd got him.

I sat there for ten minutes or so until I couldn't feel my hands or feet for the cold. A storm was brewing and I could feel rain in the air. Best head home before the heavens opened. Would Travis regret throwing me out like that? Okay, so asking him to sack her was wrong of me but the rest of it wasn't unreasonable and surely he'd see that when he calmed down.

* * *

Mum and Dad were engrossed in a mini-series on the TV when I arrived home and didn't question my mumbled excuse that I'd needed to come back early because I'd forgotten one of my textbooks.

The storm broke as I made it upstairs, the wind howling round the house and the rain battering against my window.

I'd been seething in my room for about twenty minutes when a text arrived from Scarlett:

✉ From Scarlett
Best birthday gift ever. Check your email.
Thanks Chloe!

What was that supposed to mean? Stomach churning, I opened my emails. At the top of my inbox were three messages from Scarlett. I clicked on the one with the subject line 'Open me first' and gasped.

The image showed Travis on his bed in the caravan. He was wearing a deep red satin sleeping mask, his wrists secured to the headboard with matching fluffy handcuffs. He was bare-chested and there was no mistaking Scarlett's trademark red lipstick across his mouth and torso. The photo was thankfully cropped at the waist. I didn't need to see further evidence of where her filthy mouth had been.

Even though I knew I was only torturing myself, I clicked on the second email. It was a selfie of Scarlett and Travis kissing. He was still wearing the sleeping mask so could have been oblivious to her taking the photo but did it matter either way? He'd obviously jumped straight into bed with her the moment he'd got back and that hurt.

Sighing, I clicked into the final image. It was a video clip and my stomach lurched. The photos were bad enough without seeing a film. Yet I couldn't stop myself.

Travis was still handcuffed to the bed and still wearing the sleeping mask. As with the first photo, only his face and chest were revealed and there was no sign of Scarlett, but it was pretty obvious from the ecstatic expression on his face what she was doing to him. I felt sick. Yet I couldn't bring myself to stop the video.

'Who's better in bed,' Scarlett purred off-screen. 'Me or her?'

Travis shook his head. 'I'm not answering that.'

'It's pretty obvious. One of us knows what she's doing and the other doesn't,' she teased.

'That's not fair.'

'But it's true.'

Travis's smile confirmed it and my jaw clenched. We all had to start somewhere and he'd certainly never complained.

'Is it definitely over between you?' she asked.

'I don't know.'

'How can you not know?'

'I was pissed off with her earlier, but—'

'Don't you dare say you love her because I know you don't. What you loved was playing the knight in shining armour but where's the passion? Where's the fire? Where's the excitement and adventure?'

I willed him to correct her. To tell her it was true love. But he said nothing.

'You love me, Travis. I know you do.'

'Can't I love you both?'

'Yes, but you don't. You love me and only me. Don't you think it's time you started being honest with yourself?'

I held my breath as I waited for Travis's response.

'Okay. You win. It's you.'

I curled my legs up to my chest, unable to peel my eyes away from the phone. *Please tell her you're joking.*

But Scarlett obviously wanted to dig the knife in even further. 'And you don't love Chloe?'

'I... erm...'

He gulped and I allowed myself a brief moment of hope.

'Say it,' she prompted.

Travis sighed. 'I thought I did but... I'm not sure how or when it changed but I fell out of love with her and in love with you.'

'Good. Because I love you too, Travis.'

Scarlett's face filled the screen. She pointed her finger towards the camera – at me – then screwed her hand into a fist and wiggled it against her cheek mouthing 'boo hoo'. She dropped her fist and grinned at the camera as she waved goodbye before the recording stopped.

My phone slipped from my hand onto the duvet and I pulled my pillow towards my mouth to stifle an agonised scream. Rocking back and forth, releasing gasping sobs into my pillow, I'd never felt pain like it. I loved him so much and I'd believed he loved me but he'd only seen me as a damsel in distress who needed rescuing and he'd mistaken that for love. Until the real thing came along with long nails, bright red lips and all the moves in bed.

An hour later, with no tears left to cry, I lay on my back and stared at the ceiling. There was no point fighting for him, not that I had any fight in me after those photos and that video. The battle had been lost the moment Scarlett saw him. As Lorna said, 'What Scarlett wants, Scarlett gets.' Well, that was it. I was saying goodbye to cute, sweet Chloe and I was going to be more like Scarlett. It was time to forget Travis, forget Scarlett and move on. From now on, what Chloe wants, Chloe gets.

34

A month or so later, I discovered that moving on was going to be a little more problematic than anticipated because Scarlett's 'great idea' had left me with more than regrets and bad memories.

Pregnant. I slumped back on the seat in the supermarket toilets, staring numbly at the stick in my hand. Something else to add to my list of regrets for that night. Lose boyfriend, lose friend, lose dignity, lose self-respect, gain baby. How was that fair?

The external door opened and I heard a young child talking animatedly about the presents on her Christmas list and how she hoped Santa Claus would bring her lots of surprises too.

Christmas. I stared at the stick again but the positive verdict was still there, challenging me. This was certainly a surprise and it definitely wasn't on my Christmas list.

I needed some air.

* * *

Half an hour later, I leaned against the sea wall on North Bay, gulping down deep breaths of fresh sea air. The dull grey waves were turbulent, like my thoughts. Larger waves intermittently crashed against the wall sending salty spray onto my cheeks and hair but I didn't care. At that moment, I didn't care about anything.

When had it happened? *That* night, of course. Who? I hadn't a bloody clue. How could I? Not that it would make much difference if I had known. Neither of them were in my life anymore and I didn't want them to be.

My relationship with Travis wasn't the only one to end. Scarlett dumped Greg and, given the content of the abusive messages he bombarded me with before I blocked him, Scarlett had obviously told him it was all my fault.

For the first week or so after Scarlett's emails, it was her I hated with a passion I hadn't known was possible. All of this had been about her getting what she wanted – *my* boyfriend – and I apportioned full blame on her for all the pain and heartache. She'd used Greg, she'd used me and she'd manipulated Travis. I still loved him so much and kept hoping he'd get in touch and tell me he'd made a huge mistake. I was pretty certain he hadn't known Scarlett was taking photos or recording him and managed to convince myself that he'd only said he loved her and not me because she had him handcuffed to the bed and anything he said was influenced not by his heart but by another part of his body.

For hours, I'd scrutinised the video, looking for where she might have edited it to make it appear that he'd said he loved her when he really hadn't. Eye strain and headaches were the only outcome from that. Even so, I still didn't want to believe it was true and obsessively checked my phone at all hours hoping to hear from Travis. Until one Facebook post made my blood run cold and my heart turn to stone.

She'd tagged me in, of course. It was Sunday 2nd December and they were clinking glasses at the staff Christmas party and looking disgustingly happy together. The photo was bad enough but it was the caption that broke me: *First leg of our travels booked. Can't wait to start a round-the-world adventure with this gorgeous man on 27th Dec. Best Christmas present ever!*

A small damp dog jumped up at me, barking, bringing me crashing back to my current predicament. I acknowledged the apologetic owner, who clipped a lead on the dog and dragged it off, then turned back to the sea and counted off on my fingers when the baby would be due. It was six and a half weeks since *that* night. Nine months from then would take me to early August. Summer holidays.

I'd always wanted children but not like this. Not in my teens. Not while I was still at college. And definitely not when I had no idea who the father was and didn't care after the way they'd both treated me.

The sky darkened and the clouds burst. I sprinted along the promenade, past the beach huts, towards Blue Savannah to seek shelter but I paused outside, taking in the enormous Christmas tree, colourful garlands and twinkling lights. Laughter. Fun. I couldn't face it. Pulling my scarf more tightly round my neck, I pulled my hood up and traipsed home, my feet and hands numb from the cold and wet.

Mum and Dad were still at work. I gazed round the gloomy lounge and couldn't bring myself to switch on the tree lights to brighten the room. I made a cup of tea then left a note in the kitchen to say I wasn't feeling well so I'd gone to bed.

I heard Mum arrive home from work and, shortly after, my door opened but I feigned sleep. Dad arrived home a little later. I tried to imagine their reactions if I told them I was pregnant. Shock. Disappointment. Panic. They'd tell me they'd support me, but how could they? Money was tight as it was without another mouth to feed. But it wasn't going to come to that anyway. I'd Googled it and there was a ten per cent chance of a miscarriage. The risk fell to five per cent at twelve weeks but I didn't need to think about that because my pregnancy wouldn't get that far. It was all a big mistake and it was going to go away. It had to.

35

CHLOE

Present day

I looked up at Sam and my voice caught in my throat as I whispered, 'It didn't go away.'

She pressed her hand against her throat and gulped. 'I'm so sorry. I had no idea. This was your first year at college? No wonder you were so...'

'Horrible to everyone?' I suggested when she fell silent. Because I had been. I'd been foul. I was angry with the world and everything in it, including myself.

I didn't miscarry and my new strategy was equally ludicrous and uncontrollable: ignore it and it will go away. It wasn't hard to ignore either. I was young, fit and healthy and didn't suffer any of the pregnancy complications I'd had with Samuel. I had no sickness and the slightest feeling of nausea passed quickly with a healthy snack. I continued to play sports and eat well and, with the tiniest of baby bumps, I could believe it wasn't happening to me. Almost.

'I was going to say distant,' Sam said gently.

'I didn't know what else to do. I didn't want *anyone* to know. I kept thinking you'd all guess what was going on so I avoided spending time with anyone. Especially you. You knew me too well. If we'd spent as much time together as we had before I met Travis, it wouldn't have taken you long to find the truth.' My voice cracked and I shuddered. 'I'm sorry I hurt you all but it was the only way. I'd have said or done something to make you guess or you'd have caught me at a vulnerable moment and I'd have spilled the beans. If I said it aloud, it would make it real and I'd have to face up to what had happened and I didn't want to do that.'

'So nobody knew?' Sam asked, doubt in her tone as her eyes flicked from me to Auntie Debs and back again.

'I knew,' Auntie Debs confirmed.

Sam didn't look surprised but I was sure I detected a flicker of hurt across her eyes. No wonder. Auntie Debs barely acknowledged her own daughter's existence yet she and I had been so close that spring and summer, united by my secret.

'It wasn't intentional,' I quickly added. 'My head was all over the place. I didn't want anyone to know, yet I felt annoyed that nobody had guessed. It felt like nobody cared. Like I was invisible.'

'That's because we never saw you. You wouldn't let us.' Sam frowned and I could hear the understandable frustration in her voice.

'I know. It was completely my doing but I just got more and more annoyed with everyone. Deep down, I think I wanted someone to guess so I wasn't in it alone but I was equally terrified of what would happen if they did.'

'So you guessed?' Sam asked her mum.

'Yes, and before you say anything, I thought Chloe should tell her parents but I understood why she didn't want to. I wasn't going to force her and I wasn't going to break her trust.'

'I *wasn't* thinking that.' Sam was clearly hurt by the suggestion.

'I was wondering how you guessed because I certainly didn't pick up on anything.'

'Chloe came round to our house one evening. She'd had another run-in with her mum and needed some headspace. You and Jonathan were both out. We were on the sofa talking about nothing in particular when Chloe suddenly squealed and put her hands on her stomach.'

I remembered the moment so clearly. During April, I'd felt the first movements – a gentle fluttering like a baby bird ruffling its feathers in my tummy – and it terrified me. This was real and no amount of wishing or hoping was going to stop it from happening. Until that day with Auntie Debs in mid-May, the baby hadn't kicked and what a huge kick that first one turned out to be.

'I couldn't think of an excuse quickly enough, not that Auntie Debs would have believed me anyway. It was obvious what had just happened. So that was it. My secret was out and, in many ways, it was a relief. Your mum asked what I planned to do. I needed my qualifications to get a job and I wasn't even halfway through college. I had no money and I couldn't expect Mum and Dad to support me when money was already tight for them. Plus, I hated not knowing who the dad was. Every time I thought about it, I felt sick. I didn't want Greg's or Travis's baby. I hated them both so much by this point that I couldn't imagine loving a child from either of them. I told her there was no way I was keeping it.'

Sam frowned again. 'You couldn't have had an abortion, though. Not if the baby was kicking. You'd have been too far along.'

I nodded. 'I was.' My 'ignore-it-and-it-will-go-away' strategy meant I naively never even looked into terminating the pregnancy and, by the time Auntie Debs knew, Sam was right; it was far too late. The decision had been taken out of my hands.

'So you had the baby?' Sam asked.

'I didn't want it. I couldn't. Adoption was the only option left. So

I... erm...' I couldn't find the words to say what happened next. The tears tumbled down my cheeks once more and I looked at Auntie Debs in desperation. She took my look as a request for help and picked up the story. Or at least the story as she knew it.

'Chloe had already made contact with an adoption agency who'd found a suitable family in Cumbria. All the arrangements were made and we found a lodge at a holiday park where Chloe could spend the summer until the baby came. You all thought she had a summer job there.'

Sam gasped. 'Oh, my gosh. That explains so much. Nobody understood why you'd even looked for another job when you already had one lined up at Kellerby Cliffs.'

I hung my head, tears dripping onto my jeans. So many lies.

Mum went mad when I broke the news that I'd be spending the summer at Lakeside Glen Holiday Park in the southern Lake District. Why would I travel all the way to Cumbria when I already had a job lined up practically on our doorstep at a holiday park I knew and loved? It might have made sense if Travis and Scarlett had still been working there but they'd gone travelling and she thought my excuse that there were too many bad memories was 'feeble and childish'.

We had a blazing row about it, finishing with her saying, 'You can do what the hell you like, Chloe. That's all you seem to have done this year anyway. But you're on your own. Seeing as you think you're adult enough to spend the entire summer away from your family, then you're adult enough to pay your own way because we certainly can't afford it.'

'Fine by me! I don't want your help anyway,' I yelled before storming out of the house and slamming the door. I didn't make it far before the anger eased and the guilt set in. I hated all the lies but at least that argument had proved one thing: I'd been right about not keeping the baby. It would have financially ruined my parents.

'I hated the thought of her being on her own all summer,' Auntie Debs said. 'I tried to book some time off work but I was too late to get the dates. She didn't want me there, anyway. Said it was easier that way. The adoption agency were there for her and the new parents were even at the birth.'

'I'm so sorry, Chloe. I can't believe you went through all that alone.'

I gulped as I looked up at Sam and saw tears glistening in her eyes.

'Alone? It's what she wanted,' Auntie Debs snapped. 'Everything about this was how Chloe wanted it.'

Sam winced. 'I know. I wasn't having a go. I was thinking more about Chloe keeping this a secret for months before you found out and, even though it's what she wanted, it still had to have been tough being all alone that summer, especially when—'

'That's not my fault. If I'd taken any time off work, I'd have lost my job and then we'd have been stuffed because I wouldn't have been able to repay the loan I took out. Stop blaming—'

'I am *not* blaming you,' Sam cried. 'For once, will you just put a lid on the insults? This is about Chloe, not about you. She's asked you to come here today to support her while she talks about what happened and the last thing she needs is to witness one of our petty squabbles. So either do what you came to do and support your niece, or leave.'

I had never seen Sam stand up to her mum like that. I nervously glanced from one to the other. Sam was sitting tall, her jaw tense, her eyes narrowed and she looked set for a fight.

Eventually Auntie Debs conceded. 'I'll stay,' she muttered, shoulders slumping.

'Good. Glad that's sorted.' Sam looked at me and the anger disappeared from her tone as she asked, 'What did you have?'

'A girl.'

'And what were the adoptive parents like?'

I hung my head and the tears flowed once more. 'I don't know,' I whispered.

'What are you talking about?' Auntie Debs said. 'They were at the birth.'

'They weren't.'

'You said they were. Was it just the people from the adoption agency then?'

I shook my head again. 'They weren't there either.'

'So who was?'

'Just the hospital staff.'

'I don't understand. Why weren't they there?'

This was it. This was absolute truth time. 'Because I never arranged the adoption.' The words sounded strange, alien, as though somebody else had spoken them.

'What? Of course you did! I saw the letters and the portfolio. It was full of photos. The Maythorpes. Tim and Amanda Maythorpe.'

'They don't exist! I made them up!'

Auntie Debs clapped her hand across her mouth, her eyes wide as she muttered, 'Oh, my God!'

I pulled my knees up to my chest and wrapped my arms round my legs, rocking back and forth as I gulped down deep, painful sobs.

'Chloe? What did you do with the baby?' Sam's voice was full of trepidation. 'Look at me! Concentrate. What did you do with the baby?'

36

Twelve years ago

My body ached and my eyes felt so heavy that I could have fallen asleep standing up on the wooden veranda of Fern Lodge. I focused on the overcast sky through the trees while Auntie Debs fumbled with the key.

'We're in!' she declared, finally pushing the door open. 'No idea why that took me so long.'

Her shaking hands might have had something to do with it. The closer we'd got to Cumbria, the more apprehensive she'd become. Beads of sweat had trickled from her brow and I hated that I'd done that to her, but there was no going back now.

It was the Friday at the start of the summer holidays and college had finished on Wednesday, giving me a day to pack before leaving Whitsborough Bay for the summer. I'd had to be careful not to look like I was packing too much so, across the past fortnight, I'd been a frequent visitor to Auntie Debs's with so many additional clothes, books, DVDs and art supplies that, when she picked me up this morning, her car boot was already full.

We'd been so lucky finding the lodge and I couldn't help thinking it was time that something went right for me. Tucked away on its own and surrounded by trees in a quieter part of the large holiday park, it had been become available last minute when the owners' sale fell through.

'You look beat,' Auntie Debs said. 'You go for a lie down and I'll bring the stuff in.'

She wouldn't take no for an answer so I gratefully curled up on the double bed and, within minutes, exhaustion took me.

* * *

The following morning, Auntie Debs and I ate breakfast in silence then she suggested a walk round the site to help me get my bearings before she headed home.

I felt a sense of familiarity as we ambled along pathways between caravans and lodges. It wasn't as big as Kellerby Cliffs and there was a greater ratio of lodges to caravans but the facilities were pretty much the same, minus the fun fair.

Lakeside Glen was on the northern shore of Lake Windermere and had a jetty down to the lake with large boulders on either side. Auntie Debs and I each sat on one, admiring the stunning view across the lake.

I picked up a pebble, skimmed it across the water and counted five leaps before it sank. 'I'm sorry for making you lie.'

Auntie Debs was silent for a moment and I wondered if she was angry with me. I was about to offer another apology but she spoke, her words slow and careful.

'Sometimes things happen and a few white lies are the only way to deal with them. I'm sorry you've found yourself in this position. I only wish I could do more.'

'Like what?'

'Stay here with you.'

'You know you can't. I need to do it this way. It's for the best. But please don't feel you haven't done enough. You've been amazing. You've kept my secret. You found this place. You drove me here. You even took out a loan for me.' I had some wages saved from working at Kellerby Cliffs but they weren't going to stretch far and I was too young for a loan or credit cards. Auntie Debs had saved the day by opening up a new bank account and taking out a loan in her name, keeping it hidden from Uncle Jonathan. She'd used it to pay for the lodge and had given me the debit card so I could withdraw cash and pay for meals.

'I'll pay you back as soon as I start working.'

'When you can afford it. Don't you be worrying about money for now. You've got more important things to focus on.'

We sat in silence as the minutes ticked past, watching the lightest of breezes send ripples across the lake. When a young family appeared with an inflatable dinghy, Auntie Debs stood up and reached for my hand. 'I'd better go.'

Arm in arm, we made our way back up to Fern Lodge. I sat on the veranda steps while she gathered her belongings. When she stepped out of the lodge later, her eyes were red and briming with tears.

I stood up and wrapped my arms round her and clung to her tightly as silent tears rained down my cheeks. 'Thank you for everything,' I whispered. 'Please don't worry about me. I know what I'm doing.'

As she pulled away, I waved to her with a big smile but a heavy heart. Know what I'm doing? Far from it. I didn't know anything anymore. I was lost and alone and absolutely terrified.

37

CHLOE

With Auntie Debs gone, I stood in the middle of the open plan lounge/kitchen/diner and fought the urge to sink to the floor, sobbing. I couldn't spend the whole summer in tears. I was going to have to get used to being alone and keeping myself occupied.

I was already panicking about food. Auntie Debs had asked if I could cook. 'I'm a dab hand in the kitchen,' I'd responded before rattling off a load of dishes I could make. I had no idea how to make any of them. Unless they came in a plastic tray with a film lid and needed five minutes in the microwave.

I wandered into the bedroom, stripped down to my underwear, and gazed at the curve of my stomach in the full-length mirror. According to the NHS's pregnancy calculator, I was a little over thirty-eight weeks pregnant, with a due date a week on Tuesday. But I could pinpoint the exact date of conception without a shadow of a doubt. It would be thirty-seven weeks tomorrow since the 'great idea'.

I'd looked up images of women at thirty-seven weeks pregnant. Some bumps were enormous and I'd been worried I'd look like that and my secret would be out but it hadn't happened. My bump was small and neat and it was amazing what swing dresses, maxi dresses and oversized hoodies could hide. And avoiding your family.

For as long as I could remember, I'd wanted a big family. Even though I'd always had Sammie in my life and she'd been like a sister to me, I'd have liked siblings. Never in my dreams about my future family had I imagined that my first pregnancy would end up like this.

Since finding out I was pregnant, I'd been hell to live with. Angry, snappy, sarcastic. Everything was a fight. I'd pushed away all the people who could have supported me with this, but I knew why. If they'd known, they'd have found a way to keep the baby and I didn't want it. It was bad enough that my head was full of memories of Travis and Greg without a living, breathing reminder of the biggest mistake I'd ever made. People made enough assumptions and judgements about me as it was.

Before Auntie Debs found out, I had debated whether to tell my parents. I prepared speeches ranging from simply blurting it out to asking how they might react if I ever found myself in that situation. Then they invited our next-door neighbours, Stewart and Anne, round for a barbeque. My bedroom overlooked the back garden and, through my open window, I could hear Mum chatting to Anne as they sat on the bench below, drinking wine.

'Ooh, you'll never guess what Elaine's daughter has gone and done,' Anne said.

My ears pricked up. *This should be good.* Elaine lived a few doors down and her daughter, Tegan, was what my dad called a 'hell-raiser'. She was a year younger than me but had already been suspended from school twice, run away from home on at least three occasions and been in trouble with the police numerous times. I was intrigued to hear about her latest escapade.

'She's only gone and got herself pregnant.'

I bristled. *Got herself pregnant? I think you'll find there was a man involved somewhere.* I held my breath, waiting for Mum's reaction.

'Stupid girl,' Mum said, her tone full of disgust. 'She'll be the death of her poor mother.'

'You're not wrong there. I feel so sorry for Elaine,' Anne gushed. 'She was in bits. No idea what to do. I asked her who the father is but Tegan wouldn't say. Doesn't know, more like, the daft, dirty little slapper.'

I'd never particularly liked Anne but now I hated her. It took a hell of a lot of restraint not to shout out of the window that sometimes mistakes happened.

'That's a bit harsh,' Mum said, calming me a notch. 'Although I definitely agree with the daft part. There's no need for an unwanted pregnancy in this day and age with so many options available. It's careless.'

'I reckon it was deliberate. Could you ever see that one passing her exams and holding down a job? She'll be after a house and benefits courtesy of our taxes.'

'You're probably right.'

Seething, I stuck my earphones in so I didn't have to listen to any more of their drivel.

I didn't work out any speeches after that. I was definitely alone in this one and time was not on my side.

A couple of weeks later, Auntie Debs found out. I didn't play it fair with her. She insisted at first that we tell Mum and Dad. No way. I suggested that, if the truth came out, it was unlikely I'd stick around for the fall-out. If Auntie Debs was worried about me already, how would she feel if she had no idea where I was? That kept her quiet.

* * *

The first week at Lakeside Glen dragged by in painful nothingness. It didn't take me long to work through my DVDs. Twice. I'd packed a few books but I couldn't concentrate on reading. I took out my sketch pad on several occasions but didn't feel inspired to draw anything.

Although there was a good Wi-Fi connection, social media was a no-go zone. I couldn't post anything and I couldn't be seen as 'active', destroying the illusion that I was busy working. I'd unfriended and unfollowed Travis and Scarlett but they both kept posting pictures of their travels without privacy settings and I stupidly kept torturing myself by looking. Tanned and grinning at the camera, it broke my heart to see Scarlett with everything that should have been mine. Everything she'd stolen from me.

Some days I sat on the veranda steps or at the small table, watching the distant activity on the lake. Fern Lodge was in an elevated position so I could see a myriad of boats navigating up and down Lake Windermere but I never ventured down to the shore until dusk fell and I was more likely to be alone. I didn't want to be round people. If I felt lonely in the lodge, I'd have felt even lonelier in a crowd. Happy families. Couples in love. Not for me.

There was a minimarket with a good supply of fruit and salad and a reasonable range of ready meals onsite. There were also a couple of takeaways. I tried cooking. I attempted a lasagne but the mince was still red when I dished it up. Thinking I'd been too ambitious, I bought a jar of pasta sauce for my next attempt but the pasta was still crunchy and I somehow burned the sauce.

I think I could have lost my mind if it hadn't been for yoga and meditation. I'd taken up both at the start of the year as a way to stay calm while my world fell apart. With so much anger pulsing through my veins, I dread to know what would have happened without them. Every time I started to panic, they saved me.

So did Auntie Debs. She phoned me every day – sometimes two or three times – to check I was okay, that I was eating and that everything was still going smoothly with the adoption process. It disturbed me that I'd become such a dab hand at lying.

* * *

At the start of week two, I looked in the mirror again and didn't recognise myself. The bump was still compact but even the loosest of clothes weren't going to hide the fact that I was pregnant. This was it. This was real. And, actually, the baby could make an appearance at any point and I wasn't fully prepared for what needed to happen next. Better get to work.

When Auntie Debs found out and asked me what I planned to do, I just blurted out adoption. I hadn't given it any consideration but it struck me it was my only remaining option. I didn't want her to talk me out of it so I told her plans were already underway for a couple in Cumbria to adopt. They weren't. I have no idea where I plucked Cumbria from.

Back at home, I searched online, found an adoption agency website and it scared me shitless. Going through court was frightening enough but then I read that the baby had to be at least six weeks old before I could make the final decision. I slammed my laptop shut, gulping down deep, panicked breaths of air. What was I supposed to do with the baby for those six weeks? The birth would fall into the college holidays so I could invent a job on a holiday park in Cumbria to have the baby in secret but how could I explain staying there throughout September and missing the return to college without Mum and Dad finding out? And if I had the baby with me for six weeks, I couldn't imagine ever wanting to let go and no way could I risk that.

Why was it all so complicated? I curled up on my side on my

bed, staring at my bookshelves on the opposite wall, frantically trying to think of a way out of my predicament. My eyes rested on the spine of a novel I'd read last summer and my heart started racing. I rolled off the bed, grabbed the book and scanned down the blurb, recalling the story of a woman desperate to protect her baby from her violent boyfriend and give it the better life it deserved. Could I? For the first time all year, I felt a frisson of excitement. It might actually work. No. I had to believe. It *would* work.

The priority had been to get Auntie Debs to believe the adoption story because I was going to need her help. Over the next few weeks, my pet project was creating the perfect family to adopt the baby. Amanda and Tim Maythorpe from Cumbria, both thirty-two, childhood sweethearts, married for eleven years, unable to have children. She was a primary school teacher, he was a bank manager, and they were going to call the baby Ava Jasmine if it was a girl and Jack if it was a boy although they hadn't yet finalised his middle name.

The Maythorpes became my obsession. I created a flashy portfolio to show Auntie Debs full of photos of them, their house and their extended family, all copied from a mix of Google Images and some random couple I found on Facebook who posted everything public.

I created letters from the adoption agency confirming the arrangements, ensuring I threw in enough legal jargon to sound plausible and enough warmth to reassure Auntie Debs that they had my best interests at heart and would look after me during the birth.

Some days I allowed myself to imagine the life the baby would have with the Maythorpes. A better life. Much better than anything I could offer. They'd be so happy. It was the right thing for everyone. I was giving that lovely couple the child they'd always longed for and I was giving the baby a chance.

But on those days, I went to bed and sobbed into my pillow. Because it wasn't real. The Maythorpes didn't exist. There were no arrangements in place. But there would be. My baby needed to get its chance in life. It would be better off without me. And right now I needed to stop moping around. The baby could make an appearance any day and I needed to be ready.

I grabbed my laptop and a notebook and sat at the dining table. Although I'd considered alternatives, a hospital birth was really the only option. Trying to go it alone carried far too many risks as well as being terrifying.

I'd already researched the best hospital and had confirmed it in one of the fictional letters I'd shown to Auntie Debs. Lancaster and Barrow-in-Furness both had maternity wards and were similar distances from Lakeside Glen but I could only get to Barrow by changing trains in Lancaster, making Lancaster Royal Infirmary the logical choice.

I scribbled down all the train times, checked out the distance from the holiday park to Windermere station and Lancaster station to the hospital. I added the numbers for taxi companies local to the holiday park and looked up B&Bs a short walk from the hospital.

There'd be questions. Lots of them. Who was I? Why was I alone? Why didn't I have any medical notes? Why hadn't I had any scans? Auntie Debs had asked about that. I'd told her I'd had one done in York and had produced yet another letter confirming this, but had told her I hadn't wanted to keep a photo; too hard.

It helped that Auntie Debs had already thrown so many questions at me but the hospital weren't going to accept the answers I'd given her. If this was going to work, I needed to have my story straight and stick to it. This was the most important role I'd ever play. My attempt at being Chantel Delacroix had failed but only because I'd lacked any time to fully prepare and get into the character. This time it would be different.

I was Rosie Kathryn Lennox, recently turned nineteen, married last October in a small civil ceremony to childhood sweetheart Kieran Mark Lennox, age twenty-one. Make that Private Kieran Mark Lennox of the Duke of Lancaster Regiment, currently on tour in Afghanistan. I'd ideally wanted a bigger wedding and had suggested waiting but he was determined to make me his wife just in case anything happened overseas because I had no family. It was just as well as it turned out I was pregnant...

By the end of the week, I knew everything about our life together, from how we met to what I wore on our wedding day to the style of wallpaper I wanted for our lounge when we moved into the army barracks on his return next month.

We'd moved around after Kieran left college. My Gran, who raised me, had passed away and he was my life so I was happy to go where he found work. A plumbing apprenticeship hadn't worked but he'd found his place in the army and we were excited about settling somewhere.

I couldn't remember the last time I'd registered with a doctor. Never seemed to stay in the same place long enough. Of course I would have if I'd realised I was pregnant but I only found out a couple of weeks ago. I thought the extra weight was comfort eating until I caught sight of myself in a full-length mirror for the first time in months. What a shock!

And so it went on, building my character, learning my lines. I only left the lodge to seek out food, skim a few stones into the lake on an evening, and for one trip into Windermere for a few essentials to take to the hospital. Otherwise, every waking minute was spent being Rosie.

My drama teacher would have been proud of me. Method acting at its best. Over the next week or so, Chloe Olsen ceased to exist and Rosie Lennox took charge. Strong, confident, equipped to deal with anything life threw her way including an unexpected –

but very much wanted – pregnancy. Sammie would be proud, too. For the first time in my life, I was studying as hard as she did. Scrub that. Sammie wouldn't be proud at all. There was nothing at all about what I was going to do that could possibly make anyone proud.

38

CHLOE

I was staring blankly at the TV on mute, running through my former addresses for what felt like the millionth time, when the first mild contraction hit. It was shortly after 9 p.m. on a Tuesday evening and I'd been at Lakeside Glen for three and a half weeks. Hours of research about what to expect revealed that contractions felt different for different women but there was no mistaking what it was when it came; a dull ache in my lower back and a tightening then softening of the stomach. The baby was on its way.

For a moment, I allowed Chloe to feel the fear and shed a few panicked tears before Rosie stepped in and took control. It was going to be fine. We had a carefully constructed plan to follow.

I calmly switched off the TV and consulted the list of B&Bs. The first couple I rang were fully booked but the George Tavern – a boarding pub a short walk from the hospital – had one room available. It was on its own above the bar so could be noisy, the landlord warned, but that couldn't have been more ideal so I secured it for one night only, confirming it was okay to pay cash on arrival. Then I called a taxi to take me to Windermere train station. I picked up the small black backpack containing only the bare essentials for me and my bag for life holding the basics for the baby and made my way to the holiday park entrance to wait.

* * *

Thank God my room was on its own or there'd have been complaints about me pacing the floor all night. I sat or stood and meditated as much as I could but, as the contractions intensified, moving seemed to be the only way to cope with the pain.

How many times did I pick up my bag intending to barge over to the hospital to beg them for an epidural? But I channelled Rosie. Calm. Controlled. Organised. I could do this. I could wait. I had to. Because if I was admitted too early, there was too much opportunity for them to interrogate me. To see through my lies. To know what I was up to.

As the sound of traffic on the street outside intensified for the morning commute, so did my contractions. I gripped onto the edge of the sink, biting down on my flannel, as another took hold. Moments later, there was a pop and fluid trickled down my legs onto the tiled floor. It was time.

My hands shook as I wiped the tiles and threw the soiled towels in the bath. I rumpled the bedding so it looked like the bed had been slept in and, leaving the key in the door, left the pub via the side entrance the landlord had shown me.

* * *

Baby Girl Olsen, aka Ava Jasmine Lennox, was born at 9.33 a.m. on Wednesday 13th August weighing 5lb 11oz.

As the midwife handed me the tiny bundle wrapped in a towel, I gazed down at her and felt a rush of love but I pushed it away. She wasn't mine. I ran my hand over her head. She had a downy covering of blonde hair. Could have come from me. Could have come from Greg. I'd never know for sure and it didn't matter anyway.

'You did really well.' Ruth, the midwife who'd led the birth, smiled warmly at me. She appeared to be a little older than Mum, with dark hair greying at the temples and rosy cheeks. 'Just the placenta and then you're all done.'

'What happens after that?' I asked.

'We need to see if we can track down those records of yours before we move you onto the ward.'

My heart started to race and I fought to keep my voice light and casual. 'Why do you need my records first?'

'It's just procedure. We need to—'

A knock on the door interrupted her. A younger midwife stepped into the room and smiled at me. 'What have you had?'

'A girl. Ava Jasmine.'

'What a beautiful name. Congratulations.' She turned to Ruth. 'Can I have a quick word?' She looked serious and my stomach lurched. Had I somehow been rumbled? This had been part of the plan over which I had no control. I could reel off addresses till the cows came home and lead them on a wild goose chase round the country but if they couldn't release me off the secure delivery suite until they'd absolutely confirmed my identity, I was stuffed. Being so close to the birth when I'd been admitted, the priority had been on the safe delivery of the baby but she was here now and everything I'd so carefully planned could easily unravel.

There was a back-up plan if they called me out on my lies – escaping from an abusive boyfriend who didn't know I was pregnant – but I really didn't want to use that as surely it meant involving the police and/or social services. The fewer people I came into contact with, the better.

'I swear it always happens on a full moon,' Ruth said, bustling back into the room.

'What does?'

'Crazy time on the delivery suite. There's apparently a queue and they've already had to postpone two inductions so we're going to need to move you both out as soon as we've delivered that placenta.' She smiled at me. 'It's like Piccadilly Circus out there. But don't you worry. We've got a bed for you in post-natal upstairs.'

* * *

Forty minutes later, I was shown to my bed in a four-bed bay on Ward 17. My bed was in the far corner by the window. The other three were all occupied. A midwife who introduced herself as Cecile brought me a jug of water and checked if I needed anything immediately, apologising that everything was a bit hectic that morning with a run on births.

When she left, I glanced round the ward. I didn't want to get into a conversation with any of the other new mums so I was relieved that the woman opposite me seemed engrossed in a magazine, the woman next to her was sleeping with her baby in a crib by her side and the woman in the bed next to me was breastfeeding.

'Do you mind if I...?' I asked her, reaching for the curtain between our beds.

'That's fine,' she said, smiling.

I had no idea if I was allowed to do it but I didn't care. I needed to be alone. I pulled the curtain round the side and end of my bed, sank onto the mattress, and crumbled. I held Ava close to my heart as my body shook with silent, painful sobs.

Time passed – maybe ten minutes or so – as I fought to compose myself. I jumped as the curtain was pulled back into place.

'All a bit overwhelming for you?' asked Ruth, giving me a sympathetic smile.

Be Rosie. 'Just a bit. It's such a shame Kieran couldn't be here.'

'Have you sent him a photo?'

'Yeah. He said he's in love already.'

'I bet he is. She's such a beauty. Comes from good genes, that one. Right then, how about we try feeding her?'

Damn! I hadn't thought about that. 'I, erm... I don't want to feed her myself.'

'If you're worried, we can show you what to do.'

'No. I know it's best for the baby but money's tight. I'm going to have to start working as soon as Kieran's back next month. I've got a job offer to work in a call centre so Ava will be in part-time childcare. It just seems easier to go with the bottle from the start.'

It sounded like a feeble excuse and it was. How could I have planned so much yet missed that part out? There was no way I could feed her myself, though. I could already feel an attachment from holding her and couldn't risk taking that further. Where would we be if I did? She deserved better than being saddled with a failure like me.

I thought Ruth was going to try to persuade me but someone called her name. 'It's your choice,' she said smiling at me. 'We can sort out some formula for Ava shortly.'

'Thank you.'

I bit my lip as I watched Ruth walking away. Call centre? Where had that come from? But I'd noticed that, if you threw in enough detail, people would believe anything and, right now, I was the queen of make-believe.

* * *

After bottle-feeding Ava and changing her nappy – both with the help of Cecile – I nipped to the bathroom and washed and dressed. I'd chosen the plainest clothes I had: black cropped leggings and a long white T-shirt with my trainers.

Returning to my bed, I French-braided my hair and checked my backpack. Jacket. Baseball cap. Wig. My fingers brushed against the note I'd prepared and I shuddered.

The lunch trolley came round. My stomach was in knots and I couldn't face eating but I smiled and took the sandwich and yoghurt, eager not to do anything that could arouse suspicion. I took a bite of the sandwich but it felt like a chunk of brick being forced down my throat and, confident nobody was looking, I wrapped the rest in a tissue and shoved it in the bedside cupboard.

I was on tenterhooks with every passing minute, terrified they'd have guessed, half-expecting a delegation of hospital staff, clergy and police to march towards me, demanding that I confess. I held my breath every time I saw Ruth approach but she was frequently whisked away before getting to me.

Visiting time was two till four and that was my chance; all those extra people coming and going. I'd pull on my cap and slip out unnoticed. Hopefully.

As 2 p.m. approached, I felt sick with nerves. My palms were clammy and beads of sweat prickled my forehead, but my mouth was so dry.

Ava was sound asleep in her crib by the bed, a Peter Rabbit comforter next to her. Sammie and I had always loved Beatrix Potter and, on my trip into Windermere, I'd been unable to resist. The Lake District was, after all, where she'd lived and written many of her books. I hoped they'd keep it for her as a memory of me. Not that I'd deserve to be remembered.

I crouched down beside her and ran my finger across her soft cheek. 'This is goodbye,' I whispered, my bottom lip trembling as I swiped at the ready tears. This was so much harder than I'd thought. I'd spent all year feeling completely detached, wanting the 'problem' to go away and feeling loathing when it didn't. Yet now... I brushed the tears away once more and took a few deep gulps of air, trying to force down the lump in my throat, willing Rosie to take control again.

It's for the best. It's for the best. It's for the best. You have no job, no money. She has no dad. She'll have a better life without you. She'll be taken care of. You're doing the right thing. She's on a maternity ward, for God's sake. Where better to leave her? She'll have a good life. Without you.

Cries of delight and laughter announced visiting time. I placed my cap on the bed, reached into the backpack and closed my fist round the note. *You can do this. It's for the best.*

Through a blur of tears, I stroked Ava's cheek once more. I kissed my finger and lightly touched her lips with the kiss. *Be a good girl. Be happy. Be brave. Be loved.*

I slipped the note down the side of the blanket.

Please take care of her because I can't.
Keep her safe and loved.
I'm so sorry.

I glanced towards the end of the ward and could see several people milling round. The new mums on the ward were preoccupied, greeting or preparing for their visitors. *Now! You need to leave now!* I wiped my streaming eyes and nose, blew one final kiss towards my baby girl then pulled on my cap and shuffled towards the exit.

My heart thumped uncontrollably, waiting for someone to call my name or place a hand on my shoulder. The door opened and an elderly couple holding a 'new baby' balloon and a large teddy bear stepped through. The man held the door for me and that was it. Three paces. Two. One. Outside.

Head down, I hurried along the corridor, down the stairs and out into the fresh air. *Do not look back. Keep going.*

Away from the hospital and down a back alley, I dumped the cap in a bin by a restaurant. I pulled my denim jacket out of my backpack, checked everything was still in each pocket, then pulled it on. Clipping my plait on top of my head, I pulled on the dark bobbed wig and sunglasses and dumped the backpack too, then hastened to the station, the flood of adrenaline keeping my weary body moving.

I only started to relax after I'd changed trains at Oxenholme station and was on the last leg to Windermere. Pressing my forehead against the window, I stared out into the passing countryside, tears blurring my vision, feeling a darkness descending on me. I was broken. I wasn't sure I could ever be fixed. *But it's for the best. It is. It has to be.*

39

Present day

I was so shocked, I couldn't speak. Had Chloe really just admitted that she'd abandoned her baby and kept that secret for twelve long years? What must she have been going through, pregnant and alone, and how desperate must she have been to abandon the baby? I couldn't quite believe she'd done that. The stress of making a decision like that had to have taken its toll. And she'd only been sixteen when she fell pregnant, seventeen when she'd had Ava. She had to have been terrified.

I couldn't see the familiar strong, confident, cocky Chloe in the woman in front of me. With her face pale, her cheeks damp with tears, and her slumped shoulders, she appeared broken and was it any wonder? What a thing to go through and what a secret to keep!

So much from the past now made sense: Chloe's bad mood that Christmas and her detachment from me across the year, her arguments with Auntie Louise, her closeness to Mum and disappearing to work in Cumbria when she already had a job lined up at Kellerby Cliffs. She'd told me it would give her experience of working in another kids' club, which would be great on her CV. It seemed so plausible.

My head was spinning with so much unexpected information. I wished Chloe hadn't pushed me away or that I'd not let go so easily. The worst thing was that the reason she'd cited for not going down the formal adoption route was invalid. I had a basic knowledge about the process from a former colleague who'd adopted a baby and, while it was true that the final decision couldn't be made before six weeks to allow time for either parent to change their mind, the baby could be taken into foster care during that time. Chloe could still have gone down that route and had access to the support she needed, confidentially. I certainly wasn't going to make a difficult situation worse right now by pointing that out.

I glanced at Mum. Also pale-faced, she had her hand pressed across her mouth, her eyes wide.

'I'm so sorry, Chloe,' I said gently. 'How are you feeling?'

Head still down, she merely shrugged. I couldn't think what else to say. I didn't want to bombard her with questions. She probably needed some quiet time after finally sharing the truth.

Mum looked up at me and drew in a deep breath.

'I think that cup of tea might be a good idea now, Samantha,' she said, finally breaking the silence.

'Yes. Good plan.'

With the kettle boiling, I dropped teabags into mugs and discreetly glanced over to where Chloe and Mum were huddled together in hushed conversation. What must Mum be going through right now? She'd been part of this yet it hadn't happened how she'd believed. She was probably even more in shock than I was.

What would happen next? Was telling me like a dry run for telling James? I frowned as the kettle reached boiling point. How did James fit into all of this? She was meant to be explaining why she'd run out on him and, from what I'd heard so far, there was no connection to him whatsoever. I was going to have to ask.

I made the drinks and carried them over. They both muttered a thank you.

'Are you okay?' I asked Chloe.

'A bit numb. Thanks for listening and not having a go. Both of you.'

'As if we'd do that. Oh, my gosh, Chloe, you were only a teenager and very likely terrified. You did what you thought was best for the baby.'

Her bottom lip quivered and her eyes filled with tears again. 'Do you think they'll have found her a good home?'

'I'm certain of it.'

'That's all I ever wanted for her.'

'I take it James doesn't know any of this?'

She shook her head.

'I don't know if this is the right time to mention this but I think I'm missing something. What's Travis and the baby got to do with you leaving James?'

'Everything.' Chloe took her mobile phone out of her handbag, pressed a few buttons, and handed it to me. 'I know I shouldn't have looked but James left his phone behind when he went shopping and I found these.'

I scanned down the photos of three emails, frowning:

To: James Turner

From: Genevieve Enderby-Bowes

Subject: Your Counselling Session

Thank you for your voicemail earlier. I understand that you wish to explore an additional area of concern. This is no problem. Even when a client comes to me with one clear goal, doors frequently open to other issues. Sometimes they're connected and sometimes they're not.

This may lead to additional sessions in order to explore your issues fully. I hope this reassures you. I look forward to meeting you.

To: Genevieve Enderby-Bowes

From: James Turner

Subject: RE: Your Counselling Session

Thank you for your prompt response. I have two more questions:

I thought I'd only need support for the cancer but things at home have deteriorated since I booked so I think we probably will need extra sessions. Do I need to book them now?

Am I actually permitted to discuss the challenges with my home life without my wife being present?

Apologies for bombarding you with questions. This is all new to me. Thank you.

To: James Turner

From: Genevieve Enderby-Bowes

Subject: RE: RE: Your Counselling Session

I'm happy to help.

No. We can add those in after your first couple of sessions. We can always cancel them if we feel they're not needed.

You can talk to me about anything you wish although the focus will be on you and your behaviour. It may be that you would want to consider marriage guidance as a couple at a later date but we will start by focusing on you.

'I'm not getting the connection.' I scrolled up and down shaking my head. 'What am I looking at?' As far as I could see from the emails, James was struggling with his cancer diagnosis and needed some help through counselling but wanted to take the opportunity to talk about issues at home too. I could see that Chloe might be upset by reading that. I'd be hurt too if I discovered that my partner was seeing a counsellor to discuss problems in our relationship without my knowledge, but I'd also be glad that he cared enough to talk it through with a professional, presumably with a view to finding a way to fix it. Casting all that aside, I still couldn't see the connection to Chloe's past. There was nothing in those emails that explained or justified running out on James like that.

Chloe took the phone back from me. 'The name! Genevieve Enderby-Bowes! She's Travis's bloody sister!'

'Oh. And?'

She gaped at me as though I was stupid. 'And I've met her. Several times. And don't say it might not be her because that's far too unusual a name for there to be more than one of them.'

'I agree that it's pretty distinctive. But I still don't see why that would make you pack your bags and leave.'

'What if it all came out? What if they realised the connection?'

'How? Genevieve might not be a common name but Chloe is. You're her brother's girlfriend from thirteen years ago and you don't even have the same surname now. I don't think she'd make any connection at all and, even if she did, what difference would it make? Travis never knew about the baby so his sister didn't either.'

'But she's his sister.'

'I get that but there's no obvious connection. Unless it's just me missing it.' I looked pleadingly at Mum. She'd never backed me up on anything before but I hoped she could see past our toxic relationship and understand that this was about Chloe who she obviously loved very deeply to have kept her pregnancy secret for twelve years. She was good at keeping secrets, though. She'd kept her own for more than thirty years.

Mum took the phone and scanned up and down then returned it to Chloe. 'Sorry, but I'm with Samantha on this one. I see that she's Travis's sister but I think you've let your imagination run away with you here. You've seen the name and panicked.' Mum supporting something I'd said was a first.

'But...' Chloe's face paled. 'But if he mentioned me and Whitsborough Bay, she'd...' She tailed off, shaking her head.

I felt sick for her. Mum was right. She'd panicked and fled for no reason. 'If Genevieve did make a connection that you were her brother's ex-girlfriend, she'd need to refer James to a colleague because it's a conflict of interests. She wouldn't be allowed to tell him she knew you.'

Chloe looked as though she might faint at any moment. Mum obviously thought the same as she put her arm round her while I dashed to the sink for a glass of water.

'So I did all this for nothing?' Chloe whispered when she'd taken a few sips.

I couldn't answer. What good would a 'yes' do?

'Oh, my God! I did all this for nothing!' Her voice got louder and higher with each word. She leapt up and started counting off on her fingers. 'I took Samuel, I left James, I shouted at Mum, I was horrible to you and now I've told you both everything.' Her voice was bordering on hysteria and her breathing was rapid. 'And it was all for *nothing*! I need some air.'

'Chloe!' I called as she ran out of the barn.

I stood up to run after her but Mum grabbed my hand. 'Leave her.' She tugged me down and I slumped on my chair, devastated for Chloe but also a little overwhelmed. Mum had touched me. I knew it wasn't out of affection but it still had a profound effect on me. I couldn't remember the last time we'd had any sort of physical contact.

'She needs a moment,' Mum said. 'She'll be back when she's ready. It's a lot to process, don't you think?'

Was that an actual conversation starter? Could this day get any stranger?

'I can't imagine what she must have been going through all these years. Abandoning a baby like that. That has to leave some serious scars.'

'It's all my fault.' Mum's voice cracked and I was shocked to see tears in her eyes. I'd never seen Mum cry; not even at Nanna's or Gramps's funerals. 'I should have realised.'

'You couldn't have known,' I said gently. 'By the sounds of it, she gave you no reason to doubt any of it.'

A tear trickled down her cheek and she swiped it away with the palm of her hand, sniffing. 'She was just a kid, Samantha. I was the adult. I should have taken care of the adoption for her or I should have phoned the company and checked it out. What was I thinking, letting a teenager sort out something like that?'

'You can't blame yourself, Mum. We both know what Chloe's like when she makes up her mind about something. She pulled out all the stops to convince you she was fine and everything was under control. She said so herself.'

More tears fell and Mum didn't even try to wipe them away. 'Thank you. But I was still wrong to do what I did. I stand by the first part. It was Chloe's baby and her decision about who to tell and what to do and, if I had to do it all over again, I'd do that part the same. Looking back on the adoption, though...' She sighed and shook her head. 'I should have known. Alarm bells should have gone off. I can't believe she abandoned her baby like that. Louise and Simon would have supported her somehow. We could have...' Mum's voice cracked and she properly sobbed.

I wanted nothing more than to rush over and put my arms round her, but fear of rejection kept me rooted to the spot. I swallowed hard on the huge lump constricting my throat. 'Please don't punish yourself. You were the only one who was there for Chloe when she desperately needed someone. You helped her through what was probably the worst time in her life and the hardest decision she's ever had to make and you respected her wishes all the way through it. At the time, you did the right thing for Chloe.'

Mum looked up and my stomach churned as I waited for a snide remark. I was sucking up to her or I didn't understand or she was sick of listening to me wittering on. But she said nothing. She just stared at me, tears pooling in her eyes, and then she whispered, 'Thank you.'

I couldn't hold back my own tears at that point. Mum had actually thanked me for something. She'd listened to me and she hadn't snapped back.

'Right pair we are,' I said, grabbing a box of tissues off the treatment table, helping myself to a couple, then offering the box to Mum.

I sat back down. 'I'm seriously concerned about her state of mind. To have abandoned her baby in the first place is worrying but she's kept it hidden for nearly twelve years and just seeing the name of Travis's sister has triggered all of this. Mentally and emotionally, she must be at the end of her tether. She might have been for a long time.' I bit my lip. Mum had always pushed back any time Dad or Auntie Louise had suggested she seek professional help, so she wasn't going to react well to this suggestion, but it was absolutely what Chloe needed and I was prepared to fight for it. 'None of us are qualified to give her the sort of support she really needs. She needs professional counselling.'

Mum opened her mouth and I steeled myself for an objection but she closed it again and looked down at her hands.

'You're right,' she said looking up eventually. 'It's too big and too deep for us to handle on our own. But is it too late?'

I needed to choose my words carefully. If I picked well, it could help Mum face up to her own demons. 'It's never too late to get help. It won't be easy. It'll likely be painful and heartbreaking but it *will* be worth it. Something that happened in the past doesn't need to control a person's future.'

She nodded slowly. 'We'll get something sorted. We'll get her the help she needs. You know who else she needs to tell?'

'Her mum and James?'

'Yes, she does, but that's not who I was thinking.'

I raised an eyebrow questioningly.

'It tears me up to say this but she needs to tell the police.' Mum dropped her gaze to Samuel, who was now stirring. 'There's a little girl out there who's almost twelve years old and she has no identity.'

40

SAMANTHA

Mum and I agreed that Chloe needed some space and she'd come back when she was ready. Samuel didn't share our opinion. Having stayed asleep while Chloe revealed the secrets of her past, he was now wide awake and crying. We did our best to soothe him but he needed feeding and only Chloe could do that.

I found her on Thomas's bench, transfixed on the meadow, presumably lost in her memories.

'"HOT TIP" tip just in,' I said gently. 'There's a woman sitting on a bench who has a family who loves her very much and will be here for her every step of the way. She doesn't need to go through any of this alone. Not anymore.'

She looked up at me, tears glistening in her eyes, then jumped up and threw herself into my arms. I held her tightly as agonising sobs shook her body, making her gasp for breath.

'It'll be all right,' I whispered, stroking her back.

'I gave my baby away,' she cried.

'I know. And I can only begin to imagine how hard that was for you.'

'I had to. It was for the best. I couldn't have...' She gasped for breath again.

I pushed down the lump in my throat. 'I know. We understand.'

When her sobs eased, I released my hold. 'Samuel needs you. Do you think you're up to feeding him?'

'Is he crying?'

'Yes.'

She took a deep shaky breath. 'Do you think they'll take him away from me? Tell me the truth.'

We hadn't discussed the police in Chloe's presence but she'd obviously realised that the authorities would need to be alerted. I could see the fear in her eyes and I wished I could give her some assurance but I was afraid of what any false hope might do to her. Ignorance was the best approach for now.

'I don't know what will happen next. I'm really sorry but I've got no experience of this situation.'

'What's your gut feeling?'

My gut feeling was that abandoning a baby was a criminal offence. She'd been young, scared and desperate and I was sure they'd take her mental health into consideration and be sympathetic, but there would still be repercussions. No way was I going to alarm her by telling her that.

I put my arm round Chloe and steered her towards the barn. 'I honestly don't know. Come on, Samuel needs you. Let's focus on that for now.'

While she fed Samuel, Mum suggested that Auntie Louise should come over and hear the truth. Chloe agreed without hesitation but didn't want Mum to go home. Mum glanced at me.

'You're very welcome to stay. And obviously Auntie Louise can too. We're short on beds but we'll work something out.'

I looked at Chloe. 'What about James?'

She shook her head slowly. 'Not today. I can't even... I *will* tell him but... Just Mum for now please.'

I patted her arm. 'Okay. I know how tough this was for you.' There was no way I was going to push her to contact James until she was feeling emotionally stronger.

Mum went outside to phone Auntie Louise and ask her to pack a bag for each of them. They'd both need to take some compassionate leave for at least the rest of the week to support Chloe.

She returned to the barn to confirm that Auntie Louise would be across as soon as possible and that she knew there was big news but she'd need to wait until she got here to hear it.

With two more bodies to accommodate at the farmhouse, I phoned Josh to ask whether there was a single bed at the veterinary practice house, Alder Lea, which could be brought over for Chloe's bedroom. Josh and I could both stay in the barn and Mum, Auntie Louise and Chloe would have to distribute themselves across Chloe's bedroom and ours. It didn't feel right for anyone to be assigned to an airbed after such a shock.

'The house has been empty for over eighteen months,' Josh said. 'I wouldn't like to vouch for the mattresses. But leave it with me. I might be able to come up with something. Are you okay? You sound drained.'

'You'll understand why when you get home. It's too complicated to go into now but Chloe's told us what happened and it's a bit of a shocker.'

'Not just a Chloe over-reaction then?'

'Definitely not. She's going to need lots of care and attention to get through this.'

'Sounds serious. While you're taking care of your cousin, promise me you'll also take care of yourself.'

I could feel his hug down the phone. 'I will. I promise.'

Josh phoned back fifteen minutes later to say that one of his customers ran a furniture warehouse and he'd arranged for them to drop off an ex-demonstration double bed and mattress for Chloe's room at 7 p.m.

When I hung up, I sat with my head in my hands at the treatment table, feeling helpless. Chloe wanted to be alone until Auntie Louise arrived and had taken Samuel up to her room. Mum also wanted to be alone and had gone for a walk. And I had a job to do but couldn't bring myself to open my laptop. All I could picture was a teenaged Chloe all alone in a holiday camp lodge psyching herself up to leave her baby in hospital. Tears dripped onto my hands and onto the table as I imagined her loneliness, desperation and pain.

'Oh, Chloe!' I whispered. 'We could have helped.'

My head was thumping and my eyes were bloodshot when Josh returned home from work, coming straight into the barn. He held me tightly while Chloe's story tumbled out between sobs.

'I can't believe it,' he said. 'Poor Chloe. How's she doing?'

'Not good although I think it's been a relief to let it out. She wanted some space but I should probably check on her now but...' I glanced towards the hedgehogs.

'I'll sort out our patients. You get over to the house.'

'Auntie Louise should be here soon. And I've texted your dad and Beth to suggest that they might want to go out for a meal tonight as everything has gone a bit crazy here and I'm not sure what we'll do about food.'

'Do you ever stop thinking about others?' he asked, cupping my face and gently kissing me.

'I can't help it.'

'I know you can't and it's one of the many reasons I love you so much.'

Feeling brighter with Josh home, I returned to the farmhouse. Beth and Paul confirmed they were heading out for a meal. Ten minutes later, Auntie Louise arrived and I was so relieved they had gone out because I'd have hated them to overhear what happened next.

41

CHLOE

I'd felt sick this afternoon when I told Sam and Auntie Debs the truth. My heart had pounded and I swear I thought I might faint at several points, yet I somehow got through it. I'm not sure what was worse: telling the full truth for the first time or admitting how badly I'd betrayed Auntie Debs after everything she'd done to help me.

Yet now, relaying the same information to Mum, I felt calm. I'd asked her to listen without any interruptions, which helped, and I'd asked Sam and Auntie Debs to be there so I knew they'd support me if Mum took it badly.

What I wasn't prepared for was her turning on Auntie Debs.

It was obvious she was shocked to discover I'd been pregnant because, like Sam, she hadn't suspected a thing. She was full of apologies for not being there for me and regrets that we'd fallen out that year. I didn't want to keep any part of it from her so I told her about the conversation I'd overheard with our neighbour, Anne and she was mortified.

'It's all my fault,' she whispered, clutching her hand to her throat.

'It isn't. I'm certain nothing would have changed even if I hadn't heard you. My mind was already made up. I couldn't keep her.'

But when it got to the part where Auntie Debs found out, Mum's eyes widened, her shoulders stiffened and she absolutely hit the roof. She didn't even know the rest of the story. That one piece of information was like lighting the touchpaper. The shock, grief and anger poured out of her in a tirade of abuse directed at Auntie Debs. She shouted, swore, pointed her finger, stamped her feet. At one point, I even thought she was going to lunge at her. And Auntie Debs simply sat there, red-faced, head-dipped and took it all.

I felt sick once more as I clung to a cushion, staring numbly at them. I knew I was going to have to speak. This was all my doing, after all.

'I'm so sorry, Mum,' I said in a small voice. 'But it wasn't Auntie Debs's fault. She wanted to tell you and I wouldn't let her. I told her I'd run away if she did.'

'She should have taken that risk,' Mum snapped. 'You were only seventeen.'

'I think you should let Chloe tell you the rest,' Sam suggested tentatively.

Mum looked at me expectantly as I twiddled with a lock of hair. 'I agree but, Mum, if you shout at me like you just shouted at Auntie Debs or if you have a go at her again, you'll have to leave because I can't deal with that right now. I know you're angry and hurt and I understand why but we can't change what happened. If you want to shout and swear, there's a cow shed past the barn. Go in there and do it.'

Mum stared at me for a moment then nodded but she didn't look at her sister. What had I done to them? Auntie Debs would be devastated at Mum's reaction. I was certain she'd be already blaming herself for what I'd done and having Mum blame her too might be too much to bear. But Mum needed to know. No more lies.

'Prepare yourself because you're not going to like this...' I said.

42

SAMANTHA

Auntie Louise kept her promise to Chloe and didn't shout at anyone again after the full truth came out but there was no mistaking that she held Mum entirely to blame for what had happened.

'You were the adult. You should have known better,' she'd hissed.

The atmosphere was unbearable and I could feel the strain taking its toll on me. My headache had intensified and I felt dizzy. The last thing we all needed right now was for me to faint.

'I think we could all do with some time out,' I said, standing up slowly. 'Anyone fancy pizza?' I was conscious nobody had eaten and hoped some food might help me feel a little better.

My suggestion was met with disinterest. 'Well, I'm hungry so I'm going to get Josh to order a takeaway if anyone wants some, otherwise you're welcome to raid the kitchen.'

I went into the kitchen and opened the fridge, breathing in the cool air for a few moments before pouring myself a glass of fresh orange juice then texting Josh to say it would just be the two of us for pizza but best order extra just in case.

After finishing my drink, I returned to the lounge. Chloe and

Auntie Louise were cuddled up on the sofa staring at the TV in silence while Auntie Louise stroked Chloe's hair. Mum was rigid in the chair, also staring at the TV. I looked round at the three of them, fear clamouring at me that this could be the start of another family rift. We'd barely made it through the last one.

I glanced at the Peter Rabbit comforter beside Samuel and my throat tightened. I knew Chloe had bought him that. Had it been a conscious reminder of the one she'd left for Ava?

Mum stood up. 'I think I'll get my bag and head back home,' she said to nobody in particular.

'Do what you like,' Auntie Louise muttered, keeping her eyes fixed on the TV. 'Like you always do.'

Mum's jaw tightened but she didn't retaliate. 'Chloe, I'm so sorry for everything. Take care of yourself.'

Chloe rolled off the sofa and gave Mum a hug. 'I don't want you to go.'

'I think I'd better. The focus needs to be on getting you some help; not on your mum and me arguing.'

'Can't face the truth about your part in this mess?' Auntie Louise challenged. 'That's so typical of you. Bury your head in the sand while everyone else is left to pick up the pieces.'

I winced. There'd been so many digs this evening about Mum's past. It seemed like Auntie Louise was baiting her, wanting her to reveal her big secret too. It wasn't fair on Mum or Chloe – who had no idea what Mum had been through – and I wasn't going to stand for it.

'Right, that's enough. It's been a difficult day for everyone but that's nothing when you think about what Chloe – and Mum – have been through, so let's stop it with the accusations and bitterness and try to be here for each other as a family so we can all support Chloe through this. Mum, Auntie Louise, I'm sure there are things you need to say to each other but how about they're saved for another day when things are less raw? As for you leaving, Mum, Chloe wanted you to stay earlier and I think it's up to Chloe now.' I looked at my cousin and she gave me a weak smile.

'I want Auntie Debs to stay. I need her here.'

I looked at Mum who nodded, then at Auntie Louise, who shrugged. 'Good. Glad that's sorted. I'm going to put the kettle on.'

Mum joined me in the kitchen while I was squeezing out the teabags. 'Thank you for standing up for me,' she said, taking me completely by surprise, yet again.

'You're welcome. How are you holding up?'

'I've been better. I'll stay for Chloe but is there somewhere I can go now to give them a bit of space? The tension's killing me.'

'There's a TV in my bedroom. You're welcome to go in there. Or if you want something to distract you from all of this, I'm heading over to the barn as soon as I've dished out the drinks. You're welcome to join me and find out more about the rescue centre. You could maybe even have a go at feeding the hoglets if you want. Completely up to you.'

She was silent for a moment, as though weighing up her options. 'I'd like to come to the barn.'

That really wasn't the response I'd been expecting, and she must have spotted the look of surprise on my face.

'Only if that's okay,' she added.

'Yes, of course. I'd love to show you what we do and you can meet my fiancé, Josh.'

Her eyes flicked towards my hand. 'It's a beautiful ring. Congratulations.'

'Thank you.'

'I might just change into something warmer and I'll come over in a bit.'

I told her where to find the bathroom and my bedroom for changing.

She'd no sooner headed upstairs than the bed arrived, so I pointed the delivery men to the top floor then took mugs of tea into Chloe and Auntie Louise and let them know I'd be in the barn if they needed me.

* * *

I was about to close the front door when Auntie Louise stepped out of the lounge and followed me outside, closing the door behind her.

'I'll walk over to the barn with you.'

We walked in silence until we reached the farmyard, out of earshot of the house. Auntie Louise stopped and turned to face me.

'I'm sorry about landing all this on you and for all the disruption. I just wanted to check you're okay. You've barely had time to settle in and get the rescue centre up and running and now you've got a house full of people and problems.'

'What's the good in having a seven-bedroom farmhouse if six of the bedrooms are empty?' I smiled at her. 'It's fine. I'm not worried about me. I'm worried about Chloe and what might happen next. I've been speculating all week on what could have caused her to leave James and I certainly didn't come up with anything like this. How are you holding up?'

'Still in shock. I can't get my head around it all. It doesn't feel real.'

'I know. It probably doesn't feel real to Chloe either. I have no idea how she's managed to keep that buried for so long. She's going to need a lot of help and I'll do whatever I can to support her and you too.'

'Thanks, sweetheart. You've always been so kind. Right from being a little toddler, your Uncle Simon and I always knew you'd grow up to be a nurse or a teacher or a vet like your dad. Caring for others is part of who you are.'

My throat felt tight. Until last year's rift, I'd always had a good relationship with Auntie Louise, but she'd never said anything like that before and it felt good to hear it.

'Thank you. And because I care so much, I need to say this. Don't let this come between you and Mum.'

Her expression hardened, as did her tone. 'She should have known better.'

'Why? If the positions had been reversed and it had been you discovering it was me who was pregnant, begging you not to tell my mum, would you have done anything different? Mum did what Chloe wanted her to do and she supported her as best as she could. I'm kicking myself for not spotting anything and for letting Chloe push me away, so I know you'll be feeling guilty too, but imagine how much worse Mum must feel. She believed the baby had been adopted. I'll bet she's been running through everything that happened that summer, searching for signs she missed that Chloe was struggling with her mental health and was about to abandon her baby. I can't even begin to think what that level of guilt must feel like. Can you?'

Auntie Louise shrugged. 'Probably not.'

'You have every right to feel upset and angry but, as Chloe said earlier, we can't change what happened but we can make sure it doesn't affect us for the rest of our lives. Mum's going to need you, you're going to need her and Chloe's going to need you both. Chloe's confession is just the start of it. There's going to be a tough road ahead.'

'What do you think will happen to her?'

'Chloe asked me the same thing earlier and I honestly don't know. I didn't say this to her because I didn't want to risk spooking her and have her running again but I do know that what she did is a criminal offence.'

Auntie Louise clapped her hand across her mouth. 'Oh, my God! Are you saying she could go to prison?'

'They'll look into her age and her state of mind and I'm sure they'll show understanding and empathy. Let's face it, anyone who abandons a baby is not thinking clearly and definitely needs help. We've got to give Ava and her family some closure on wondering where she came from and we've got to think of Chloe. She's already hidden this for nearly twelve years. She can't keep hiding it.'

'I agree. What do you think James will do?'

'It's a hard one to call. If it was just about the past catching up with her, he'd be as shocked as the rest of us and he'd probably need some time apart from Chloe to process it. After all, this is his wife and this is a huge secret she's kept from him.'

'But you think it's more than that?'

I sighed. 'For James, it will be about Chloe running out and taking Samuel. It's refusing to speak to him and not even seeing him when he came here. It's arguments, mood swings, accusations of an affair, checking his phone. And all that while he's struggling with his cancer diagnosis. I actually think the situation with James will be harder than with the police.'

Auntie Louise closed her eyes for a moment and breathed in deeply.

I hugged her. 'We'll get through it together. And that includes Mum.'

'I'm fuming with her.'

'Nobody's asking you not to be. Just maybe, for Chloe's sake, find a different way to convey that.'

As she walked back to the farmhouse, I paused in the farmyard and looked round. Thomas used to say Hedgehog Hollow was a family home. Now it was full to bursting with family. I bet this wasn't quite what he had in mind.

In the barn, I checked my emails and picked up one from Adam, the accounts tutor.

To: Hedgehog Hollow Rescue Centre
From: Adam Fox, Business & Accounts Tutor, Reddfield TEC
Subject: Student Bookkeeping Volunteer
Hi Samantha,
Great news! I have a volunteer for you. A few students put their name forward but the most conscientious one (who also has her own transport – bonus!) is Phoebe Corbyn. She's quiet but exceptionally bright and very focused.
Short notice but is there any chance you could come to the TEC to meet her in the morning? We're both free 2nd period. If not, it might have to be next week. Let me know either way.

To: Adam Fox, Business & Accounts Tutor, Reddfield TEC
From: Hedgehog Hollow Rescue Centre
Subject: RE: Student Bookkeeping Volunteer
Thanks so much. That's brilliant news! I'll meet you in reception at 10.15 a.m.

'It'll do you good to get away from things for an hour or so,' Josh said when I told him.

'I wondered whether I should stay but Chloe's got Auntie Louise and Mum. I can't put everything here on hold for her.'

He gave me a reassuring smile. 'Don't worry about them. They'll understand.'

* * *

Josh and I were tucking into takeaway pizza a little later when Paul and Beth appeared in the barn, each holding a sleeping child.

'Is it safe to go back inside?' Paul asked.

I put my slice of pizza down. 'I'm so sorry for asking you to go out. I feel awful.'

'Honestly, don't worry about it,' he said. 'We were planning to go out anyway for my last day at Langton's.'

'It's just as well you did. Things got pretty heated.'

'Do you need us to move out?' Beth asked. 'Give you more space?'

She sounded casual but the worried expression on her face contradicted her tone. It was the last thing I wanted, especially with Paul starting chemo again next week.

'Gosh, no! It should calm down now that we know why Chloe left James but I wouldn't like to put a timescale on how long they'll be here. We've had a shift round and there's room for everyone. My Auntie Louise and Chloe will be in our room with Samuel, my mum's on the top floor and Josh and I will be sleeping over here.'

'Promise you'll let us know if we're in the way,' Paul said. 'We could maybe move into Alder Lea.'

Josh shook his head. 'You were invited here for a reason. You'll need the support next week and, if anyone needs to leave, it'll have to be Chloe. Your recovery needs to come first.'

'That comes from me too,' I added. 'Even if Chloe can't go back to James, she's got other options.'

'Thank you.' Beth smiled gratefully. 'We're going out for the day tomorrow but please don't think it's because we feel pushed out. We're taking the kids to a petting farm, which was always the plan.'

They bid us goodnight and went to put the children to bed. Despite Beth's reassurances, I couldn't help feeling guilty. We'd invited them here so they could have help and so they could both rest and recuperate yet the farmhouse was anything but restful at the moment.

With the truth now out, Chloe seemed calmer but the tension had moved to Auntie Louise and Mum instead. Hopefully Auntie Louise would sleep on it and they'd make their peace in the morning.

* * *

Josh and I were clearing away the pizza boxes when there was a knock on the door and Mum stepped inside.

'Did you mean it when you said I could come over?'

'Of course! Come in. Are you hungry? We've got some pizza left.'

'No, thanks.' She came a little closer and the smell must have tantalised her. 'Actually, if you're sure there's some spare.'

I indicated the boxes. 'Knock yourself out. There's a microwave if you want it a bit hotter. This is Josh, by the way. Josh, this is my Mum, Debbie. Everyone calls her Debs. I don't know if...' I tailed off. Mum and I didn't have a relationship so it felt weird telling Josh what to call her.

'I'm happy with either,' she said.

'It's good to meet you, Debbie.'

'So this is where you keep the hedgehogs?' She nodded towards the crates, a slice of pizza poised near her mouth.

'Yes. Welcome to Hedgehog Hollow Rescue Centre. When I inherited it, it was a one-storey barn but, after it burned down, the locals rebuilt it with two storeys, which gives us loads of flexible space. We take in sick and injured hedgehogs and abandoned hoglets. At the moment we have twenty-seven adults and twenty-eight babies.'

'So many? Already?'

'We've had fifty-three admissions in total but that's nothing compared to some rescue centres. Established centres can be treating several hundred at a time and we've got the space here if it ever comes to that.'

Mum had never shown any interest in anything I'd done before yet she genuinely seemed to want to hear all about Hedgehog Hollow. She asked questions, she helped feed the hoglets, she stroked Gollum and wanted to know how he'd ended up bald and if his spines would ever return. She told me about seeing hedgehogs in the garden at Meadowcroft when she'd been little and she even joked about some of the names she and Auntie Louise gave them. She asked Josh about his practice and how Dad was settling in. It was the strangest thing having such a lengthy normal conversation and even some laughter with her. I kept expecting an alarm clock to sound, indicating it was all just a dream.

Shortly after 10 p.m. she yawned and announced it was time to head over to the farmhouse for bed.

'Hope you manage to sleep okay,' I said. 'If you need a break from the intensity of it all tomorrow, you're welcome to come over here again any time from 11.15. I'm going to a meeting but I'll be back late morning to prepare for a school visit in the afternoon.'

'I'll see what Chloe has planned in the morning.' She walked towards the door then stopped and turned to face us. 'It's been a tough day today and this has been exactly what I needed to take my mind off it. Thank you both. What you do here is pretty special.' She looked directly at me. 'Your Nanna and Gramps would have been very proud of you.'

Without another word, she left the barn and I turned to Josh, my mouth agape.

'Bet that's not something you ever expected her to say,' he said, putting his arm round my shoulders and cuddling me to his side.

'Nothing about today has been expected. Am I living in some sort of parallel universe?'

'I thought she was going to say *she* was proud of you although, when she said your grandparents were, I'm pretty sure that's what she meant.'

Tears pricked my eyes. Yes, I'd thought that too. What an unexpected twist in the strangest of days.

We finally settled on the sofa bed a little after midnight. 'How are you doing?' Josh asked, his voice full of concern.

'Still feeling like I'm in a dream. I know I shouldn't dwell on it but I keep going back over that first year at college. Like I said to you the other night, Chloe was really distant but we all thought it was because it had ended with Travis and she'd fallen out with Scarlett. I can't believe she went through most of her pregnancy completely alone. And it breaks my heart so much to imagine her all alone in the Lakes, making plans to abandon her baby. She must have been so desperate to even think about that, let alone go through with it. Tell you what, it certainly explains some of the things she's said and done over the years.'

'Yeah, I was thinking the same. What a thing to have kept hidden for all these years. Her head must be mashed.'

When I didn't respond, Josh tightened his hold on me and kissed my forehead. 'You know there was absolutely nothing you could have done at the time, don't you?'

'I can't help wondering if...' I sighed. 'You're right. Chloe didn't want anyone to know. Mum only knew because she saw the baby kick. I'm just grateful that someone was there for her.'

'And everyone's here for her now. She's got so much support round her and she'll get the help she needs.'

'It explains a lot about Mum and Chloe's relationship over the years, too. You should have seen Mum earlier. I felt so sorry for her. It must have been hard enough for her carrying Chloe's secret alongside her own for all this time but, when Chloe admitted what she really did with the baby, she looked so defeated. My heart broke for them both.'

'Must have been a hell of a shock for her.'

'And a major guilt trip but it led to the first civil conversation I can remember us ever having. She listened to me and she even agreed with me and then you saw how she was tonight. What a transformation.'

'She certainly surprised me. I actually quite liked her.'

'So did I! And before you go worrying that I've got my hopes up that everything's changed and Mum and I will be the best of friends from now on, I'm not daft. Today has been emotional for everyone and she probably didn't have the energy to fight with me. She said herself that learning about the hedgehogs was the distraction she needed so it was probably more about her than me. But, even if nothing changes between us, I'm grateful that, among this mess, the one chink of light was that Mum and I connected. Just for a few hours.' My voice caught in my throat and the last sentence was barely audible.

Josh changed position to hold me closer. 'You never know. It could be the start of the ice thawing. From what you've told me of your Auntie Louise's reaction, your mum might need you now.'

I swallowed on the lump in my throat. 'I'd like to think so, but I'm a realist now when it comes to Mum. I've got my hopes up far too many times before.'

'Someone told me recently that it's never too late to start over. Who was it now? I think it was a badass hedgehog saviour.'

My heart swelled with love for him as I kissed him. 'Thank you.'

'I don't want you to get hurt again but I watched her with you tonight. It was like she was seeing you for the first time as this amazing woman who's there for her family no matter what and who's set up this incredible facility instead of seeing you as the child she felt she had to shut out.'

I couldn't speak for the lump now blocking my throat. I tightened my hold and kissed his chest. Once again, he'd known exactly what to say.

43

CHLOE

'I woke up and you'd both gone.' Mum sat down beside me on the bench at the back of the farmhouse the following morning. 'I panicked for a moment.'

Samuel was sitting on my knee, his Peter Rabbit comforter scrunched in his hand. I handed him over to Mum for a cuddle.

'I'm not a flight risk, Mum. I know and accept that I did a bad thing and I'm going to face the consequences, whatever they are.'

I'd fallen into an exhausted sleep last night but, after waking in the early hours to feed Samuel, my mind was active and I'd been unable to drop off again. I Googled what would happen to someone in my situation. Weirdly, it didn't shock me. Neglect and abandonment apparently. It deserved a prison sentence. What upset me more than that was the phrase for what I'd done. Baby dumping. You dumped a crap boyfriend when you'd had enough of him. You took old carpets and broken toasters to the tip and dumped them. You didn't dump a baby. Yet that's exactly what I'd done. What sort of person does that?

'It's beautiful out here,' Mum said. 'You can see for miles.'

'I've never really appreciated views like this before. Sam's very lucky living here. I feel I need to absorb it. Just in case they lock me up.'

'Oh, sweetheart, I'm sure it won't come to that.'

'It might. I've got to be realistic about this. I thought I was doing the right thing for Ava at the time, but who am I kidding? I hope she's happy. I hope she went to a good family like my fictional Maythorpes.'

'Would you want to see her? I don't know if it'll be an option but, if it was, would you want to?'

I'd thought about that a lot during the night. I pictured her as a toddler with blonde curls and wondered whether they'd kept her name, where she lived, whether she was sporty and artistic like me.

'I'm not sure,' I said eventually. 'I don't think it's my decision anymore. It would be up to Ava... or whatever her new parents called her.'

'How are you feeling now that it's out in the open?'

'A right mishmash of emotions. Relieved, scared, guilty, tearful, calm. I seem to ricochet from one to the next.'

'That's understandable.'

We sat in silence, gazing out at the meadow. I recognised daisies and buttercups but I had no idea what any of the other flowers were called. Sam would know. She was good at stuff like that. I didn't know what any of the butterflies were called either. Or the birds chirping. I'd never paid any attention when we'd visited Nanna and Gramps at their home in Meadowcroft. I'd always wanted to move on and do something but Sam would happily sit for hours taking it all in, a look of wonder on her face. If I'd been more like Sam – calmer, considered, restful – instead of chasing the new and exciting, I'd never have agreed to Scarlett's suggestion. I'd be in a very different place right now.

I closed my eyes and pushed that thought out of my head. If only... Two little words but so relevant to every part of my life and I had to stop thinking about what could have been. If I hadn't gone along with Scarlett's suggestion, my life would never have brought me to James and I wouldn't have had Samuel. I'd still do it all again to have them both in my life.

Would James still be in my life when he knew? Would Samuel? The thought of losing them scared me way more than the thought of months or even years behind bars. Because, without them, my life would be over.

I wiped some drool from Samuel's chin with his bib. 'I'm going to text James to ask if he can take a day off tomorrow so I can explain it all to him and, once that's done, I'll speak to the police.'

'So soon?' I could hear the panic in Mum's voice but I felt strangely calm. For now, anyway.

The following morning, at Reddfield TEC, Adam appeared with a student who he introduced as Phoebe. A slender, pretty eighteen-year-old with long dark hair and big blue eyes, I'd never met anyone quite so timid. We grabbed a drink in the canteen, and it was just as well Adam was there with his prompts and encouragement, or Phoebe might never have spoken. She seemed completely overwhelmed to have been given the opportunity and kept staring at me, wide-eyed.

I offered to drop the paperwork off at her house but, in the longest sentence I'd heard from her, she said she'd prefer to come and collect it herself over the weekend and would text me to check on a suitable time. We exchanged phone numbers and she scuttled away, clutching her bag to her chest.

As soon as she was out of earshot, I raised my eyebrows at Adam. 'You said she was quiet, but that was off the scale. Are you sure she wants to do this?'

Adam smiled. 'Don't worry. She's really enthusiastic. I asked the ones who were interested to put together a proposal as to how they'd manage the accounts and hers was brilliant. As soon as she gets to know you, she'll be fine and I promise her work won't disappoint.'

'Okay. I'm happy to work with her but please can you keep checking in with her and make sure she's happy to stay working with me? I'd hate her to feel she's being pushed into something.' I had enough drama in my life at the moment without adding into the mix a timid teenager being made to do something against her will.

* * *

Paul's car had gone when I pulled into the farmyard. I'd seen him and Beth before I'd left for college and wished them a lovely day out but there'd been no sign of anyone else up and about at that time.

I was about to unlock the barn door when I spotted a car on the farm track so I waited. The driver's rescued hedgehog presented with another case of flystrike. It was the most common reason for admissions at the moment and, as it was more common in the summer, I suspected cases would keep escalating. It was lucky I'd laid out the barn ready for the school visit as it looked to be quite a severe case, so I'd be working on my new patient right up till the children arrived.

I'd only just weighed her when Mum appeared in the barn. 'You said last night that I could come over again...' Her voice was tentative.

'Of course! Come in. It's perfect timing because I've just had a rescue arrive. Are you squeamish?' It was bad that I didn't even know that about my own mother.

Mum came closer to the treatment table. 'Not really. Why?'

'You'll soon see. This is Shelley, named after *Frankenstein* author Mary Shelley. She's an adult female with a bad case of flystrike and a few of the eggs have already hatched into maggots.'

Mum seemed intrigued rather than disgusted and the next hour flew by while we worked together to clean Shelley up. Although there were a lot of eggs and several maggots, they were isolated to one cut on her back and hadn't spread, so it didn't take quite as long to sort her out as I'd initially anticipated. Mum asked a few questions about treatment but there were extensive periods of silence. They weren't uncomfortable because we had a task to do, but I couldn't help thinking it was a reminder that we didn't have a relationship and I should proceed with caution.

Mum prepared a crate for Shelley under my guidance and placed her among the strips of fleece.

'Shelley will stay here until her cut's fully healed and she's put on weight, then we'll release her either on the farm or in one of the local villages where we know there's a hedgehog population.' I moved the crate to join the others. 'And now it's time to feed the hoglets.'

'Do you ever stop working?' Mum asked.

'Hoglets season means we have through-the-night feeds but the hoglets are getting bigger now so that's easing, although we'll go through it again in the autumn. As for the rest, there's a constant rotation of feeding, cleaning and medication but it depends on what's admitted, which obviously we have no control over. I can have a few days where I have no new patients and then I can suddenly get several in at once and I have to prioritise.'

'So a hedgehog could arrive while you're doing the school visit?'

'It's a definite possibility but the school is prepared for that and all it means is they get to see me working on a live case. Right, hoglets time.'

My very first hoglets – Leia and Solo – had recently moved onto solid food so could eat in their crates but most of the others were still too young and needed formula. They weren't able to generate their own body heat until they were a month old, so I still needed the heat pads. The loudest squeaking was coming from the Brontë hoglets, so I opened their crate and smiled at the sight of five of them scrambling over each other, clearly desperate for sustenance. I placed them one at a time on the heat pads and a quick inspection of Brontë's cut suggested it was healing well.

Cathy hadn't been in the scrum and my pulse started racing. She hadn't taken much formula during the night and Josh and I had suspected she might not make it through to morning. I'd checked on her when I rose and she'd been holding on but might we have lost her since? I tentatively peeled back the strips of newspaper and fleece and my heart sank. She was curled up at the back of the crate. Still. I gulped and blinked back the tears as I lifted her out.

'What's up?' Mum asked.

'We've lost one.'

'Oh, no!'

I gently placed her in a metal tray and covered her in a piece of blue paper towel. I'd make sure I moved her before the children arrived.

'Are you okay?' Mum asked.

The obvious concern in her voice made me want to cry even more. I nodded and took a couple of deep breaths. 'It happens. She was tiny and struggling to eat so it was inevitable but it still hurts. The only way to make peace with it is knowing that none of the six would have survived if Hedgehog Hollow didn't exist so, even though I couldn't save Cathy, her siblings are still with us.'

Mum didn't say anything but she looked thoughtful as she helped feed the others.

Fizz arrived as we finished, wearing a pink 'hedgicorn' T-shirt in the same design as yesterday, and I introduced her to Mum.

'I've never met a Fizz before,' Mum said. 'Is it short for something?'

'Felicity, but nobody dares call me that. Felicity Kinsella sounds really posh, don't you think?'

'Kinsella? I was at school with an Adrian Kinsella. Any relation?'

'He's my dad! Oh, my God! What was he like at school?'

Mum smiled – a proper smile that lifted my heart. 'A bit of rebel, as I remember. He was always in and out of the Head's office, in trouble for one thing or another.'

'That's hilarious because do you know what he does for a living?'

Mum shrugged.

'He's a police sergeant.'

Mum laughed; a sound I'd heard so rarely over the years that I'd begun to wonder whether she knew how to laugh. 'I would never in a million years have predicted that.'

'I'll have to tell him I've met a school friend of his. What's your name?'

'Debbie Wishaw, but it was Danby back then.'

Mum had just introduced herself using her married name, which surprised me. It would be quite some time before the divorce was through but I'd assumed she'd have reverted to Danby. I glanced down at her left hand and noticed that she was still wearing her wedding and engagement rings. Dad still wore his wedding ring, too. I'd asked him about it and he'd said it didn't feel right to remove it while they were still officially married. How strange that neither of them had taken that step.

There was a knock on the barn door and Chloe entered holding a tray. She looked surprised to see Mum with me. 'I thought you and Fizz might be hungry, but I didn't realise Auntie Debs was here too. There's food for you in the house.'

'You've made lunch again?' I asked, touched that she could even think of preparing us all lunch at a time like this. 'Thank you.'

'It's just a few sandwiches and some crisps.'

'Sounds ideal. Are you okay this morning?' I was conscious of not saying too much in front of Fizz. I'd wondered if it was worth asking her to run a 'hypothetical situation' by her dad to see what might happen to Chloe but I didn't want to do that without speaking to Chloe and Auntie Louise first.

'I'm doing okay at the moment, thank you. Would it be all right if I invite James over to the farm tomorrow if he's free?'

'He's welcome any time.'

'Thank you. And would it be okay if my dad comes over later? He won't stay but I'd like to see him.'

'Of course he can. He can stay if he wants. There's always the airbed.'

'We'll see. I'll bring your lunch over, Auntie Debs.'

'It's okay. I'll come over for it in a few minutes.'

'Thank you. Okay, so enjoy your lunch and I hope the visit goes well.'

She left the barn and Mum and I exchanged concerned looks. Although she'd said all the right things, there was no mistaking the toll this had taken on her. It was as though all the fight had left her and she was on autopilot, trying to be polite and careful. And how many times had she said 'thank you'?

'This looks yummy,' Fizz said, grabbing a plate from the tray, clearly oblivious to the strangeness that had just occurred.

* * *

The second school visit went really well. It was easier this time as we had a better idea of the timings. Mum decided to stay in the barn to help out – a decision that I suspected was very much about avoiding Auntie Louise – and stuck with the same group of children so she could see what both Fizz and I were doing.

The three of us cleared up after the children left.

'I've got some coursework due in tomorrow,' Fizz said when we'd finished. 'I'll have to love you and leave you. Sam, I might be able to come over for a bit on Sunday but I'll let you know.'

'Thanks, Fizz. Don't worry if you have too much on. You've done loads already this week.'

She gave me a hug then left the barn with a wave.

'I can't believe her dad's a policeman,' Mum said as soon as the barn door closed. 'He used to steal sweets from the local shop and sell them at school. Your Nanna used to say he'd either end up behind bars or putting people behind bars. I thought behind bars but I'm glad he went the right way.' Her smile faded. 'I hope they don't come down hard on Chloe. I think she's punished herself enough over the years.'

'Same here. She looked haunted earlier, didn't she?'

Mum sighed and nodded. 'You went out with James. How do you think he'll react?'

'Auntie Louise asked me the same thing and I'll say to you what I said to her. I think he'd have been shocked about the baby but he'd have understood she was desperate, but I think the way Chloe has treated him this week might be the sticking point.'

'You might be right. The last thing Chloe needs right now is for her marriage to fall apart on top of everything else. Let's hope he's in an understanding and forgiving mood. Speaking of which, I'd better go and face my sister.'

'Good luck.'

She gave me a weak smile then headed for the door.

I boiled the kettle then sat down at the treatment table with a well-earned cup of tea. Mum and I had spent nearly five hours together and she hadn't made a snide comment or given me a dirty look once. I still wouldn't get my hopes up too much but the early signs were encouraging.

45

CHLOE

I sat cross-legged on the bench that evening, a mug of tea next to me, my phone in my hand, trying to psyche myself up to make contact with James.

Dad was in the lounge with Mum and Auntie Debs. Mum had given him the basics over the phone last night but had told him not to rush over as I needed a bit of time. He'd driven over straight from work tonight and had given me the tightest of hugs, setting me off crying again.

'There's no need to go through it all with me unless you want to,' he said. 'I know it must be painful. I've got the gist and I'm here for you.'

His reaction was welcome and reassuring but it made me wonder yet again what the hell I'd been thinking when I was sixteen/seventeen. Why hadn't I let my parents in then? Yet another 'what if'.

Auntie Debs had nipped out to the supermarket while we were talking and came back with the ingredients to make fajitas for everyone. I was extremely hungry by this point. Paul and Beth joined us, so there were eight adults round the kitchen table tucking into the meal, which meant lots of chatter and laughter, but I felt so disjointed from it, as though I was hovering above the table in some sort of dream-like state.

After we'd eaten, I went to collect the plates for dishwasher duty but Josh insisted he'd do it.

'Might it be a good time to contact James?' Mum asked me discreetly when everyone had finished eating and mugs of tea were being poured.

I glanced at the wall clock. He'd be on the train home. It was as good a time as any. Which was why I was outside on my own now, looking at the text I'd composed.

⊠ To James
I cannot even begin to say how sorry I am for
the distress I've caused you this past week but,
if you're ready to hear it, I'm ready to explain
what happened. I know it's short notice but is
there any chance you can come to the farm
tomorrow morning at 10am to talk? xx

I kept reading and re-reading it, removing the kisses then adding them in again, adjusting the wording then putting it back to how it had been.

'Bloody hell! Send.'

My phone started ringing a couple of minutes later. I knew he'd do that.

⊠ To James
I'm sorry but I'm not going to answer my phone
because you'll want to get into a conversation
and it needs to be face to face. And NOT tonight
so please don't drive over as I won't see you.

You'll understand why when you know the full
details.

He rang again a few minutes later.

✉ To James
If you ring again, I'll switch my phone off. Can
you come tomorrow or not? xx

He replied:

✉ From James
Why does it always have to be on your terms? Why
can't we do this tonight?

✉ To James
Because there's a house full of guests who won't
be here tomorrow so we'll have more opportunity
to talk then. Or Saturday if you can't get the
day off xx

✉ From James
I'll come tomorrow but at 8am.

I nearly agreed but it wasn't fair on Paul and Beth. I hadn't
paused to consider how awkward they might be feeling, but Mum
had pointed out that they'd had to go out last night and had been
out all day today. Over dinner, they'd said they had plans for
tomorrow too and, even though they told Dad they were making
the most of family time before Paul's second round of chemotherapy started, I couldn't help wondering whether they'd have
gone out for full days if it hadn't been for me.

✉ To James
I said 10am. Not a minute sooner. Please bring
Samuel's buggy so Mum can take him out for a
walk while we're talking xx

✉ From James
I want to see my son

✉ To James
You will. You can spend as much time with him as
you want but I want him to be out while we talk.
Hope you understand that xx

✉ From James
I don't understand anything right now, Chloe.
See you tomorrow and it had better be a damn
good explanation for what you've done this week

I could hear the sting in his words and, once again, picture his face at the airport before he walked away. The absence of kisses on any of his texts cut deep too. Taking a deep breath, I typed in a final text:

✉ To James
It is xx

That was it. Tomorrow morning, he'd know the full truth and it was very likely that my marriage would be over. If only I hadn't run. If only... Story of my life.

Friday morning arrived. The day of my confession to James.

It was only five days since I'd seen him, but it felt like five months. After feeling reasonably calm yesterday, I was now a bundle of nerves. I'd already dashed to the bathroom several times, thinking I was going to throw up, but the sensation had eased each time and I'd splashed my face with water before returning to Mum and Samuel declaring a 'false alarm'.

Now, as the minutes dragged painfully, I began to regret insisting he wait until ten. Would I have been better just letting him come over last night and getting it over with? But I could also argue that I'd have been better off confronting him on Sunday. Or telling him before we married. Or after we met. My life was full of moments where I could have/should have done things differently and dwelling on them wouldn't get me anywhere. I'd created my own mess and the time to sort it out was now.

'Are you sure you don't want me to stick around when he gets here?' Mum asked ten minutes before he was due.

'I need to do this on my own. I don't want him to feel he can't react how he wants because you're there. He needs to be able to tell me exactly what he thinks and I need to hear it.'

I'd suggested Mum might like a trip into Reddfield with Auntie Debs while James was here, but she'd refused. She said she wanted to be nearby in case things became fraught and I needed her. While I knew that was true, I suspected another reason was avoidance of her sister. They'd sat apart over dinner last night. When I returned to the lounge after texting James, Paul and Beth had gone upstairs to bathe the kids, Sam and Josh had gone over to the barn, so there was just Mum, Dad and Auntie Debs. And an atmosphere I could have cut with a knife.

Auntie Debs kept trying to make small talk but all she got from Mum was a 'yes', 'no' or short answer that shut the conversation down, usually accompanied by a sigh. I tried too but didn't fare much better so gave up and focused on playing with Samuel, glad of the distraction. Auntie Debs obviously gave up too. She muttered something about going to bed early with a headache. Headache, my arse. Mum's attitude towards her sucked. Couldn't she see it was only making it worse for me? I couldn't face another argument by pointing that out but I wasn't happy about it. They were usually the best of friends, in agreement on most things. Like most siblings, they had their moments, but they were soon forgotten with a hug and a smile. Not this week. Another thing that I'd messed up to add to my big list of failures.

'Nearly time,' Mum said, bringing my focus back to James's arrival.

I looked out of the front window and my stomach did a backflip at the sight of his car in the farmyard.

'He's here.' I picked up Samuel from his playmat. 'Will you answer the door?'

'If you want.'

'No. I'll do it. No. You do it.'

Mum placed a hand on each of my shoulders. 'Breathe.'

James walked past the window, pushing the buggy, but he didn't look in. Even though I was expecting it, the doorbell ringing still made me jump.

'I'll get it.' I felt sick again. The last time I'd felt this nervous was making my escape from the Royal Lancaster Infirmary nearly twelve years ago. 'Wish me luck.'

'You've got this.' Mum fixed her eyes on mine, squeezed my shoulders and gave me a gentle push towards the lounge door.

Boosted by her words, I stepped into the hall and opened the front door. James looked awful. Taking in the untrimmed beard, unruly hair and dark bags under his eyes, my first reaction was that the cancer had returned, filling me with panic.

'Are you okay? Is it the cancer?'

'Is what the cancer?'

'You look like...' I tailed off. Of all the opening statements I'd planned in my head, insulting his appearance hadn't been one of them.

'I look like shit?' he suggested, eyebrows raised. 'Hmm. What could possibly have caused that, I wonder?'

The bitterness was hardly surprising. I deserved it. I thrust Samuel towards him. 'He's missed his daddy.' It was a sneaky tactic but I wanted to deflect his anger away from me for a moment. There'd be plenty of time for that when Samuel was out of earshot and James heard the truth.

'And I've missed him too,' he snapped, cuddling Samuel close to him. 'And I shouldn't have had to miss him if my wife hadn't run out and refused to see me.' He kissed Samuel's head then narrowed his eyes at me. 'As I put in my text, there had better be a bloody good explanation for this week.'

I gulped. 'Why don't you come in?'

'What do you want me to do with the buggy?'

'Leave it out there. Mum's going to take him for a walk round the farm while we talk.'

'I'm not leaving here today until I've spent some quality time with him.'

'You'll get that. I promise.'

He raised his eyebrows again. 'A promise from you doesn't seem to be worth much at the moment.'

I deserved that. I moved aside so he could step into the hall.

'Tea or coffee, James?' Mum asked, her tone flat. She'd obviously heard the whole exchange and wasn't impressed.

'Hi, Louise, I didn't realise you were here.'

'Clearly not, or you might not have spoken to my daughter like that. Tea or coffee?'

'Tea, please.'

When she stepped into the kitchen, he widened his eyes at me in a why-the-hell-didn't-you-tell-me-your-mum-was-listening kind of way. I shrugged and led him into the lounge.

We sat in silence for a few minutes until Mum appeared with drinks then disappeared with Samuel and a reminder to ring her if I needed her.

'Am I somehow the bad guy?' he asked when the front door closed.

'She's just protecting me. She was hoping for a happy reunion as that would make the next part a little easier. I told her not to get her hopes up.'

'She seriously expected that? You run away with my son with no note, no explanation and, for nearly a week, you refuse to see me or even speak to me and your mum really expected me to turn up here with a smile on my face and a big hug, ready to forgive and forget?'

'Maybe not quite that. But...' I shook my head. 'Never mind. I asked you here so I could explain why I left. I know what I did was cruel and thoughtless and... well, that's always been a bit of a theme for me. I shouldn't have run out and I shouldn't have pushed you away but something happened on Sunday that completely freaked me out. I panicked and I didn't pause to properly think any of it through. Again, story of my life.'

James folded his arms, eyebrows raised, clearly frustrated with my rambling. 'What happened on Sunday?' he demanded.

'I promise you I've never done it before but you left your phone behind when you went to the supermarket and it was too tempting. I looked through your texts.'

He didn't look surprised. 'I thought you maybe had when I realised I'd left it behind but that doesn't explain why you ran out. All my texts are boring. Don't tell me you thought I was having an affair yet again? I thought we sorted all that out after Samuel was born.'

'We did. It was stupid of me. I honestly didn't think you'd found someone else but I did wonder, because of how it had been between us over the past few months, whether you might have fallen out of love with me. We hadn't even kissed since Samuel came home and I suppose I was looking for something that might confirm that because I was too scared to ask you straight out.'

'How could you even think that?'

'I've just told you. Because of how things were. We were always arguing. I knew it was my fault. You must have dreaded coming home from work, wondering what I was going to moan about next.'

James looked as though he was about to protest, but I got in first. 'Don't try to make out it wasn't that bad because we both know it was and you obviously thought so too because you were going to talk to a counsellor about it.'

His eyes widened. 'You checked my emails too?'

'Only from one person but it was enough.'

'So let me get this right. You took our son and left because you were snooping on my phone, looking for evidence that I didn't love you anymore and this was a conclusion you'd jumped to because of a few cross words and a lack of intimacy, despite that being something that happens to pretty much all new parents.'

Colour rushed to my cheeks. I sounded so stupid and paranoid when he put it in simple terms like that.

His voice became louder and angrier as he continued. 'You found a couple of emails between me and the counsellor I'd arranged to see about my cancer where I happened to mention that I also wanted to talk about a few problems at home and you instantly concluded that... I don't know... I wanted to slap you with some divorce papers? So you upped sticks and left without even thinking to ask me about it.'

'It wasn't that. I mean, it *was* the email, but that's not exactly why I left.'

'Good. Because if you'd bothered to ask me, I'd have told you that I'd arranged to see a counsellor because I've been having panic attacks about the cancer coming back and me dying and leaving my wife and son alone.'

I clapped my hand over my mouth. 'Oh, James. You never said.'

'Of course I didn't, because every moment I spent with you, you were too tired to talk or you were tearful or we were bickering so how could I add in the added complication of me having panic attacks? I wanted to speak to Genevieve about how I could broach the subject in a way that wouldn't upset you even more.'

My stomach lurched. 'Are you still having panic attacks?'

'Three this week. You know why getting a day off today wasn't a problem? Because I was sent home on Tuesday and I've been signed off sick for a fortnight. So tell your mum that I'm sorry I disappointed her by not giving you the happy reunion she wanted but I'm up to here with your shit this week...' He held his hand way above his head to indicate his point, '... and I'm not feeling particularly happy about anything.'

What had I done to him? I had to be the most unsupportive wife ever. He'd hidden his cancer diagnosis from me in the first place because my pregnancy was so stressful. Why? Because I'd got myself worked up about being pregnant again, constantly terrified that a medical professional would make some comment about this not being my first pregnancy or that something would go wrong as my punishment for what I'd done to Ava. When I started spotting last year, I'd really thought it was the end. Of course, James hadn't known any of that; he'd just assumed it was a difficult pregnancy. And now he'd had to hide his fears of his own mortality from me; fears that had resulted in panic attacks. What if he'd had one of those while he'd been driving to or from the station or while he'd driven over here in the storm on Monday? Or perhaps this morning?

'I can't even begin to tell you how sorry I am for everything you've been through. I'm not trying to make excuses because there really aren't any for what I've done but, when you hear what I have to say, you'll understand. Or maybe you won't understand but you will have an explanation.'

'You're not making any sense.'

'Sorry. Let's go back to the emails. It was not about you speaking to Genevieve about our home life that was the problem. It was that you were speaking to Genevieve. When I saw her name, I panicked, because I know her and I thought things about my past that I hadn't told you – or anyone else for that matter – might come out. The crazy thing is that there's no way they could have come out because Genevieve didn't know them but I saw her name, added two and two together and got five thousand and six and I ran. And I realise I'm still not making any sense, am I?'

James stared at me blankly.

'Okay. Let's start from the beginning.' I ran my shaking hands through my hair and gulped. 'Genevieve Enderby-Bowes is the sister of Travis Enderby-Bowes, who was my boyfriend when I was sixteen. I told you that, before I met you, I'd been in love once. It was with Travis...' My voice shook and I instinctively considered playing a part to give me strength but tossed that thought aside. From now on, there'd be no more acting. I needed to find the real Chloe Turner and, right now, she was scared and vulnerable and she wasn't going try to hide it.

James's tea sat on the table beside him, untouched, while he listened to me telling him how I met Travis and Scarlett that summer. I took care not to place much emphasis on my feelings for Travis but that did nothing to ease James's stony expression as I spoke.

He nodded at various points but didn't speak. All I could think was: *If he hates this first bit, he's going to loathe the rest. He has no idea what's about to hit him.*

When I reached the part where I returned to the holiday park over the October half-term holiday, my heart started to thud.

'I hope this is relevant,' he said, running his hand across his beard when I told him about Scarlett's birthday. 'I know we both have pasts but I'd rather not hear the graphic details about yours.'

'It is relevant because, a little later, I discovered I was pregnant and had no way of knowing who the father was.'

James sat forward in the chair, eyes wide. 'You were pregnant when you were sixteen?'

'Yes.'

'Shit! Chloe! Why did you never tell me?' His voice was full of empathy rather than anger, which threw me a little.

'Because I didn't tell anyone. The only person who ever knew was Auntie Debs.'

'You didn't tell your mum?'

'I was too ashamed.'

The clear expression of sympathy on his face was hard to bear because I knew it would soon be replaced by confusion and then disgust.

'So what happened to the baby? You had an abortion?'

I shook my head. 'I left it too late to even consider that. I went through with the pregnancy...'

I'd told myself I wouldn't cry but I couldn't help it as I relayed the final part. I watched his expression throughout and I'd been right about the change from sympathy to confusion.

'Please tell me you're making this up.'

'Why would I make it up?'

'I don't know. Why would you swap partners when you claim to be in love with your boyfriend? Why would you not tell your family you were pregnant? Why would you lie to your auntie about arranging an adoption? None of this makes sense!' His voice became louder with each question and the last statement was shouted, accompanied by him flinging his arms in the air.

And then came the statement I'd been dreading but, from his reaction in the airport, I'd known was coming. 'Who are you, Chloe? Because you're sure as hell not the woman I thought I'd married. I don't recognise you at all.'

He leapt up and started pacing the room, running his fingers through his hair and shaking his head. 'What were you thinking? What sort of person abandons a newborn baby like that?'

I sank back onto the sofa, clinging onto one of the cushions for comfort. Me! I was the sort.

'You hear stories like this on the news but these are women who are scared and desperate.'

I gasped. 'You think I wasn't scared and desperate?'

'But they're really young or they have no money, no job, no father.'

'All me!' I tossed the cushion aside. 'I was still at college so I had no money and no job. Mum and Dad have never had any spare money so I couldn't expect them to help and I didn't know who the father was. I couldn't look after a baby and I wanted her to have someone who could. I wanted her to have the best start in life.' I was shouting now but I couldn't help it. I needed him to understand.

'And the best start was abandoning her in a ward full of strangers?'

'I know how it sounds now but, at the time, I thought it was.'

'And do you still think that now?'

'Of course I don't. What do you take me for?'

'Do you really need to ask that?'

No, I didn't. It was written all over his face. As predicted, the confusion had turned to disgust.

'I needed help and I still do. This has been haunting me for years. What happened has affected everything I've done since.'

'How? We've been together for two years and I've had no inkling that anything like this was lurking in your past. I should have known there was something wrong with you. I mean, who seduces their cousin's boyfriend within thirty minutes of meeting him? You were hardly going to turn out to be a role model, were you?'

How dare he throw that back in my face? I wanted to leap up and slap him across the face like a scorned woman in an old movie. 'So love at first sight for both of us is now me seducing you, is it?'

'It's what it feels like now that I've heard about your sordid partner-swapping past.'

'Oh, my God, James! I can't believe that you're actually more bothered that I partner-swapped when I was sixteen than you are about the baby.'

'I'm not more bothered about that. I just...' He pressed his fingers to his temples. 'Christ, Chloe, it's a lot to take in.'

I lowered my voice. 'I know. I get it. It's huge. But please will you sit down so we can talk about it properly? You're making me dizzy.'

'Oh, I'm sorry. Is my pacing bothering you? Because I think I can probably trump you on the being bothered stakes right now.'

The withering look he gave me could have made me crumble but instead it gave me strength. I stood up, marched towards the door and flung it open. 'You say you don't recognise me but I say ditto. When the sensitive, caring man I married is ready to have a serious conversation without the insults and the sarcasm, you let me know.'

'So that's it? When the going gets tough, you run away or you throw me out?'

I softened my voice. 'Why don't you go and find my mum and spend some time with Samuel while we both take a moment? I'll be on the bench out the back if and when you're ready to continue the conversation calmly. If you need some time to process it and want to talk again another day, that's fine too, but you should know I'll be speaking to the police tomorrow so things may get a little crazy after that.'

'The police? What for?'

'Because baby dumping is a crime which carries up to five years in prison. So, when you're asking who does what I did, believe me, it *really* is someone desperate who's at the end of their tether and unable to think straight.'

'Chloe, I...' His face softened and he reached out a hand towards me.

I flinched and stepped back and into the hall. 'I expect Mum will either be on the farm track or in the cow shed. The echoes make Samuel smile. He'll be ready for a feed around noon so don't go too far. I got help feeding him, by the way. Turns out that horrible midwife was right and I *was* doing it all wrong. Plus, I had mastitis so that was fun.'

That sympathetic look and the tilt of his head was there. I

couldn't bear it. Aw, poor little Chloe can't cope with anything life throws at her. Bless her.

I yanked the front door open and forced myself to look at James. 'The good news is he doesn't need feeding quite so often now so, if you want him again after his lunchtime feed, you could even take him out somewhere.'

He nodded and I could sense a battle raging. Shout at me? Lecture me? Hug me? Walk away?

Be you. Be honest. Be real. 'Look, I know it's been really hard on you. I didn't think about how much it would hurt you not being able to see Samuel. I didn't really think about anything. I hope you know it was never about me trying to hurt you. It was about trying to protect us all and I know I screwed that up too.'

I was aware I was babbling but I needed a moment to focus on something different. The suggestion he find Samuel wasn't just because he was angry and needed to cool down. It was because this was harder than I'd expected. I'd imagined accusations and raised voices but even in my worst-case scenario, he'd still been the man I loved. He'd still hugged me. I didn't know what was real anymore. Me? Him? Us?

He stepped closer to the door, which meant he was closer to me. I could smell his pine body spray and it set my heart racing once more, a scent so delicious and familiar. I still yearned for him to hold me and, as he moved closer still, I wondered if he would.

Then he stepped outside and, without another word, headed towards the farmyard, shaking his head. I closed the door behind me and rested my back against it, then sank to the tiled floor, sobbing.

I'd just lost him. Actually, I'd done that on Sunday when I ran and, as I'd feared all along, the truth was simply the final nail in the coffin.

* * *

Mum found me on the bench about ten minutes later.

'James has got Samuel,' she said, slumping down beside me. 'I'm guessing from his expression that it didn't go well.'

'I'm not sure it could have gone much worse.'

'I'm so sorry, sweetheart.'

She put her arm round me and I rested my head on her shoulder. I had no tears left and no energy to cry them even if I had.

We sat like that in silence for a while.

'Where's Auntie Debs?' I asked. 'I haven't seen her since first thing.'

'I don't know. Her car's gone.'

My stomach sank. 'She hasn't left, has she?'

'How am I supposed to know?' Mum muttered.

I stood up. 'I hope she hasn't. Don't you get it? I've destroyed so much already and I can't have a rift between you two on my conscience too.'

'It's not your fault. It's hers.'

'No, it isn't! Mum! When did you become so unreasonable? It's like the pair of you have had a role reversal. Auntie Debs did *exactly* what I wanted her to do at the lowest point in my life. Now, when things are close to being that low again, you're doing exactly what I *don't* want you to do. We need to find Sam and ask where Auntie Debs has gone and, if she's gone home, you're going after her and bringing her back.'

I stormed off to the barn without waiting for a response. Sam looked up in surprise as I burst through the door.

'Is everything okay?' she asked, an edge of panic in her voice.

'Yes. No. Have you seen your mum?'

'She stopped by earlier to see how Shelley was doing – the hog that came in yesterday – and now she's gone to Reddfield to meet my dad for lunch.'

'Oh.' I frowned. 'Your dad? I wasn't expecting you to say that.'

'Me neither. He apparently rang her last night to check she was okay with things. They chatted for a while and he asked her out for lunch.'

I spun round to face Mum who'd followed me into the barn. 'See! Even Uncle Jonathan's concerned about her. He gets it. Why don't you?'

'Fine! I'll speak to her when she gets back if that's what you want.'

'No, Mum. You'll speak to her if that's what *you* want; not because I've told you to.'

'Dad sends his love to you too, Chloe,' Sam added. 'He wanted to come round but I told him not to as we had a house full. I hope that was the right thing to do.'

I nodded. 'He knows everything, though?' I'd given Sam permission to tell him. It wasn't right to have him as the only family member clueless as to what I'd done, especially when it was his daughter's doorstep to which I'd brought my troubles.

'He does. He says he's got a big hug waiting for you when you're ready.'

I thanked Sam and left the barn with Mum.

'I'm not trying to get rid of you, Mum, but I could do with some time on my own to think about what happens next with James. Why don't you take off somewhere for the afternoon? You could drive round the villages or go for a walk if you don't fancy going into Reddfield.'

Mum looked as though she was about to argue so I pre-empted it. 'I can always call you if I need you, and Sam's here.'

She sighed. 'Okay. I'll give you some space.'

'And think about what I said about Auntie Debs.'

* * *

James brought Samuel back to me shortly before twelve.

'He started grizzling a few minutes ago,' he said as he lifted Samuel out of the buggy and handed him to me.

'Have you had a good time with Daddy?' I asked him, kissing his head. 'Let's get you inside and get you fed.'

'I'm sorry I got so mad. I've just been so worried.'

'About Samuel or about both of us?'

'Both of you, of course.'

'This is the problem, James. For me, there is no "of course". I don't know how you feel about me anymore. Obviously how you feel about me right this minute is very much clouded by the confession to end all confessions that I hit you with earlier, but I don't know how you felt about me before that.'

'Where's this doubting of my feelings suddenly sprung from?'

'It hasn't "suddenly" sprung from anywhere. It's been how I've felt since our honeymoon.'

His eyebrows shot up. 'Since August?'

Samuel started crying and I gently rocked him, hoping to placate him for a few minutes longer.

'Since you walked out on me at the airport, nearly ending our marriage, then said you'd come back for our baby.'

'I said I'd come back for you both.'

'I know, but I wasn't convinced you'd have bothered if it had just been for me. After that, I was treading on eggshells waiting for you to leave me because that's what the people I love do.'

'That's why you thought I was having an affair? That's why you looked at my phone?'

Samuel's cries were getting louder and I had to raise my voice to be heard over them. 'I love you so much. I thought nothing could match how I felt about Travis, but along you came and you absolutely eclipsed that. What I felt for Travis was like puppy love by comparison but I knew that, one day, either I'd mess things up and push you away or you'd realise you'd made a mistake and let me go. And here we are with both of those things happening.'

'I haven't let you go.'

'You have, James. You just haven't admitted it to yourself yet.'

Samuel was screeching now, his face red and his fists flailing.

'Sorry. I've got to feed him.'

The last thing I saw before I stepped into the farmhouse was James's eyes full of tears and, when I finished feeding Samuel and looked out of the front window, his car was gone.

I cuddled Samuel close to me and kissed his head. 'Your daddy's a good man. The best. But he was too good for me. Once a failure, always a failure.'

'Happy first birthday, cutie!' I exclaimed, scooping Archie up into my arms on Saturday morning and spinning him round as he giggled.

'I can't believe he's one already,' Beth said when I put him back down on the lounge floor.

We watched him attempt a lap of the room. He could only manage a few steps before splatting down on his backside but it didn't seem to faze him and he clambered to his feet and tried again.

'He's so close to walking properly,' I said. 'Next minute, he'll be running.'

'With Lottie chasing after him. So many precious moments.' Her smile faded and tears clouded her eyes. 'Oh, God, I promised Paul I wouldn't get upset.'

I gently placed my hand on her arm. 'It's understandable. You've had a tough year.'

'I keep trying to be positive but I see Archie making this amazing progress and I can't help worrying that Paul won't be around to see Lottie doing the same.'

'Aw, come here.' I enveloped her in a hug, blinking back my own tears. 'You can't stay strong all the time when facing something like this.'

She held me for a few moments then stepped back, wiping her cheeks. 'I needed that. Thank you.'

'How's Paul doing?'

'Putting a brave face on it but he's scared. We've talked about the worst-case scenario. That was a tough conversation. He sorted his will and arranged his funeral when he was first diagnosed so the practical stuff's all done. I know we have to be prepared just in case but the thought of losing him...' Her voice cracked and I hugged her again.

'Sam, have you seen my—' Chloe stopped dead. 'Sorry. I didn't mean to—'

'It's okay. You can come in. Beth's just a bit upset about Paul's diagnosis.'

'Is it Tuesday he starts treatment again?' Chloe asked.

Beth nodded. 'Just have to hope it works this time or we can find a stem cell donor match.'

'We've got the first testing programme next week, so fingers crossed. The more people we test, the more likely it is we'll find a match.' I turned to Chloe. 'Were you looking for something?'

'My phone charger, but I've just remembered where I left it. Sorry for interrupting.'

'Honestly, Chloe, you weren't.' But she'd already closed the door.

'She looks shattered,' Beth said. Chloe had given me permission to tell Beth and Paul what was going on, which made things easier with us all living under the same roof.

'It didn't go well with her husband yesterday and she's phoning the police today. I doubt she's slept much.' That made two of us. I'd had yet another nightmare in the early hours, waking up drenched in sweat once more. I hadn't screamed so Josh didn't wake up, but I felt nervous and shaky, imagining the Grimes boys lurking in dark corners. I ended up having to put a lamp on before I could settle again. Although I didn't want to admit it to Josh, I could feel the pressure building and was genuinely fearful of a relapse. But with members of both our families facing situations so much worse than mine, I was going to have to somehow find the strength and energy to keep going. They all needed me and I couldn't let them down.

'Are you sure it's still okay to have the barbeque later?' Beth asked. 'There's so much going on at the moment that Paul and I honestly don't mind cancelling. I know it's a joint birthday and engagement party but it's not like Archie will remember and we'd understand if you'd rather celebrate your engagement when things have settled.'

I gave her an appreciative smile. 'I talked to Chloe and she was adamant it should go ahead. I don't think she wants to feel guilty about us changing our plans on top of how bad she already feels.'

Paul came into the room with Lottie. 'She's all changed so we're good to go.' He passed Lottie to Beth then hoisted Archie onto his shoulder.

'What time do you want us back?' he asked me.

'We'll aim to have food ready for about six but don't feel you need to stay out all day.'

They left the farmhouse for a day out in Whitsborough Bay and I went into the kitchen to make a drink. The house was very quiet. Josh had gone out to get food and drink, Mum and Auntie Louise had gone for a walk round the farm together – Auntie Louise's suggestion – and would hopefully return as friends. Chloe was calling the police. Hand-holding had been offered but she said it was something she wanted to do on her own.

The barbeque had been planned last Saturday – the day before Chloe turned up – after we'd had notification that the wooden patio furniture we'd ordered to match Thomas's bench would be delivered today. Paul and Beth had been wondering what to do to celebrate Archie's first birthday – especially when they didn't know any families in the area – so we'd suggested a low-key joint event. We'd invited my dad, Lauren, Connie and Alex, Hannah and Toby, Rich and Dave, Fizz, and Josh's good friends and honorary brothers, Lewis and Danny. At the time, I'd hesitated whether to extend the invitation to Auntie Louise, Uncle Simon, and Chloe and James after Chloe's cool reaction to the engagement news. Now they were coming by default, although James wouldn't be here. To my knowledge, he hadn't been in touch since he left at lunchtime yesterday. I never imagined Mum would be a guest, though. I hadn't made an assumption she'd want to join us just because she was staying at Hedgehog Hollow but she'd seemed quite pleased with the invite. I just hoped she and Auntie Louise were putting aside their differences because we could all do with a fun, relaxing evening after the week we'd had and the week that lay ahead.

Leaving a note on the kitchen table for Chloe, I headed over to the barn to watch out for the furniture arriving and for Phoebe. She'd texted to say that she'd stop by at about 11 a.m. to collect the accounts paperwork.

Bang on eleven, she pulled into the farmyard on a pale pink moped.

'I could have dropped the paperwork off for you if I'd known you were on a moped,' I told her.

She removed her pink helmet and shook out her long dark hair then fixed those big blue eyes on mine. 'I like riding it and I wanted to see the hedgehogs. Is that okay? Sorry. I probably should have asked first. I can just get the paperwork and go if you're too busy.' It saddened me that every word dripped with an apology. She clearly had major self-esteem issues.

'It's no problem at all. Let's go into the barn. I'm about to feed some hoglets. You can help if you want.'

She gasped. 'Really? I'd love that.'

The paperwork was in a folder waiting on the table, so I passed it to her and she secured it in her backpack, then I spread the heat pads out and explained what I was going to do. She nodded but didn't ask questions.

'Can you wash your hands for me? I'll give you some gloves but it's an extra precaution.'

She moved over to the sink and jumped back as the water came out a bit faster than she must have expected.

'You might want to take your jacket off,' I suggested. 'Save it from getting wet.'

'I'm always cold. I'll just push up the sleeves.'

With the Brontë hoglets out, I picked up Heathcliff and showed Phoebe what to do, then passed her Emily, who was the least wriggly one. She held Emily firmly in her left hand but her right hand shook as she dripped formula anywhere but the hoglet's mouth.

'Sorry,' she muttered. 'I didn't mean to make a mess.'

'It's fine. It took me a few attempts. Just try to relax.'

The formula dripped on Emily's belly, Phoebe's gloves and the table.

'I'm sorry. I can't do it.' She thrust the hoglet and formula back at me and hastily peeled off her gloves. 'I'm so sorry.'

'Don't worry. There's a knack.'

She grabbed her bag. 'I'll get the accounts back by the end of the week. I'm sorry.' Then she ran towards the door.

'Phoebe!'

But she was gone. I couldn't run after her when I had five hoglets spread across the table and, even if I'd been able to, I didn't want to scare her. She wasn't Fizz, comfortable round animals and eager to dive in. It might have been the first time she'd ever handled animals and, knowing that she lacked confidence, I should have given her a chance to watch rather than have a go. Lesson learned.

I was about to start on the next batch of hoglets when a small lorry pulled up, so I went outside to direct the furniture delivery to the garden. Chloe was sitting on Thomas's bench with her hands clasped round a drink, Samuel in his buggy beside her with the sunshade over him.

I sat down next to her. 'Have you done it yet?'

'Yes, but there's nothing they can do at the moment. I never thought about a weekend being a problem but apparently they have a trained specialist in these things and she doesn't work weekends so someone will be in touch on Monday.' She took a sip of her drink. 'The good news is that they didn't feel the need to blue-light it straight over here and drag me away.'

She gave me a genuine smile and it filled me with relief that, in the darkness, she could find something to laugh about. 'Have you let James know?'

'You'd be proud of me. I rang him. He didn't answer, though. I left him a message and invited him to the barbeque. I probably shouldn't have done that.'

'He's more than welcome.'

'I'm thinking more for me. I'm going to be constantly watching out for him, hoping he'll appear, even though there's no way he will. Not after how we left things yesterday.'

'He's shocked and hurt and he needs time. I know he loves you.'

'Do you? I wish I believed that. Before we married, I never had a moment's doubt but then I ruined it all when I showed him how petty and jealous I can be. I think he'll be relieved I've given him a way out.'

'You still love him now?'

'More than ever. I feel like part of me is missing.'

'Then why aren't you fighting for him?'

48

CHLOE

I frowned at Sam. Why wasn't I fighting for James? Because I was running on empty. I was physically and emotionally drained. There was no fight left in me, if there ever had been in the first place.

'Is he worth fighting for?' she prompted when I didn't respond.

'Yes.'

'So why are you sitting on a bench talking to me when you could be telling him how you feel?'

'But you said he needs time.'

'And I stand by that. He does. But from what you've told me about your conversation yesterday, you'd already thrown in the towel because you thought he had. Put yourself in his shoes. You left him, you ignored him, you revealed a massive secret, then you told him your marriage was over. I know you said that because you thought it was how *he* felt but did you tell him how *you* feel? Did you explain how terrified you've been of losing him? Did you tell him how hard it was to stay away from him when he was here on Monday night?'

I re-ran yesterday in my head. 'I told him I loved him but that was it.'

'Then what do you expect from him? Poor guy probably has no idea where he stands. Let him have time to come to terms with all of this but let him have that time with all the facts on the table.'

I looked at Sam's eager expression and couldn't help smiling. She made a good case. 'Are you suggesting I go now?'

'There's no time like the present.'

'What about Samuel?'

'Take him with you. James will be home. If he's signed off sick, I doubt he's in the mood for much socialising.'

I hesitated, my stomach churning with nerves. 'Are you sure this is a good idea?'

'Do you have a better one?'

'I thought I was meant to be the impulsive, reckless one.'

'You usually are and now is the time for that person to hold her own. And it's not reckless. Impulsive, but definitely not reckless. Reckless would be not trying.'

Feeling inspired by her words, I kissed her on the cheek then ran into the house to pack a bag. Samuel wasn't due a feed for a couple of hours, so the timing was good. For the first time in ages, I actually felt excited about something. Sam was right. The decision about our future was down to James but, before he made it, he needed all the information. If he still wanted to walk away, at least it wouldn't be because he believed I didn't care.

* * *

The sun shone brightly as we drove. With the radio playing back-to-back summer-themed songs, I felt lighter than I'd felt since the wedding but, as I reached the outskirts of Whitsborough Bay, nerves kicked in. I pulled into a layby and took several deep breaths. The voice of doubt was loud: *Don't put yourself through this. Turn round and drive straight back to the farm.* But I could hear Sam's voice shouting over it: *Poor guy probably has no idea where he stands. Let him have time to come to terms with all of this but let him have that time with all the facts on the table.* I could do this. I wasn't going to add not fighting for my husband to my long list of regrets.

As I rounded the corner into our cul-de-sac, my heart sank at the sight of an empty drive.

'We'll just have to hope your daddy's gone shopping and will be back soon,' I told Samuel as we pulled onto the drive.

It felt strange being back in the house. I actually felt like an intruder in my own home. It also seemed so small after the enormous rooms and wide-open spaces of Hedgehog Hollow.

Outside, I'd felt uncomfortable with so many houses round me, feeling as though all the neighbours were watching my every move. They maybe were. They'd probably seen me frantically tossing binbags into the car last weekend and disappearing for a week.

The lounge was immaculately tidy. So was the kitchen diner. The place looked like a show home; all clean and staged. And after the comings and goings of so many people at Hedgehog Hollow, it was eerily quiet. I gave a little shudder.

'I might as well pick up a few things while I'm here,' I told Samuel, carrying him upstairs in his car seat.

Our bedroom was also tidy but, in Samuel's room, the cupboard doors were still wide open and the drawers were hanging out just as I'd left them, as though James hadn't been able to bear spending time in the nursery, thinking about what I'd taken from him.

The roll containing the last few binbags was on the window ledge where I'd left it, so I tore one off and filled it with Samuel's bedding.

Half an hour later, I'd filled another two binbags with some of Samuel's toys, books, hooded towels and his playmat and some more clothes and toiletries for me.

I hoped James wouldn't appear while I was still packing as it would be typical that he'd see the bags and accuse me of sneakily packing up all of Samuel's belongings while he was out. My heart thumped as I loaded them into the boot of my car – one eye fixed on the entrance to the road – but James didn't appear.

'I'm not sure what to do now,' I said to Samuel when I went back inside. 'You'll want a feed in about half an hour, so how about we watch TV and hopefully Daddy will appear? If not, we'll have to go back to the farm. We should maybe leave him a note this time, though. What do you think?'

Samuel just stared at me, wide-eyed.

'Yes, I agree. Good idea.'

I lifted him and his comforter out of the car seat and we settled down to watch a Winnie the Pooh cartoon. All the while, I kept my eye on the window, waiting for James's car to pull onto the drive. It wasn't looking promising.

I'd fed Samuel, changed his nappy and was pulling his trousers back on when I heard the front door open. I froze, my heart thudding.

'Chloe?' James called.

Angry? Confused? Pleased? I couldn't gauge anything from that one word. 'In here.'

The door opened and he looked at me completely blank-faced. 'What are you doing here?'

'I wanted to talk to you.'

He raised his eyebrows. 'More secrets to reveal?'

'No.'

'Good.' He looked down at Samuel kicking his legs on the floor and reached out his arms. 'Can I?'

'You don't have to ask.'

He picked Samuel up and kissed his cheek then cuddled him.

'Where've you been?' Crap. That sounded like I was suspicious of him. 'I'm not prying. You don't have to answer.' I pulled myself up and sat down on the sofa.

James sat on the chair and I tried not to read anything into the distance.

'For a walk along North Bay beach.'

'Busy?'

'Very.'

'Any more panic attacks?'

'No.'

'And you got home okay yesterday? Stupid question. Of course you did. You're right here.'

'I got home safe and sound.'

Small talk wasn't going well. The silence screamed at me until I couldn't bear it any longer. I'd have to just say my piece and leave.

'I rang the police this morning and I need to speak to a specialist so someone will call me on Monday. I left a message on your voicemail to say that. I don't know if you've listened to it yet.'

'I have.'

'Good. Erm... I'll let you know what happens on Monday. Unless you don't want to know. I'm assuming you do but maybe you're not bothered and—'

'You're babbling.'

'I know. Sorry.'

'You obviously didn't drive here to tell me you'd phoned the police because you'd already left me that message. So why are you here?' He sounded exhausted.

'I wanted to apologise for yesterday and tell you that, although you might not think it because of the way I've treated you this week, I do love you so very, very much and I don't want to lose you. I know you have loads to think about and where we go from here has to be your decision. Unless, of course, I get sent to prison in which case it's the judge's decision and not... Sorry. Babbling again. What I'm trying to say – very ineloquently – is that I don't want you to make any decisions thinking I don't care about you or our marriage because that couldn't be more wrong.'

'Chloe, I—' His voice was soft.

'Please let me finish.' I pleaded with my eyes and he nodded. 'I love you more than you could ever imagine and a whole pile more on top of that. When you were at the farm on Monday, I nearly came downstairs so many times. I was awake all night, thinking about you. I saw you leave and I wanted to run after you. I know it seems like I was being selfish and unreasonable but my logic – probably quite twisted logic – was about trying to hold onto you for as long as I could, knowing that I'd lose you when the truth came out. Does that make any kind of sense?'

He was silent for a moment, then he sighed. 'Yes. I can sort of see where you're coming from.'

'Thank God! Because it all made sense in my mind until I started to try to explain it. I'm going to get some help and I'm willing to do anything you want to make this work. We could do marriage guidance or couple's therapy or whatever it's called.'

'The thing is...'

My stomach did a somersault. That wasn't a good sentence-opener. 'Go on...'

He sighed once more. 'The thing is, I don't know how I feel about any of this and I don't know how I feel about...' He bit his lip and gazed down at the floor.

I gulped down the lump in my throat. 'It's okay. You can say it. You don't know how you feel about me.'

He looked up again with sadness in his bloodshot eyes. 'I'm sorry.'

'It's fine. It's expected. Don't worry about it.' I stood up. 'We'd best be making tracks.'

James stood up too. 'I'm not saying it's over.'

'I know.' My voice was a little higher than usual. 'I guess you won't be coming to the barbeque tonight, then? I'm sorry. I don't know why I said that.' I reached across for Samuel. 'Right, young man, let's leave Daddy in peace.'

James followed us to the door. 'Can we talk next week?'

My hopes soared.

'About me seeing Samuel regularly,' he added.

My hopes crashed and burned.

'You can come to the farm and spend the day with him tomorrow if you want. I'll stay out of your way.'

'I can't. I'm going to Toby and Hannah's.'

'We're not far away if you want to visit before or after...' I tailed off at his grimace. 'I'll speak to you next week.'

'Chloe!' he called as I reached the car.

He ran up to me and leaned forward. I held my breath, thinking he was about to kiss me or at least hug me. But then he bent down.

'Samuel dropped this.' He handed me the Peter Rabbit comforter.

'Oh. Thank you.'

He took a couple of paces back so I could secure the car seat, but I was all fingers and thumbs, fumbling with the seatbelt. I thought I'd clicked it in but it retracted and then, when I tried again, it kept locking.

'For God's sake!' I cried, tears burning my eyes.

'Here, let me!' James leaned across. I pressed myself against the door as he deftly fastened the belt. *So close. Heart thumping. Can't breathe.*

He stood up, bringing his face tantalising close to mine once more, then stepped away a few paces. I swallowed down my nerves and closed the back door.

'You do understand me needing time, don't you?' he asked gently.

I made a strange sound. A sort of yes-turned-squeak accompanied by a subtle nod of the head.

'It's just that so much has changed between us over the past year that it's hard to know what's real anymore.'

I made that strange sound again.

'I'm not saying it's just you. It's me too. The cancer and now the panic attacks. There's been...' He shrugged.

I'm not sure if he would have tailed off anyway or whether he could see how close I was to crumbling. I threw him a half-smile and then did that 'call me' signal with my hand. I've never done that in my whole life but I couldn't open my mouth to speak as I knew a sob would escape.

As I pulled off the drive and along our road, I could see him in the rearview mirror, hands in the pockets of his jeans, shoulders slumped. Was his heart breaking like mine? Silent tears rained down my cheeks and soaked into my T-shirt.

Driving slowly back to Hedgehog Hollow, I thought about the evening Travis drove me home in silence and Scarlett sent me those emails. That hurt so badly but this was a million times worse. This was comparable to the darkest moment of my life so far and the worst decision I ever made – walking away from baby Ava. It was perhaps fitting that my actions on both of those bleak days had directly caused how I was feeling right now. It was true what they said: you could run from your past but you could never hide.

49

SAMANTHA

I was on my own at Hedgehog Hollow on Saturday afternoon. The atmosphere between Mum and Auntie Louise seemed to have relaxed following their walk this morning and they'd decided to visit a local stately home together while Chloe was over in Whitsborough Bay. Josh had gone out again to get a gas cylinder for the barbeque. I hardly noticed the quiet as the rescue centre was busy with collections and arrivals.

Potter had come in a week into May with a dog bite which was now fully healed, so the couple who'd found him collected him to release him in their garden. I mentioned that I was going to release another two hedgehogs on the farm and they offered to take them too, leaving me with twenty-five adults.

Terry, a regular visitor who'd brought in three hedgehogs over time, plus a box of six hoglets he'd found abandoned in a box on his doorstep, arrived with another adult in need of care.

'You're my best customer, Terry.' I smiled at him as he followed me into the barn to see what was wrong with the hedgehog.

'It's our Wilbur. He sniffs them out.' Terry's dog had found Arwen tangled in goalpost netting and she'd been an emergency admission on our Family Fun Day during opening weekend. 'This one was hiding under a bush. I think it's got ticks.'

I lifted the emaciated hedgehog out of the box. It was a boy and there were large patches of white and grey blobs between its spines. 'Spot on with your diagnosis. Definitely ticks. Horrible little things.'

'Do you think it'll be all right?'

'Hard to say. Hedgehogs will often pick up ticks and can be fine with a few of them but this many usually indicates they're quite poorly. I'll remove them and clean up any wounds but it depends on what else is wrong with our little friend.'

'I'm sure you'll work your magic, lass.'

'I'll do my best. Thanks for bringing him in. I'm naming the hogs after classic authors at the moment. Do you have a favourite?'

'I'm not much of a reader but I read *Twenty Thousand Leagues Under the Sea* when I were a lad. Jules Verne. Loved it.'

'Verne it is, then. Do you want to stick around?'

'I've got our Wilbur waiting outside the barn. We're off to the coast. Let us know how you get on.'

I waved Terry off and set about preparing what I needed to remove Verne's ticks. As soon as I'd done that, I needed to get some fluids into him. Even though he was emaciated – making him an oval shape instead of the lovely roundness of a healthy hedgehog – and clearly in need of food, subcutaneous fluids were needed to rehydrate him first before we could think about food. A starving hedgehog can't handle a sudden intake of food and can potentially die as a result.

I'd no sooner got Verne settled in his crate than Rhys Michaels, our gardener from Whitsborough Bay, arrived. Dave had recommended him and he'd done an amazing job of taming the overgrown ivy on the farmhouse and landscaping the garden before Thomas died. I'd kept him on since then and I had a new project for him so he'd asked if he could call in this afternoon to see and measure the space ready for starting work in a week's time.

'I want to create an intermediate home,' I told Rhys as we stood in the unused space at the back of the barn. 'The idea is to replicate the environment a hedgehog would encounter once released, but for it to be completely enclosed so I can still bring them in and house them in the barn overnight. I imagine it as a training ground for the hoglets before they're released so they know what to expect in the wild as well as giving space for injured adults to move round and strengthen their limbs.'

Rhys removed a retractable tape measure from his jeans pocket. 'And you want it to be the full length of the barn?'

'Pretty much. If that works. And probably a similar width.'

I helped him measure out the space and he scribbled something down onto a small notepad.

'You'll be wanting hedges and shrubs and the sorts of plants that will attract food for hedgehogs like slugs and beetles?'

'Exactly. And I also want things they can nest under like palettes and log piles. I've got a few website links I can send you.'

We chatted some more about ideas. I wasn't bothered about making it beautiful; it needed to be practical. Beatrix, who'd come in earlier this week with a broken leg, could use the space to get her strength back once her bandage was removed and she could also help train her litter. In the wild, mother hedgehogs would spend some time training their young in how to forage before turfing them out the nest and sending them off to live a solitary life. We had another mum, Trinity, who could do the same with her triplets and I'd need to hope that the abandoned hoglets could make sense of it themselves. They'd have far more chance of survival if they were prepared for what to expect first.

I also envisaged the space as being perfect for our bald hedgehog, Gollum. I had no idea whether his spines would ever grow back and, if they didn't, there was no way he could survive in the wild as the spines were the first defence against predators. He'd therefore need to live with me permanently and a hedgehog house in a large outdoor space was infinitely preferable to him seeing out his days in the barn.

Rhys pushed his tape measure back into his pocket. 'I've done some research already but, if you can email me those links today, I can check I'm thinking along the same lines as you. I'll work up a sketch and have it to you by Tuesday night and, once you approve, I can order the materials. It'll be all digging at first so we've got plenty of time to finalise the plans.'

'Brilliant. Thank you.'

He scribbled a few things down on his pad and I looked over the space, trying to visualise it. At the moment it was predominantly long grass interspersed with a few clumps of mud and stones, so probably not too challenging to work with, but what a transformation it would be and how amazing for our patients to have this space.

Suddenly the silence was punctuated by the sound of swishing grass, like someone running through it. That noise! My heart started racing and beads of sweat pricked my forehead. The sky darkened and I was back on the night the barn was attacked, anxiously searching for Misty-Blue, hearing someone running through the long grass but unable to see them. I heard her howl, saw a hooded figure run past me. My breathing came fast and shallow and my legs felt shaky.

'Don't hurt my cat!' I yelled.

'I'm nowhere near your cat.'

'I can hear you. I'll call the police.'

Someone grabbed me and I screamed before sinking to the ground.

* * *

Someone was calling my name.

I opened my eyes and squinted.

'Rhys?'

'Oh, my God! What happened?' I could hear the panic in his voice.

I slowly rose to a seated position and licked my dry lips, feeling totally disorientated. I jumped as Misty-Blue clambered onto my knee. 'Where did she come from?'

Rhys crouched down beside me. 'She was running through the grass and you yelled at me not to hurt her and that you'd call the police and then you dropped to the ground. Are you okay?'

The grass. It was only Misty-Blue running through the grass. Nobody was going to hurt us.

I looked up at Rhys. 'Can you get me some water from the barn?'

Moments later, he was back and a mug of cold water was pressed into my hands. I gratefully took a few gulps.

'Sorry. I feel silly now. Can you help me up?' I reached out my hand and Rhys gently eased me to my feet. 'Remember I told you about the barn getting attacked? That night, I could hear someone running through the long grass and, when Misty-Blue ran through it just now, I had this weird flashback thing. I'm sorry for shouting at you.'

'The shouting didn't bother me. It's the keeling over I'm worried about. Should I call an ambulance?'

'Honestly, Rhys, I'm fine. I'll have five minutes on the bench and I'll be right as rain.'

He sat on Thomas's bench next to me. Misty-Blue jumped up and draped herself across my knee.

'She's a beautiful cat,' Rhys said, his tickling of her ears being rewarded by deep purrs. 'Are you sure you're okay?'

'Embarrassed, but all right. Talk to me. Take my mind off it. How's Callie and the kids?' I'd never met Rhys's wife and children but I'd always tried to make time to enjoy a mug of tea with him each time he'd worked here so I'd found out a bit about his family.

'Callie's not too good just now.' His eyes shone with excitement. 'But she always struggles with sickness for the first four months of pregnancy.'

'Oh, my gosh, Rhys! Congratulations to you both. That's brilliant news.'

'Thank you. Esme's really excited but Tyler says he wants a puppy instead.'

'Then he's going to be pretty disappointed. How old are they now?'

'Tyler's two and a half, Esme's five, and Megan – my daughter from a previous relationship – is nine.'

'You'll have to bring them all to the farm when the hedgehog garden's finished.'

'They'll love that, especially Tyler. He's obsessed with animals.' Rhys glanced at his watch. 'You look like you've got some colour back.'

'You don't need to stay with me. I feel fine now and Josh will be back any minute. Thanks so much, Rhys.'

We said our goodbyes and I stayed on the bench for a few minutes more until I'd finished my water. This was getting ridiculous. Nightmares, being jumpy and now two flashbacks, although they'd felt more like reality than memory. What was happening to me? I thought about a recent conversation I'd had with Connie about my suspicions that Mum had Post-Traumatic Stress Disorder. Was it possible I had it? I'd have to ask her at the barbeque tonight if we got a quiet moment because, if that's what it was, I needed to get it dealt with quickly. I spent so much time alone at the farm. I was fortunate that there'd been somebody around for both the incidents so far, but what if I had another episode like that while I was on my own? I shuddered at the thought.

* * *

An hour or so later, Hedgehog Hollow was full of life. Everyone had arrived and it was lovely to hear the laughter and chatter in the garden following such an intense week. Paul and Beth looked happy and relaxed after a day at the beach and were touched that so many of the guests had brought a gift for Archie.

'You have such lovely friends and family,' Beth said, carefully peeling back the tape on a gift from Rich and Dave to reveal a soft toy hedgehog. 'They barely know us and they've brought gifts.'

'They're an amazing bunch.' I looked round the group, smiling. It was incredible to think that more than half of them had only come into my life during the past ten months, yet I couldn't imagine them not being around.

They'd all brought us engagement presents too despite being specifically told not to. We had flowers, champagne and some lovely gifts for the farmhouse.

I left Beth and Paul opening the rest of Archie's presents and sought out Lauren.

'How's my replacement working out?' I asked her.

'Alice is brilliant but I miss seeing your smiling face every day. I was just saying to Connie that the three of us should go out somewhere together. We're worried you never stop working.'

I smiled at her. 'The hedgehogs don't feel like work but, I must admit, a night out would be brilliant. Let's get one organised soon.' I glanced across at Mum and Dad, deep in conversation. 'Do you know how lunch went for those two yesterday? I haven't had a chance to ask Dad and I wasn't sure how to raise the subject with Mum.'

Lauren's smile slipped and she screwed up her nose. 'You'd probably better ask your Dad.'

'What's that expression for?'

'I'm just a bit worried about him. I know how cut up he was after it ended. With me being twice divorced, we've talked quite a lot about the process and how it can feel and I can't help thinking he regrets going down that route.'

I took her arm and led her away from earshot of anyone. 'You think he wants to get back together with Mum?'

She shrugged. 'I don't know. He's never actually said that, but look at them now.'

They were laughing together; a sight I hadn't seen for a very long time. It was a little unnerving. Dad had given his all to their relationship, trying to make it work under the most difficult of circumstances. If he still harboured hopes of recovering it, was he only setting himself up for more heartbreak? And what about Mum? She'd changed so much since splitting up with Dad, suggesting it had been the best thing for her. She'd styled her hair, changed her wardrobe and settled into a new house. That all suggested relief at their relationship ending.

'They're probably just finding their way back to some sort of friendship,' I said. 'It's been amicable so far.'

'I'm sure you're right. Ignore me. I'm probably reading far too much into it.'

'Do I detect a hint of jealousy there?'

Lauren stared at me for a moment then laughed out loud. 'You are funny. Your dad and I are just good friends. He's like a big brother to me and our Connie. It will *never* be anything romantic so you stop that imagination of yours running wild. I'm the expert on meddling; not you. I need a top-up.' She walked away to refresh her drink, chuckling to herself.

I watched my parents for a little longer. It was so alien to see them deep in conversation and even stranger to see them laughing. I had that sensation of being in a dream again. Everything was changing and I could barely keep up.

Connie and Alex were talking to Uncle Simon and Auntie Louise. I definitely needed to have a word with Connie about the two flashback episodes at some point.

I couldn't help noticing the adoring glances passing between Connie and Alex, and the occasional touch. They seemed to radiate happiness, reminding me of how Chloe and James had been right up to their wedding day.

Chloe still hadn't returned from Whitsborough Bay. I desperately hoped that was a good sign and that she and James were properly talking now that he'd had time to recover from the initial shock. Their relationship was worth fighting for. It was obvious from the moment they first saw each other that there was something special between them.

'I think my Uncle Alex is smitten,' Dave said, coming up beside me and making me jump.

'They both are. It's lovely.' It really did warm my heart seeing them like that. 'So how are things with you?'

'Good. Busy. But I have an opening in my diary and I wanted to talk to you about it.'

'Sounds intriguing.' I led him to Thomas's bench and we sat down.

'I don't want to push you into anything but I've had a building project fall through. A client I do a lot of work for can't get the planning permission he needs, which means August and September are unexpectedly free. When we moved Paul and Beth's stuff across from Wilbersgate, we talked to Josh about the other barns here and the subject of holiday cottages came up. I don't know if you've had a chance to discuss it yet.'

'Do you know what? We've started that conversation so many times and we always seem to get distracted but, yes, I love the idea of holiday cottages. They could be a good income stream for the rescue centre. Is there enough money in the pot?' Thomas had been a wealthy man after building up a business from scratch and selling it for an eyewatering amount. He'd left money for Dave and his team to convert the barn into the rescue centre, refurbish the farmhouse, resurface the track and farmyard, replace the fencing alongside the track, and had suggested there'd be enough in the pot to work on some of the other outbuildings.

'Unless you're after a luxury finish, there should be enough to convert two barns. Each one could easily create two decent-sized rentals and they could be up and running for October half-term, but we'd need to source a new architect as my mate's snowed under.'

'Fizz has an architect friend. I'll get his number. Sorry I haven't sorted it sooner. It's been so busy.'

Dave looked at me with concern. 'You're still enjoying it, though?'

'Oh, yeah. I love it. There's just a lot going on right now.'

'You've certainly got a house full. Could you imagine Thomas's face if he saw this place now? He'd have loved it.'

'I was just thinking that myself the other day. It's how he always imagined the farm. Full of life.'

'And you've done that. But don't forget to take some time out for you. Rich and I worry about you doing everything for everyone else and exhausting yourself again.'

I rested my head on his shoulder. 'I'll take care of me. I promise. Lauren was just saying earlier that she and Connie want to take me out one evening. I'll probably wait until Paul's settled into his chemo, first.'

Dave rested his head against mine. 'There'll always be something. Get that date in your diary and do it soon.'

'Yes, Dad,' I joked.

He clinked the neck of his bottle of lager against mine.

'Josh says it's a ten-minute warning on the food,' Lauren called to me.

'Thank you.' I stood up and stretched. 'That's my cue to cut the burger buns open.'

Dave followed me over to the large table.

'Can you empty the salad into bowls while I slice the buns?' I asked him, picking up a bag of burger buns. 'I thought we had some sausage ones.'

I looked up to see something hurtling towards me. My heart thudded and my legs shook. Somehow I knew I needed to duck but fear rooted me to the spot and, as the item hit me, I released a blood curdling scream and sank to my knees.

'Sam? Are you okay?'

They were back. The Grimes boys or their friends. They'd come to finish the job. 'Leave me alone!' I screeched as I retreated under the table. 'We owe you nothing!'

A hand reached towards me and I screamed again. Spots swam before my eyes and the ground started spinning. And then everything went black.

* * *

I could hear whispering. My knees were throbbing and my head hurt. I tried to put my right hand up to my head but something soft was covering me.

'Sammie? Are you awake?'

'Josh?' I murmured.

'I'm right here.' I felt him squeeze my other hand.

'Where am I?' I tried to open my eyes but there was a bright light above me making me squint.

'I'll dim the light.' It sounded like Connie. The brightness faded.

'Sam, it's Hannah. Can you open your eyes?'

I squinted at the faces above me.

'I'm just going to shine a light in your eyes for a moment,' Hannah said. 'And now I'm going to check your pulse.'

It was going to be fast. I could feel my heart racing.

'What happened?' I asked after Hannah confirmed my rapid pulse rate.

'You fainted again,' Josh said, 'but it was different. You screamed. You looked terrified.'

'They were here,' I whispered.

'Who?' he asked.

'The Grimes boys.'

Josh shook his head. 'They're in prison.'

'What can you remember?' Connie asked.

'They threw something at me.'

'I think I know what's happening.' Connie crouched down beside me. 'Have you been having nightmares recently? Been jumpy?'

I nodded.

'It could be PTSD,' she said.

I released my right hand from beneath the throw and rubbed it across my clammy forehead. 'I wondered that myself. Something happened this afternoon when Rhys was here and during one of the school visits. I wanted to ask you about it tonight.' I quickly described what had happened.

'Definitely sounds like PTSD,' she said.

'Can we get help?' Josh asked, gently squeezing my hand again.

'We'd need to get Samantha properly assessed – first with her doctor and then with a specialist – but it's curable.' Connie turned to me. 'Like I told you before, it's my special area of interest so I can give you lots of information, but I'm not qualified so I can't diagnose you or treat you and, even if I could, it would be a conflict of interests. I can get you referred, though.'

I shuffled to a sitting position with Josh's help and Hannah rearranged the cushions to make me more comfortable. 'I feel silly, now. Did I really scream? In front of everyone?'

'Don't feel silly,' Connie reassured me. 'We're all friends here.'

'But I ruined the party.'

Josh stroked my hair back from my face. 'You didn't. The party's still going on. Archie's chatting up Amelia again and everyone's fine.'

I smiled at the thought of the babies together.

'Although I did think your mum was about to keel over too,' Josh continued. 'She went white as a sheet. She thought you'd had a heart attack.'

'She was worried?'

He smiled and nodded. 'Strange new world, isn't it?'

It certainly was.

'Sounds like I missed all the drama last night.' I sat beside Sam on the bench on Sunday morning. Mum and Auntie Debs had driven through to Little Tilbury. They wanted to take Samuel for a walk past their childhood home, Meadowcroft. Samuel wouldn't have a clue what was going on but I think they wanted to reminisce about simpler times. Their friendship seemed to be back on track, which was a huge relief.

'When did you get back?' Sam asked.

'About half five, but I wasn't in the mood for celebrating.'

'It didn't go well?'

'Not really, although it could have been worse. He says he needs time but it didn't sound positive. I told him how I feel and I'm glad you pushed me to go. Ball's in his court now.'

'I'm so sorry.'

'You're not the one who messed things up. So what happened yesterday?'

'Dave throwing a packet of bread buns at me triggered a PTSD episode. Or at least we think that's what it was.'

'Shit! That doesn't sound good.'

'It's not great and it was pretty terrifying at the time, but it's treatable. I need to have a few stress-free days. Josh is going to take a couple of days off work to run the centre.'

'How does a packet of bread buns trigger a PTSD episode?' I didn't know anything about PTSD but this struck me as such a random thing.

'It took me back to the night the barn got attacked when I had the box of eggs thrown at me.'

My stomach sank. 'I don't know anything about the eggs.' Why didn't I know that? Because I'd been completely self-absorbed, as usual. 'I'm listening now if you're up to it. You can tell me how you ended up leaving your job, too.'

'Make me a cuppa and you're on.'

I stood up. 'I'm sorry I haven't been a good friend. I promise that's going to change.'

For a moment, I thought Sam was going to object and tell me I was a great friend, which would have been a blatant lie, but she gave me a weak smile. 'You don't need to change. You just have to be the lovely version of you. Remember when you packed me a box of gifts when I started university? That was so thoughtful. I've still got the photo frame in my office with a picture of you and me in it. That's the real Chloe.'

Tears pricked my eyes. 'You really think so?'

'I know so.'

I gave her a grateful smile. 'One mug of tea coming up.'

'Can you make it—?'

'In a hedgehog mug? Consider it done.'

* * *

While the kettle boiled, I ran upstairs and into Sam's office. I immediately spotted the seaside bunting I'd made strung across the wall above the window, the cushion and the noticeboard. She'd kept them all these years! I was so touched by that.

On the bookshelves were three silver-framed photos. The first showed Nanna and a woman I didn't recognise with Sam as a six- or seven-year-old. The middle one was a selfie of Sam and Gramps which, from their outfits and the balloons, I could tell was from his seventy-fifth birthday party. The last was an elderly man wearing six paper hats from out of a Christmas cracker. Presumably Thomas, who I'd never asked Sam about. I needed to rectify that.

A soft toy hedgehog sat on another shelf and, next to that, was the sparkly photo frame I made, just like she said. It contained a photo of us each wearing our school uniforms and licking giant ice-creams. It had been taken on North Bay seafront after our final GCSE exam. I picked it up and ran my fingers down the glass and across the gemstones and sequins on the frame. We'd been so happy back then, with exciting futures ahead of us. And just a few months later, one stupid decision changed everything.

'I'll dig deep and find the old Chloe,' I whispered. 'She's still in there somewhere.'

* * *

I carried our drinks out on a tray with a huge plate full of chocolate biscuits.

'Wow! Someone's hungry!' Sam exclaimed, eyeing up the pile as she took her mug from the tray.

'We've got a lot to talk about so I thought we might be here for a while.' I put the biscuits down on the bench then sat down. 'So, take me back to last August and my wedding day. You were lost and you stumbled across Hedgehog Hollow, where you found Thomas collapsed...'

Sam looked at me, clearly confused.

'There's a "HOT TIP" just in. There's a woman staying on a farm in Huggleswick who's had a hell of a wake-up call recently and has realised she's been really spoilt and selfish because she's been so angry with the world for a couple of huge mistakes she made when she was a teenager. She's keen to make amends, especially with the cousin who she loves very much.'

Sam's eyes sparkled with tears. She gently touched my arm and whispered, 'Thank you.' Then she took a deep breath. 'Well, the bride and groom had this crazy idea to send me back to Whitsborough Bay to collect a plant, of all things and, if I wasn't such a pushover, I'd have told them where to shove their plant. And to add insult to injury, it turned out it was for my nemesis Great-Aunt Agnes and I wish I *had* shoved it somewhere pretty special, given what she did to us both that day. So, I was lost with no mobile signal and the worst satnav in the history of satnavs when I stumbled across Hedgehog Hollow and was thrust into the life of one of the most amazing men I've ever met…'

Josh looked up from the treatment table and smiled at me. 'I thought you were meant to be resting today.'

'I was, but I thought you might be hungry.'

'You've made me some lunch?'

'Actually, Chloe did.' I placed the plate of sandwiches on the side then sat down opposite him. 'Without being asked and without complaining.'

Josh raised his eyebrows. 'Overnight personality transplant?'

'Lightbulb moment, I think. We've been sitting on Thomas's bench for the past few hours. She realised she'd completely lost touch with everything going on in my life and wanted to catch up. It was lovely. It reminded me of how things used to be. We'd walk along the seafront talking for hours. Conversations were usually more about Chloe than me, mind you, but this morning was pretty special.'

'I'm dead chuffed for you. Do you think she can keep it up?'

'I hope so. It's not like she's being fake. She genuinely can be really lovely and the great thing about her and James together is he brought that side of her out much more often, or at least he did before their wedding. If she can show him that's who she really is, maybe there's a chance for them. Oh, well. Only time will tell.'

I looked down at the hedgehog he was working on and realised I didn't recognise it. 'New arrival?'

'This is Prickles.'

'Remind me what literary masterpiece Prickles wrote.'

Josh laughed. 'A woman and her little girl brought him in, and the girl had already named him. She was really excited about it, so I didn't have the heart to tell her we were doing literary classics. Plus, I realised we never had a Prickles when we were using hedgehog-related names at the start.'

'Prickles it is, then! What's wrong with him?'

'He was found curled up in the middle of their drive. He's definitely dehydrated but I'm still checking him over and then looking forward to my sandwich. Are you not eating?'

'Chloe and I have been stuffing our faces with biscuits so I'll have something later. Do you need a hand with anything?'

'No. It's all under control.'

I went round to his side and gave him a hug and kiss then returned to the farmhouse to make a cup of tea. Mum and Auntie Louise were tucking into lunch at the kitchen table and Chloe was picking at a bunch of grapes, with Samuel on her knee playing with a set of plastic keys.

'Josh says thank you for the sandwich.' They were all staring at me. 'What's going on?'

'We're going to head back to Whitsborough Bay this afternoon,' Chloe said.

'Really?' I pulled out a chair and sat down, feeling strangely disappointed. 'Why?'

'Your mum and I need to be back at work tomorrow,' Auntie Louise said.

'And it makes sense for me to go back home.' Chloe sighed. 'By which I mean Mum and Dad's house rather than *my* home. It means James has easy access to Samuel and I'm nearby for whatever happens with the police.' She stroked Samuel's head. 'I'm sorry if me being here this week contributed to what happened last night.'

'Oh, Chloe, don't blame yourself for that. It had been building up for a while and it would have happened anyway.'

'But all the added stress probably didn't help. There's one more thing I need from you before we leave. Can you do one of those stem cell tests on me?'

I nodded, feeling quite tearful. It was moments like this that reminded me why I'd held onto my friendship with Chloe, even when she tested me to the hilt.

* * *

I was in the farmyard half an hour later when I spotted Phoebe approaching on her moped.

'I've done the accounts,' she said as soon as she'd stopped and removed her helmet.

'That was quick.'

'I didn't have any college work to do.' She got off her moped, removed her backpack and handed me a folder. 'I've emailed you the spreadsheet but my printer's broken so I couldn't print it out for you. Sorry.'

'That's no problem. Thank you so much. I'll have a look at it later. Did you have any queries?'

'It was all straightforward and it tallied with the bank statements you gave me but I couldn't find one receipt so I've put a Post-it note on the bank statement to say what's missing. Everything's all organised in this file by date order and I've numbered each receipt.' She sounded so confident but then she faltered and bit her lip. 'But if you don't like the way it's organised, just say and I can change it next time.'

'I'm sure it'll be fine. Thank you, again. I really appreciate you volunteering. It's one less task for me to worry about.'

'I love accounts. Anything to do with numbers is awesome. My friends laugh and call me a geek but I'm not bothered. At least I know what I want to do with my life.'

'That's a great attitude to have.'

She looked as though she wanted to say something else so I smiled encouragingly.

'I'm so sorry for running off yesterday.'

'That's okay. I'm sorry if I pushed you into doing something you didn't want to do.'

'Oh, no!' She shook her head vigorously. 'I wanted to have a go but I panicked when I made a mess of it. Sorry.'

'Like most things, it just takes time and practice.'

She nodded, wide-eyed. 'I'd better go. Thanks so much for the chance to work on a live set of accounts, especially for somewhere as special as this. I'm so grateful.'

'Absolute pleasure.'

She smiled, then pulled on her helmet and set off back down the track. I opened the folder and flicked through the pages. Everything was beautifully and logically organised. Adam had been right about Phoebe – bright and focused but quiet. I loved how confident she'd sounded when she described what she'd done. I'd do what I could to build on the tiny sliver of confidence she had and encourage her to stop apologising.

* * *

I was on Thomas's bench a little later, idly stroking Misty-Blue's belly while I gazed out over the meadow, when I heard someone clear their throat and looked up.

'Mum! Sorry, I didn't see you there.'

'You looked like you were miles away.'

'I was. We're getting a couple of the barns converted into holiday cottages and I was trying to imagine how they'd look. So, are you all packed?'

'Louise is just helping Chloe with the final few bits. Can I sit down?'

'Of course!' I shifted my book and empty mug to give her some space.

She rested her hands on the bench either side of her, and leaned forward, shoulders tense, as though she was trying to decide on a conversation opener.

'How are you feeling after last night?' she asked eventually.

'My knees are still sore from where I fell, I'm feeling fuzzy-headed and I had another bad dream last night, but I'll get some help and I'll be fine.'

'If it is PTSD, what will treatment involve?'

'A visit to my doctor for an initial assessment, then a referral to a mental health specialist and probably psychotherapy.'

'Will that make you forget what happened?'

I shook my head. 'I was doing some research about it last night. I'm not going to ever forget the fire or the assault or anything else the Grimes family did but the idea behind psychotherapy is to help me think differently about what happened and react differently.'

From the intense expression on Mum's face, she was clearly absorbing all of this and presumably thinking of it in relation to her own past. I selected my next words carefully. 'Quite often, those with PTSD can blame themselves for what happened or be fearful of it happening again, so it's about finding a way to better control their fear or distress. The great news is it's curable, no matter how much time has passed after the traumatic event.'

There was silence and I wondered if Mum would open up, but she stood up after a while. 'I hope it gets sorted. Will you let me know?'

'If you'd like me to.'

'I would. Thank you for standing up for me this week and for teaching me all about the hedgehogs. I'd forgotten how much I liked those spiky little creatures.'

'Thanks for listening.'

'I'd better see if they're ready.'

She wandered off and I smiled to myself. My mum just thanked me for the second time in the space of a few days. I never thought I'd ever do anything she thanked me for, let alone two things. I looked across to the meadow.

'Was that you again?' I asked Thomas, then blew a kiss over the wildflowers. It had been one heck of a tough week for everyone but it seemed that the worst was behind us and we could all move forward now. Fingers crossed.

Seven weeks later

I pushed Samuel's buggy along the promenade in North Bay. Now almost six months old, he was very aware of his surroundings, twisting his head in the direction of new noises, uttering a steady babble of indistinguishable sounds.

Whitsborough Bay would have been busy anyway, being ten days into August and the height of the tourist season, but the cloudless sky and bright sunshine had brought even more people flocking to the beach. Most of the colourful beach huts seemed to be in use, there was barely any space between sunbathers on the beach, and loads of people were in the sea, splashing in the waves, playing on bodyboards, and even braving a swim.

The whole place was alive with activity: shouts, cries, squeals of delight and general chatter. I liked the vibrancy but I missed the calm of Hedgehog Hollow. I missed Sammie, but we spoke on FaceTime several times a week and kept in touch by text. I was usually the one to call her, but I'd stopped reading anything into that. It wasn't that she wasn't thinking about me;

it was just that her life was so much more chaotic than mine right now.

We reached the end of the promenade and I bought myself a soft drink from the small café there. One of the benches overlooking the sea had just been vacated so I made a beeline for it. I angled Samuel's buggy so the low sun was behind him, handed him a sippy cup and tapped my drink against it.

'Happy wedding anniversary to me,' I whispered.

I took a sip of my juice and sighed. Before Samuel was born, I'd wondered how James and I would spend our first wedding anniversary. Would we leave the baby with my parents and go for a romantic weekend away, just the two of us? Or would we be such a happy family unit that we couldn't bear the thought of leaving the baby behind? I never imagined it would just be Samuel and me and no marriage left to celebrate.

I'd stupidly allowed myself a little fantasy of James turning up today with a bunch of flowers and a declaration that he still loved me and wanted to try again. I'd told myself I hadn't brought Samuel out for a walk until now because it was too hot earlier, but who was I kidding? I'd wanted to be at home just in case flowers arrived. Chocolates, perhaps. Even just a card. By the time we reached 6.30 p.m., I was crawling up the walls and had to get out.

James had done nothing to indicate that a reunion was even the slightest possibility, so I was annoyed with myself for letting my imagination run wild.

After I'd moved out of Hedgehog Hollow, I texted him to let him know I was back in Whitsborough Bay and had received a short but telling response: *Good. That will make it easier for me to see Samuel.* I'd phoned on the Monday to let him know I'd spoken to the police and was meeting the specialist officer the following day. He'd thanked me for the update and told me he wanted to see Samuel that afternoon and I'd need to start expressing milk so he could have him for full days. It was a reasonable request but it felt so formal and official. And cold.

After that, most communication was by text with a quick information-based handover of Samuel on the doorstep. But as the weeks progressed, the handover conversation became longer and less stilted. I discovered that he was back at work, the panic attacks had ceased and he was finding counselling helpful in coming to terms with his cancer diagnosis. I hoped he was finding it helpful in coming to terms with our situation, but I was too afraid to ask in case he told me it had helped him reach the conclusion that it was definitely over.

Despite the awkwardness between us, I still loved him more than ever. Sammie told me to keep the faith but it wasn't easy. The last seven weeks had taken it out of me. I felt as though I'd regressed to childhood, back in my old bedroom, crying myself to sleep at night and having my mum come in to hug me and tell me things would work out okay eventually. I managed to hold onto that belief most days but, lying in an empty single bed at night, I ached for James and our life together.

There'd been good news from the police. I wasn't going to be prosecuted. I ugly cried that day, weak with relief. The specialist officer I was assigned had clearly graduated from the Sammie Wishaw School of Kindness, showing me nothing but respect and understanding. She hugged me when she gave me the news, which made me cry even more.

I discovered that Ava had been placed with a foster family before being adopted by a couple who'd been unable to have children of their own and that she was happy and well-adjusted. They didn't give me any details of her name or where she lived. I didn't know whether they could have done but I'd made it clear from the outset that I didn't want them; I just needed to know she was part of a loving family. I felt that I had no right to find out any more about her. I'd given up that right when I'd abandoned her and it wasn't fair on her or her parents. If she sought me out one day, I'd be happy to meet her and explain things from my perspective, with no expectation she'd want anything to do with me beyond that. It was strange to think that she'd be turning twelve on Wednesday; just two days away.

I sat there a while longer, staring out towards the sea, feeling lost. I had no idea what the future held. I'd be returning to my job at pre-school after the October half-term but that was my only certainty. Although Mum and Dad insisted they loved having us, Samuel and I couldn't stay there long-term. We needed our space and they needed theirs but I wasn't sure I was strong enough to go it alone. No, that wasn't it. I didn't want to go it alone. I didn't want to be a single mum; I wanted to be a family unit with James.

I no longer felt like a failure with Samuel. Sorting out the feeding problems had lessened the sleeping challenges, which had massively increased my ability to function during the day. I'd stopped thinking that my tough pregnancy and my difficulties with Samuel were my punishment for abandoning Ava and I wasn't afraid to ask for help now if anything did get on top of me. Asking for help wasn't a sign of weakness.

I'd made the early months as a new mum way more difficult than they needed to be. Fear of losing Samuel out of my life – like I'd lost Ava – had made me clingy and unable to bear being away from him, never able to settle unless he was close, yet I felt stifled by my actions, longing for some me-time yet being unwilling to accept it when I had the chance because that meant time away from Samuel. Vicious circle.

The only occasion I'd ever let him out of my sight for any significant amount of time was when I'd helped run the craft stall for the children on Sammie's Family Fun Day and he'd stayed home with James. Although I'd enjoyed the activities, I'd hated every moment of being away from Samuel, terrified I'd return home to find him gone. Completely irrational. I knew that now.

With each passing week over the summer, I felt more organised and in control of my life. I'd taken Samuel out on several day trips all by myself; something I'd never been brave enough to do before in case I somehow messed up and lost him. Also irrational.

We'd been over to Hedgehog Hollow several times and, again, I didn't mind that I was the one making all the effort because that wasn't really how it was; it was simply easier for me to go to see Sammie and Josh than it was for them to come to Whitsborough Bay. I'd had several long chats with Sammie and had apologised for various things I'd said or done over the years, including how horrible I'd been when she'd visited me in Whitsborough Bay a few weeks before I ran out on James. Looking back on that visit, I'd only been interested in the things that were going wrong in her life – me wanting to know I wasn't the only one struggling with things – and I could see now how badly that would have come across.

I was surprised at how much I liked Josh. It was obvious how much he loved my cousin and how he'd do anything to ensure her beloved rescue centre kept running so she could have the time out to get the help she needed for her PTSD. I couldn't have been happier for her that she'd found what she called her 'forever', after everything she'd been through. In full disclosure mode, I'd almost admitted to Sammie that I'd originally thought Josh was only with her for the farm, but I'd learned enough from her about kindness to know that there were certain things that could hurt others and were better to remain secret.

Another reason for visiting Hedgehog Hollow was to see how Paul was getting on. When my results came back for my stem cell test, I wasn't a full match but I was close enough for consideration. Unexpectedly, I felt more elated at that news than I had at the news about not being prosecuted. In my mind, I deserved to be punished for dumping Ava but Paul didn't deserve what he was going through, especially when he had a young family, so I was willing to do whatever it took to help him out. As it happened, I wasn't needed. Sammie and Fizz had organised some local testing programmes, which had turned up a much stronger match. A nineteen-year-old from the Young Farmers' Club Fizz's brother ran – or something like that – and the procedure had taken place last week. Hopefully it would work.

I took my phone out of my shorts pocket, kidding myself I was checking the time when I was really checking to see whether James had been in touch. Glancing back out towards the sea, I smiled as a man and a woman drifted past on stand-up paddleboards which reminded me of my first date with Travis. An important aspect of moving on had been to learn from the choices I'd made but not to let them control or ruin my life. I needed to let go of my hatred of Travis, Scarlett and Greg. Despite everything, I was glad I'd met Travis. Because of him – even if not fathered by him – a couple somewhere had the daughter they'd longed for and I had Samuel, even if I didn't have James.

I watched the paddleboarders drift out of view, stood up and stretched. 'We'd best be getting you back to Grandma's for your bath,' I told Samuel, taking his cup from him and replacing it with his Peter Rabbit comforter. I wondered if Ava still had hers.

A weariness took hold of me as I pushed him back towards the car. It was just as well I had the buggy to hold onto as I barely had the strength to put one foot in front of the other. I'd give myself tonight to wallow but, tomorrow, I'd work on a plan. The future wasn't what I'd hoped but it wasn't what I'd feared it could be either when the truth came out. I'd been very lucky and I was going to make the most of my freedom and stop dwelling on what ifs.

* * *

'How was your walk?' Mum asked, appearing in the hall, wiping her hands on a tea towel.

'Nice. It was busy down there but we grabbed a bench beyond the beach huts and people-watched for a while.'

'Something came for you. One second.' She retreated into the kitchen.

Flowers? My heart leapt, then sank again as she passed me a cream A5 envelope. The envelope was handwritten and there was no stamp so it had to have been hand-delivered, but the writing wasn't James's.

'When did this come?'

She shrugged. 'I spotted it on the mat about half an hour ago.'

I ripped the envelope open and took out a stiff piece of folded A4 cream paper with the letterhead for Sanderslea House Hotel at the top of it. Typed onto it were the words:

10th August
9.00 p.m.
Room 626
A car will pick you up at 8.30 p.m.

I turned the paper over, frowning, but there was nothing on the back.

'From James?' Mum asked, peering over my shoulder.

'It doesn't say, but who else could it be? It's where we met.'

All day I'd longed for some grand gesture from him and now I felt completely deflated. Was this some sort of game? I didn't like games. Scarlett had played a game with Travis and me and I'd lost. I wasn't going to set myself up for failure again. I was done with being a failure.

I sighed as I folded the paper and put it back in the envelope. 'But it doesn't matter because I'm not going.'

'You can't mean that. You've been pining for him for nearly two months and he's arranged all this and you're not going to go.'

'Arranged all what? All I've got is an unsigned piece of paper with a date, a time and a room. For all I know, he's going to slap me with some divorce papers.'

'James wouldn't do anything that crass.'

'How do you know? Or are you in on this?'

She held up her hands. 'Honestly, I know nothing about it.'

I adjusted Samuel's position on my hip. 'I'm going to bath this one and settle him in bed, then I might have a bath myself.'

'Chloe! Aren't you even curious?'

I paused halfway up the stairs and looked down on her. I had no fight left in me. 'I'm knackered. It's been a tough day and I just want a bath and an early night. When the car shows, can you send the driver away, please?'

* * *

Samuel was bathed, fed and settled in his cot by 8.15 p.m. I filled the bath and sat on the edge of it, still wearing my scruffy, ripped denim shorts and coral vest top from earlier. My stomach was in knots. Was I being selfish and stubborn? Should I go? The invite – if it could be called that – was definitely from James. I'd recognised the room number immediately. It was the turret room where we'd got together the night of Gramps's birthday party; the place it all started. But had he chosen it to indicate a fresh start... or an ending?

There was a gentle knock on the door and Mum pushed it open. 'The car's arrived.'

'I'm not going.'

'If you weren't going, you'd have sunk under those bubbles ten minutes ago.'

I looked down at my outfit. 'It's too late. I've no time to change and I can't go out like this.'

She looked me up and down and shook her head. 'No, you can't. I reckon you'll need a cardigan.'

I smiled at her. She'd been such a rock since I moved home. We'd never been closer and I often felt she understood me better than I understood myself.

'I was just about to say there's something else missing, but there it is! That beautiful smile. If James loves you and wants you back, you shouldn't have to change for him and I mean that in every sense of the word. These past couple of months when you've been make-up free and wearing casual clothes, you've seemed more relaxed and more yourself than ever. It's as though you've stopped trying to impress anyone or be what you think they want you to be and you've just been yourself. And that's the person we all love. If James doesn't want you back, isn't it better to find out now? And if that's really his decision, then he never deserved you in the first place.'

With a huge lump in my throat, I stood up and hugged her. 'Thank you. I don't know how you put up with me, but thank you.'

We broke apart and Mum smiled at me. 'Remember that message I sent you after I'd seen you at Hedgehog Hollow? I told you that you were and always would be my proudest achievement and the most important person in my life. That's never changed. So get in that car, face the future and make yourself proud.'

* * *

My heart thudded as I crept along the corridor on the sixth floor at Sanderslea House Hotel. I paused outside room 626 and looked down at my tatty flip-flops and the chipped nail varnish on my toes, suddenly feeling very self-conscious. I pulled the bobble out of my hair and shook it out but Mum's words came back to me. Sod it. If he wanted me back – and it was a big if – then he could take me as I was, make-up free with messy hair and skanky clothes because Mum was right; this was the real me. Chantel Delacroix, Rosie Kathryn Lennox and all those other characters I'd tried to be over the years were no more.

I scraped my hair back into a very messy bun, took a deep breath and pushed open the door.

As I climbed the winding staircase, I could hear music and recognised it as the song we'd chosen for our first dance at our wedding. My sweaty hand slipped off the wooden handrail. The same track started playing again as I rounded the corner and I held my breath as I spotted James standing with his back to me, looking out of the window. He obviously hadn't heard me enter. Maybe I should have knocked.

He was wearing jeans and a maroon short-sleeved shirt. I'd often told him how good he looked in shades of red. Had he chosen that shirt just for me?

Our wedding music and my favourite colour on him pointed towards a reconciliation, but I wasn't going to get my hopes up only for them to be dashed.

'Fancy seeing you here.' I cringed. What a stupid line.

James spun round, surprise on his face. 'I didn't hear you come in.'

'Stealth.' I pointed to my feet. 'It's the flip-flops.'

His shoulders relaxed and he smiled. 'Come up.'

There was an ice-bucket on the coffee table. Champagne? A celebration? But as I got closer, I could see it was white wine and the nerves took hold. I was going to have to go through with this, but the urge to turn and run down the stairs was strong.

'Wine?' he asked.

'Yes, please.' I perched on the edge of one of the chairs while he poured. I couldn't bring myself to look at the chaise. I vividly recalled what had happened on there the last time we'd been in this room together.

He handed me a glass. 'I wasn't sure if you'd come.'

'Until the car showed up, I wasn't planning to.' I swept my hand down my body to indicate my outfit, then pointed to my bare face and messy hair. 'As you can probably tell.'

'You look really good.'

I was about to put myself down – natural instinct – but I pushed back my shoulders instead. 'I feel more me like this, which was unexpected. Turns out I was trying to be someone I thought I needed to be. You look good too but I always did like you best in red.'

It was adorable the way his cheeks coloured but I refused to let myself read anything into it.

'Thanks for coming.' He raised his glass towards mine. 'Cheers.'

I put my glass down on the table and shrugged. 'Cheers to what? Why am I here, James?'

He put his drink down beside mine and slumped back in the chair. 'Sorry. I imagined this going differently.'

'What did you imagine would happen?'

'I don't know. I thought that if we went back to the place where it all started, maybe we could recapture the magic we both felt that night. I thought we'd look at each other and...' He shook his head. 'Sorry. It was a really lame idea.'

The song came to an end, plunging us into an awkward silence, then started again. James reached for his phone, presumably to turn it off.

'Leave it,' I said. 'It wasn't a lame idea. It's probably really romantic and, in a movie, it would work perfectly. But we're not in a movie.' A scene from *Notting Hill* popped into my mind, where Julia Roberts turned up at Hugh Grant's bookshop with a painting and an apology and asked him to love her and Hugh Grant turned her down. James was Julia Roberts in our scenario but the difference was that he hadn't told me how he felt. He said he'd wanted to recapture the magic so the intention was there but was he apologising now because he didn't feel the magic and therefore it was over? I needed to find out.

'Tell me what you want to say. Don't worry about it being the right words. Just say it from the heart and I promise I'll listen, even if it hurts.'

He ran his fingers across his beard. 'Okay. I've been talking a lot to my counsellor and she's helped me see what an idiot I've been; my words, not hers. I've been focusing all my energy on the wrong things. Mainly the past. I've done it with my cancer, thinking about how tough it was not being able to share my worries with you when I was diagnosed—'

'That's not fair. I knew nothing about it.'

'I know. That was my decision. A stupid one, as it turns out. Anyway, I was focusing on that difficult time instead of accepting it was behind me and the future was what was important. Then, with your secret out, I kept focusing on you being in love with Travis and then being with another man and, yes, I was jealous about it all and I know I had no right to be because I've got a past too. Instead of thinking about how desperate you must have been when you gave up the baby, I kept thinking about the angry, jealous, bitter individual I didn't recognise on our wedding night and thinking that was the same person who'd abandon a baby. What I wasn't focusing on was any of the positives about the past and I certainly wasn't looking at the future – a future as a family and a future without cancer. Everything got muddled up and the negative stuff dragged me down to the point where I heaped it all on you. I blamed you – unfairly – for everything that was wrong in my life and, for a while, I couldn't bear to be around you.'

'And now?'

He looked at me with such tenderness, my heart began to race. 'And now I can't bear not to be around you. Whenever I have Samuel and he does something cute, I turn round to point it out to you and you're not there and I know that's my fault. I know it's not going to be easy and we're going to need some help to sort our shit out but I never stopped loving you, Chloe. We joked that Cupid shot us both through the heart the evening we met downstairs. I don't know how you feel anymore but that arrow's still lodged in my heart and I don't ever want to remove it. If you'll have me back, I'd like to try again. I'm just hoping I'm not too late.'

I bit my lip, emotions whirring round inside of me. He'd just handed me what I'd longed for and it had been a pretty damn perfect movie-style speech. But I was scared.

He ran his hand over his beard once more and grimaced. 'A long silence like that probably indicates a no.'

'A long silence indicates I'm thinking. What I said when I drove over to Whitsborough Bay after the truth came out still stands. I love you more than ever and then some. But you fell in love with someone who doesn't exist anymore. I'm not the angry imposter you didn't recognise but I'm not the person who whisked you up here on the night we first met, either. The real me is a mix of those two people and the terrified teenager who made some bad decisions and has spent a lifetime so far paying for them. You might have some shit to sort out but I have a great big cart full of the stuff and I've barely managed to rake out the first dollop. Do you really want to have to deal with that?'

James stared at me for a moment, his expression unreadable, then he picked up his glass and smiled. 'I think our first wedding anniversary present to each other should be a shovel. Would you do me the honour of shovelling some shit with me?'

Laughing, I picked up my glass and clinked it against his. 'I don't think I've ever heard a more romantic line.'

We both sipped on our wine, smiling at each other.

James nodded towards his phone. 'What do you know? They're playing our wedding song. And we didn't end up doing our first dance a year ago.' He put his glass down and held out his hand towards me. 'Care to dance?'

I placed my glass next to his. 'Better late than never.'

We shuffled round the room, arms round each other. I could hear his heart thudding in time to mine. How it should be. And how it would be from now on. No more secrets, no more lies – from either of us – and a fresh start. As he tilted my face towards his and gently kissed me, there was no denying the magic was still there. It had just been buried for a while – like the past – and now we'd rediscovered it along with our future. He was right that it wasn't going to be easy but, as Nanna had always said, nothing worth having comes easy.

I squealed with excitement when a text came through from Chloe on Tuesday morning while I was walking over to the barn:

✉ From Chloe
Despite early indications to the contrary, it turned out to be a happy 1st wedding anniversary after all. It's not going to be smooth but we're both ready and willing to make it work. James has a day off work and we're heading out for a family day but I'll FaceTime you at 8.30 tonight with the full details xx

I felt so lifted by Chloe's news and couldn't wait to tell Josh but he was away at a conference for the day so I'd have to wait until tonight.

It had been hard keeping Chloe's spirits up all summer while James remained so distant. Unable to bear seeing how miserable they both were, I'd decided an intervention was needed and I *happened* to be at Hannah and Toby's cottage one evening when

James visited. Toby went upstairs to put Amelia to bed, leaving James alone in the lounge while Hannah and I were in the kitchen, and I *might* have mentioned in a rather loud voice how proud I was that Chloe had volunteered to be a stem cell donor for Paul without any persuasion and how it was amazing to see the transformation in her over the summer under such difficult circumstances.

After I left that night, James had admitted to Hannah and Toby that counselling had helped him conclude that pushing Chloe away had been a mistake and my 'very loud and completely unsubtle revelations' had simply supported that. He just didn't know how or when to tell her and whether he might be too late. In my mind, it was never too late to right a wrong and that was exactly what they'd told him so we'd all been anxiously waiting for him to make his move. Thank goodness he finally had.

I unlocked the barn and, as I cleaned the hedgehog crates and dished out medication, I reflected on a summer of highs and lows. With Chloe's great news this morning and Paul's stem cell transplant going well last week, hopefully we were heading for a much more positive autumn. It was unlikely to be plain sailing for Chloe and James but I was convinced they'd come out the other side stronger and more in love than before.

Paul had a long road ahead but the prognosis was good. He'd remain in hospital in isolation until late September then recuperate at Hedgehog Hollow. Beth was now fully recovered from her fall and we'd organised nursery places for Archie and Lottie to take the pressure off her when Paul came home.

Connie continued to inspire me with her strength and compassion. A great believer in the saying 'everything happens for a reason', she recognised and embraced how much happier and more fulfilled she was now compared to when she'd been with Paul. She didn't gloss over the hurt he caused, she didn't make out that what they did was acceptable or forgivable. She simply choose to move on and start afresh, grateful that the hurt had ultimately led her to a better place. I loved seeing Josh embrace the same approach and was certain his relationship with his dad would keep growing stronger.

Which brought me round to Mum. Despite the lack of tension between us when she'd stayed at Hedgehog Hollow and despite her thank you when she left, I'd been right in my prediction that we wouldn't suddenly become the best of friends. The whole family had been over to the farm on a couple of occasions and, although it had been polite and civil, I wouldn't say we had a relationship. I still felt the distance, even if I didn't feel the contempt radiating from her anymore. It saddened me but, as Josh pointed out, it was more than I'd ever expected and Mum still had wounds to heal. Maybe one day.

* * *

'I thought I'd find you out here.'

'Josh!' I put my mug of tea down on the arm of Thomas's bench and jumped up to kiss him. 'I didn't hear your car.'

'Probably because you were too busy chatting to Thomas and Gwendoline.'

'I was telling them about Chloe and James.'

'I'm so chuffed for them. Do you know any details yet?'

'Not yet. She's FaceTiming me at half eight.'

'In that case, you've got time to look at your gift.'

We sat down and he handed me a gift bag with a large butterfly on it.

I untied the bow, lifted out my gift and gasped. 'Oh, Josh! It's gorgeous.'

'I had it especially made for you.'

'Sammie & Josh's Wedding Planner,' I read, lightly running my fingers over the rose gold lettering and the stunning cover illustration of a pair of hedgehogs, one wearing a wedding veil and the other wearing a top hat.

'It's perfect! Thank you so much.'

'We said we wouldn't plan anything until Dad had gone through his treatment but he's gone through it all now. He and Beth have started making plans for next year and I thought it was time we started making a few of our own.'

'Does that mean you want to get married next year?'

He cupped my face in his hands and kissed me with such tenderness, I felt like I was floating on a cloud.

'I'd marry you tomorrow if I could,' he said, taking my hand in his, 'but I'm happy to wait till next year, the year after or even longer if you prefer. There's still loads happening with my dad, your counselling, and the cottages being built. The last thing I want to do is add any pressure on you to squeeze in a wedding too, but I thought we could have this planner set by for whenever you feel ready.'

Josh kissed me again and we snuggled up together on the bench looking over the meadow. 'I'm happy with whichever date you choose and wherever you choose to do it.'

My eyes rested on a kaleidoscope of butterflies flitting between the wildflowers and my heart soared. 'Here. I want to get married here.' My voice cracked as emotions engulfed me and I took a shaky breath as I turned to Josh. 'This place brought us together. Thomas and Gwendoline brought us together. I want to get married in front of them. What do think? Is that a crazy idea?'

He shook his head and I could see him battling with his emotions too. 'I think that's an amazing idea.'

'And I want it to be next year. May the second.'

Josh's eyes glistened. 'The anniversary of opening day.'

I nodded. 'And what would have been Gwendoline's eightieth birthday.'

'I think we've just created the first few entries for our wedding planner.'

As Josh wrapped his arms round me and kissed me again, everything felt so right with the world. Next year, a year after opening Hedgehog Hollow, I'd say 'I do' to my forever in the place of our dreams. The incredible couple who'd made that happen would be right in front of us and I couldn't think of a more perfect way to celebrate the legacy with which Thomas had entrusted me.

Over Josh's shoulder, I blew a kiss towards the meadow. Thomas had always wanted the farm to be full of life. A wedding would certainly achieve that. I couldn't wait to look into getting a licence and to starting my second year at Hedgehog Hollow as Josh's wife.

EPILOGUE

'Hi Sam! How was Christmas?' Fizz asked, running down the barn towards me three days after Christmas, arms outstretched.

'Amazing,' I said, squeezing her tightly. 'I had a moment on Christmas Day when we raised a glass to Thomas and Gwendoline but it was fantastic. How was yours?'

'Awesome. Barney had us all up at the farm and it's always a riot.'

'I'm liking the red hair.'

'Thank you. I thought it was more festive than pink.'

'Suits you.' I looked down the barn past her. 'Where's Zayn? I thought you were picking him up.' Zayn, my work experience student, had impressed us during his fortnight in June and had stayed on as a volunteer.

'I did. He's on his phone. He'll be in soon.'

'Great. Phoebe's dropping by to collect the receipts and invoices shortly. I told her she didn't have to do them over the Christmas break but you know Phoebe.'

Fizz smiled. 'Reliable as always.'

I still didn't know what to make of Phoebe. Fizz and Zayn were open books, constantly chatting about family, friends and hobbies, but I had no sense of who Phoebe was outside of her passion for numbers and a wish to become an accountant. I felt like I overwhelmed her every time I saw her which was an odd feeling when, coming from a nursing background, I was so used to putting everyone I met at ease.

Her work was superb, though. She was reliable and punctual and always polite. She'd proved herself to be trustworthy too. I'd given her limited admin rights for online banking so she could keep on top of bill payments for me and I checked the account religiously but she'd given me no cause for concern. She'd saved us money by regularly switching energy supplier and had secured some small grants too, all off her own back. She now pretty much managed all the finances and it was certainly a weight off my mind.

* * *

'Hi, Phoebe,' I called down the barn when she arrived a little later. 'How was Christmas?'

'Quiet but okay.' She glanced nervously towards the table where Fizz and Zayn were busy treating a dog bite on a hedgehog that had just been admitted. 'Sorry. I didn't know you'd have people here.'

'Only Fizz and Zayn,' I said as she came closer.

Fizz looked up and smiled. 'Hi, Phoebe, how's it going?'

'Fine, thank you.'

'I don't think you've met Zayn yet but he goes to the TEC. You might have crossed paths.'

Phoebe shrugged. 'I don't think so. Hi.'

Zayn looked up, grinned, then focused his attention back on the hedgehog.

'The receipts?' Phoebe prompted. 'Sorry. I need to get back.'

I handed her a plastic folder. 'All in there. Thank you.'

'I'll get these back to you quickly. See you later.'

Shoulders hunched, she scuttled out of the barn.

While Fizz and Zayn finished up, I boiled the kettle and watched Phoebe heading down the track on her moped. I wished there was something I could do to make her feel more relaxed around me; around any of us. Maybe I was expecting too much but it had been six months now. Although if Fizz – the world's bubbliest person – couldn't get much out of her, I shouldn't be too hard on myself.

With the hedgehog settled in his crate, Fizz and I sat down on the sofa bed with our drinks a little later and Zayn pulled up a chair. He shoved a chocolate digestive into his mouth whole.

'Oh, my God, Zayn!' Fizz cried. 'You're such a pig.'

'Party trick,' he said, showering biscuit crumbs onto the floor. He finished eating it. 'Guess how many marshmallows I can get into my mouth at one time.'

I grimaced. 'I don't know. Thirty.'

He grinned and pointed towards the ceiling.

'Thirty-five?' Fizz suggested.

'Forty-two!' he declared proudly.

'That's gross,' I said.

'The Guinness world record is fifty-six but I'm improving all the time. One day, I'll be a record breaker.'

I laughed. 'It's good to have goals. Fizz's goal is to become a veterinary nurse, mine is to have enough people using the holiday cottages to fund this place and Phoebe's is to be an accountant, but I think most marshmallows in the mouth eclipses all of those.' I clapped my hands and Fizz joined in, laughing.

'That reminds me,' Zayn said. 'Phoebe. I'm surprised you'd have her working here.'

'I thought you didn't know each other.'

'We don't but I know who she is. Not that it's any of my business, like, but it's a bit brave, especially if she's got access to your bank accounts.'

I sat up straight. 'What are you saying?'

'I am on the right person, yeah? Phoebe Corbyn-Grimes?'

My stomach lurched. 'Grimes? Did you just say Grimes?'

'Yeah. Although she maybe doesn't go by her full name. The tosser who torched this place – Cody Grimes – is her stepbrother. So's Connor, who I'm pretty certain got banged up again for vandalism here. Is that right?'

I nodded numbly. She couldn't be related. She just couldn't.

But Zayn was on a roll. 'If I've got this right, Phoebe's dad married Cody and Connor's mum, making her Corbyn-Grimes, but he died a few years back and... Are you okay? You've gone really pale.'

'Oh, shit!' I ran to the table, grabbed my phone and clicked into my banking app. With the chaos of Christmas, I hadn't checked for several days.

Security tests passed, I stared at the balance. Shaking, I sank down onto the nearest chair. 'Oh, no! It can't have.' But the balance on the screen – £7.86 – told me it had. Feeling like I was in a slow motion, I twisted to face Fizz and Zayn.

'It's gone. It's all gone.'

'What has?' Fizz asked, rushing over to me.

I thrust my phone at her. 'That's the rescue centre account. There was nearly thirty grand in there. It's been emptied.'

ACKNOWLEDGMENTS

Thank you for taking another visit to Hedgehog Hollow for the third book in the series. *Family Secrets at Hedgehog Hollow* was originally meant to be the final book but, as you'll have guessed from the cliffhanger, there's more to come and I'm really excited about bringing you a fourth instalment in early 2022. We'll continue to find out how Samantha is getting on running the rescue centre and dealing with PTSD, but there's another character whose story needed telling... I'll leave you guessing as to who that might be! There were several options but one voice was louder than the others!

I feel as though I've been living and breathing hedgehogs for the past year. I wrote *Finding Love at Hedgehog Hollow* in the first half of 2020 then moved on to *New Arrivals...* then straight onto *Family Secrets...* but I love being at the farm, gazing at the meadow, breathing in the fresh grass, hearing the hedgehogs snuffling. And it seems my readers do too. Well, most of them.

If you read the acknowledgements for *New Arrivals...* you'll know that it was a tough book to write, partly because it was written in the midst of the Covid-19 pandemic, which made creativity challenging, and partly because the story wasn't quite working until I turned it into a dual perspective one. And, on that subject, my books remain a Covid-free zone. I write uplifting stories that provide invaluable escapism and will continue to do so. I know that Covid is part of our reality but I choose for my characters not to live in a socially distanced world when this is a reality from which most of my readers wish to escape.

I'd love to say that book three in the series has been much easier, but it has also presented challenges. I finished writing the first draft in late November 2020, so it was still written during the dark first year of the pandemic. I was quite far through writing it when book two – *New Arrivals at Hedgehog Hollow* – became available on NetGalley seeking advanced reviews from the reviewing/blogging community. The first few reviews were gorgeous, but then two came in together that stopped me in my tracks. Both reviewers declared that it had been a big mistake turning the first book into a series and one called book two 'cringeworthy' with 'nothing to add, just padding' before concluding that she was 'very disappointed'. Wow! How was I supposed to continue writing a third book when I'd read something like that? The answer is, I couldn't. I was creatively paralysed for days. I'd pitched the idea to my editor for a fourth book by that point but was now questioning whether I should even finish writing the third one. Yes, I'll admit it, those reviews made me cry.

But my amazing husband and daughter built me back up and helped me focus on all the positive ones instead and I slowly clawed my way back into the story. A massive thank you to them for picking me up and to all the readers who have shared their love for the first and second books in the series and who have expressed their excitement about the third. I'm ever so grateful.

During the editing process, I hit another stumbling block. When I wrote *Finding Love at Hedgehog Hollow,* I needed to do a significant re-write after a conversation with my sister-in-law revealed a huge plot problem. I swore to research things more thoroughly in future, yet I got caught out again with this story. My amazing editor, Nia, wanted me to be absolutely sure about all aspects of Chloe's hospital stay, so I put out a plea on Facebook for help from an NHS midwife. My great friend Nic Bennett put me in touch with a friend of hers called Hannah, whose brilliant information about processes and safeguarding helped me realise that my plans were flawed and I'd made some careless assumptions. She let me bombard her with emails full of what ifs and alternative scenarios until I proposed something that was accurate and plausible. Hannah – I cannot thank you enough. Obviously practices will vary across hospitals and trusts and if anything has been misrepresented here, that's my error... or deliberate creative licence on my part. This is, after all, a piece of fiction and sometimes we do have to bend things a little.

This book, just like the second in this series, is dedicated to a family member who we've lost recently. My second cousin, Gary, died shortly before Christmas, aged only forty-two. I am heartbroken for his mum (my cousin) Janice, his stepdad Richie, his sister Lucy and the children, nephews and niece he leaves behind. RIP, Gary, with love, xx.

Enormous hugs to my mum, who remains the biggest supporter of my work. She's always checking my chart positions and championing me to her friends. It's appreciated so much. Love you lots, Mummy Bear xxx.

A massive thank you goes to my fabulous friend, Sharon Booth, for helping me work through a plot point around Chloe's backstory. On the back of the negative feedback, I'd started doubting myself and Sharon helped me massively. Sharon's an extremely talented author, so do check out her gorgeous books.

Another great friend, Sarah Thorpe, was a brilliant source of information about the National Federation of Young Farmers' Clubs. It was a small plot point in this book but I wanted it to be accurate. Thanks again to Tracy Underwood for some further expertise on counselling and my Auntie Gwen, hedgehog rescuer, for the original inspiration.

My final research thank you goes to author and friend, Helen Phifer, and to good friend, Jackie Bradley, who are my go-to sources for police-related information. Although you weren't directly able to help me with Chloe's backstory, I appreciate you both trying. I found loads of valuable newspaper articles and websites about child abandonment and was quite shocked at the numbers of cases, which rise every year.

Thank you to my amazing editor, Nia Beynon, for your praise, encouragement and helpful editing guidance which, as always, have strengthened this story. Also an enormous thank you for being there with reassurance when those couple of bad reviews make me panic and for the emergency phone call when I had a very last-minute re-think about the ending. You are the best! And thanks so much to the whole team at Boldwood Books for continuing to make all my writing dreams come true.

To Cecily Blench and Sue Lamprell, thanks for the amazing work on polishing and perfecting my prose and to Debbie Clement for yet another absolutely delicious cover.

If you've listened to the audio version, I hope you've enjoyed it. Emma Swan has brought Samantha's voice to life for the whole series so far, and it has been a thrill to have Lucy Brownhill join her on this recording for Chloe's perspective. Thank you so much to both of you for such incredible narration across all my audiobooks. Thank you to ISIS Audio and Ulverscroft for the recording and distribution.

A huge thank you to Rachel Gilbey for organising another superb blog tour, all the bloggers and reviewers who took part or who have read and reviewed this book independently of the tour, and to you, my amazing readers, for your love and support.

Finally, we ran a competition where a subscriber to my newsletter could name a hedgehog in book two. I was so delighted with the name – Snoop Hoggy Hog – that we ran it again for this book. Congratulations to Kaye Dunn, who suggested the gorgeous name of Prickles. He makes his debut appearance in Chapter 51.

I have a Pinterest board for each of my books so you might like to visit that to see some of the images that have inspired this story. You can find it at: www.pinterest.co.uk/jessicaredlandauthor

If you'd like more insights into the world of Whitsborough Bay or Hedgehog Hollow, you might like to join my Facebook Readers' Group. Just search for 'Redland's Readers' and answer a couple of quick questions to join.

If you've enjoyed your third trip to Hedgehog Hollow, a lovely review or even a rating would be amazing and recommendations to friends and family are invaluable. You might also like to check out my other books, if you haven't already done so.

Big hugs,
Jessica xx

HEDGEHOG TRUE/FALSE

Hedgehogs are born with spines

FALSE - Imagine poor mum giving birth if they had spines! Ouch! When hoglets are born, their skin is covered in fluid and, after a few hours, this is reabsorbed and soft white spines erupt from the skin

Hedgehogs are good swimmers

TRUE - They're really good swimmers and, perhaps even more surprisingly, can climb trees. They do sometimes drown, though. It's not the swimming that's the problem; it's the getting out again

Baby hedgehogs are called hoglets

TRUE - Isn't it cute? They're sometimes known as piglets, pups or kittens but the official term is hoglets

Hedgehogs are nocturnal

TRUE - They are nocturnal although. It's not unknown for them to be out and about during the day but this is often a sign that something's wrong

Hedgehogs can run in short bursts at speeds of up to 3mph

FALSE - They're even faster than that. They are surprisingly nippy and can reach top speeds of 5.5mph in short bursts. Go hedgehogs!

Hedgehogs lose half their body weight during hibernation

FALSE - It's actually just over a third but that's still a significant amount and hedgehogs fresh from hibernation are going to need some major feasts to build up their strength quickly

Hedgehogs got their name in the Middle Ages from the word 'hygehoge' which translates today as 'hedge' and 'pig' combined

TRUE - The name does what it says on the tin! They snuffle round hedges for their foot and this snuffling/grunting is just like a pig

Hedgehogs have good eyesight

TRUE - It's often believed that their eyesight is poor but it's not the case. They simply don't use their eyes because they don't need to. They have a keen sense of smell, taste and hearing and it's these senses they will use far more than their eyesight

Hedgehogs are quiet eaters

FALSE - They're very noisy when they eat. They love their food and will slurp, crunch and lip-smack with their mouths open. Not the ideal dinner guest!

HEDGEHOG DOS AND DONT'S

Food and Drink

DO NOT give hedgehogs milk to drink. They are lactose intolerant. Dairy products will give them diarrhoea which will dehydrate them and can kill them

DO give hedgehogs water but please have this in a shallow dish. If it's in a deep dish, the risk is that they'll fall in and be unable to get out again

DO give hedgehogs dog or cat food - tin, pouch or biscuit format - but not fishy varieties

DO try to create a feeding station for a hedgehog so that other garden visitors (including cats) don't beat the hedgehog to it. You don't need to buy anything expensive. There are loads of tutorials and factsheets online around creating your own simple station

Your Garden

DO avoid having fences with no gaps under them. Hedgehogs can travel a long way in an evening and they rely on being able to move from one garden to the next. Or you can create a hedgehog highway in your fence

DO place a ramp by a pond so that, if a hedgehog falls, it can easily get out

DO NOT let your dog out into your garden during babies season (May/June and Sept/Oct) without checking there are no hoglets out there first

DO build a bug hotel and DO plant bug-friendly plants. It will attract all sorts of delicious food for your hedgehogs

DO NOT use slug pellets. Hedgehogs love to eat slugs so pellets reduce their food supply and/or poison hedgehogs

DO have a compost heap or a messy part in your garden. If you can have some sticks/wood piled up in a safe corner, this makes a perfect habitat for hibernating

DO check your garden before strimming or mowing. Garden machinery can cause horrific accidents or fatalities

DO NOT leave netting out as hedgehogs can become trapped in it. If you have football goals in your garden, lift the netting up overnight and secure it safely to avoid injury or fatalities

DO always check bonfires before lighting as there may well be hogs nestling in there

Finding Hogs

DON'T assume that a hedgehog out in the daylight is in danger. They usually are but watch first. It could be a mum nesting. If it's moving quickly and appears to be gathering food or nesting materials, leave it alone. If this isn't the case, then something is likely to wrong. Seek help

DO handle hedgehogs with gardening glove - those spines are there to protect the hogs and hurt predators - but keep handling to a minimum. Stay calm and quiet and be gentle with them. Transfer them into a high-sided box or crate with a towel, fleecy blanket or shredded newspaper (and a thick layer of paper on the bottom to soak up their many toilet visits). This will help keep them warm and give them somewhere to hide. Make sure there are plenty of air holes

DON'T move hoglets if you accidentally uncover a nest but, if mum isn't there, do keep an eye on the nest and seek help if mum doesn't return. Hoglets won't survive long without their mother's milk. Put some water and food nearby so mum (assuming she returns) doesn't have far to travel for sustenance. If the hoglets are squeaking, this means they are hungry and you may need to call help if this continues and there's no sign of mum

MORE FROM JESSICA REDLAND

We hope you enjoyed reading *Family Secrets at Hedgehog Hollow*. If you did, please leave a review.

If you'd like to gift a copy, this book is also available as an ebook, digital audio download and audiobook CD.

Sign up to Jessica Redland's mailing list for news, competitions and updates on future books.

http://bit.ly/JessicaRedlandNewsletter

ABOUT THE AUTHOR

Jessica Redland is the author of eleven novels which are all set around the fictional location of Whitsborough Bay. Inspired by her hometown of Scarborough she writes uplifting women's fiction which has garnered many devoted fans.

Visit Jessica's website: https://www.jessicaredland.com/

Follow Jessica on social media:

f facebook.com/JessicaRedlandWriter

twitter.com/JessicaRedland

instagram.com/JessicaRedlandWriter

BB bookbub.com/authors/jessica-redland

ALSO BY JESSICA REDLAND

Standalone Novels
The Secret To Happiness
Christmas at Carly's Cupcakes
Starry Skies Over The Chocolate Pot Café
All You Need Is Love

Welcome To Whitsborough Bay Series
Making Wishes At Bay View
New Beginnings at Seaside Blooms
Finding Hope at Lighthouse Cove
Coming Home To Seashell Cottage

Hedgehog Hollow Series
Finding Love at Hedgehog Hollow
New Arrivals at Hedgehog Hollow
Family Secrets at Hedgehog Hollow

ABOUT BOLDWOOD BOOKS

Boldwood Books is a fiction publishing company seeking out the best stories from around the world.

Find out more at www.boldwoodbooks.com

Sign up to the Book and Tonic newsletter for news, offers and competitions from Boldwood Books!

http://www.bit.ly/bookandtonic

We'd love to hear from you, follow us on social media:

facebook.com/BookandTonic

twitter.com/BoldwoodBooks

instagram.com/BookandTonic